To Dave

REVENGE, ILLUSTRATED

Part 1: unearth the underdog

Revenge rests with the underdog.

BARRY COCHRANE

REVENGE, ILLUSTRATED
Part 1: unearth the underdog

Copyright © 2023 Barry Cochrane

All rights reserved. No part of this book may be reproduced, scanned or transmitted in any forms, digital, audio or printed without the prior written consent of the author.

This is a work of fiction. Names, characters, businesses, places or events are either the product of the author's imagination, used in a fictitious manner or are entirely coincidental.

ISBN: 979-8-8643-7587-7

DEDICATION

To Gerry.

ACKNOWLEDGEMENTS

Without the following people, this book would never have made it to the e-shelves and print shop.

Firstly, to my wife Tracey – moon and stars – it all came from you. From encouraging me to even start this daunting journey, to spurring me on to continue evolving it over the months, and for always being with me at every single step to finally get it over the line.

Kelly Redgrave – for everything! All your feedback and pointers from a time-served reader of a thousand books, to a newbie writer. All at a tragic time. My sincere thanks.

Sas – for taking the time out a super-busy schedule to proofread and provide pointers.

G-Mac – for animal inspiration!

My family – for being there for me all the time and being the wonderful individuals who you are.

To my sister, Maggie – for being both the most generous and the strongest person I know. I love you.

To readers of this book – thank you in advance.

Chapter 1 – 1999

He was 10 months old when Justin Howard finally picked up the spoon that had seemed to dodge the grip of his chubby little fingers for so long, and he fed himself. It needed dexterity and finesse, things he'd excel at in later life. But for now, he was obsessed with this beautiful, red plastic spoon. Small, vibrant, smooth and perfectly curved. How the same colour changed as he moved it. It was clear that he took more interest in this than his food.

His parents, Mike and Deborah watched on obsessively. As new parents, quite naturally they absorbed what he liked and didn't, but they were, however, more concerned in what he took interests in. Of course, that happens with all new parents, but not like this. This was rather different, and every day required full attention. This wasn't the actions of your average super-proud, baby-smitten parents, or of an overly risk-aware mom and dad. It was infatuation. And for a reason. A hidden reason, one so sinister, they'd never mention it to anyone. This had to be kept secret, and no one could ever know.

Toys for Justin comprised of building blocks and toy cars, and as he grew older, action figures, a cowboy costume complete with holster and gun and an electric train set with scenery and some figurines. To his parents, those things were all safe, and he could play alone or with a friend. But if they ever gave him pencils or crayons to draw things with, he was never allowed to do this unsupervised.

One of his parents would keep a close eye on Justin at all times, especially after he'd finished drawing, or finished colouring in. Any picture he drew, was immediately taken from him. Taken to be lovingly 'kept forever' – they'd tell him with a smile – a faked one. In reality, they were all destroyed in a hurry. Only then, would the Howards breathe normally again. Nonetheless, drawing was the only thing Justin ever seemed to take a really fond interest in. But this worried the Howard's, and for good reason – there was untold history behind it all.

Many a night, only after they were certain Justin was asleep, would they secretly discuss the possibility of an infamous, generations-old family curse repeating itself. Surely not. 'Please not our child', they'd pray. In the beginning, the chances of this happening to their boy were so distant, so remote, it was hardly worth thinking about. They needn't worry. But they did worry. In fact, over time, Deborah had worried herself ill.

As time passed and Justin grew older, doubts had slowly but surely crept in and they accumulated. With Justin growing up, their odds of having a normal family life, whatever that was, would seem less certain. Their revolving roulette was a wheel of misfortune, and the section they wanted to land on just kept on passing them by, forever spinning past, and the ball never lands anywhere – at least not for now. There was evil on that roulette wheel, and both parents were all too aware of it. Still, each night they prayed in hope that this evil they feared above all else, hadn't returned to curse the Howard family. Surely it hadn't inflicted their child – their only child?

The Howards had tried for a second child, but after three devastating miscarriages over seven years, they decided to stop. The initial bliss and excitement of pregnancy, a gorgeous little blob on a screen, slowly and inevitably morphing into a lifeless one, and being told by medics in a private room the all-too familiar tragic news they'd now become accustomed to, had turned their hopes and excitement, into hopelessness and despair. The radiographer's job was mostly one of exciting news, but not always. The Howards couldn't bear it again, especially Mrs Howard, and over time, they accepted that Justin was destined to be an only child.

In the early years, they decided to take turns and share the exhausting supervision of their boy. They made rules to follow, and as long as they were kept to, things would be okay. Justin's father, Mike, was a very slim man with wavy black hair, and he always had gel in it to hold it in place. He worked as a mid-distance lorry driver, transferring cattle from one state to another for slaughter. He'd often be away a few days at a time, sometimes away for a week or more. When he got back to the family home, he was shattered, but so was his wife, as she'd been the one on continual guard and it was exhausting. She was done.

For years, she'd been a stay-at-home mom, all pre-discussed and pre-agreed years ago. She always wanted to be a math teacher, but put this idea on hold when she was pregnant with Justin. She loved the idea of that job and yearned for it to happen, partly for some adult conversation the school's staff would bring, but mostly just to restore some kind of normality and a sense of worth, that had become distant. 'Adult conversation', was one thing she missed so much during the days when she'd been alone with her toddler, and she craved it in the evenings when Justin was in his bed. She needed someone to offload her day's troubles to, and to listen to their day, or at least appear to, but it never happened.

She had slowly grown out of touch with things, and wasn't the type to go out much, even when her husband was back home. She hardly ever fussed about her looks, did something nice with her hair or put on make-up, unless she was going out somewhere, like to attend an appointment with the school. Even then, her hair was just pulled back and held in place with a rubber band. Her appeal to others, the attractiveness she knew she once owned, had slowly faded and she was aware of it. Her focus had been elsewhere.

Deborah's parents had moved to Montana many years ago, this being the result of a bitter family feud, all over a combination of Justin and their own religious beliefs. Neither of Justin's parents had any siblings, so apart from Mike's parents – Stuart and Sarah, now Grandpa Stuart and Grammy Sarah, there were no other family to help out with baby-sitting of young Justin – but given what they suspected, maybe that was a good thing.

From time to time, when Mike had been home for a few days, they had considered getting a local babysitter, someone from the neighbourhood perhaps? But no. These discussions never lasted long. They felt they couldn't trust anyone with Justin. If they ever were to speak their rules – their strict rules, to anyone, any babysitter or any neighbour, then they'd just appear weird. It would have changed how people viewed them.

A babysitter would, most likely, tell their friends at school their stupid rules and, quite rightly, have a good laugh doing so, ridiculing the Howards and their crazy do's and don'ts. What if they told their own parents this stuff? Word couldn't get out about this. Safer just to not trust anyone and keep this secret to themselves.

When it had become time for Justin to go to the local preschool, if all had gone well, the plan was for Deborah to go back to work, maybe just a few hours at first. Partly to help pay for preschool, but largely to free her of this 'watch', which had increased in intensity as Justin got older. It had become an obsession to her, and it had taken its toll. Deborah was not always like this. Photographs she'd kept revealed she had been one of the girls, craving the city's weekend, sometimes wearing a semi-daring outfit, showing off her tanned arms and legs, her slimline physique and her gorgeous chocolate-brown hair while she danced around her purse. In contrast, now she barely wears make-up at all.

At a visit to the preschool, the Howards were shown around and they observed. As new parents, this was all novel to them.

"Nice tree, Jamal!", a teacher would complement. "I love that rainbow over it."

"Lovely picture, Dean! Is that the sea with a big fish in it?", another would say with a huge smile on her face, her eyes just as big.

"That's a *gorgeous* sky. I love the sun!", another teacher expressed to a kid who had just finished it, yellow paint still tacky.

The Howards envied the innocence of it all. A place full of compliments and encouragement where kids could do no wrong. How nice it would be to have no fears. But what if someone drew a dinosaur, like they saw on telly? What if one of the kids drew two dinosaurs, fighting? What if an asteroid was drawn, speeding towards earth – head on? What if?

Upon joining, the Howards told the preschool that Justin had a rare allergy. He couldn't have nuts and he'd react to certain chemicals found in most of the general art sets that were available to buy. They said his skin was so sensitive, that he had to be kept away from all of these things and his reaction would be so severe that it could bring on anaphylaxis – a life-threatening reaction that would require immediate medical attention.

Instead, they supplied the preschool with their own 'special' pencils, crayons and paints and their own 'special', 'allergy-friendly', colouring-in paper. So they claimed. Their paper was mostly the colour-by-numbers sets. However, these things simply don't allow for Justin to express his imagination, and that conflicted with the preschool's Policy on 'child development', but their Policy, merely words on paper, got trumped by the safety of a child.

However, this was all lies. Their boy didn't have any allergies. What he did have, was an overly vivid imagination, and maybe – just maybe, he also possessed a curse his parents prayed hadn't been passed onto him, and they couldn't take chances.

Justin had always enjoyed stories read to him, always been allowed to watch some TV, and he'd always been allowed to make up his own stories and play with other kids in the street. However, if he was out in the street playing or in a neighbour's back garden, it would normally end abruptly. Somehow, one of Justin's parents would come to collect him a bit earlier than expected, usually the first kid to go home.

The Howards had been the type of people who mostly kept themselves to themselves, not socialising in the evenings with neighbours. In those early years and until Justin reached fifteen, they'd never quite fitted in to neighbourly life in Indiana, and many a time, the neighbours had talked. They were viewed as being a bit weird or just strange, certainly overly possessive, and careful with Justin. But back then, no one could ever have guessed what was going to unfold in the years that lay ahead. If they did, they would have moved away themselves whenever they could.

Chapter 2 – 1974

Damian Keefer was a tough lad. He had to be. His biological father had died of a drug overdose when he was very young. His parents had been habitual heroin addicts, gradually adding a bit more each hit, or splitting and adding-in whatever they could get their hands on, usually drinking cheap vodka before the jab. It happened the very first time that Damian's mom had been offered fentanyl, a new drug at the time, and much more powerful than heroin. She purchased it on the streets in plain sight. It didn't come with instructions and she wasn't stopping for user advice. Later that evening, they both injected each other with it. She only remembers waking up in hospital and trying to free herself from some tubes they'd connected her to.

Damian had grown up barely remembering what his real dad had looked like. His mother, devastated by this accident, suffered a downward spiral, and never went back to work as a waitress. They lived off welfare allowances and didn't have much of anything.

As a young teenager growing up, Damian hadn't approved of his mom's boyfriends. To stabilise things a bit, she eventually got married again. This time to Rodger. Damian despised him and the daughter he brought into the family, Katrina, now his stepsister. Katrina was just fourteen years old and she hadn't fitted into school life nor had many friends, apart from some other goths she hung about with. It allowed her to be 'different' she insisted, but Damian insultingly told her that all goths looked and dressed the same, so she wasn't different at all. It hadn't gone well from there.

Rodger was now Damian's stepfather, and they argued and fought frequently. Damian was big for his age, as tall as Rodger was and he was stocky and strong, with a shaved head and a few homemade tattoos. Rodger had beaten him up from time to time, mostly when he'd come home drunk, and Damian bore the scars on his back from the metal buckle of his stepdad's belt. The scars were a permanent reminder which of them was the tougher. He had actually lost a tooth one night when Rodger had come back from the pub so drunk, he couldn't manage to undo his buckle, and punched Damian in the face instead. He hadn't realised what had happened until he sobered up the following afternoon and had been told about it.

These events toughened Damian up and he chose to spend most of his time on the streets. He had never known what caring family life was. To Damian, his current family was false. It seemed like pieces from different jigsaws had been forced together.

So when he got friendly with Stuart Howard, he viewed him as his brother. In his world of chaos, this was his only stable relationship and the closest thing to family that Damian had. The pair had grown up together, initially knowing each other from school bus rides over the years, both getting off at the same stop, living in the same block. They met most days after school but not always, as Stuart had been kept back two full years at school and he had been forced to stay inside some evenings and study. Stuart had focussed all his energy on artwork, which he excelled at. He just didn't get anything else.

With a few other guys in similar positions, it wasn't long before they formed a gang. They were all teenagers, a difficult age for youngsters, but an age where Damian could stay out until late and avoid Rodger.

Things changed when word of rival gangs forming in the neighbourhood spread. Proper gangs, not just play stuff like they were. Damian said they'd have to get tougher – it was do or die. Caleb and Simon were also in the gang, Simon being the one they spent the most time convincing to join. Caleb just went along with the rest.

The new rules were the same for everyone – a fight. Stuart recalled the time when Damian challenged him to a duel, in front of the other two, bare chested. This was an initiation thing, to see if they were tough enough – worthy of belonging to their group. With his heart thumping, he took off his jacket and they circled each other, until the clinch. It wasn't a boxing match, and no striking was allowed either. This was simply a grappling-type contest to see who got the better of the other, although none of them were trained in wrestling or jiu-jitsu.

The winner would be the one who got the other to submit somehow, signalled by a verbal submission, or by a hand-tap somewhere on the other person. Stuart remembers being grabbed by Damian's grip and just how firm that grip was, then being tripped, forcing the two of them to the ground and landing on Damian's arm, where his grip released. A scramble resulted, and Stuart somehow found himself on his side with Damian in front of him.

Before Damian could turn round, he grabbed his neck from behind with his forearm and had him in a choke hold, his other hand pressing hard on the back of Damian's head. Damian struggled for a few seconds, trying to get free but he couldn't. He tapped on Stuart's thigh three times, and the grip was instantly released. The 'tap' was a signal they'd all agreed to, and it meant the game was up and the tapper was submitting. A manly cuddle ensued, followed by a few laughs, each recalling their version of what had happened. Stuart was worthy. He'd done okay.

Over the next couple of years, they landed themselves in a bit of trouble from time to time, nothing too serious though. Nothing worthy of being locked up. However, it had become clear that Damian was turning into the type of lad that would push them all a bit more each time, and eventually towards the limit, trying to get maximum buzz, thrills and of course, credibility with other gangs. Other kids innocently passing through what they claimed, '*their*' territory, had been stopped, harassed, and robbed – some beaten up.

Vehicles of neighbours they hadn't liked had been damaged, one had been taken for a ride and dumped miles away, and anything of value robbed. A few homes had been broken into, carefully scoped-out in advance to discover when the owners would be away and how best they could get in.

Against his better judgement, Stuart had gone along with all this at first, partly due to peer pressure, partly due to other gangs out there and he thought he'd be better off belonging to one of them than not, and of course, well what else is there to do in Westfield? It was nothing too serious after all.

But things did get more serious, and when they did, Stuart wanted out. He just couldn't carry a knife and use it. He wasn't going to burn someone's car they'd stolen for thrills. Stuart had been no angel growing up either, and this group had certainly brought some adrenalin rushes and some cash, but growing older meant getting even tougher, if he was going to stay.

Stuart, though, wasn't a tough guy. He really wanted a career in art. It was the only thing he was good at. Occasionally, his mind wandered, and he'd slip into a daze, envisaging himself as a successful painter, showing off his latest display in a posh gallery with tall ceilings, with posh critics in dinner jackets judging one of his 'pieces', red wine swaying gently in pristinely clean diamond-cut glasses, pondering where they'd hang it back home – the asking price wouldn't even be discussed. But that was a light year ahead. First, he had to escape that head-lock Damian had had him in for years. He'd been holding him back from pursuing this dream.

But recently, there was another reason to escape Damian's grip. He'd been chatting with a girl at school a few times, and he liked the way she spoke to him, brown eyes focussed on his. Her mannerisms hinting she was interested in Stuart, and for more than just chat.

"Hey Stuart,", she said while wandering along the school corridor, close to the exit and about to leave school for the day. "I saw your painting in the art class – the Pepsi can.", she clarified, referring to the hand-crushed can of Pepsi that was sweating on a tabletop. "That *was* you, wasn't it?"

"Eh, yeah", came Stuart's reply, shell-shocked that she'd even bother speaking with him, and almost within touching distance too. "Do you like it… Sarah? It is Sarah, isn't it?", making sure to add the fact that he *definitely* knew her name. He knew fine her name was Sarah. They'd spoken in art class once before.

She nodded with a smile, answering both his questions. "It's stunning… really. That's why the teacher hung it on his wall, I suppose. You're brilliant… I mean, your art stuff is."

They both smirked. It was clear they were going to be friends, at least.

"Just thought I'd mention that Stuart. Got to go. Bye." And with a smile on her face, she left. He watched as she was leaving, eager to see if she'd turn around one last time or not. She didn't.

He liked that during their chat, a nearby sports car's V8 engine had started, and the driver had revved it hard, showing off its snarl, and she hadn't even glanced away. In fact, he almost did. But his eyes remained fixed on her. The car had sped away, frustratingly interrupting their brief conversation, which had come easily, but he paused until it had gone, glancing annoyingly at it as it left. She appreciated this. Although brief, it had been good speaking with her, and it all felt real. With his 'so-called' friends, he immediately realised none of that had been real. No need to pretend to be tough with her. No swearing required. No showing off and no fighting.

The jackpot came when, during another conversation with him, she had innocently slipped in where she lived, and it was only a few blocks away from his home, easily walkable.

His mind had been taking over and he was ready to turn over to a more exciting chapter of his life that was maybe about to begin. He found himself frequently thinking about her, about her welcoming smile when she noticed him, about her silky-smooth, glossy dark-brown hair she twiddled in the last of the Autumn sunlight, her soft voice, her smooth skin and her appealing femininity. Going on a date, spending time doing things was the next step, but he wanted to be certain she'd accept his offer.

He'd done some scary things in the past, so why was he dreading a simple conversation with a girl that had been nice to him? Someone like her in his life was, perhaps, but just perhaps, becoming a real-life possibility, and he found his thoughts racing ahead of him. They'd only spoken a few times together, but it felt like the start of something. At night in bed, out of all the things he could have thought about, he imagined her. He imagined innocently holding her hand on a walk together, and finally kissing her and how good that kiss would be. This was desire, and he wanted her in his arms – instead of at arm's-length, that had been the case so far.

He found himself reliving the conversations they'd had. Was the way she was softly looking at him, through the top of her brushed eyelashes, with her head slightly tilted to one side, just her normal way, or was she sending him a message? If so, what was she saying? Did she like him, or was she just being nice? 'Fuck me – this is tough', he'd think. Dare he make an idiot of himself and take the first step? Rejection would sting.

The crux of it was that he knew he'd have to clean up his act if he was to have any chances with this classy girl who'd shown attention to him, when there were loads of other blokes at school. Other guys Stuart knew were more worthy of her than he was. Stuart was a confident guy, about medium height and with dark brown hair which wasn't groomed to any particular style, and stubble that never sat evenly. He wasn't a good looking guy, but she seemed to look past that, and past the bumpy nose he hated and the ear that stuck out more than the other.

Obviously, Sarah didn't know what he'd been getting up to in the evenings and weekends, and the brief conversations they'd had didn't go there. The violence, the break-ins, the fights, all had to come to an end. He could never tell her his past. If he did, how could he justify that? 'Because there's nothing to do in town', or 'Everyone's in a gang', is just lame. She could never find out, so, in effect, he'd have to lie to her. Not the best way to start things off. Boy was he regretting it all now.

Late one evening, he'd been in his room, chatting with Simon when a powerful image just barged its way through and into his thoughts. He felt compelled to make a drawing of it before it vanished. He grabbed a notepad and a pencil, and he quickly sketched a picture, and finished it off by signing it, just like he would do if he'd been that successful artist, selling his paintings in a chandeliered gallery, just like he'd visualised.

Simon saw that he'd drawn a black panther, escaped from the local zoo, now roaming a park in Westfield, its hungry yellow eyes prowling and a child nearing it. The picture looked real, as if the big cat had just froze – keeping completely still, so not to be seen. Soon after, Stuart felt drunk, his eyes spinning the room, and he told Simon he was just needing an early night. That night, when Stuart had fallen asleep, he dreamed about the drawing he'd made. Every dream feels real, but this was *way* more real.

In his dream, there was a hole in the fencing and one of the panthers had escaped from its enclosure. The zookeepers had only just noticed after counting them at feed time, and sounded the alarm. The escaped panther had made its way to the nearby park that the lads went to all the time. The cat was specifically looking for him, stalking *him* down, and *only* him, not bothering with nearby children, nor their mothers who were too scared to intervene.

People were panicking. Screams could be heard. Then, the panther vanished from sight – just like his picture. It was getting dark, and the black cat was shadow-blending. Then, in the distance, he saw its yellow eyes appear… then they disappeared. Where was it? His ears could just about detect it panting, and that panting was now getting louder. He slowly turned round to check, and it was right behind him, just ready to pounce on him, its claws unsheathed and extended for the kill, catching the moonlight. The hunter opened its jaws wide open, showing its lethal curved teeth. But it didn't jump. It didn't snarl. It just stood there, looking at him. Then, very slowly, he approached the beast, cautious step – by cautious step, respecting its superiority and never daring to break eye contact.

Its jaws began to close. Its claws now retracting into their sheaths, taking the moonlight shine with them. A calmness fell over it. He extended his arm out towards it, not knowing what move this killer-cat would make, but when he got closer, it licked his hand. He felt its raspy tongue on his fingers, all wet and rough. He offered a smile, symbolising peace – not threat, then approached closer still, and, with his hand now damp with its slavers, he gently gave it a stroke, from head to neck. The panther closed its eyes as he did so. It was a truce, and neither of them were dying that day. Then, they both heard the unmistakeable sound of crisp, dry leaves being crackled, as someone steadied themselves on them, raising the sharp end of a rifle their way, and it immediately bolted off into the distance, its tail slapping him in the face as it passed.

Stuart woke up, glistening with sweat. The bedcovers were sticky. He thought for a minute, debating just how real that cat seemed, and how real its fur had felt on his fingers. Finally, he got out of bed, and headed for the shower as he needed one. He found himself staring into the bathroom mirror, gazing into his confused head which housed a dull ache, watching himself shaking that head gently, feeling stupid. The dream had felt so ultra-real. But what he noticed in the mirror, startled him, and made him squint to focus.

Between his fingers, were a few threads of jet-black fur, about four inches long. They weren't his. He thought he must still be dreaming, so he splashed some water on his face, washing away the fur down the sink hole as he did. He went back into the bedroom, and pulled back the covers, just to check. Nothing was there, apart from sheets that needed a spin in the machine.

'What the fuck is going on?', he thought. He never mentioned this dream to anyone. They'd think he'd gone crazy. Shower can wait till morning.

The following afternoon, as the four boys were in the park at their usual bench, they heard the town's Police issue a warning over their tannoy system. A black panther had escaped for real and had been seen in the park. People had been told to go inside and lock their doors. This caused bedlam, and people ran in all directions screaming in fear. But the boys didn't. They all retreated to the safety of the trees, desperate to see this roll out.

Around ten minutes later, as the Police were hunting it down, they saw that a young child had wandered off from its mother, and had strayed towards the panther, unaware of the dangers at her age.

"Emily!", her mother cried. "EMILY! Come to mama!" But she didn't hear mama.

The panther approached the toddler calmly. The girl's mother was now screaming tears, pleading with the Police, who were holding her back, to shoot it. The cops had rifles in their hands, but the child was in front of the cat and the risk of shooting the child was just too high. The mother was now hysterical. This fully grown predator looked enormous next to the child. Easy pickings for it, should it wish. But it didn't. Instead, the child toddled from around the side, to the front of the cat, fascinated by features it hadn't seen before. She extended her arm towards the cat's face, ignorant of the risk.

"Shoot!", came the order, and a rifle blast went off. The panther got tagged with a tranquiliser dart. It stumbled around, then lay down shortly afterwards. The town folk had been terrified, but it was now over. No one got killed, and no one was injured, but many had feared for their lives. An elderly man in the park had actually fainted, but it hadn't harmed him either. Stuart rewound back to his identical sketch, knowing he hadn't detailed anyone dying, not even the cat.

People in town spoke about that for months, but the boy's gang got together the very next day and quizzed Stuart. They were in awe, but sceptical. Did this just happen?

"Fuck me! Stu, you drew that!" Simon was lost. It was spooky, but surely it was just a coincidence.

Being hyper-charged, then puzzled by this, Stuart was enticed by the gang into making another picture, and only the gang crew would know about this one. Being a Friday night, and no school tomorrow, he conjured up an idea with a darker side. This time he would draw something that no person could possibly set-up or make happen, like letting the animals out of their cage on purpose. This would have to be different.

It had been drizzling all day, but out of nowhere, it started raining heavier, so Stuart brought the lads into his dad's garage for some shelter from the heavens – and nosey passers-by.

"Hey, you got any beers?", said Simon, jokingly, but of course, serious too – his delayed expression, hanging on Stuart's answer the giveaway. Caleb waited too.

Stuart fetched a can of beer for each of them from the garage fridge, and four hisses went off. Yesterday had been a weird day, and some beers were indeed called for. A second round happened within a few minutes, as most of them guzzled down the initial can in no time.

"Keep the noise down, or we'll get kicked out.", he whispered.

Now they were alone, his concentration grew stronger. The inspiration he required for this image rushed in, and he asked them all to stay silent. With no chatting, they all heard the patter of rain on the garage roof, and the water running through the guttering pipes.

From the bottom drawer of a dusty filing cabinet, he removed some drawing stuff he had hidden there. Paper, pencils and colouring in pencils. Although legal, to him it had felt like stashed contraband, after overhearing his parents quarrel one night.

"What you got in mind Stu?", asked Damian.

"Shush", came the reply with Stuart's hand in the air, his eyes remaining focussed on the paper.

While using a bench as a table, the rest gathered round. He quickly outlined their little town, making sure to include the nearby park and a shop they were all familiar with. He added a bit of colour to the trees, grass and their park bench. The sky was silence-black. Then he looked at all three of them. This was the most ominous look he'd ever given any of them. No words were spoken. To finish it off, he selected some different coloured pencils, and his hand approached the dark sky. He started drawing what looked to be a huge jaggy star. Stuart rapidly transformed it into a meteor, speeding passed overhead, right above their little town.

The boys looked on with confusion, and glanced at each other, but remained silent. Once finished, he checked the picture over for completeness, then he grabbed his signing pen. As his hand approached the right-hand bottom corner, where he'd sign all his work, his hand struggled to get there, feeling resistance like two opposite sides of a magnet forcing his hand away. It was like a warning not to sign it.

His hand was trembling. The rest looked on, questioning their very eyes. They suspected that the drawing, or something inside it seemed to be alive, and communicating with Stuart, issuing him with a caution against him authorising this event.

The delay had prompted him to a moment of reflection. Stuart's eyes rotated between the rest of them for any signs he should quit. No one said a word or shook their head.

'Do you still want to proceed?' It seemed like there was a third party telepathically interacting with him – through his artwork. A third party who could grant his command and make his drawing happen for real.

After a pause, and one very deep breath, he tried again, this time with a firmer grip and a bolder stance. But he didn't need to. The resistance had vanished. He'd been warned. The drawing had lowered its guard and Stuart quickly signed it – 'Stuart Howard'.

Almost immediately upon signing, the rain stopped. All four of them noticed this, and with the last of the rainwater trickling into the drains, outside fell eerily silent. Caleb, nearest to the garage door, opened it up, eager to see the nightline from outside. It was now well after 11pm but it seemed earlier, with the black clouds full of water all but gone now, leaving just the lighter ones remaining, and some were beginning to float away.

One by one, the group ventured outside, more cautiously than they entered, each one looking up. Everything started to change. The remaining clouds started to part, and as they did, they seemed to be making way for something. All four of the group found themselves sky-gazing in disbelief.

They'd never seen anything like this before. Shortly after, they all made their way back over to the bench in the park, sat – and began their wait.

It was just after midnight when the lads were still persevering outside, waiting anxiously for something to happen, when Simon announced, "Guys, that's now midnight. I'm calling it a day. Let's meet up tomorrow?", and started walking away.

Caleb shouted out, "Fucking hell, LOOK!", as he pointed, far away in the distance." No one else could see anything. "There, in the distance, I see it! It's coming this way."

Simon turned around. He'd resigned this event to being a non-starter, but he'd wait a bit longer if something was just about to kick off. The other two also looked up.

"I don't see anything. Where?", shouted Damian, annoyed after waiting so long.

Unable to prevent the small grin growing on his face, Caleb said, "Don't you all see it? Right there, next to the flying saucer."

It wasn't funny. They were all tired and the group were far from impressed as they all were beginning to lose faith in Stuart's 'so-called' ability. The escaped cat was just a coincidence after all – or a set up. Maybe Stuart would be flung out the gang.

"This is bollocks! Fuck it – I'm off. I'm knackered.", Simon angrily declared, but not shouting, being aware of the time of night.

"Guys, I'm going too. I'm almost sleeping on my feet!", Caleb said, being the next to declare he was retiring for the night. But before the pair left, the two of them looked at Stuart, expecting a nod of acceptance.

Instead of seeing that, they saw Stuart's eyes gradually beginning to glaze over, as if he had cataracts, his eyes wide open.

"Stu!", said Caleb, to alert him. "STUART!", a bit louder this time and with a worrying look, as Stuart hadn't responded. "Guys, what's happening?"

Stuart's neck gave way, and his head tipped over to the front. He was out cold, unconscious while still sitting on the bench that the four of them had occupied for the last hour. None of them knew what to do.

Then, suddenly, the jet-black sky started to brighten up. It caught the attention of the rest. The brightness intensified to almost daytime levels. Then, they all heard a deep rumbling, way off in the distance. All three of them looked around in different directions to see if they could spot anything. All three tough-guys were now looking rather timid. An unknown phenomenon was about to start.

Then, out of nowhere, it happened. Damian spotted it first. "Guys, look!" The pair looked to where Damian was pointing.

It was appearing from the East. Far off in the distance, the trio could see the beginnings of a bright light, a bit hazy as it was a hundred miles away and they couldn't focus that far. All of their eyes were now fixed on this marvel, like a fighter jet would lock-on to an enemy target in combat. They couldn't look away – they seemed hypnotised by it. It was now speeding directly towards them, and as it did, it got bigger, bit by bit.

The noise intensified as it neared. The guys covered their ears with their hands to block out the scream it was making. The thing was now turning the entire sky dazzlingly white, and they squinted through near-shut eyes, desperate to catch a glimpse of what was coming.

It was approaching fast – really fast. Damian budged Stuart with his elbow to alert him, to wake him out of the trance he seemed locked into, so he could witness all this too. It was his doing after all. It looked as if it was about a mile above the earth's surface, yet it was still absolutely enormous. The ground was now starting to shake.

They heard windows smashing with the intense rumbling and shaking it was causing, and the lights from every nearby lamp post went out. Electricity must have failed as they noticed that most of the homes went into darkness. As it passed overhead, all three of them dropped to the ground, as if it was close enough to the earth to clip them as it raced past. Not quite.

Then, it shot directly over and past the group in an instant, revealing just how fast it had been moving. It screamed at the top of its voice as it rocketed by, deliberately alerting everyone to its presence. It sounded like a Space Rocket's Rolls Royce engines being throttled to the limits as it soared its way over them.

It had been relatively still outside, but this thing charging past had created its own wind. The boys noticed the branches of trees being forced to bend over so much, the trunks of some of them snapped.

And then, as quickly as it arrived… it was gone. It had thundered its way over the horizon and out of sight. Its presence only evidenced by a trail of space dust left in its wake, and, for now, they were still airborne in the sky, glistening with a yellowish orange tint. The lads found themselves being lured to these beautiful sparkling particles, ensnared by their glittering dance, in an otherwise blank and empty sky. But after a few more seconds, they all faded into nothing, disappearing before their eyes. It was the most intense spectacle they'd ever witnessed.

They could see that the lights in the nearby street started to blink back on, one at a time. A few people were seen peering out through their glassless windows.

It was all over in less than fifteen seconds. Although the noise had been deafening, Stuart hadn't woken, and he'd been the only one that'd remained sitting throughout it all. The other three looked at each other, each one looking stumped and waiting for one of the other two to speak first. They approached Stuart. Only now it was over, did he appear to be waking from this deep sleep. More like a coma.

"Stuart!" Damian almost gave off a caring tone. "STU!", he repeated, "… are you okay buddy?" Damian put both hands on Stuart's shoulders, rocking him gently.

With one blink, Stuart's eyes switched to brown again. He paused and looked around, startled by the damage that hadn't been there before he closed his eyes just moments before – before something possessed him. He was absorbing the strewn rubbish mixed with tree leaves, some still settling to the ground, now this thing had gone.

"I'm fine.", he eventually said after a self-scan, but a hand on his head said differently. "What happened?"

The other three looked at each other. He hadn't seen it.

"What happened? Stu! Fuck me! You missed it all. It flew right over us – just like you drew! A shooting star!", explained Caleb, pointing at the sky while he spoke to remind a groggy Stuart he'd been the author of these events.

"It wasn't a fucking *shooting star*, dipshit! It was a meteor – or, or a fireball. It was on fire!", Simon argued, correcting Caleb's ignorance.

"Stuarty boy… we don't know what it was… ", Damian added, "… but it was just like you drew it!", exhaling loudly with laughter with those last few words.

Stuart gingerly tried to stand up, but he staggered and almost fell. He would have done, had it not been for the reflexes of Damian's hand that'd caught his arm. This firm grip brought an old memory back, from the first day in the revised gang, and he found himself recalling that entire memory, but much quicker than it happened in real life.

He immediately sat back down on the bench, even then, searching for balance. The others were more hyped than he was. "Fuck me. Ahh."

"You okay bud?", Damian asked.

"No. Oh, Jesus fuck!" With his vision spinning, Stuart rolled off the bench and onto the ground, where he managed to mumble, "Headache… *SEVERE* headache."

Stuart didn't really need a narrative. While out cold, he'd envisaged the events in his mind playing out before it happened in reality. He'd drawn it too. He was only checking-in with them that it had worked. But this headache was more intense than anything he'd ever had before. He'd been warned these may happen, from his own Grandfather William, who'd called them 'ultra-migraines', but they faded quickly.

For both these occasions, he'd seen a mini-trailer to the event at some point after signing, but this one was accompanied with a killer-headache – the first one was just a dullness. He discovered that they'd last around half an hour before they eventually started to disappear. He'd never suffered from migraines before. These had to be connected. Now, he was positive they were.

Sketching a third event was inevitable, and despite there being a price to pay for exercising his talent, he was fast becoming addicted.

Migraines were a punishment by a higher power he'd never meet. A punishment that he'd bear alone. But this was only the half of it – these were just short-term punishments. In time, he'd learn of a much higher price he'd pay for using this gift.

Chapter 3

A few eventful months later, Stuart knew he'd have to split from the group. That would need planning. He'd break the news to Damian, and do so in private. It wouldn't be the right thing to do any other way. Finally, his better side was edging him out of this dodgy, going-nowhere gang, and onto a cleaner path. Now, he regretted joining in the first place.

He'd always felt different – like he had a purpose in life, something deeper, something more than just being good at drawing. Over the last few months, he'd felt changes. His body had sent its first dire message, communicated in a different way, a way he didn't even know existed. It was a strange feeling, and he couldn't express himself to the others.

Now he knew for sure that his gift came at a cost – but altering the future – making things happen that weren't going to happen otherwise, and all he got was a black-out? No way! He rightly suspected that there would be a higher price to pay, but he didn't know what, and he didn't know when that day would come. To him, this ability was like a double edged sword, and the second, sharper edge would hunt him down later.

His mother told him to visit his grandfather during those months, and the news his sick Papa Will gave him was grim. With his mind properly messed-up by it all, he soon realised that he'd need to ration the rolling-out of his fantasies for the sake of his sanity, or quit completely. But Damian wasn't about to let that happen. No other gang member had this talent on their CV. When Stuart joined the gang around two years earlier, no one had known this thing then. And despite Stuart having his hand raised after winning that initial ceremony battle, they all realised that they wouldn't need his strength or his wrestling skills. Rather, Stuart's gift would be utilised instead, and Damian's mind had swelled full of ideas on how to use it to his full benefit.

They used it to get other gangs caught by the cops. They used it to make sure cops were elsewhere when they broke into homes, and they used it for other heists too. But over time, Stuart had begun to feel used himself. They were all benefitting, but only one of them was suffering, and no one seemed bothered.

What Stuart hadn't known, was that each time he utilised it, later on in life he'd also suffer another terrible curse, and over those months, it had been growing more potent, accumulating with each score they took. But recently, with frequent use, it had been taking its toll on him so much, that he'd been drained. Enough was enough. It just wasn't worth it anymore.

He reached a point where he needed to stop. It was a scary thing to possess anyway. Better just to see how things unfold, he thought. Let nature take its normal course of events. But he knew it wouldn't last. He knew when the time came, if he really needed to, he'd go back to his old ways and use his gift again, but this time, for his own benefit.

No one else suffered. None of the gang got hurt. They just counted the cash, or sold whatever they got away with at the last score. He'd always known that when the time was right, he'd leave and go it alone. So just after their latest, but unsuccessful late-night raid that he'd completed together with Damian, he realised that moment had arrived.

"Fuck this, Damian. I can't do this shit anymore." His heart still racing from the getaway run, legs cocked in sprint-ready mode, aware they may still be getting hunted by the owner of the home, or the cops if he'd rang them. With the cover of the bridge – their main hub and go-to place if they ever split up to evade capture, now seemed the right place and time for his departure. "We almost got caught, for fuck's sake!" The bridge's cave-like echo hammering home the closeness of capture, and resonating the emptiness of hollow pockets.

"What the fuck are you saying, Stuarty?", Damian snarled, clearly the tougher of the two, despite being a bit younger. Of course, he knew fine what Stuart was telling him. "We didn't get caught!"

"… yeah, so far… ", interrupted Stuart, before Damian could add anything else, "… we've just been lucky Key, and next time… who knows what'll happen… and for what – fuck all."

They'd ran from the home they were robbing before they could take anything this time. Ran scared as the owner walked down the stairs, shotgun in hand, ready to protect his family at all costs. This light sleeper had somehow been alerted to their unwelcome presence, perhaps from the twiddling of the back door's lock.

Stuart was thinking ahead, and knew Damian would blame him for not thinking it all through and 'fixing' things like that, and including this in his sketch – sorting it in advance. Although he was leaving, or asking permission to leave, he needed to sound firm.

"Christ almighty, the cops might be on to us!", he added, referring to the last time when a Police car had rolled past them, a bit slower than usual, suspicious eyes peering.

"Fuck the cops… ", came Damian's reply, "… they've got nothing on us – you see to that!", he concluded with confidence, winking at Stuart as he finished.

No reply echoed back.

"... Quitting while you're ahead?" He knew he'd leave sooner or later.

"Yeah, I guess so, Key. It's the right thing to do. It's been fucking me up... you *know* it has. You get out too.", attempting to sound more like a suggestion, than an instruction. He knew better than to tell Damian what to do.

Damian had been the Alpha male among the small group of four they used to be, until Simon had also left the group just a month ago, Caleb being forced to stay, by their leader. This would leave just two of them if Stuart departed, or got permission to. Hardly a 'gang' they once labelled themselves. And without their formidable member playing an ace every now and then, this gang's future was most certainly over. Each one of them would now be especially vulnerable to other gangs. Targeted by them, payback for things they'd done earlier.

Being wary of what Stuart could do, Damian had always been careful not to cross a particular line. He certainly didn't want him as an enemy. With a small grin developing across one side of his cheek, and beginning to nod in acceptance of his departure, he paused and said, "So you're doing a Simon! ... All right... but.... I'll be seeing you around."

Damian extended his hand out, fingers above thumb, as if to sanction the exit, his approval as leader being required, and, without that, nobody's departure was authorised. Stuart's hand quickly joined Damian's, but it wasn't genuine. It wasn't met with the same grip strength or enthusiasm as normal, Stuart distinguishing his look of disappointment, from good luck. And while never breaking eye contact, Damian's fake smile, which had revealed his missing tooth just to the side of the two front ones, quickly vanished from sight. This Alpha male wouldn't let go until he'd had the last word. While gripping harder, he repeated with intensity which *was* genuine, "See you around."

Chapter 4

Around three months later, Damian contacted Stuart and told him to meet him in the park at the usual bench they all knew as their alternate, rendezvous safe-place. It was just the two of them. Damian was already sitting on the bench by the time he arrived, but he wasn't late.

"How you been?", Stuart asked, sitting down opposite as he spoke.

"I need a favour, Stu." He got straight to the point.

Stuart saw a different side to Damian's demeanour. He was serious. "Sure, Key. What do you need?"

Damian let out a long sigh. "You know that girl I've been seeing?"

Stuart paused, briefly scanning his memory for any sign of seeing him with someone. "No. What girl?"

"Em…" He was normally a fluid speaker and never stuttered or paused. "Okay. Well, there's this girl… well, I've being meeting up with a girl from out of town." He let out another sigh, this time shaking his head as he done so. "She's fuckin pregnant man!"

Stuart knew his old pal well enough not to congratulate him. This was a problem, and Stuart didn't smile or grin at all, but he did look up at the sky. He wasn't religious, he never went to church, and he didn't believe in God, but he looked up anyway. No help was offered.

"What you gonna do?"

"Nothing!", came the instant reply. "That's where *you* come in."

"Me?", gasped Stuart, with a hand on his chest. "What the fuck do you want *me* to do? I don't even know who you're talking about!"

Eyeing his former friend he said, "Stuart, we all know about your gift. Your... *ability*... to make shit happen."

Stuart could now sense the smell of drink coming from his old pal's breath. 'Fuck me', he thought. Yes, he could make things happen, but he couldn't undo this.

"Key. What the fuck are you saying?", came a snappy reply. No one got away with speaking to Damian this way, but in the here and now, it was Damian that was crawling back, seemingly demanding a miracle.

Damian looked directly at Stuart. "I need you to make it go away."

"And how exactly am I going to do that?"

"This girl, Stu, has got fuck all. She wants the baby. Christ, I can't seem to talk sense into her. She's only 15, Stu!"

"Fuck sake!"

"... and she won't have an abortion. I could get the money but she's not having it. She just wants the child! Desperate for a child with *anyone*, the whore, and it wouldn't matter who. You know the type. And I'm telling you, she's just a child *herself*! I'm not ready to be a dad! I don't want a kid! I wouldn't be a good dad anyway. Seeing my kid on a weekend only, while she went out partying. I've got no money. I don't have a job. Stuarty, listen to me... she's fucking blackmailing me."

"How?" The lack of response suggested otherwise. "Key – how?"

Looking desperate with his head cupped in his hands, Damian exhaled loudly. "She says she'll tell the cops I raped her! She's only 15. FUCK! I never asked her age. I just... I thought she looked older. Jesus, you don't ask do you! *She* came onto *me*! Stu, I could go to prison!"

Stuart was witnessing a new side to Damian. Only now, Damian seemed to be realising the consequences of rash actions. That didn't sound like the Damian he'd known. With Stuart out the gang, it seemed Damian had ventured into other, deeper waters. What had he gotten himself involved in now? Was he telling the truth? Had he become a pimp? Stuart couldn't bring himself to ask. Actually, he didn't want to know.

"What's done – stays done Key! You know that! I can't... *reverse* time!"

Damian knew what he really wanted Stuart to do. It wasn't long before he said it. "I need you to draw her giving birth to a stillborn baby." It must have been the first time, but he couldn't look at Stuart when he spoke. He knew the sick gravity of this request.

"You are, of course – fuckin joking?"

"She's too young to be a mom anyway. A kid would ruin her life for fuck sake!", justifying his atrocious plan. It was all so simple to Damian. A quick fix, almost implying this was the one and only thing he'd ever asked from Stuart. Nothing could be further from the truth. Stuart was spent. He'd been used, over and over. Sucked in, chewed up and spat out. It'd been all take and no give.

"Stu – I NEED this! I can't be a dad, and I can't go to jail... she's a fuckin manipulating... "

Stuart put his hand up to obtain some thinking time, but he'd already got there. "Are you fuckin deluded? I'm not God! For fuck sake, Damian!"

Damian faced the ground again. For the first time ever, he looked ashamed. Not of what he'd gotten himself entangled in, but of what he was asking his pal, rather – begging his former pal, to do for him, and he wasn't in control. His lips opened and his mouth moved a bit, but nothing came out.

Stuart had been blackmailed by Damian before. It was to stay with the gang after they found out about his gift. If he'd left, Damian threatened to tell everyone about it. And if that happened, Stuart thought everyone would see him as the son of Satan, or some kind of freak, and he'd be taken away and locked up in some underground research chamber, with Government officials secretly performing experiments on him, with leads connecting him to machines that lab experts in white jackets would be monitoring, taking notes on their flipboards. Once again, his mind raced ahead. He had to stay a member of the gang back then, but he was in charge now.

"Do you even understand the consequences for *me*?"

Despite feeling a bit sleepy from the liquor he'd knocked back prior to meeting Stuart to make this a bit easier, he was awake to the fact that his request wasn't going to be granted. Then, after a moment's pause, he said, "Yeah! You black out and… and get a headache.", downgrading his side effects, appearing magnanimous as he did so.

"No – No – FUCKING No! Let me stop you right there! For me, it's *much* more than that!" He paused to consider revealing it. "Fuck it, I'm not even going to tell you. There's consequences for *me*, Damian! *Serious* consequences – it's not just a fucking *headache*!"

"Stu, this is my *life*, man. I'm *begging* you!"

Stuart remained deep in thought, prodding his brain to find an alternative way out.

"Stu, you're the only one that can do this… and you still owe me, man."

Stuart's head remained where it was, but his disgusted eyes immediately darted towards Damian's, explaining his disgust on his behalf. Now Damian was cashing in his chip.

Was he referring to Stuart's 'ability', and he'd not told officials about what he's capable of doing, so far? Of course, sunglass wearing agents from the Government hadn't snatched him and dragged him into the side of a black van and sped away. Not yet. Or was Damian referring to the time, years ago, where Stuart was on the ground, getting beat up in an alleyway by three lads from a gang out of town, and he'd intervened, kicked the one of them who was kneeling over him so hard in the face that he heard the boy's jaw dislocate, leaving him screaming in agony, and then rescuing Stuart from the ground and quickly getting out of their territory? Did it even matter?

Stuart thought he'd paid up in full, and then some. 'Sorting' it, that other gangs got snared in the various traps he'd set to pave the way clear for them to do whatever they wanted and get away with it, within reason, of course. It all had to be viable.

It wasn't too long after that beating, when they decided to make their 'group' a proper 'gang' and toughen the fuck up. These thoughts took only an instant to weigh up, then Stuart replied.

"If I do this thing… If I even *could* do this…" Damian began nodding in acceptance of his former friend's terms, despite not knowing what they were yet. "… then it's the final time.

The very last fucking thing I do for you.", pointing at him. "And then – I'm finished, forever. It's over! Because… essentially, you're asking me… you're asking me to murder a fucking baby!"

Stuart was committed now. "You can't tell anyone. *ANYONE – EVER.* Understand?"

Damian nodded, still not looking at Stuart but making sure he saw his accepting gesture. Now it was time for Stuart to turn the bribe table around.

"Key, listen to me. I'm fuckin deadly serious man! This would ruin my entire life. Only me and you will know about this, right?"

"Yeah, of course!" It was a kind of 'whatever' reply, quickly blurted out now he'd got his way.

"So, if I hear a word about this from a single soul – then it can only have come from you. In that case, I'm coming out fighting, and I'm looking for you. Do not make me do it. We're even, after this, right?"

Stuart offered his hand, a normal gentleman's handshake, and they shook on it. It was Stuart that had the firmer grip this time.

"I'm not doing a stillbirth, though." That got Damian's attention. "It's too far in the future."

"Shit." Damian hadn't thought about that.

"If I do this, it'll be today."

From six months away, to right now – today – tonight even, Damian felt an instant chill. It shook him like he was plugged in. Now, this thing was hitting home hard – very hard – that there's no time to prepare or get ready. The immediacy of this plot made things deadly real, and it stopped him in his tracks. He hadn't thought this far ahead. Typical. Maybe he'd regret afterwards that he was deleting his very own child from history. Or more like he'd blame Stuart. Typical. And once the reality of it all set in, and the finger of blame extended, there would be repercussions. And it *would* set in.

"When I do this… ", Stuart continued, shaking his head, "… it will happen within 24 hours. It always does. Christ almighty please forgive me.", he begged, while looking up at the sky again. He hadn't heard the geese that had been flying overhead, but he saw them now. He envied their liberty, how free they were to do what they wanted, and go where the air under their wings took them, sailing through the air. Like them, Stuart had felt free the last few months. Now, invisible iron bars were forming around him again and they were bending the logic of his thoughts, and he needed to think straight.

Now he'd been recalled back to his No 2 role in the gang again, for one final hit. Those last few months in the gang had been torment for Stuart. The others had envied him, but that was out of ignorance. It was a sombre inducing moment, a place he didn't want to be.

"Where does she live?"

"In a flat, just outside town."

"In that case… tomorrow, she's falling down a flight of stairs, or… being shot, or… No! It will have to be something else. I'll need to think. Key, make sure you're somewhere else, far away, and make sure you're seen by people. You need a strong alibi. Understood?"

With that, Stuart insisted that he be given all the details that he'd need for this to happen. Who she was. Where she'd be. The layout of the block of flats, etc. It was against his better judgement, his morals and his conscience. Just the very thought of this was making him ill. His new girlfriend could never, ever know about it, so he didn't write anything down. He'd have to remember it all instead.

"Leave it with me. We won't see each other again." And with that, Stuart got up and walked away.

Of course they'd meet again – Damian didn't have anything else.

Damian's head was up his arse, but while Stuart's thoughts un-muddied themselves on his walk home, he realised that when the dust settled and reality set in, Damian would come charging back, leading a solo stampede, and seeking revenge for killing his child. And before the day arrived when Damian twigged onto that concept, he'd have to do something drastic.

Chapter 5 – 2014

It wasn't until thirty-two years later, that the peace had been shattered and Stuart had been reminded of the past life he'd tried to forget. He'd been truly ashamed of it all, but in his unique mind, he'd boxed-up all those shitty memories and sent them into outer space. Over time, they'd all faded away. It was as if the gangs, the stealing, the beatings and everything else had been sketched with disappearing ink – that is, apart from one.

Living with extreme guilt is a terrible thing – it can consume you, especially if you keep it to yourself. But Stuart was now a changed man, and although remorseful, he'd never shared his guilt with anyone. He'd never found a way to do it. Who'd believe him anyway?

Now 52, he'd led a decent life, consciously trying to make up for the ills of his past, most of which hadn't made the journey to 2014 with him. He'd never forgiven himself for killing that unborn baby, and he'd only used his gift one more time since that awful night. It was too much power that had been handed to him. Too much power for one boy to cope with.

He'd set a 44 year timer inside his head, and it'd been constantly ticking away, annoying him all the time. He knew the peace in Westfield was going to end sooner or later, but a decade or more later, and maybe he'd have taken his family far away by then? He wasn't told it'd happened, but he'd felt that prison's iron gate creak open, just in time for Christmas.

During all these years, Stuart had married his childhood sweetheart Sarah, and raised a family of one, a son named Michael. Mike was now a man himself – a married man to Debbie and they'd had a son, Justin. Debbie was beautiful inside and out. Apart from her obvious physical attraction and her soft, feminine physique, she never smoked and she never took drugs. She barely even swore, certainly not in front of others. Best of all, they just clicked effortlessly, and they got on without having to try.

During the years that Justin had grown to fifteen, Debbie never revealed his secret to anyone. It had taunted her since his birth, slowly nibbling away at her sanity. She loved her son, but hated this thing inside him. She viewed it as an omen, and it had slowly consumed her, robbing her of joyous mom-hood, unwelcomingly stalking her down, like wolves' hunt deer.

All those years, they'd remained in that little village of Westfield. Moving away seemed like betrayal to their roots, and to Stuart, moving would be costly, in more ways than one. To him, it would be running away from his past, and he knew it would chase him down. It would be like waving a red rag to a bull, and he'd resigned himself to the fact that he'd just have to face his bull – eventually. In the background, that timer had always been counting down, nearing zero, but it had suddenly skipped 12 years, and the alarm had rung early. All of a sudden, they'd ran out of time.

Chapter 6

Westfield had quickly become a place you don't want to live. It had a bad feel to it now, and it wasn't safe, especially when it got dark. Synonymous with prison, Stuart imagined. It had all turned sour since Damian got released and kids vanished. Were they eventually going to bring in Mr Keefer? He wouldn't answer a single question until his lawyer arrived anyway. Holding Damian would be risky. Maybe seen as 'harassment'. Maybe he'd sue again? They ran on a tight budget as it was, without having to fork out compensation payments yet again, to a piece of shit like him.

It felt as if Damian was waiting, biding his time, and had been thoroughly expecting them to break down his door all heavy handed, suited-up, knocking him to the floor and tightly ratcheting up the cuffs – just like all those cell-raids – then speeding off to the interrogation room with lights flashing, leaving neighbours gossiping. But it never happened, and the weeks were passing.

Damian had gotten smart inside, and had spent the years wisely. Uneducated and near-illiterate, he'd bettered himself and made the most of his time. He read books. He helped other cons to read too. He wasn't quite a lawyer himself, but he'd read all the law books he could get his hands on, and everything else.

He'd also learned to listen, a skill he didn't have before, and over the years he'd become friendly – but not friends, with a few other convicts, each one with a different story to hear. Inevitably, they'd chat about their crimes on the free side of the wall, revealing how they'd escaped or beaten the prosecution. But of course, they all had their own 'bank job' to tell of, and they'd open up about how they got pinched. Cell-rehab, consists of cons teaching other cons to be better crooks, and over the decades, Damian had listened to dozens of stories. Once back on the outside, he was never getting caught again.

And when others slowly rotted away, had gone insane with worry about what their wives were getting up to while they stewed the years away, one by torturous one, or got bullied for smokes and, of course, their ass, Damian hadn't. He hadn't had anything worth losing on the outside anyway. Fuck them all. And who's going to bully Damian? He *was* the bully. Prison was never going to be tough for a hornet among bees.

But when a young man loses his liberty, that's not all he loses. Most convicts are greeted by someone when released. Family, normally. Family that had stood by them, through everything. He'd been freed to no one. He'd caught the bus, and that was it.

For the first time in over three decades, his time was now flying past. He'd travelled solo again, bussed it South, unsupervised at last and headed homebound, all the time his eyes scanning the land, noticing changes to it. For over thirty years, he'd been ordered what to do. Now, he was his own professor again, and no one was pulling his strings. And during his final few months inside, knowing the most senior Judges would be desperately trying to find something, anything to deny his appeal – but failing – he'd made his own release plans.

Chapter 7

Westfield was known for being a sleepy little town, teetering on the edge of boring some would say, but safe. The cops had next to nothing to do, apart from the odd house call for loud music from a party, or issue the occasional speeding ticket. Since Christmas, things had changed drastically. The local newspaper had reported that three children had been kidnapped from Westfield – all local to the community. Twin boys in late December and a fourteen year-old girl just a few weeks later. The twins were almost thirteen.

Now that it'd turned February, and the Police still had no one in custody, everyone was on edge, some panicking about what was next, and desperation was setting in for relatives of the missing. Some ignorant minds suspected the newly freed Mr Keefer – but why would he risk being carted straight back to prison? Many of the local's fingers pointed towards the odd Howard family, mainly Mike and his father Stuart, despite the break-in to Stuart's home just over a week ago. And so began a cruel onslaught of taunting and revenge from the townies.

Yes, they *were* a bit odd, but they didn't look the kidnapping type, but then again, you can never tell. Thank God, a few people were on their side. One of them was Justin's best friend and his parents who'd they'd spoken with at school a few times, mainly while waiting for the kids to rush out. A bit more logical thinking, and not personally affected or related to the missing kids, they hadn't taken sides. Innocent until proven guilty, kind of thing. The last thing the Howards needed was the entire town on their backs. Having one decent family talking reason among the others, was like a hung jury.

Nevertheless, in the street, just outside Justin's home, sometimes people had gathered and would shout things.

"Fucking evil scum!" "Get out before we burn your home.", had been a death threat that the Howards simply couldn't ignore.

They'd drawn their drapes in fear, as if that would help dampen the volume of the chanting somehow, or put a stop to it. They'd squatted down, clamping their ears, occasionally glancing at each other in the dark, trying to give the impression they were out. But there was no hiding from this. The town folk had spoken, and they'd had enough.

These threats were not to be taken lightly. At the end of January, Justin's grandparent's home had been burgled. The place had been messed-up, personal things taken. All of Grammy Sarah's jewellery had been stolen, not that it was worth much. Things precious to them, such as old, framed photographs had been left strewn on the floor, the broken glass revealing they'd been hard-heartedly trampled over, in the process of thieving or ruining what was there.

But worse than that, and sickeningly so, their mattress had been urinated on, as if to make a statement. The stench was awful. Even after a removal firm took the thing away and after they had replaced the entire bed with a new one, it had still taken over a week before the stink had finally gone, the noxious smell of bleach on the floorboards taking over.

The smell would eventually fade but the image of the act itself remained vividly imprinted on both their minds. Who would do such a thing? They had talked this through, but only once. Sarah got the impression Stuart had been holding something back from her, with his abrupt responses suspiciously sounding pre-rehearsed.

This event affected them differently. Sarah was more shocked than Stuart, and she had puzzled over why this had happened to them and not anyone else in their neighbourhood. It wasn't a series of break-ins, and they didn't have valuables. She got an unnerving suspicion that they'd been targeted. But her husband knew it was a warning. The lifting of the jewellery was a red herring. Sarah didn't have anything worth stealing. It was simply made to look like a robbery. The 'thief' had been there for an alternate reason.

Stuart wasn't psychic, but he damn well knew who was behind this. Peeing on beds was a sort of 'calling-card' he was all too familiar with from memories afar. Memories he'd thought he'd wiped clear from his mind. A disgusting MO, from an equally disgusting man with a point to prove. An old acquaintance, who'd served serious time for armed robbery at a bank in the city many years ago, which had gone wrong, and he'd been caught.

The resulting 12-day trial had seen the jury find him guilty of this crime, and of brandishing his sawn-off shotgun, using the butt of it to break an overly resilient teller's nose, and threatening to fire it in her face as she lay bleeding on the floor, her tears diluting the blood on her blouse. This threat was leverage, to get the Manager to open the vault and do it quickly. His resolve quickly vanished, and the keys were passed over by a trembling hand to a calm one.

However, the Police had already been alerted to this robbery and they'd arrived early. The resulting shoot-out sealed his fate to a much longer jail term. He'd been sentenced to 44 years in Pendleton Correctional Facility in Indiana, a maximum-security prison catering for extremely violent offenders.

This bank heist was something they were both firmly involved in, but Stuart walked free and he hadn't. At some stage, just as the Police arrived, Stuart had removed his mask and pretended to be one of the bank's customers instead. None of the other customers had seen Stuart's face as they'd both arrived with masks on, and no one seen him take it off either, as they had all been ordered to lie on the ground, face down, eyes shut.

The bank's CCTV system had somehow stopped working twenty minutes before the pair stormed inside. The cops knew it was a two-man job, and had discovered Stuart's involvement, but they used him as leverage. He'd been bribed to shore-up their fabricated version of events, rat out Damian and help put him away for good. It was a deal he had to make, as he'd recently discovered that Sarah was pregnant. Quite simply, Stuart needed the money the bank job would have brought, but now they'd been caught, he couldn't do hard time inside.

The cops were aware of all of this, and strategically played their hand, forcing Stuart to testify he was merely a bank customer, and after the shots were fired, he hid in a corner, trembling with fear. He swore he saw Damian shooting at the Police – which of course, didn't happen. Damian had sat quietly in the dock, smiling at Stuart during Stuart's made-up bullshit evidence, declaring he had merely gone to the bank alone to open a savings account for his unborn child, and he was simply in the wrong place at the wrong time.

Stuart was lying as much as the four cops had been and he couldn't look Damian in the eye during the trial, just the odd glance. When he done so, he saw Damian grinning directly at him, realising his former friend's betrayal and that he'd now stand no chance of being found not guilty. He understood Stuart's reasons, but his fake smirk revealed there would be consequences, payback at the first opportunity and this would not be forgotten. It was terrifying. Damian never ratted anyone out, and he took the 5th throughout questioning and the hearing, as a 'fuck you' to the cops, and the system.

Damian had attended the trial in a rented suit, and with his hair grown much longer and now combed neatly into a side shed, where it had merely been shaved all over by his mother at home for as long as Stuart could remember. Make up had covered the tattoos on his face and neck. Glaringly obvious defence tactics to sway the jury into thinking that he was a decent man, not a man that could have committed such an atrocious crime.

The Police's main focus had been to nail this thug at whatever cost, a notorious small time criminal who'd now stepped into the big time league, and a big time sentence is all that would suffice the Judge. But also as Damian had, allegedly, '… aimed his sawn-off shotgun at the Police and had discharged it, to the reckless endangerment of the lives of innocent bystanders and Police Officers.', and it was, '… only due to the Police's professionalism and expert training that they, and the bank's customers and staff were unharmed.', the Judge summed up.

But Damian had now been released on appeal, his committed hot-shot lawyer recently finding a loophole in the legal system via the details of a new, and unrelated case and exploiting it to the maximum. A forty percent commission fee will do that. Something to do with the way crucial evidence had been improperly stored by Officers, then it vanished, coupled with the testimony told by two Police Department Officers who said they'd only used 'reasonable force', given the circumstances, and they justified beating-up the armed suspect, because they'd 'feared for their lives'. They'd used this reasonable force given the immediate danger, and it was proportionate.

The sucker punch coming for these Officers, when it was ruled that the prosecution could produce footage filmed by a passer-by on his mobile phone, clearly showing the suspect wasn't armed at all, and the cops beat him up as he lay spread-eagled on the ground in surrender mode, and they also stole his wallet in the process. It should have been settled out of court.

Perjury is a sackable event for all Indiana Police, and the two Westfield Police Officers were indeed dismissed. But these very two Officers had been part of the original four who'd given matching testimony to the court when Damian had been sent down 32 years earlier. The Court obviously believing the word of four decorated Police Officers, and a witness, against the pathetic, optimistic, and implausible 'Not Guilty' plea of Mr Keefer, a notorious ex-convict who was responsible for seeing Westfield town's crime rate rise and embarrassing Westfield Police Department in the process. It was the only words he'd spoken during his trial.

And with that new case, 'State versus O'Hara, 2013', Damian's final appeal was there for the taking, and release papers bearing his name had been working their way through this maze of a system – full of red tape, locked doors and barricades. Although he'd spent 32 years inside, he was now a free man, and had received $3.3 million dollars compensation by the state due to the Police Department's staff lying, desperate to see this criminal went down at any cost, and falsifying evidence in the process. They'd settled out of court. All four Officers had since been dismissed, and they were now all facing charges of their own, the hearing set for late 2014.

Damian was out. A free man now, but a tormented one, seeking payback, and this had been his way of letting Stuart know he was back in town. Message delivered. He'd stewed in prison for decades and had years to reflect on his knee-jerk request to Stuart about the pregnancy of his unborn child and firmly decided that Stuart, being the smarter of the two, should have told him to fuck off home, sober up and think all the consequences through, before coming back.

His full name was Damian Adam Keefer and he was a year and a chunk younger than Stuart. For a lad of 19 years old at the time of his sentencing, he was tall and well built, with a few tattoos. He'd been a tough and cocky guy, always having an answer for everything, and when he didn't, the outcome of a fight usually ended up deciding who was right. Mostly so, just his proposition of one.

This tough guy had now gotten much tougher, something prison does for many who serve serious time. It's either that, or crumble. His tattoo collection had also evolved while inside, and on his chest, he bore the Devil who is shown cutting his own wrists with a knife while laughing.

Being imprisoned, he'd been deprived of his chance of raising a family of his own, all down to a few corrupt cops, who he'd be paying a visit soon, and the corresponding words of his former pal who'd sealed his fate to a much lengthier sentence and at a much tougher jail. He accepted his guilt, but he'd taken the full brunt of an overzealous Judge's rant all by himself.

While getting his home's locks changed, it'd become obvious to Stuart that the prison's rehabilitation programme wasn't working. This leopard didn't even try, and was out to avenge him *and* perhaps his family – the family Damian never got to raise. This was a chilling prospect and the events that would follow would leave Stuart, and his entire family devastated forever.

Chapter 8

Sarah had packed a bag for the night and left. Since the break-in almost a fortnight ago, that'd become more common. Away for the night, out on a drive to meet up with another friend in the city, she'd assured him. He'd never been invited, but these stayovers and time away from all this stuff would be good for her, Stuart thought.

All alone, it'd been a solitary ice cube sailing around his glass of Jack Daniels that had broken a minute's silence as he sat in his rocking chair, a place where thoughts came to him best – but always in random order. And as he closed his eyes, seeking out the past, he went there…

Through their entire married life, he'd never cheated on Sarah, or even tried to. In fact, he never even considered it. However, he hadn't been completely honest with her. He'd never revealed his past life and his ability to her, and as the years rolled by, he'd kept it that way, trying to block those memories out, hoping it might all just… go away. The right time to tell her, simply never arrived. Now he wished he'd let her in from the start.

He allowed his mind to drift back to the time when making his son's girlfriend most welcome in the home. And when an excited Debbie and Mike made their pregnancy announcement, he and Sarah were overjoyed, champagne was uncorked and tears shed. He'd been a witness to her health deteriorating as the years rolled on. His guilty hand took another sip…

He rocked up a bittersweet fact. Young Justin had grown up knowing only one set of grandparents. 'That would be me and Sarah', as disdain returned again. Deborah's own parents had disowned her years ago, before their announcement. Her parents were deeply religious, and they hadn't approved of her relationship with Mike right from the very start. They were Jehovah's Witness worshipers and went along to the meeting hall at least once every week, usually more. They saw the other witnesses as their 'brothers' and 'sisters'. Their own daughter was soon to have a son, their first grandson – their *only* grandson, and a *real* grandson by blood and DNA. However, Mike wasn't religious at all, and hadn't accepted any of their persistent offers to join their congregation.

His searching mind found the day when baby Justin had been born at the local hospital. Debbie's parents didn't even show up. It was only him and Sarah who'd been supportive, paradoxically being the faithful ones – loyally devoting themselves all through her pregnancy and all through labour's final hours. Nonetheless, showing forgiveness, he knew Debbie and Mike had taken their new son to visit them in their home, as they hadn't visited Justin since he'd been born two months earlier.

There were no hugs, or pictures taken of the new baby. No champagne corks were sent flying. Their focus was always elsewhere, usually preparing for the next meeting at the hall, Mike had told him, and that continued for months. Debbie and Mike decided not to push things, so as not to antagonise anyone. After their latest, disastrous visit to Debbie's parents, they decided to wait until they contacted them, hoping they'd long to see their one and only grandson again, and take him a walk in the park or feed the ducks. It never happened.

Debbie had committed to Mike and her own little family, and she'd given up trying to fix ties with her parents. It was better for all sides that this battle was over. Her parents were happy with their 'family' and unhappy when their real family was visiting. The Howards were happy with their own little family, and they felt like intruders when they visited her parents. Some problems are best left unfixed. Ties were cut, and baby Justin never saw his second set of grandparents again. 'My boy's now fifteen', he smiled.

Debbie insisted she gave birth first, then the wedding could commence a few months afterwards. Of course there would be pictures taken, and she didn't want to look 'fat' in her words. But those pictures would tell another story – if only someone had looked closer. Time for another sip until the next memory arrived…

In 1999, Justin was born into their strange world. He knew it was the happiest he'd ever been. More than anyone else, he was the most proud. He knew his grandson and him would have a bond like no other. And as he rocked in that chair, it brought back visions of gently rocking his baby grandson side to side on his knees.

Mike and Debbie got married in the following months. Not a church thing – Mike had never stepped foot in one. Theirs was a small one, not bothering to spend more than they needed on fancy photographers, expensive cars and cakes. They managed all this between themselves, and the end result was just the same.

It was now just a small family of the five of them. They were all quite young for their place in the family, as neither Grammy Sarah nor himself had reached forty yet when Justin was born. Young and healthy grandparents growing up with their young family, in Westfield, Indiana. Although abandoned by half his grandparents, young Justin had grown up fine. In fact, their small family had a very special bond. Tight ties, and for all the right reasons. It had all seemed so perfect. But the past can't be erased, and that story is embarrassing – but not for *his* family.

His glass was sweating. He tipped up another memory, misting the glass on the inside too with his breath. Oblivious to everyone in town, he'd made a secret deal with the cops before the trial – a sort of coalition partnership. Since then, he'd been seeking redemption, working with the Police as a secret informer in the state, in return for immunity. Time for another sip…

The Police had known fine well that he was involved in that bank robbery, but only as a second 'lookout' – and the escape driver of the stolen car. Regardless, the cops wanted him siding with them – not with Damian, as it was Damian they were really after. So they struck a deal, and they'd been utilising this 'alliance' for years now.

Most weekends, late at night, he'd either be tasked with driving around a town they'd told him to scope out, or just be somewhere, blending-in with the innocents, being their eyes and ears, sometimes wearing a wire. He'd wait until Sarah was asleep before venturing out. After a few hours, he'd return home and slip silently back under those cold covers. She never mentioned if she'd noticed, but she must have.

If there was anything worthy of note, he'd meet a plain clothed Officer at a pre-determined destination, just as if it was two old friends meeting up for a coffee. If he had nothing to report, he simply wouldn't show up. Over the years, the cops had begun trusting him more. The alliance they'd formed meant that they never hassled him about anything, in fact their relationship bloomed and even the odd parking ticket simply vanished. Many scores in Indiana had been foiled, criminals caught and tried, and crime rates were at an all-time low. The town had become a safer place to live and a better place to bring up kids. Shops had returned to Westfield and the town had begun to thrive again.

But these recent kidnappings had foiled everyone, and the townies had gradually lost confidence in the Police again. It was as if the Police themselves had been locked up, unable to do anything. There was still a lunatic on the loose and no one was safe anymore.

However, for him, a whole new side to this thing had been activated. Without making any drawings, he'd received a vision. A vision in relation to one of those kidnappings. The taking of a little girl from the town, Sarah-Jane Preston. It wasn't as vivid or as clear as they were years before, when he'd been the author of these events, but it was an image, nonetheless. A bit fuzzy, yes. A bit out of focus, yes. But revealing. Sickening. *And* – he knew who was behind it, yet he hadn't informed the cops. He hadn't even noticed, but a smaller ice cube now sat redundant at the bottom of his empty glass. God, he knew how it felt.

Chapter 9

Four days later, when Stuart woke to another day alone, he looked over. She wasn't there but her smell was – he just couldn't bring himself to wash the bedcovers. He moved over to her side and just lay there, inhaling her. He knew the car had driven perfectly fine only the day before, as he'd driven it himself to nearby shops. It seemed apparent that no one wanted to dig a little deeper and uncover the reason behind this, and discover why it had turned into a death trap overnight, and why his wife had been taken long before her time, at just 49 years old.

Apart from not suffering, if there were to be any positives taken from this tragedy, you could say it ended a strange torment for Sarah Howard. She'd discovered something very troubling about her husband recently. Deeply concerned, she needed time on her own to think things through and had been going for regular drives into Indianapolis – and other places, insisting to go alone, her thoughts deep in overdrive as she cruised there and back.

Stuart hadn't been aware that she'd found something out, and the fact he never mentioned his secret to her, the one person on earth that secrets shouldn't be kept from, will haunt him till they meet again.

He'd suspected Sarah of cheating on him. He was almost three years older than she was and he'd got a bit out of shape in recent years, preferring a more relaxed lifestyle as he approached retirement, as if he was rehearsing for it.

Naively, he'd assumed her complete devotion, essentially taking her for granted. That was a mistake, he now thought.

Just a couple of weeks before the crash, she'd gone out and bought a laptop, a thing they'd never owned before. She'd joined Facebook, and she'd been looking up old friends and chatting with them online, often staying up late at night. Up till then, they'd had a healthy habit of going to bed together, cuddling up under the blankets, reciting the day's events in a spoon.

But he hated her newly-found, nocturnal interests. Not because it was putting an end to their bedtime routine, but because he wasn't part of it all, and hadn't been invited in. With his wife still hooked on her new and engrossing evening routine, focussing on a screen instead of him, he'd been demoted to 2nd place. He'd been going to bed alone now, auto-pilot controlling his mind, thinking the worst... 'Who is she secretly chatting with? What *other* websites is she visiting? Had she been tempted elsewhere and was he losing his wife?'

Conversations between them had become more forced – and it was normally him who'd been the initiator. She'd become less interested in him, preferring to focus on what she'd found online and on what she'd left in lock-mode since last night's finger-tapping. He felt like he'd been pestering her. That was the beginning of the end.

He saw their relationship like a game of cards, full of risk, right until the end, never knowing what's coming next. Sarah had been a good looking girl at school, and she'd grown into a good looking woman, with a slim and feminine physique. At almost 50, she'd been aware that she was a grandmother. She'd made the best of her looks and was a keen runner, often going out jogging around the nearby parks. Stuart had always punched above his weight, accepting that at any time, she could meet a better man than him and leave.

That didn't happen though. However, each time he'd approached her recently, she'd turn the laptop away, shielding the screen's contents from his view. Even when she'd gone to the bathroom, she'd always close the lid, or lock it – and he didn't know the password. Like the unknown password was locking him out of the laptop, he's began to feel locked out of his wife's secret affair.

Jealousy is a damaging emotion, and whether she was flirting online or not, whether she was being pursued or not, whether she had been chatting with an 'old flame' or meeting with a new one, mattered, and it mattered massively. If that's what it was, then that's what it was and he'd accept it. But not knowing is even more damaging, and she never told him anything – and he never asked. This new time-consuming 'Facebook' thingy, something they'd never done before, was beginning to look like a marriage breaker. The thing is, he had a secret himself, and had hidden it from her for decades. It would be wrong to hypocritically accuse her of cheating.

After the break-in, she'd suspected him of knowing more than he let on. Unaware to him, she'd been doing her own research, joining the dots. In her mind, characters had been forming and they all had a story to tell. She'd been more eager than the Police to discover who'd broken into their home and her research was sound. This new internet thing was a useful tool.

Sarah had been busy contacting, connecting and chatting. Some people were still right here in Westfield, but many had left and moved town, or even moved States. She'd been travelling to meet them, to see what she could find out, realising that the further they'd moved away, the more likely they were to talk. As a result, she'd unearthed many buried secrets, some difficult to hear, and she'd unravelled the mystery far enough to work out who was behind this, and why. She'd discovered enough about Mr Damian Keefer, to realise why her husband was on edge, and she'd been ready to forgive him. Sarah had been busy contacting, connecting and chatting – but not cheating.

Towards the end, he'd chat with her about nothing in particular, and noticed her fidgeting, her mind elsewhere, itching for him to disappear. He no longer commanded the same attention span from her as he once did, her distant eyes revealed a mere pretence to be listening, staring at something that wasn't there when he spoke. Now she was gone, his gaze only saw half a man in the mirror, full of regrets about how he'd handled things, and her passing had spun him off his axis and was forcing him back onto that perilous path of years ago. This would be dodgy, but he'd hardly ever backed down in his past, and wasn't going to now. He was being offered another card on 20. 'Twist'.

Chapter 10 – March 2014

Around three months since the twins went missing, some Westfielders assumed it would be Damian behind the kidnappings. However, the Police simply let him be. Whoever it was, had been hiding their tracks well. Some townies suspected the Howards. They'd always been a bit strange – verging on weirdos, maybe. But if they'd been involved somehow, then how come no arrests?

Seemingly desperate for the town folk's forgiveness and seeking redemption, Damian Keefer had joined-in with a few families who'd faithfully been out at nights, searching for those missing children, despite the anticipated unwelcome looks and harsh comments from some, not wanting to mingle with an ex-prisoner. He'd soaked up those comments and hadn't bitten back. He was now showing the town a different man – a changed man.

Damian knew people suspected him. From the moment he was released in December 2013, it had all went down. Just bad timing maybe, but he had an idea. Focussing on those three kids that had gone missing, he'd called a meeting at the town hall for 7 o'clock on Wednesday evening, and put notices up everywhere. When the time came, it seemed as if half the town turned up. They arrived in numbers, each with a measured degree of scepticism on their face, and arms folded. The noise level grew as the numbers did.

Front and centre, he saw scores of faces, eager to hear what he had to say. Those faces looked distantly familiar. He found himself being transported back to the time when he was almost deafened to the thumping sound of the side of the Police van that had carted him away, with angry faces jeering and spitting. He'd woken at night in prison many times, recalling this. These were now the same people, just a bit older, but they'd aged better than he had.

Damian stood up at the front of the room, microphone in hand that he'd purchased.

"Thank you everyone.", he said, kicking clear the wires that were looping their way to the hall's speaker system. "Can you all hear me?" He waited a second or two till he had their attention.

"I know everyone will have questions about what's been happening right here in Westfield. We've had three children taken from us in recent weeks. *Three…* and the Police are doing nothing. I want to help."

"What can you do?"

Before he could answer, another voice shouted, "You're that bank robber. How can we trust you?"

Damian was prepared for this – it was inevitable. "You're correct, mam. I did do that. I was guilty, and I went to prison. I was just a young, stupid boy when I did that. Every single day since then, I've prayed to God for forgiveness. I wished I could change what I did that day, but I was on a road to destruction. I deserved prison – because I would just have continued on that road. I'm glad I got sent away, actually. I am truly sorry for what I did, and I served my time."

Addressing the whole room, he preached, "But I'm a changed man now. I've found Jesus, and he's in my heart. Jesus has shown me a better road – a road that offers salvation, forgiveness and hope." The cross on his chain shined through his shirt that was intentionally unbuttoned at the top. "I want to give *back* to this town, and I hope you'll let me do it. I want to help find those kids – the kids that were taken from us – the kids that we've all been praying for their safe return to their families. Jesus gave *me* hope – now I want to pass that on. That's why, with Jesus guiding me, I have bought some things that may help us find them, wherever they may be. You see, up till now, people have been out, looking, calling their names. I want us to do these searches better. I want everyone to coordinate their efforts when out. We stand a better chance that way. I think we need small groups out there, each one searching a different area. There's over six hundred people in this town, and everyone wants to help find those kids, right?"

The crowded hall was listening intently. A few were nodding and he was beginning to win some of them over.

"My daughter's been missing two months – in fact, *exactly* two months today.", came an angry yell from the rear of the hall, as she pointed to the floor. "It's *my* daughter, not yours. Who put you in charge?" It was Mrs Preston, and she looked pale and skinny, and she wore the worry she'd endured.

"Mam, firstly, let me say this. May Jesus be with you and your daughter.", he said as he convincingly placed his free hand across his chest. "Listen, I'm *not* in charge. I'm just trying to help. Mam, the same cops you trusted with your kid's safety – the same *bent* cops that lied to put me away and are guilty of perjury… well I don't trust them for lying – why should you? I was just a kid when they lied and put me to jail for 44 years. They don't care about kids. Police Officers lied in court under oath to send me away for good. That's been proven now and I'm sure you've all read the papers. You know it's true. Those very cops you trusted – *they* deserve to go to jail – and I'll be there at *their* trial, watching."

It was a small town, and everyone knew this story anyway. They knew what he was saying was indeed true, but perhaps not *quite* the way he was telling it. He saw people looking around, considering. The town was disgusted with the Police and the recent revelations.

"The cops are getting nowhere. We've got to do something, right? Something as a town. I say, we coordinate our efforts and find these kids. What we need are small groups of about ten, and someone to volunteer as Team Leader, and lead that small group. We all meet here – 6pm each night before going out, get ready and head out in teams. I've bought some stuff to help. I've got warm jackets for everyone, I've bought thirty radios so we can communicate with each other, and I've got dozens of torches, and a map of the town for each group, flares and whistles."

Damian paused for a second, reached inside one of two bags he'd brought and grabbed two large posters and held one in each hand. He'd arranged for large waterproof posters to be made up, with rivet holes in the corners for easy tying. One of them showed the twin boys. The other showed the girl. Much better than the posters someone printed off at home and laminated.

"I got these from a sign maker in town. They'll catch people's attention. I say spread the word, and get as many of us as we can to meet here every night after dinner around six, and we head out then. I'm searching too and I'm going out weekends as well, straight after church. And I've asked this hall to lay on some hot food for all of us, each search. We may need the energy."

He paused for a bit to allow them to think. "Please. Let me help too.", he offered. He held aloft one of the radios, and a jacket in his other hand, eager for someone to be the first to collect.

"We all deserve forgiveness.", came a voice from the back of the gathering, an elderly churchgoer, who then walked up to Damian as the crowd opened up to let her through. "I've seen you at Westfield Parish Church. Whatever you did son – or didn't do – I for one, will forgive you, if you help bring those kids home."

Damian knew everyone is always welcome at Church, and had become a regular inside prison. The one place in a super-max jail that provided some tranquillity, in an otherwise ruthless den.

"Thank you mam.", nodded Damian with a gentile voice. He knew her name but wanted to sound respectful, and he handed her one of everything. "Who's next?", he said eagerly, as his actions began converting some more.

Mumbles rippled through the crowd. "I'm in too. The Police are bloody useless.", came a voice from the pack.

"Me too.", committed another.

Some people walked to the front to meet Damian. Stuart saw a few leave. With a bit of hesitation, a man extended his hand towards Damian's, and they shook. With the first handshake, came another, then another. This was now happening.

Stuart was somewhere in the crowd, skootching down, and had been listening on sceptically. He immediately saw this for what it was – a way of diverting the angry mob's attention away from Damian himself. 'A changed man? Yeah, right!' He quietly disappeared through a side door that had been left open to allow air in.

Chapter 11

In April, Justin and his parents had moved to Redleaf, a little town on the skirt of Divernon, in Illinois, as Justin was approaching 16. That was a big step for them, and moving to a new State for anyone would be daunting enough by itself, but they knew it'd be tougher for them. It was around 300 kilometres away from their previous home and Justin's papa in Westfield, Indiana. Far enough to feel safe from the horrors they'd left behind – close enough to visit.

They remember everything that had happened in their old town, and like the luggage they'd brought with them, they'd packed up those memories too. Westfield had been decent, until those last few months. Gram and papa had lived just around the corner, through one of the wooded areas. But after those two kidnappings, the Westfield locals had been warned not to play in, or even pass through any of the woods or the array of parks alone, and certainly not at night. Now safe from the epicentre, Justin remembered more clearly…

HAVE YOU SEEN THIS GIRL?
MISSING SINCE 18th JANUARY 2014.
IF SO, PLEASE CONTACT THE POLICE

Notices had been stapled up on trees everywhere – showing a picture of a local schoolgirl, Sarah-Jane Preston, who'd been missing for three months. And not a month earlier than that, twin boys had vanished too. Witnesses said the boys had been playing in the park with a frisbee, and were coerced to a van by a man wearing a dark jacket and baseball cap. The van's side door simply slid shut and it quietly made its way off with the boys inside. No one saw the man's face. Parents and relatives had been left devastated. Hope was fading with every day that passed without news. The twelve year old boys had become teenagers in captivity. Instead of celebrating, their birthday was just another day of searching. Sarah-Jane's parents in particular, were now at breaking point.

The villagers had suffered losses and the locals had been doing whatever they could to safeguard loved ones. The village of Westfield had fast become a notorious place, for all the wrong reasons. But that's not why they left.

On one of her journeys into the city early February, Sarah crashed her car. She died within minutes. It was reported that the brakes on her car had suddenly failed, leading to the tragic accident. The whole family was numb.

In an attempt to leave this all behind them and start afresh, Justin's parents had taken him away, and the Howard family had moved to the nicest neighbourhood they could afford to buy with the money given to them by Mike's father, Stuart. He'd stayed behind, and Justin missed him – and his Gram Sarah.

Justin recalled his grandparents being old-fashioned and liked the simple life. They were one of the remaining kind where they listened to sleeved vinyl records on an old stereo with a turntable, and their furniture looked the same age. They didn't have much money. They had enough, but not much, and nothing valuable in their home or on their wrists. A small family of Justin, his parents, and his dad's parents, they'd all been happy enough, meeting up frequently and always helping each other out. The five of them had been grateful with what they had. Now, it was just the four of them.

They'd owned an older car. Stuart saw to it that it was taken care of and was always seen checking fluid levels and other stuff under the hood. He frequently picked up his grandson from school, took him fishing, sometimes not returning back until late in the evening.

This old vehicle had to be safe, and it had actually been serviced at a local garage just a few weeks earlier and it drove fine. So it came as a huge shock when their car had slammed heavily into the van in front, on the Interstate Highway, I-465.

There were no air-bags or fancy safety systems like in today's elaborate cars. The force of the impact had caused Sarah to thump her head so hard on the steering wheel that she died at the scene. 'Catastrophic impact to head and torso' was mentioned in the official coroner's report for the cause of death. The impact had caused a large fracture to her skull and her brain had swollen quickly. There was nothing anyone could have done.

A few days after the crash, the Police had visited Stuart at his home. A cop local to the area, who Stuart had known for years, Officer Roberts, and his trainee partner, had rolled up quietly to the home. With hats under their arms as a mark of respect, they walked up his pathway and gently knocked the door. Stuart hadn't been expecting them. Maybe someone said they'd turn up – maybe not. It'd been a few blurry days, battling constant confusion. What he knew for sure was that this wasn't the end of things – far from it.

Trying to decide on the best course of action while on sleeping tablets the doctor had prescribed, washed down with nothing but bottled spirits, in the pursuit of blanking out the pain, just wasn't working. Normally a deep thinker, he'd been stuck in limbo and everything was distorted. He'd eaten virtually nothing since the crash.

From previous encounters, he associated the cops with flashing lights and sirens, but not that day. Reluctantly, he'd waved them inside as he shielded sunlight from his watery eyes. They tried to look compassionate, but it wasn't working. While inside, they told him of his crumpled vehicle, a station-wagon, and how it'd been towed away for forensic analysis.

"Mr Howard.", began Officer Roberts, "I'm sorry for your loss." His steady tone being noticeably softer than Stuart had been accustomed to, from days gone by. He took the lead, with his female partner looking around the room, not writing anything down – but making notes.

Stuart's eyes looked up from the sofa he'd occupied, upwards through a few fingers that had been shielding his reddened face to the unwelcome cops who hadn't been invited to sit. "Have you got any idea what happened yet?", he asked, not sounding hopeful of any positive leads. To some degree, they'd visited to ask Stuart the same question.

"Not yet. We're keeping an open mind."

It'd been raining that day, and the crime scene notes showed that the soles of her shoes had been found to be damp.

"Maybe her foot slipped off the brake pedal?", his partner suggested while analysing his cupboard, not even looking round to face him.

"BULLSHIT!", Stuart immediately shouted. "I fucking KNOW the brakes had been tampered with."

Officer Roberts gestured to his new and rookie partner to wait in the Police car. Her exclusion would now allow for a more sincere conversation between the two of them – and some bits could be 'off the record'.

After she'd left, and the screen door had hit against its frame, he apologised to Stuart. They could now speak freely.

Continuing in a calmer tone, allowing Stuart the space he needed, he added, "The brakes *did* fail, Stuart. Sarah's not to blame – we *know* that now. There was no brake fluid left. Initial findings are that it looks like the brake-line's been cut, but we can't tell for sure. The car was mangled."

Realising his words could have also been chosen more wisely after his partner's antagonising verbal blunder, he continued, "Stuart, we don't know the full extent of this yet, but we're looking into it. You've got my word on that."

At least he sounded sincere, and the fact that it was one-on-one now, helped drain the tension. Stuart didn't say anything.

"Mr Howard… ", he said, interrupting Stuart's thoughts, and pausing until he looked up at him. "… have you *any* ideas who's behind this?", gently lowering himself onto a nearby chair opposite as he spoke, almost asking permission to sit with his delay. It now seemed like the cops were treating this as deliberate sabotage, tampering with a vehicle, reckless endangerment, attempted murder, or whatever they'd be writing in their little book. The cops knew of Stuart's prior ties with Damian and that he'd been released recently. Stuart knew he was being asked if he thought Damian was behind it.

Stuart paused. He wondered if it had been the right thing to do in *not* informing the Police when his home was broken into just a couple of weeks back, and if he should tell him now. He still couldn't think straight, but they were obviously linked.

'Fuck it. The less they know the better', he thought to himself, this now being the second time he'd deprived them of the information he knew about his former friend, who was now walking the streets again as an innocent man.

The silence was increasingly becoming harder to bear and Officer Roberts could hear his watch's second hand twitching round. He put his other hand over it, in an attempt that it would dampen-down its ticking. It seemed like the hand must have rotated a full minute before Stuart responded.

"No.", this time staring directly at the unwelcome cop, of course, being certain of his suspicions, but unwilling to share them. Breaking into his home and urinating on his bed had clearly been a two-week warning he hadn't heeded. "I've got no idea."

Roberts knew full well he was lying, but his wife had just been killed, so he let it be, and Stuart got a pass. "Sir, … but you *will* let me know if you think of something. Won't you?"

Stuart thought if he did this by the book, then Damian would get questioned, maybe arrested, maybe a trial, and maybe go away again. Too many 'maybes'. Feeling pessimistic now about the useless Police's chances against Damian and of course, his hot-shot lawyer, he thought otherwise. "Off the record?"

"If you need it to be.", showing the palms of his hands.

"I'll deal with this myself." His message wasn't welcomed.

"No you won't, Stuart. We've got our best people on this… What do you mean by that anyway?"

Stuart allowed an eerie pause to pass. "I mean – I'll deal with *grief* myself." He stood up, indicating this was the end of the unwelcome visit inside and it was time for him to join his colleague in the car. Officer Roberts caught-on and mirrored Stuart's movements in rising to his feet, but just a moment or so after Stuart stood, and smirking a little as he did.

"Stuart. Let us do our work here."

"Yes, of course I will.", he replied, in a tone as calm as he was asked, but unconvincingly so.

The visit had been a formality. A 'box-ticking' exercise for the record. Both sides knew all too well who was behind it, and it seemed to worry them both, and for different reasons. Stuart knew his family was in danger and he'd been forced to get them to safety. And as for the Police – well they seemed powerless to the good people of Westfield – but why? There was a reason, but they weren't privy to it.

Chapter 12

Stuart didn't join any of the search teams, but he was curious to see what Damian had got them doing. That curiosity got the better of him, and just like those townies that Damian re-invited back to the town hall at 6pm to start the searches, he also went along, but he didn't go inside.

When the groups started coming out, sporting matching jackets and radios, he followed behind one of them, covertly keeping his distance just far enough back, so as not to be seen. He saw them all looking around their designated area, and heard the calling of the missing children's names. The volunteers seemed re-energised, desperate to be the one who found something.

After around two hours of walking through the parks and well into the woodlands, whatever little pessimistic hope he'd been fooled with, just vanished. He'd had enough, and knew the group wouldn't be finding anyone, at least not where they were being told to look. He stopped following, and waited until they had all disappeared behind some trees, then he turned around and walked back the way they'd all came.

He sat down on a park bench, knowing the group were searching in vain, and that Damian was now wriggling his way back in among his old town. The same town he stole from all those years ago. The same town folks that he'd personally beaten up, or robbed from. The same town that sent him to prison for 44 years. Were they forgetting all that? He wasn't.

It must have been over half an hour later, but while deep in thought, it had felt more like just five minutes. He saw the group wandering back, smiles absent. *Of course,* a wasted effort. Conned by a conman. As the group neared, he noticed that some of the team were looking at him, eyeing him with disgust. Disgust for not helping.

"You not joining in the search, sir?", one of the younger members said, obviously not knowing who Stuart was.

"He doesn't help anyone. Just himself.", said another.

Just as they passed him, Stuart felt forced to yell out. "You're wasting your time folks."

The group slowed down, and when the leader stopped walking, they all did. "What do you mean by that? We're wasting our time looking for missing kids?", the Team Leader quizzed, illuminating his face with the torch.

"No mam. You're looking in the wrong place."

"What do you mean by that? Aren't you Mr Howard?", one of the group asked.

"Yes. Listen, where you've been told to look… the kids aren't there."

One of them neared Stuart, and came a few steps closer. "Where are they?"

"I don't know where they are, but you won't find them. Not here you won't."

Concealed inside the group, was the missing girl's mother. She made her way to the bench and sat beside him. "Mr Howard. I'm Jane Preston. I'm looking for my little girl, Sarah-Jane. Where should we be looking? Do you know something?"

Stuart sighed. He didn't know where they were, but he had a hunch. "I know who you are mam. Listen, I don't know where those kids *are*, but if I were you, I'd be looking closer to home."

"What do you mean by that – closer to home?"

As much as he sensed her desperation, he was desperate too. Desperate to be more specific, but if he said what he'd envisaged, he'd be seen to be in on it himself. "Mam, you're all being led way out here… ", he gestured with arms wide open, "… out here – in the middle of nowhere!" It called for a moment of reflection. "Can I ask something?"

"Anything."

"How many teams have you got out there?"

He saw her eyes roll north-east. "There are about… eight groups tonight."

"We're group DELTA.", the group's leader said proudly. Someone had suggested using the phonetic alphabet system. It made them appear and feel, as if this whole thing had been a bit more professionally organised.

"What groups are searching Westfield itself?"

The group members all looked at each other. It sounded like a daft question. Then it wasn't. All the teams had been sent out away from Westfield town. Directed outwards in all directions. Arranged to leave Westfield by its organiser and sole funder, Mr Keefer.

"No one is searching Westfield.", Mrs Preston said, whatever look of hope there had been on her face now substituted with a worried one. The penny dropped.

Stuart stood up, now level with them all. Before he left, he repeated her words, "No one is searching Westfield!"

Stuart started walking away. He'd made his point, but Mrs Preston wanted a bit more. "Sir?" She waited till he'd turned round. "Mr Howard, what are you saying, exactly?"

This had to be said. "Mam. You're all following instructions, right? And not a single group has been told to search back home. Think about it!" Stuart then turned and walked off, and as he did so, he could hear the DELTA group mumbling among themselves.

Chapter 13

Late on, after the search missions were over, some of them had come back out, this time with no group rules. Misguided hope had turned to anger, and some of that anger had pointed towards the Howard family that never joined-in. The town had come alive at night with revenge seekers, vigilantes wanting payback and targeting Justin's parents.

In those last few weeks, if the Howards had ventured outside, it was always daytime. Someone would spit on the ground in front of them. Shop owners hardly making eye contact at the till, and no small talk.

One day when Debbie had been home by herself watching the local news in hope of a breakthrough, she got the fright of her life when there was a massive thump on the living room window. It almost broke. A few eggs had been thrown at the home by kids, the yolks cementing themselves permanently to the walls. She rushed outside to confront whoever had done it and saw a group of three teenagers, now walking casually away.

"HEY!" She waited for them to turn round. "Did you just throw eggs at my house?" She already knew the answer and immediately felt out her depth, that initial rush of adrenalin-fuelled rage had now retreated and turned into fear of retaliation – as if she'd provoked them.

"What the fuck did you say – witch?", came a reply shouted from the assumed pack leader of the trio as he walked confidently towards her, arms stretched outwards, desperate for her to bite.

Mike had been working away for now, and she felt especially vulnerable without him there. "Please stop doing it", her reply – softer now, almost sounding apologetic. They'd triggered a tipping point that she'd reached herself some time ago. But after seeing their young faces, she feared that her son might be targeted by them if things escalated.

"Get the fuck back in your house", came the reply, the lad eager to have the last say on this. "**Get the fuck back in your house**", he barked, as she hadn't moved yet. She'd been frozen till then, almost glued to the spot with dread, but quickly obeyed him this time, making certain she didn't mouth anything else and being just as sure to lock the door with the key. Police needed evidence but the townies didn't. They knew what they knew.

That was then. With everything that had happened, Mike, Debbie and Justin needed to move somewhere else. So the timing of Stuart's policy payout, about two months after Sarah's death, was such a relief. Stuart had, of course, been the insurance beneficiary and had received the money from his wife's death.

Deep in thought in his silenced home, Stuart sat on his rocking chair and recalled how he had gifted Mike the entire payout, with only one condition – that they fled Westfield and relocated somewhere else, somewhere safe and build a new life.

"Mike, you need this money", he'd said, "Use it wisely. I'm staying put. My Sarah's gone. I'm gonna put an end to this."

Mike had gazed ominously at the cheque he was holding, as he heard his father's message. "Come with us dad…" he pleaded, "We'll make room for everyone. There's only four of us."

"There's *three* of you Mike, and it's *your* family you need to look after now.", came the no-nonsense reply with remnants of his youth. "I was born and grew up here. I'll die here too, and I'll die happy, son."

Debbie's eyes had welled up, tears almost spilling over the edges. She realised the gravity of what was happening and, if she was reading him right, then they may not see Mike's dad again. She used the back of a finger to collect them and protect the little make-up she had applied for this visit.

"Let me see if I can make things a bit easier for you", he said convincingly, switching his focus to Justin and winking at his grandson through a forced, but admiring smile as he did so. Justin rushed to his grandfather for a hug, almost forcing him backwards, squeezing him much firmer than ever before. There was indeed a special bond between the two.

"Will we still go fishing? You *will* come and visit us papa, won't you?"

Only then did it hit Stuart, that Mike and Deborah hadn't told their son everything. While still in his final embrace with his grandson, and looking at Mike and Debbie, he felt compelled to restate his words.

"I'm staying here", Stuart repeated, this time in a softer voice, the matter being closed now, and not up for debate anymore. "Go, and make a good life elsewhere, and pray to God this doesn't follow you!", almost sounding like some kind of preacher now with these words, despite the Howard's never being the church-going type.

Now the difficult talk had been done, he seemed more relaxed in his demeanour, confident that his son's, and his little family's future would be safe. He knew what he had to do, and it wasn't pleasant, but his confident look, his firm cuddles and his assuring smile hid the evils he knew were about to re-appear – but only once they'd left town.

As they were packing up the car, he wondered. He had work to do, and it was almost time to start. It wouldn't be neat, but whatever is in this mirky business? The only question that remained was did he still have that same ability? He knew the risks and accepted them. When they'd left, and had driven out of sight, he spoke a promise to a framed picture of his wife.

Chapter 14

Word had spread around town of the Howard's departure from it. After getting nowhere with the group searches, and considering what Stuart had told one of them about them wasting their time searching, Mrs Preston invited the team leaders, and a few others to her home after Friday evening's searches. It wasn't quite a 'secret' meeting, but Damian hadn't been invited. Their strategy wasn't working and it was time to discuss something.

She and her husband led the meeting, and after thanking everyone for attending, it was Mr Preston who spoke first. "We appreciate everyone's help. We're doing this in addition to what the Police are doing. It all helps. We've all been out searching for weeks now, but what have we got?"

People looked around themselves. There was nothing to report back, and that was the point.

Breaking that awkward silence, one of the leaders said, "Mrs Preston, we've not come across anything yet. But we'll keep going out though."

One of the angry parents, a relative of the missing boys blurted out, "The Howards have left Westfield – Mike and his family. They've moved away." It seemed irrelevant, but it hadn't been discussed at any official group searches.

"We met Stuart Howard one night last week. He said we should look *closer to home!*", the DELTA group leader said. "But we'd know if the kids were here, right? The Police would know. I mean, the whole town is looking for them!", she added.

"I was there, and he *did* say that.", said Mrs Preston. "He said we were wasting our time looking for the kids *outside* of Westfield. It's as if he was making a point."

"Come on!", said one of Mike's neighbours. "I've known the Howards for years. They keep themselves to themselves, and admittedly, they're all a bit strange, yes, but really? Are you accusing them of taking these kids, and… well what exactly *are* you saying?"

Mrs Preston didn't know what to think. "All I know is that Stuart Howard told us that the kids are right here, somewhere in Westfield – then his own family leaves Westfield."

"I don't get it.", said another of the Group's leaders. "If Mike had been involved, his own father surely wouldn't be telling us, would he?"

"Well what the fuck else is he telling us?", Mr Preston said. He offered up a hand of apology.

People looked around themselves. Someone said, "Wait – are you saying the Howard's moved *because* they had something to do with this, and they were… fearing getting caught?"

"You're all missing the point." Heads turned round to see Mrs Sanderson. She was the mother of Henry, Justin's best friend. "They moved because they were getting grief from locals at nights. Vigilantes we've become! People taunting them with no proof of nothing. Being shunned everywhere they went. Stuart's *wife* died, and then they get all this hassle on top of their grief! I'd leave too if it was me."

"I can't do this anymore." The FOXTROT leader had enough. "I'm sorry, but I just can't go out searching every night, if it's wasting our time. We're searching for the twins and your daughter. I've got a daughter at home too you know, ages with Sarah-Jane. She could be at risk while I'm out there, away searching hours on end. Let's assume, just for a minute, that these missing kids *are* here. They're *right* here, somewhere in Westfield. If they are, and we're all out searching elsewhere, then we're failing them. We're *all* failing them!"

The ambience changed, and guilt set in. Most people couldn't face her as she finished. As she opened the door, blame rushed in looking for owners. She took one last look at them all before leaving, closing the door ever so quietly.

Chapter 15

A realtor that Stuart recruited, had sold the Howard's home almost immediately with the very first offer, a cheeky offer it was too and a chunk under the asking price. With the Howard's inheritance, they didn't really need top dollar from the sale of their home anyway. Maybe that had already circulated? They were now miles away, and only Stuart knew where.

To feel properly safe, they'd left State completely. They had reason not to move too far away, though, and 'back home' still had to be commutable. Mike's father still lived there, he'd helped them out and it was actually him, who they feared was in more danger.

Stuart's offer had been tough enough for a proud family to accept, knowingly deserting their only family behind, a solitary middle-aged man, recently widowed, but it was impossible to refuse his offer. When they'd gone, it'd felt like abandoning a wounded soldier behind on the battlefield with only a pistol – deep down, they knew he wouldn't survive long.

Mike had telephoned. They were safe in Redleaf and he told his father about it. It was a little village, with a population of around 700. Quiet and peaceful, with just a few shops run by locals. It had woods nearby, and kids would go there and play games, parents left safe in the knowledge their little ones were okay. A welcoming place with decent folk, everyone going about their business doing their thing. It seemed like the kind of town where everyone knew everyone by name. The type of place where people would greet each other in the morning, sometimes stopping for a chat.

But Justin's parents were not good at stopping for a chat, small talk or any kind of socialising now, damaged from their past. It wasn't quite two weeks ago that they'd moved in, and delivery vans to the home were seen more than the Howards themselves.

The inheritance money, coupled with the sale from their previous home was more than they'd ever had before, and they'd decided to give Justin $15,000. A chance for him to buy some of his own things, and perhaps buy a car of his own, when he'd passed his driving test. Something he'd spoken about for a while, and now he could focus on that, instead of the past. He'd already spent some of it, ordering craft stuff online, so he could paint properly.

They'd traded in their old station wagon, and now a brand new, fancy four wheel drive occupied the driveway, sitting there handsomely. Mike saw himself in the glossy paintwork, as he busied himself with a polishing rag, half his divided thoughts back home. To their neighbours, they seemed well-off. They weren't. They appeared successful, but inside those walls, they felt like imposters. Appearances can be deceptive.

Chapter 16

Sitting in his rocking chair, glass in hand, Stuart knew his family was now safe. Damian would come after *him*, not them, and all he could do is wait, shots already loaded in both barrels. How had it come to this? As the sky stole his attention, clouds seemed like clogged rush-hour traffic, slowly making their way somewhere, hiding – revealing distant stars as they overtook each other.

His memory went back to that night in 1979, when he'd slowly trudged back to his room and considered every option. He couldn't remember what he had for dinner last night, but he clearly recalled this. He'd always tried to block that memory out, but not tonight. Mr Jack Daniels helped him go back.

He simply couldn't kill the girl *and* her baby. Double homicide was out the question. Damian had laid all the pressure on him and he'd struggled with his thoughts back then. Every scenario he'd came up with, was flawed. Finally, without overthinking it, he'd decided, and put pencil to paper. He had drawn the girl in a bathtub, with blood as water, symbolising a massive bleed. The baby would die inside her, and the medics would arrive and remove it.

The go-ahead for it, was all that remained. As he re-lived that massive struggle to sign it, the drawing telling him not to, and fighting against him, his hand trembled now, spilling some JD on his wrist. He remembered he had to leave that room and go back later. The drawing did get signed though, and he recollected trying not to get his tears on the paper.

The girl, whoever she had been, hadn't deserved it. It must have been terrible for her. Lifechanging. He knew that then, and he knew it more now. He'd been duped into doing it, blackmailed with repercussions if he hadn't, but that didn't ease the guilt.

In retrospect, Damian could have been telling him a pile of lies at the time. Maybe he raped her? Maybe she had pretended to be 18? Maybe the two of them had been high on drugs? The more he thought, the uglier it got.

What he did know for sure, was that he signed it, and it happened – like it always did. He knew that, because he felt the pain that the baby must have felt. It wasn't pain-free, like the medics say. It was a murder, plain and simple, and every murder is agony. The pain replicated itself and made sure he'd endured it too. He knew he'd deserved that extreme agony he felt, but only he survived. For decades, he'd been ridden with guilt. He'd felt so fuckin low he could have shot himself there and then. If only he'd had a gun at the time. Now, he was staring at his shotgun that was resting precariously against the wall, almost asking to be picked up. No wonder he'd tried to blank this memory out. It'd sank in, that if he ever took another life with his 'ability', that was the price he'd have to pay. He never did it again.

Over the years, he saw his visions as forcing him to see what his eyes would miss out on. He'd only ever got one vision for each thing he done, but the mystery girl would have lived through it every day. He often wondered who she was, and how things turned out for her. But he'd never find out, and part of him needed it to remain that way.

Half-way down the bottle, he'd tortured himself enough and had to come back to reality. He'd committed murder for a pal who hadn't deserved any favours. A pal who shouldn't have gotten himself in that position in the first place. A pal who should have sorted his own mess out. Maybe even a pal who should have gone to prison for raping an underage child. He was contemplating vengeance of his own – but for now, the rest of the bottle would go down neat.

Chapter 17

Families normally move state for better prospects. Sometimes a better job with a bigger company or bigger salary or to be closer to relatives. That makes sense, but this didn't apply to the Howards. They hadn't tried too hard to find work yet, as that wasn't really a priority, but after around two weeks to reflect on things, having jobs would emit a demeanour of some kind of normality.

Although their previous home in Westfield had increased in value since they'd purchased it many years back, it went for less than expected and they'd recently received the money from the sale of that home too, less fees of course. It would make them comfortable. One thing less to worry about.

Justin wasn't a good looking lad, and he accepted that. Like his dad, he also had dark wavy hair which just wouldn't be fixed into any fashionable style, and he was also a bit odd looking. Spots were a nuisance – super-visible on his face now, but they had appeared on his chest and his back too – they'd been hibernating till now. A few fluffs of facial hair were also appearing too, in uneven amounts. Justin wished this puberty thing was in the past.

On the second Wednesday there, he'd joined the local school, Auburn High School. His class year was already overfilled, so it was agreed with everyone that he'd join the year above him. It was only for a few months, then he could re-sit next year. He'd joined mid-week, agreeing with his parents that his anxiety may cope slightly better with a shorter first week. His mom's would too.

He was just a bit shorter than most other kids in his year at his new school, and skinny too, easy pickings for the usual bullies that prey on the vulnerable, just like animals do. All this, just to be seen as cool, and to fit in *themselves*, when they are also self-conscious.

He'd been a bit nervous, but he had met someone he liked the day he joined. One of the pupils he got speaking with, was a boy in his art class called Raymond. Taking a massive risk, Raymond's parents had emigrated there from Glasgow two years ago, with the hope their son would get into the world famous and super prestigious Chicago Art Institute. Ray had natural talent, a very gifted artist, and they both complimented each other's work. Justin instantly bonded with him. They got on well, and they both produced artwork of a really good standard, Ray nosing ahead.

Apart from Ray, Justin felt quite alone now. He knew he needed something more. Something that would fill an emptiness. At the dinner table, he blurted it out.

"Mom – dad. Can I get a dog?" He had thought about it. A puppy would help fill the void of losing his grammy and his best friend Henry, and help the family focus on something joyful, a good change from the past. He knew it would be good for his mom too.

"A dog?" Mike's eyes immediately switched left towards his wife for help.

"Yes. Well, a puppy really."

"We've never had a dog before, Justin. I don't know anything about dogs!" Mike held both hands aloft showing disapproval, immediately tilting towards the downside of having one. "Your mom doesn't know anything about dogs either", he reinforced.

"You don't *need* to know about dogs, dad. It would be *my* dog. I'd look after it. I'd take it walks."

"Justin… ", his father began, hoping that a strong counter-argument would come to him as he spoke – but nothing did.

"Dad. We've all got the time. There's *always* someone in the home."

Deborah couldn't help but smile. Justin was right. After all, a puppy would bring some joy to their home. It may also bring them a bit closer together. It seemed a good idea, and had it been *their* idea, they wouldn't have went looking for problems.

"We'd probably meet people taking it for walks.", she suggested, mainly speaking to Mike. "That could be good for us." She saw Justin trying to hide his smile.

"Yeah, and who cleans up the shite?", Mike asked, more jokingly than serious. His wife and Justin both laughed.

"You'll clean the shite, dad!", Justin said, laughing as he did. Deborah laughed too.

"What am I letting myself in for? If we do this… "

"Yeah!", Justin exclaimed as he put his hands up in victory.

"If we do this, you're buying it Justin, with your own money." This was the mini-victory Mike needed as head of family. "It'll be your dog, son. We'll all help out though", warming to the idea. "I suppose it can stay inside, but *you* walk it, and *you're* responsible for looking after it. Right?"

This was met with a group cuddle. A rare moment of happiness in an otherwise gloomy month they'd had. The agreement was that at the weekend, they'd all drive into the city and go along to the pet store. Justin couldn't wait. He'd never owned a dog before.

Chapter 18

The following day, Thursday, Mike drove Justin to school for his second day there, but he noticed that Justin had been a bit quiet on the journey. "Looking forward to day two, son?"

"Yeah." He didn't sound convincing. Justin was looking out the window, and was a bit subdued. Many other kids were just walking to school, all chatting with each other, the occasional push or bump and having banter. Getting a lift there meant none of that.

"Dad, I'll make my own way back today. I'll just walk it – it's just a mile or so."

They got to the school and Mike parked up. "Are you okay son?"

"I'm fine."

He was getting out the car, so Mike didn't want to contest things in front of other kids that were walking past. "Okay. Give me a call if you change your mind though."

Justin closed the door. It gave a solid thud, and he smiled from outside. Mike knew better than to embarrass his son with waiting to see him get inside, so he drove off straight away, and headed for one of the local shops, his mind full of questions that he hadn't worked out yet.

This new village was a small one, with the nearby coal mining industry closed down years ago. In fact, while many people had left Divernon for better prospects elsewhere, the Howards had deliberately moved here, despite there being no openings at the local Junior High school for a math teacher for Debbie, now she'd completed the training. Mike worried about her, but he'd be home soon. With no clear role, he worried she'd find it harder to fit in than Mike or Justin. Then, out of the blue it happened.

"Debbie… ", the next door neighbour yelled, as Deborah was walking to her car in the driveway, "Me and the girls are having a girly night-in, Friday night. Want to come?" Her head and eyes tilting towards her house, as her hands were full.

It sounded as if the night was already set, with everyone else already confirming their attendance. It sounded as if she was the last to be invited, and the other girls, after discussing it through of course, had come to the reluctant agreement of inviting her too, maybe out of sympathy, or most likely because one of their usual group had pulled out at the last minute? She was an optional extra, and her attendance wasn't essential to anyone.

Perhaps, it was more of an opportunity for them all to feed their curiosity and find out about her. She knew how women like to talk. But till now, they'd have nothing to talk about as they didn't know anything about 'Debbie', apart from a very brief introduction as the Howards were moving into the home next door, and quite frankly, 'Debbie' preferred it that way.

Debbie was the type of pessimist who just kept herself to herself. She never went out in evenings. She never socialised and she didn't have any friends. She mostly went to the nearest shops head-down as if it was raining. She never initiated eye contact with anyone, and conversations were kept strictly to minimums to avoid getting personal.

'Is she talking to me?', Deborah thought, as Sonya, her neighbour one to the left didn't really seem to be directing the invite towards her. Rather, she just seemed to be casually unloading groceries from the trunk of her gleaming white Mercedes, concentrating on them instead, and looking as if she was on the phone to one of her friends, perhaps *also* called Debbie?

She hadn't answered Sonya until she button-closed the trunk, and her and the bags were nearing the front door, when she finally turned her head towards Deborah with her fake eyebrows raised, now expecting an answer.

Up till now, no more than a mere pleasantry had been exchanged between the two of them since the Howards had moved in. She was certain she'd introduced herself as 'Deborah' a few weeks back. How dare she call her 'Debbie', as if they were firm friends?

"Oh, sorry... ", Deborah splurted out, "... *this* Friday – *tomorrow*?" pretending to be asking for confirmation of the *day*, rather than getting confirmation that the invite was for her.

"Yes hun. You free?", her sunglasses fixed in her bouncy hair, that had obviously just been done by an expensive hairdressers in the city.

Sonya was tall and slim, with pink lipstick deliberately protruding past her lip lines, and had dangly earrings which caught the light as she turned. With her green dress and matching pumps, she looked so glamorous, and if this was Sonya just popping to the shop for groceries, what would she look like on a Friday night?

The others, she thought, would also be glammed up for the night. Debbie didn't glam herself up, or make her hair sexy. Why would she? She made a conscious effort never to draw attention to herself or her family. Debbie couldn't match them, nor even come close, but maybe, with a bit of effort, she might be accepted by their group? After giving see-through apologies for two barbeques in as many weeks, this was the inevitable third invite she'd been dreading but at the same time, it may have benefits. It could lead to other things, and may help the entire family.

Considering all this in an instant, she confidently lied, "Yeah, Sonya! I'd love to come. That's really nice of you. Who else is coming?"

"Oh, just a few of the girls I know. Your boy Justin goes to Auburn High School, yeah?"

Trying to sound casual, Debbie said, "Yeah, that's right." She didn't want to look stupid, asking how she knew this, but at the same time, there was only one High School nearby. "What time you looking to start?"

"Eight o-clock, Debs. Don't bring anything – just yourself."

'Debs? Fucking DEBS?', thought Debbie, scowling behind her own fake smirk. 'Christ, I don't even let *Mike* call me that. Bitch!' That got her back up, before the day even arrived. And before she thought more about boundaries with name familiarity, she said through that fake smile, "Looking forward to that already! What should I wear?"

"Wear whatever you like, babe. Jeans, a dress, whatever, we're just staying in – not going anywhere. Sorry, gotta go, these are killing me!", spoken with a slight grimace, referring to the bags that were now straightening her arms to an uncomfortable level. "See you tomorrow 8!"

"Yeah, see you then.", came Debbie's hasty reply, thrown out just as Sonya vanished inside, almost certainly not listened to.

This was great, yet terrifying. She'd committed now, and there was no going back. It was an opportunity for her to have a get-together with friends of an almost-friend. Surely that would be a safe place? And it would only be a few hours. One of the girls might be similar to her, also coping with moderate to severe anxiety, and they may become friendly. Of course, she'd need to rehearse with Mike what to say and what their story was from Indiana, who they knew, and why they left. It all had to sound plausible and have no holes. Several girls on a Friday night, all drinking? They'd not be afraid to probe when a story didn't feel quite right.

It was time to rehearse, and she only had until tomorrow night to get everything right. Her mind was now reeling. She'd have to alter the family's story from what it was, and mould it into something believable, but she'd also have to account for moving state late-term for Justin, and where Mike had been working to Redleaf, where there were very few job opportunities and neither of them moved for work.

In its factual form, their story wouldn't make sense to any of these outsiders. However, there was a juicy version of their story to be listened to, and anything less than plausible wouldn't stand up. Maybe she had to confess just a bit, to get things off her chest? That would be good for her, like counselling? Maybe too risky. Mild panic attack. Damn, she'd now committed to going, and there was no going back. Let's just get on with it and see what happens.

Chapter 19

Art was the one class that Justin looked forward to, the only class he felt he could express himself in. No other subject made sense to him. Fractions, dates, places and chemical names. What good is that?

For the last hour, Justin had been drawing an African elephant under a tree, reaching for its leafy branches, its calf close by, learning from mom, and the light changing as the sun arose in the background, casting long shadows. He got the feeling someone had been watching him work.

"It's amazing just how quickly you can draw, Justin. That would take me ages.", came a voice from behind him, surprising him with a rarely-had compliment. It was Ray, and he'd snuck up from where he usually sat in the middle of the class to see how his new friend worked. Ray was even better than Justin at art, a truly talented, evolving artist. A star of the future, no doubt. "It's really accurate too – lifelike."

"Wow! That's cool coming from you! I've seen some of your work, Ray – awesome, seriously. I saw your dolphin too – up on the wall. I mean, fuck me!"

Justin was referring to the dolphin that had been fully painted, glass framed and proudly mounted by the teacher on his art room wall for all to see for 3 months. It was hunting a shoal of sardines that were fanning out in all directions, and you could see the sun above through the glistening sea's swell, as the artist's perspective was from below. It truly was exceptional.

"Thanks bro. Yeah, I'm hoping to go to art college – to Chicago. Hoping to get a scholarship to go. The competition's tough as fuck though."

Justin couldn't help but smile. "I've got a good feeling that you'll make it, Ray. I'd love to have half your talent."

"Tell you what… why don't you bring in your portfolio. I'd love to look through it and see what you've done."

"What you doing after school? You could come round to my place and see what I've done – just… if you like, that is. It's quite heavy, that's the thing. I've kept it from when I was young."

And that's when it all began for Justin. Out of nowhere, one guy with a few compliments made him feel better about himself in an instant. Made him feel as if he was fitting-in. Of course, he didn't need permission to ask anyone round to the home. That had already been discussed and agreed. Justin wrote down his address and told him to come round any time after dinner.

He'd been walking down the stairs, and was now in the corridor, making his way to where the lockers were.

"Justin. It is Justin, isn't it?" Before Justin could say anything, she added, "I'm in your art class. I saw your drawing – of the elephants. It's brilliant."

"Thanks. Ehm." This was now two compliments in under an hour. Overwhelming to a young lad with only one real talent. She'd been the one he'd sensed watching him.

"I'm Tammy", introducing herself with a big smile.

"Nice to meet you, Tammy. Yeah, I'm Justin."

Justin instantly noticed that Tammy was a coloured girl, mixed race most likely. She was beautiful, with long, perfectly straight, black shiny hair that fell over her shoulders and back. He instantly noticed a mysterious side to her, perhaps camouflaged within her equally dark eyes. She was worth delaying the departure from the corridor.

"I'm taking art because I like it. But it's more of a hobby. I'm not really that good at it though. Not like you!"

"I'd love to see your stuff too, Tammy – your work." He was trying to remain casual while speaking with her, but inside, he felt a strange new feeling. His heart bumping around was making him feel clumsy. He closed his locker and focussed on her. Feeling good about himself for the first time in ages, he was going to be leaving school happy. That would be shattered in an instant.

"We've got art again tomorrow, I'll show you it, and you tell me what you think, yeah?"

Just as she was finishing, she was seized from behind, and she let out a yell. Her boyfriend, Curtis, had grabbed her for a laugh. She wasn't laughing, nor even smiling. Neither was Justin.

"Put me down!", she said, annoyed at the rude, and uninvited intrusion.

"Who's this?", Curtis enquired with an overly confident smile, clearly not worrying about the competition after looking Justin up and down, chewing gum as he did. Curtis was full of himself. He was tall and good looking, with perfect toothpaste-commercial teeth and was always smiling to show them off.

"This is Justin. He's in my art class."

Justin felt it was time to go. "I'll see you in art, Tammy." He started walking away. Whatever thoughts he'd began to sketch in his mind, he'd better erase. This was a non-starter.

Curtis led Tammy away to his car, where he'd usually drive her home in the Audi his parents had helped him buy. As she walked away, she turned back, just once. She'd noticed that Justin had changed direction and was now walking back into school, as if he'd left something in class.

Tammy was all too aware that her boyfriend was a bit of a show off. Spoiled by his well-off parents who'd seen to it that he had everything he ever needed – or wanted. She hadn't noticed that about him until after he'd asked her out and they'd been dating a few times. It hadn't been good for him, but she'd tried to overlook that. Lately, it had become evident he wasn't going to change. If nothing else, the way he was, was embarrassing for her.

More often than not, Tammy would get a lift home with him. She loved his new car, the heated leather seats, the satellite navigation, and electric everything, and liked being inside it. But she'd been getting bad feelings recently. It was beginning to dawn on her that this relationship with Curtis wasn't going to go much further. This wasn't the first time she'd been embarrassed by him. She knew that when she met Justin tomorrow at school, she'd have to apologise for his interruption, and this wasn't the first time she'd apologised for him either. She'd had enough.

As he drove away, she folded her arms, looking aimlessly out her window.

"What's up babe?"

It was as if he was oblivious to what he'd done. It was as if he'd done nothing wrong at all. If this was the normal Curtis, then she couldn't bear to be with him much longer. At one time, early on in their relationship, she did have feelings for him, but he was becoming more cocky with each day that passed and those feelings had been wilting. She was now certain the guy she'd first met, hadn't been the *real* Curtis. That guy had been slowly emerging.

"I was having a conversation with Justin, and you just… you just butted in, like you always do!"

He didn't say anything, but he pulled in along the way and stopped the car. It was a dead-end road, privately secluded by hills each side and a bridge overhead. They'd been there before, but this time there was a different feeling to it all.

"Hey babe, I'm sorry. I didn't mean anything by it."

"No of course you don't. You never do!", she snapped back. "I *hate* it when you do things like that. How do you think it makes me feel?"

Tammy was now regretting accepting to go out with him in the first place. She was disliking the person she was becoming, often fed-up and annoyed.

"Let me make it up to you. Tell you what – let's go and see a movie at the weekend?"

This was further proof he didn't give a shit about her feelings. She'd asked, and he hadn't even heard. "I don't want to go to a dumb movie!" She now had her legs crossed. Legs crossed away from him, and staring out her window without focus. A couple walked by, and it stole a moment or two. Both Tammy, and then Curtis noticed them as they walked past the car. The girl was holding on to her boyfriend's arm as he cuddled her, her head against his chest as they strolled, keeping warm with her long green scarf. She was happy. They both noticed the couple silently passing, but the couple hadn't noticed the two in the car, deeply engrossed with each other. It was more than just being content – they were in love. She didn't have that feeling with Curtis, and in truth, in the eight months they'd been dating, that feeling never arrived.

Curtis was always trying it on with her when they were alone. She was sick of having to reject his attempts to get her into his bed or the back of his car, desperate to steal her virginity. She'd promised herself long before he came along, that before she lost that, she'd be in a loving relationship. She just didn't feel it. She was confused before, but it started to make a bit of sense now. She wanted to feel like that girl wrapped in the green scarf and immersed in her boyfriend's arms who'd strolled past. Tammy's body had been undergoing changes, shaking off that little girl. Her insides were re-arranging. She wanted desire – passion, and needed to be in a place where she wanted no one else. Tammy was only eighteen and had the rest of her life ahead of her. She'd now wasted almost a year with Curtis, and it had never felt like she desired him. She wasn't even content.

Curtis leaned over, his hand followed suit and met her side, just under her breast. Her eyes looked upwards in disgust. This was typical Curtis – *so* predictable.

"Give me a kiss, babe." He tried to kiss her, but she turned away. He then grabbed her chin and twisted it so she was facing *him*, rather than outside. She slapped him on his face. This wasn't the first time.

"Oh for fuck sake, Tammy! I didn't *do* anything."

She hated his blasé nature, and the fact that he was oblivious of her hurt. She knew he was a terrible listener – always speaking, never hearing, never learning. She knew that if she took this moment to ask him a few questions about her, about Tammy and her likes, her hobbies, her interests, he'd struggle to name a single thing. Everything would be broad strokes, almost fishing – it always was. But this moment called for his attention. He was downgrading this incident at school, but it was just the latest in a string of annoying stuff.

"So what's the deal? You like this guy? This… fuckin… ", he couldn't remember his name, "… this fuckin geek you were talking to at school?"

Her eyes scowled back. She slowly shook her head from side to side as she began to turn away again, almost searching for signs of the couple, but they'd gone. Tammy had had enough. "I'm walking home." And with that, she opened her door and got out. He got out too.

"Tammy. No! Come on, let me drive you home. It might even rain!"

"I'm walking. If it rains, I'll get wet – so what?"

And with that, she ran up a nearby hill, away from Curtis and his car, the engine still running and her door still open, the car sounding 'bings' to the driver. She'd intentionally left it open. The car was precious to him. She knew he wouldn't leave it to catch up with her.

Chapter 20

The following afternoon, as Justin crossed the art room's threshold, he noticed that Tammy was already there, sitting in her seat, which was just behind his. "Hey you!" His welcome was warmly received.

"Hi Justin." She stood up and made towards him. "Listen, I'm really sorry about yesterday – for what happened with… Curt." She struggled to say his name, spitting it out annoyingly.

"Hey, it's fine. Don't worry about it. I take it he's your boyfriend?" Immediately, he knew he'd overstepped the mark and surrendered his hands. "Sorry – sorry. None of my business."

Tammy shook her head. Not enough to confirm he *wasn't* her boyfriend. Just mildly enough to show her disappointment in Curtis – and herself.

"Did you bring in your work?" It felt a good time for a topic switch.

"Oh sorry, Justin. I've left it at home. I *will* show it to you though."

Mr Henderson, the art teacher, interrupts. "Afternoon to you all. Now just before I remind you about the school's art exhibition night next Friday, I've got another task for you to do. This is a task that you'll need a partner for. It's more of a bit of fun than anything else, certainly nothing too serious, but there is my mysterious prize at stake – *and* I'll award it on the last day of term, so no staying off school either!" He heard the wordless groans complaining around the room, and he carried on with an ever evolving grin.

"… and *so*, I need you all to pair up with someone – from the other sex – and make a large painting before the end of the term – now that's just over two months away. By a *large* painting, I mean four feet by three feet. You'll be learning from each other, so choose someone who's skills are different from your skills so you can maximise your chances of winning my mystery prize, but more importantly, of *learning*."

Tammy and Justin were still standing next to each other. She glanced at him, in the hope that he'd notice. He did, and smiled, after their eyes locked on. They'd already found their partner for this task.

"Now this will indeed be a large painting. You'll each be given a four by three foot canvas, and what you decide to draw and paint is up to you. It can be *anything* – still life, scenery, flowers or plants – even aliens on another planet…" A few laughs circulated. "… or anything else you wish. There are *no rules* with this one, just work together and learn some techniques, such as scale, focus, perspective, best use of colour, shade and shadows, etcetera, etcetera. All clear?"

No one replied. It was like prom day for art. Then the room immediately buzzed with classmates shyly beginning to choose their dance partners and what music they'd paint to.

"Hey, do you want to partner with me?", she asked Justin, just to confirm what she'd assumed.

"Are you sure you want to do that? Won't Curtis *stab* me to death?", dramatically lunging forward with a stabbing motion, mimicking a fencing move, and speaking almost as theatrically as the art teacher's explanation of this project.

She giggled as he motioned the killing. "That won't happen – I promise. Please?"

She didn't need to beg. Justin loved the idea. He'd noticed two of her drawings she'd left on her table. She was good, and he instantly knew where he could help. It would be a joy to work with her. What a good idea from the teacher.

"On one condition."

"Go for it!", she replied, already smiling, knowing they were now a couple, when many others were still shyly flirting.

"That we *win* of course!"

She let out a laugh. It wasn't hilarious, but the way he overly-emphasised the drama of it all, mimicking Mr Henderson's accent, amused her.

"Then *En Guard*!", she warned, as she lunged backwards, almost falling over, but for the reaction of Justin's saving grip, and they giggled as they steadied themselves.

The teacher waved. "Okay, okay. Settle down everyone," raising above the chatter, and he paused for their attention. While waiting for the room to quieten, Justin and Tammy both gave Mr Henderson their full attention with genuine smirks, and they both noticed their prom date admiringly glimpsing back from time to time.

"Just another reminder that the School's annual Art Exhibition is taking place *next* Friday evening at seven o'clock. Remember, this is a chance for all you… budding Picasso's… to show to the world, or at least your community for now, your skillset. A reminder that someone may offer to *buy* your artwork – so make it your best, and think about how much you'd be willing to accept to part with your work, and of course, where that painting will end up being hung. After all, that's what being an artist is about – displaying to the world your masterpiece! And of course, if you can make some money along the way, then great!"

"Oh, and one last thing before we start for today. It's almost the end of the month, and you all know what that means. A reminder for Justin as he's new. You can all submit a drawing, a sketch, a painting, or whatever you like to me, before the end of each month, and that's Tuesday. Whoever I think is the best – and my rules are that I will only select one – will be hung on this very wall for the entirety of the next three months, or until end of term, as is the case now. But for now, select your painting partner for this new project and select what you'd like to make a picture of." He scanned the room for raised hands, but all was clear. "Okay! On you go."

And with those closing sentiments, the noise raised from pause-mode, as people oddly fumbled around, pondering over who they'd team up with. It would be a long two months, so it had to be someone who they could get along with, someone who's not too bossy and wouldn't take over, and someone who's skills were different from their own. There was no time to waste selecting a partner though, as nobody wanted left till the end.

"When you're ready, move the tables and chairs around so you can work in your pairs."

Justin and Tammy had joined forces instantly, so while others were still negotiating their partners, they started chatting after Justin collected one of the canvases.

"So", began Justin. "I want you to decide on this one."

"Really?" Tammy knew she was not even in the same art league as Justin was, and was kind of hoping he'd lead the way with some good suggestions. She was flattered he'd offered. Flattered he'd put his faith in her judgement.

"What kind of things do you like?"

Tammy could hardly believe it. She'd never even been asked this by her boyfriend. More like her 'soon-to-be-single' *ex*-boyfriend. "I like horses."

"Well let's do it. So what I need from you Tammy, is how many horses, what type of horses they are, what colour they are, if they are running, feeding, sleeping, being ridden, are they in a stable or in a field? What time of day it is, … "

Before he went any further, she immediately knew he was way more advanced than her. She'd just been thinking of two horses, and she saw Justin smiling, registering that as she placed her order. "Just two of them, in a field, facing each other. White horses – I don't know what breed they are." As he jotted it all down, she set the scene, "It's evening and the sun is setting in the background."

With his smile growing, he let out a sigh. "Tammy, that's great. That's a great vision. We can do that no bother. What we need, is to get some pictures of horses, and you choose the type you want us to include, and we'll create our ideas from there. Sound okay?"

"Sounds great. I've got some pictures already… at home, I mean."

"Would you be okay to bring them in?"

"Yeah. I'll bring them… Tuesday. We're back here then."

Justin quickly sketched what he thought she'd imagined in her head. He drew the two horses, standing face to face only a few feet apart, with a sun setting in the background. He was communicating with her all the time, on how large they were, what side the sun would be and how high in the sky it was, and other stuff in the background. She loved how he listened, and their conversation was effortless. She'd chosen well.

It hadn't seemed like the session was up, but it was, and it was home time. She'd brought the ideas, and Justin had made the mock-up sketch. She'd asked if it had been okay to take his drawing home to show her family, and he'd agreed. There were no arguments or conditions. After all, it was only a sketch.

They found themselves chatting about all this as they were making their way out of school, and along the pathways to the busses.

"I'm just walking home, Tammy. I'm just a mile up the road.", he said pointing. Justin knew she'd get a lift home from her boyfriend.

"Hey, do you mind if I come with you?", she asked.

More than a bit surprised, he said, "Of course not." Justin's eyes scanned for signs of her boyfriend, but he didn't see him.

As they began the walk, they started chatting about the art class and the various projects that the teacher had set. Tammy wanted to chat about the individual piece to be hung on the wall, the project for both of them to complete together, the piece for the big exhibition and future plans after term. It was a great chance to spend a bit of time with Justin and maybe make up for what happened the day before.

"Hey Tammy, c'mon, jump in." Curtis was already waiting for her at the end of the street. It seemed like an order.

"I'm walking today."

"What? Don't be daft, Tammy! What you talking about?" He saw Justin beside her.

She didn't say anything more to him, instead focussing her attention towards Justin. A much more rewarding journey home with a bloke that actually appreciates her talents and hears what she's got to say. She just walked past him and never gave a reply. Now behind them, waiting for her to turn round, was her stumped boyfriend, still in his car.

The walk home was a bit of a relief for Tammy. She'd felt compelled to be driven home by her boyfriend every single day and her options to do otherwise had been stolen. She was feeling freed for the first time this semester. She almost wanted to hold Justin's arm, like she'd seen the girl do the day before, but it wasn't the right thing to do.

Their pace was quite a bit slower than normal, both of them enjoying the chat along the way as they walked. It was new. She liked that he was actually hearing her, not cutting her off, wanting to find out more, keeping it with her. Justin was a good listener, but also genuinely interested in her, her views and her plans after High School. She knew he'd listened and that was refreshing. It was so polar-opposite from Curtis, that the change almost stumbled her words a few times.

"Are you submitting something for the exhibition?", she asked. "You should do, Justin. You'll do great."

"I've got something in mind", he replied, "There's not much time but I'll manage."

"What will you do?"

"You won't laugh?"

"At *you*? No chance!"

"I'm drawing a storm. I've done something like that before, but I'll make it better this time. More realistic."

"Everything you do *is* realistic, Justin!"

What a compliment from someone he instantly gelled with. If only she wasn't dating this fuck Curtis, he thought. He'd always be sneaking around, pissing things up for him.

"So… how do I keep in touch with you Tammy – for this project. I assume we'll need to contact each other?"

Tammy tore off a piece of paper from inside her bag, and penned something on it. "Here's my new number. Don't share it with anyone else. Text me later, so I've got your number too. I'll text back."

"Your *new* number?"

"Yes, I've had to change it."

"Why change it, Tammy?"

An uneasy pause lingered before she replied, and in that moment of silence, concern for her grew. "It needed changing." But that wasn't *completely* true. "It's actually a new phone."

Justin gulped a swallow. He was good at art, but an amateur at this stuff. It felt so personal. It felt as if she was giving him permission to call her up at any time, and chat things through on a new and private number – a direct line to her boyfriend's girlfriend. Of course, Curtis would be mad at this gesture – if he found out – and Justin suspected he'd be the one to pay for it later.

"You okay?"

Her eyes acknowledged his concern. "I'm okay."

For now, that was the end of it. "So… our painting together. Was there… *inspiration* for that?" Again, a question relating to her life, her thoughts. Somewhere Curtis never ventured.

She hesitated. "My family... " This was tough for her. Maybe a bit too personal.

"Sorry. I've done it again. None of my business."

"No, it's okay." She was calculating this gamble's odds, before opening up to him. It was a risk to tell deeply personal stuff, and she didn't really talk much about her personal life to any of her friends at school. "My ancestors were original Native Americans – 'Red Indians', some people call them."

"Really?"

"You'll laugh at *me* now."

"Tammy, no way – I'd *never* laugh at you." She heard sincerity in his voice and saw it in his face. The trust she felt with him had relaxed her to reveal what she'd revealed. It was just a little bit for now anyway. He gave her the space she needed to think, and she saw he wasn't forcing things. This hurdle was one she'd have to get over sooner or later.

"Well, my family are descendants from one of the old tribes – direct descendants. They were one of the original, indigenous tribes."

"For real?" It was obvious now.

"For real."

"Wow! Tammy that's immense. I've never met someone like that. Hey, you know what you've done?" His words were said jokingly after he felt she'd struggled to go there. She smiled with eyebrows raised, waiting for whatever was coming next. "You *know* – that *now* – you've got to tell me everything!"

"And I'd love to tell you, but that's all your getting – for now!"

They both smiled. She'd reeled him in, and teased him, just a tad with some crumbs, and he'd pecked them up. This sensitive guy was genuinely engrossed.

Justin made the connection. "That's where you got the horse idea from?"

"Kinda!"

Justin had a brainstorm. It rushed to him. "Tammy, for our picture… why don't we go the whole way. Why don't we include native tribe people too… if that's okay? The clothes, the weapons? I don't know – whatever? What do you think?"

"Oh, look, no. Sorry, I shouldn't have said. I didn't mean to hijack the whole project!"

"Absolutely Tammy! In fact, this'll be *brilliant*. I've already got visions of how it would look in my mind. Let's do this – for real. Listen, I don't want to mess it up and draw *stereotypical* stuff. I don't want to offend you."

"No. You won't."

"In fact, can you get us get some pictures? I'm interested in how they dressed and… well everything, really!"

Before they knew it, they'd arrived at the point where Tammy would turn left, leading into her street, and she stopped there.

"I'll do better than that. I'll bring in some pictures, but I've got some real stuff too." She saw that he was truly fascinated – not taking the piss.

"What real stuff?"

She smiled again. She was even more beautiful when she did, but this smile was a tad naughty. A smile with her head angled slightly sidewards. Justin noticed everything. He was always drawing things from different viewpoints, and he read her body language.

"You'll have to wait for now! I've got to go anyway. I'll see you next week at School, yeah." She indeed was teasing him.

"Yeah, see you Tammy. Nice weekend."

She'd only taken a couple of steps in the direction of her home, when he felt obliged to say something more. "Hey Tammy." He waited until she turned round. "Thanks!"

She gave one nod, and turned. It was a nod of acceptance. What was he thanking her for? For teaming up for the art project with the new guy, and helping him fit in? For walking home with him instead of getting a lift home with that wank, Curtis? For opening up on the way home about personal stuff, and letting him in – even just a small bit? For the promise of more to come? Or was it for all of that, and just becoming friends? She turned and walked away. This was for Tammy to ponder over, and she did.

Justin watched her take the first few steps away from him. He knew he couldn't stare at her. But he wanted to. She was fast becoming his obsession – but staring would just be creepy. What if she turned round and saw him ogling her? So he let her go, and continued his short journey. They both had stuff to fill their minds.

In the space of one day, he was now feeling great about himself. These last few blocks would be a joy to walk now. His house wasn't far away, and Ray would be visiting him later that evening. Things were looking up.

Chapter 21

That evening, Ray came round to the house as promised. He was carrying a large folder, zipped all the way round. It contained some of his artwork. Some of his best work that he'd spent serious time on. Justin's mom was almost finished getting ready for the night-in next door, so Justin opened the door and beckoned him inside.

"Nice room man." Ray was impressed with the size of Justin's bedroom and that it had that 'brand new carpet' smell. Scanning the room, he noticed the new stereo and a large TV on his wall, a fancy hourglass and a cool chessboard with the pieces made from marble. "That's cool as fuck, man – I made a painting of a chessboard once."

"My papa gave me it – we used to play."

Then he saw the easel and lamp in the corner beside his window, and loads of pencils and paints that hadn't been tidied away. "Take it this is where the magic happens?", he said while gazing at the picture of a Coca Cola bottle that Justin had been working on. It had only been pencilled, and the colouring of it hadn't started yet.

"Homey, this is good! Jesus… this is *really* good."

"It's for the school project – the monthly thing."

"That's a great idea to include the cap. Nice touch." He was referring to the bottle's prickly top that was half-bent after being levered off. "What you using for colour?"

"Just acrylic."

"Will you get it finished in time? Needs to be handed in by Tuesday, yeah."

"Yeah, I know. I'll be working on it over the weekend."

"*All* weekend, more like!" He'd noticed some of Justin's other drawings. Some were framed and hung up on his wall. "You did these too?" He turned to see Justin's silent nod. "Wow." It was a 'wow' – rather than a 'WOW' – but a welcome compliment.

"That's *your* stuff, is it?", pointing to Ray's folder resting on the bed. Ray unzipped it, and handed it over.

"Fucking *hell*, Ray!" Ray was proud of his artwork, and especially these ones he'd brought over for his new pal to see. "Holy *shit* man!" Justin supported the folder with care on his lap, fully aware its contents were precious.

The first picture was of an old car, which was jacked up having a wheel changed by a man with a wrench in his hand. There was so much detail to see, and it'd be disrespectful to just quickly scan over it, and hurry onto the next page. Justin noticed what others would miss, and knew the steps Ray must have taken. He saw rust on the wheel arches, fluid dripping from the engine and forming an oily well beneath it, chrome lettering stamped on the vehicle's trunk, a couple walking past pushing a stroller and there were even colourful toys hanging from its frame for the baby to see. Ray had even included puddles on the ground, and they reflected overhead birds.

He could have analysed this for ages, acknowledging how it had been created at each stage. Totally engaged, but desperate to see what's over, his anxious hand turned the page, but only after he'd gazed enough, and thoroughly absorbed everything the painting was offering. The turning of the page was done delicately, making sure not to damage anything.

The next picture was of a cat, with her four newly-born kittens. They were all suckling from their mother, ten eyes closed. Even the rug they were laying on, looked as if it was real and you could reach in and feel the warmth of the material. Justin was in awe. "These are stunning. How long did these take you?"

"Well, each one of them is around a month or so. Oil paintings are much longer though. I've got an oil painting back home that I'm still working on. I've been working on that – on and off – for almost a year! I'll show you it sometime."

Justin was honoured that Ray had trusted him with it. He carefully flipped over to the next ones, commenting on them all. The folder contained six pictures, all fully finished. As he closed the folder, he realised that in his hands was around half a year's work, of a very talented artist.

"These are superb Ray. They're… photo-real!" Justin was no competition. He was really good at art himself, but not to this level he wasn't. "I bet you can't wait to see my shit! You'll piss yourself when you see this."

Justin also had a folder with some of his best stuff inside, but it felt like a bit of an anti-climax moment when Ray opened it up and flipped through the pages, noticeably spending a few seconds less than Justin had done with Ray's masterpieces.

"These are brilliant man."

"Tammy wants me to show them to her."

"Tammy?" That put a halt to things. "Her with the funny name? Tammy *Yazzie*?"

Justin noticed his concern. "What's wrong with that?", attempting to sound innocent.

Ray let out a sigh. "I take it, you like your hands to work with?"

"What's that supposed to mean?"

"She's dating that nut, Curt. You *do* know that don't you?"

Justin gave a resigned nod. Nevertheless, he was aware what league he was in with artwork, but also with girls. "We're just working together. For the school project. She picked me!"

"Bro… he's mental. Seriously man, he'll fuck you up if you even try it on."

"Come on, man. Tammy and *me*? She's my dream girl. There's no way in a million years she'd ever even notice me in a crowd – let alone go out with me! Think about it."

"And yet, she walked home with you today…" It was now Justin who was thinking about it. "… *and* she told Curt where to go, I hear – in front of everyone!"

Concern gathered on Justin's face. The consequences were already in the post.

"So what's the deal? Do you… like her or what?"

Justin didn't want to answer this question directly. "Who doesn't."

"Tammy's too good for that arse-wipe!"

"Well in that case, she's *way* too good for me!"

Ray looked at Justin. He wanted to say something like, 'Don't be daft. You're a good looking bloke. You've got a great physique. You've got a lot going for you.' But he couldn't. He didn't think that. Justin was a decent guy, and it looked like they were going to be friends, but Justin was no stud or potential Casanova. Reflecting on this, Ray worried less.

But on the other hand, Justin did have other qualities, and Tammy had already discovered some of them. Would she see past his slightly crooked teeth? Did it matter that his hair was a bit tight and curly? Surely, it had to be the case that she was just being friendly with Justin, and not giving him the come-on?

"Listen, she's a fantasy. Nothing's ever going to happen. I *am* allowed to dream, aren't I?"

Ray looked at Justin with false sympathy. "Listen, he's a prick, and she knows it. Fuck knows why she hasn't dumped the cunt yet. But here's a thing, and listen carefully, because this is gospel." He got comfy on a chair Justin had in the room. "She *will* dump him sooner or later – that's for sure. It's only a matter of time, but it *will* happen. But let her do it on her own terms, bro. In her own time. See, the thing is, if Curt thinks she's dumped him to go out with you – well then you're in for it – and he's a fuckin looney!"

Ray walked up to one of Justin's paintings that was hung on his wall. He did this to hide the worry that had spread on his face. A moment later, he turned round. "Look man. All I'm saying is – be careful, and bide your time – that's all. Don't fuck with him."

This gave Justin a lot to consider. Ray's advice was probably the right way to go about things, but the truth is, he was already falling for Tammy. It just happened. In time, he'd have to make her aware that he liked her. Maybe she needed that? If he didn't, he may just be letting her slip through his fingers and into the hands of some *other* arse-wipe. It felt best not to over-think it. His head was hurting when he did.

The day had been quite eventful, but at least it had ended safely – or rather, without a beating from this Curtis guy. He'd had a warning, and strangely enough it was from his new best friend.

Tomorrow will be a different day. Family day. They'd agreed to take Justin into the city to look for a puppy.

Chapter 22

Mike was in the driving seat, heading north to Springfield City, and on the way there, Debbie told Mike about the night-in and some of the girl's names. Maybe she'd worried too much.

Debbie had staggered home during the early hours. She remembers that she initially had tried to discover more about the girls than she gave away, always keeping answers vague. As the night wore on, and the drinks kept coming, self-control abandoned her and who knows what she'd revealed. Although she couldn't remember anything after midnight, she did remember just going for it, and letting her hair down, dancing to music played on Sonya's fancy sound system. She'd wrongly pre-judged Sonya, damaged from her cautious past. It had been a good night after all, and she was glad she went. Good things can happen here.

They'd arranged to go to a private seller they'd seen online during the last few days who'd promised to keep the last of her four puppy Cocker Spaniels until after they'd visited, as there was another potential buyer. They'd went to a pet shop first to get a leash, bedding, toys and food beforehand.

When they got there, Justin connected instantaneously with the pup at the lady's home, and played with it on her carpet. It had a gorgeous short coat of different brown shades, its floppy ears and paws looking oversized, unlike its tail. It chewed on the toy rope he'd just purchased and had licked him on his face when he was kneeling down, petting it. There was an instant connection, and he was smitten.

"Is it a boy or a girl, mam?"

"It's a bitch, son – a girl… and she's had her jabs. She's ready for a home."

Justin looked up at his parents who were sitting down, checking through the certificates. He'd already made up his mind. "Dad, I'm taking her." He knew the price and had withdrawn the money, and a little more.

"Are you sure you want to do this son?" The eagerness in his son was undeniable, but this was just for confirmation.

"Absolutely! Are you okay with cash, mam?", Justin asked, switching attention to the seller, who nodded in agreement.

Two thousand dollars was counted, and the seller wrote up a receipt and handed it to Justin, along with the certification documents. That was it – all done. The journey back home was the happiest Mike had ever seen his son. Mike noticed in the mirror that Justin was beaming in the rear seat and his eyes were focussed on his new pup, making sure she was comfortable in the bed he'd bought.

Justin had reserved the entire weekend for doing just two things. He would get to know his new puppy Cocker Spaniel, and finish his homework. He thought about painting her, but she never sat still long enough.

She was tiny, and with all her frailties and her vulnerability, Justin had decided not to take her outside for now, and let her become familiar with the home. She had her own unique smell, and it hadn't been long before her little odour was evident when you entered the home.

Justin's family had never owned a dog before, so everyone had a lot of learning to do. She was Justin's dog, not the family's, and he decided to buy two beds for her to curl up in. One of these, he placed in his bedroom, where she'd sleep at night. She rested there while Justin worked on his other job, this art task – his Coca Cola bottle which he managed to finish off before Tuesday's deadline. It was now painted and ready for the monthly competition. Certainly not up to Ray's standard, but Justin was really happy with it. He didn't go out and leave her, so he'd spent a bit more time on that while she slept.

Justin had recently moved home, left friends behind, started a new school, was making some new friends – and perhaps an enemy, he had art competitions to enter, and he had a new dog to look after. On top of that, he couldn't stop thinking about Tammy. He found himself debating if he was falling in love with her, or if he just liked her so much. He'd never been in love before, so couldn't tell for sure. With everything going on, this cute little puppy took his mind off everything else. For sure, he'd instantly fallen in love with her.

Tuesday had arrived quickly, and Mr Henderson closed over the art room door. "Morning everyone. Nice to see you all." He knew he was a bit eccentric. "A swift reminder that today is the deadline for those of you who wish to seek fame. The time limit to submit to me their piece, in the hope of being selected to get hung up on my famous 'wall of fame' has *finally* arrived. *This* class finishes at lunch, but you have just under six hours until the end of the school-day. Or of course, you can hand it in now – I've already had over twenty pieces submitted, and I have to say – the standard has been excellent."

Justin walked up to the teacher, and handed over his creation. This was the very finest piece he'd ever created, and he'd spent more time on this than anything else. Mr Henderson looked over the painting in astonishment. As he did, he blew out of his mouth. The bar had just risen.

"Thank you, Justin." It was almost as if the teacher couldn't believe that Justin really was the creator of such work. A few faint whispers went floating around the room. Then it fell silent.

"Anyone else?", as his eyes darted from side to side, skimming the room for movement, but no one else came forward. "Then if that's that, let's crack on in your pairs, and continue with your end of term project."

The room instantly burst open with life again. Many of the couples were now talking about the painting that Justin had just submitted and were commenting on the new type of expression that Mr Henderson *still* had on his face, a mix of disbelief and amazement.

For the remainder of the class, Justin acted almost like a substitute art teacher. He showed Tammy the correct way to hold the colouring pencils and how much pressure to apply to it with the grip hand for their fence line. He'd shown her his way of drawing quickly, and to include distant objects only faintly for now, as they'll either be drawn over or rubbed out later. In a separate drawing, he explained about the key subject items and the option to have things in the background slightly out of focus, to relay depth and not divert the viewer's attention.

He asked Tammy to choose a perspective, and, working from closest, to furthest away, they'd made a mock up drawing in around twenty minutes, and they'd be using this as a guide until the very end.

Justin saw to it that Tammy got involved in this and encouraged her to express her skills on the paper. He knew she had talent, praised her when she was on the right tracks, and intervened when needed, but she done most of the work that day. The lesson flew by and she felt great about herself for learning some new techniques.

There was around 10 minutes left of the class. "Let's stop there Tammy. That'll do for today, we can't start the next stage now. Tell you what – you've done great. Honestly."

She felt as if she had indeed done great. And as they cleared up their work and put everything away, they chatted quietly. "Thanks for your help Justin. I've enjoyed this today."

"No worries. Hey, you're a fast learner. I've enjoyed showing you." But he noticed her turn away. "Hey, are you all right?" Maybe she felt a connection with the drawing already. He knew that feeling all too well. He wanted to cuddle her, but he didn't have permission.

"Sorry. Not used to praise! Curtis never compliments me. He's always putting me down."

Justin didn't really know how to answer this. It wasn't any of his business and he recalled the warning from Ray. But in this moment, he felt she needed something. With the rest of the class busy finishing off, he whispered quietly to her. "Tammy, there's a lot to compliment you about. Curtis doesn't realise what he has."

She let out a long sigh. "To be honest, I'm getting fed up with him. There! I finally said it!" Yes, she'd finally said it, and to someone who wasn't one of her girly friends either. She'd chosen Justin to vent off her annoyance that had obviously been simmering for ages.

Justin had seen them argue, and her irritation at Curt. "I thought you two were quite solid?" Conversely, he knew cracks were forming.

"Solid? Ha! No chance!"

This was the first thing he'd said, to which she frowned. There was only a couple of minutes until the end of class.

"Here, look at this." He brought out his phone and showed her a picture of his new pup.

"Oh my god!", swooning over it. He'd taken loads of pictures and deleted the ones that he didn't like and wouldn't make a good drawing. He was good at photography too, but these weren't professional pictures taken with a digital SLR camera. They were just 'snaps', taken from his phone. He'd bought a DSLR camera too.

"I've got better pictures from my proper camera – they've came out superb. I can't bring the camera to school though." This wasn't quite a cryptic message, but there was the first concealed hints of asking her round to his home.

"I'd love to see them." Justin noticed that she said this without a moment's hesitation, and without a moment's thought for any consequences.

"You'll have to wait for now. Maybe one day!" He was getting his own back.

"What's his… oh, is it male or female?"

"Female."

"What's *her* name?"

"I named her Belle", he said, looking directly at Tammy. "It means beauty." He cringed inside after saying it. Only now, did that sound like a cheesy line, but Tammy didn't take it that way.

"You've *got* to send me some pictures of her. Will you?"

"Of course I will. I'll send some tonight."

"Oh! That reminds me." She went to her bag and pulled out a folder.

"This is your work?", referring to what she was now clutching. "Ah, you brought it in. Cool."

She passed it to him, and he carefully opened the front cover to reveal the first picture inside, then flipped over to the next page and then the next. There was a little gift for him inside and it slid into his hands. He smiled at her. That was exactly what he was after.

Chapter 23

They walked out the art class together and Justin said goodbye to Tammy, as he was meeting up with Ray for lunch. He turned the corridor, and saw Curtis standing against the wall, and there were two other boys opposite him, who'd propped themselves up when he appeared. His pace dropped a little as he noticed them all, realising they'd been waiting for him, and this was their gauntlet to run.

"How you doing Justin?" Curt's words were clearly rhetorical – clearly menacing.

"Wait a minute Curt. *This* fuck! *This* is the fuckin guy that's been messing around with Tammy?", asked one of his friends, a lad called Samuel.

"Hey wait a minute! I'm not *messing around* with anyone!", Justin declared innocently. "We're just doing a project together in art."

"So what's an art project got to do with walking my girlfriend home?" Curtis now removed his foot from the wall and approached Justin.

"We're just friends. Seriously."

"It fuckin better remain that way, snowflake. Right?" This was the intimidation Justin didn't need, and his rhetorical threat demanded silence. "You were going this way – so on you go.", he ordered, thumbing the way through.

The barricade they'd made opened up a little, and Justin cagily stepped through the gap, a little more towards

Curtis's friends, than to Curtis himself. As he was passing, Samuel bumped hard into Justin, sending him over the other boy's outstretched leg and to the ground. Some stuff spilled out his school bag in the direction of Curt. He'd landed face first on the floor, but quickly twisted round and was now on his back so he could see them.

Sam leaned over him. "Wanna do something? Pizza face!"

"He's a wimp – he'll do fuck all!", added Zac, the other of the three. Curtis picked up a picture that had come to rest in front of him. It was the picture that Tammy had given to Justin as part of their project. She'd only just handed it to him minutes earlier.

"Oh… nice horse!", mocked Curtis. He turned the picture round so the others could see it, and held it at the top with both hands. Then he slowly ripped it apart while looking at Justin. "Rather, it *was* a nice horse, wasn't it Sam?"

Justin's eyes were fixed from below on Curt and he watched on, as it got torn in two. He felt a strange tingling pain as it ripped.

Now staring at Justin, Curtis added, "Stay the fuck away from my girl, or the next thing I'll rip apart is you, Just-in."

He scooped up the things that had spilled from his bag. All three walked past, each one delivering him a warning kick as they did, but Sam's final kick was harder, and it hit him awkwardly in the ribs. It could have been worse, but this time, it was more of a message.

Tammy had heard the commotion and had turned back, just in time to see the kicks. She rushed to Justin's aid and knelt in front of him, shielding him from a further assault.

"What the hell was that for?" Silence. "What did I tell you about violence? You *know* I hate fighting", she yelled, not expecting a response, but one came.

"I didn't hit him!", Curtis innocently shrugged, "*He* did.", referring to Sam. "If I hit him Tammy, he'd be going to hospital." He had to sound tough in front of the other two, and signalled to them that it was time to go, and slipped away while she assessed the damage.

She noticed before Justin did, that blood was coming from his mouth now, but just a little. His top lip got pushed into his teeth when Sam collided with him.

"Jesus! Are you okay?"

"I'm fine." Justin was embarrassed to say otherwise. It was his pride that was more dented. He didn't want to appear weak in front of her.

She saw the picture she'd given to Justin, now lying on the ground, ripped in half. It was personal to her.

"I'm sorry Tammy.", wincing with the pain from the last kick. He held his ribs with one hand and passed her both pieces.

"Justin, it's me that should be apologising. Not you." Now she realised that she'd have to decide. She'd been playing a dangerous game so far, and others were going to pay.

"Was that one of your family?" The picture was an old one, in black and white. It showed a horse, saddled up, with a man in front of it, holding onto the tethers that secured it to a fence.

She nodded. "I'll tape it together."

She'd entrusted him with a deeply personal family picture, proudly handed down the family for generations, and within five minutes of her handing it to him, it was destroyed. There was nothing more to say.

"Em. Tammy, I need to go. Listen, I'll just walk home today. I'll see you later."

She watched on as Justin hobbled away, putting the blame on herself, knowing that it had been her boyfriend that hurt her friend, and destroyed her photograph.

Remembering what Tammy had said about hating fighting, Justin could only wonder why she was dating this violent prick in the first place. He needed to learn from this.

Chapter 24

The next day had finally arrived. It was the 1st of the month, the first day of May, and almost two months till the end of term. Most of the students had, as usual, arrived a bit before the teacher and the normal background chatter filled the room. But Tammy noticed her partner hadn't turned up, and her thoughts turned to yesterday's events. While she did, Justin walked in, followed by Mr Henderson. They'd been chatting in the corridor.

"Sorry for keeping you all waiting. Is everyone okay?", waiting for any replies. "First things first. As you'll know, today is the 1st of the month. And what a quick month it's been too! You all know what the new month brings… a new addition to our wall, and I've already removed the one from three months ago and returned it to its rightful owner." He'd already removed January's winner, making room for April's. There had been many entries, and the class was hanging on the silence that loomed until he announced who'd won.

"Our winner for April *IS*… drum roll please… Justin Howard's stunning painting of a vintage Coca Cola bottle and cap." He unveiled the picture that had already been hung on the wall. There were a few gasps as the painting was revealed. Everyone was clapping, appreciating his work. "Well done Justin!"

People in Justin's little circle came up to him and gave him a hug. Congratulations were deserved, because getting your picture on the wall, really was a big deal. It's something you can put on your CV when applying for college, if that's your goal.

"Fuckin hell, Justin. That's superb!", complimented Ray with a massive smile, genuinely pleased for his pal, noticing the changes since he saw it last. "Maybe we'll both get to college!"

"I thought *you'd* win, Ray."

"I didn't submit anything this month, homey!", he replied with a wink. "You would've won anyway. That's fuckin brilliant man!"

Others in the class were gathering around his work on the wall. The teacher allowed them a few minutes to gaze every month for this. Only now, could everyone see just how talented an artist the new guy really was.

"Okay class, make your way back to your pairs now."

As they all went back to their seats, Ray nudged his pal. "You should sell that shit! I'd buy from you!"

Respect from Ray – what a compliment.

"Hey you!", Tammy said when back at the table, smiling proudly at her partner. "I didn't know you were *that* good!" Her beaming smile wasn't matched with his. She'd noticed he walked to their table somewhat gingerly. "I'm sorry Justin. I didn't know that was going to happen."

"Tammy, I'm not blaming you. You didn't do anything wrong." Justin winced as he stretched out his arm to the table. He'd been struck on his right side by the boys.

After checking that no one was looking, "Let me see." She carefully pulled up his T-shirt and as a purple-red bruise revealed itself – she gasped a huge breath. "Oh Jesus fucking

Christ!" She quickly withdrew her hand and put it over her mouth, peering at Justin over her fingers.

Justin hadn't heard Tammy curse before, and she didn't look the swearing type. Maybe Curtis had brought out the worst in her.

"You'll need to do the work today. I can't work with my left hand either!", he joked, but only a wry half-smile was revealed when she dropped her hand.

"You shouldn't even have come in today, Justin. Did you report them?"

"I'll be fine. And no, I'm not reporting anything."

"I saw everything. I'll be your witness." Justin gave her an admiring smile, recognising the good-will gesture, but shook his head. He appreciated that she'd stand up for him, but it would be him – and only him – that would pay the price later, and maybe he'd wake up in hospital? Fuck that.

"Then I'm speaking to him. It won't happen again." Well intended sentiments, but it didn't assure Justin of anything. In that moment, what he did realise was that the longer she stayed with him, the longer she'd have leverage over him and the safer he'd be. But if she broke it off, then Curtis wouldn't have any reason not to give him the hiding of a lifetime.

Chapter 25

Justin hid the bruise marks from his parents, but the following morning, his mom saw him limp out the shower room with a towel wrapped around his waist and it was too obvious to miss.

"Justin!", shrieked Debbie. "How the hell did *that* happen?", pointing to the marks on his side.

He thought the towel had covered the bruise, which had now turned dark purple. "Mom, I just fell against a table at school. I'm okay – really."

He was now covering up more than just the bruise, and she knew it. She followed him into his room and saw him straining to sit on his bed, closing his eyes tightly as he lowered himself onto the mattress like a pensioner.

"Justin! Bullshit... *table*! Son, tell me what happened." Her arms had dropped the washing basket and were now folded across her body. He was rubbish at lying and she was good at seeing through them.

"Mom, it's nothing." He didn't want her involved, and he couldn't have her worrying.

"Did someone do this to you?", but as he looked down at the carpet for a reply, Belle came over, now licking the wetness off his feet. "Look – even Belle knows something's wrong!" When he reached down to pet her to say thanks, he blew out a groan. A mom knows her child. "Right, that's it – doctors.

They might be broken!" In this mood, she was not to be argued with.

"Nothing's *broken*, mom – just sore."

"Well, I'm taking you anyway. I'm phoning the school."

Justin looked up, next-level worried, shaking his head. He instantly visualised her standing up for him, ordering the Principal to hold those responsible to account. "Mom, don't. Please!"

"I'm phoning the school, to say you'll not be coming in – for today at least, until we get you checked out. In the meantime, you rest up."

She'd made the right call. She normally did. And it was just a few moments later that he heard her on her cell phone downstairs, speaking to the school's receptionist. She was only on the call for a minute, but then she made another one.

Justin heard her footsteps coming back up the stairs, and she went into his room where he was lying on the bed, Belle beside him, cuddling in.

"I phoned the School. I told them you've got a bad cold, and you'll be off sick for a few days."

Justin smiled. She'd covered for him, but it meant she knew there was more to this than he'd let on. And now she was lying to the school.

"Thanks mom."

She nodded. "And your dad's gonna take you to the docs at twenty past ten. Do you need a hand getting ready?"

"No. I'll manage. Sure I will, sweetie?" Belle's heavy eyes were falling over.

"OKAY. Right, dad's making pancakes.", she said smiling. "Be down in ten minutes, yeah?"

Justin didn't have much of an appetite, and only ate the majority of one pancake, washed down with some orange juice.

Later, when the doctor examined him, he gently pressed on each rib through the bruise marks. He watched his ribcage and muscles expanding as he inhaled and noticed him in quite a bit of discomfort as he took that deep breath. "It looks like at least one broken rib. We'll need to do an x-ray to confirm. What happened, son?"

Mike firmly stepped in. "He fell against a table." Debate over. Anyway, their job was to diagnose and fix, not to ask the 'why' or the 'how' of it.

Justin returned home with strapping around his chest, and a plastic bottle holding two week's painkillers. It was indeed two broken ribs – the x-ray showed a hairline crack in them, but it was the muscular pain that hurt the most. He'd already taken two of them on the journey home.

He went to his room and lay on his bed. Belle faithfully jumped up and licked his face. She'd been catered for by his mom while they were away, and she'd been out in the back garden discovering grass and rolling in it – for a reason only she knew. They were both tired and they both fell asleep on his bed. Justin's mom treaded silently to check on him, and turned off his light. She didn't close the door over fully, but left it ajar to allow the dog out if it needed.

When he woke up, it was just after six o'clock. His parents had agreed to just let him sleep on as he clearly needed it. He checked his phone, and noticed he had a new WhatsApp message. It was from Tammy. It said, 'Missing you at school. x'

Justin pondered over why she added an 'x'. Did it mean something? Was it a digital kiss? Was this just the way she ended every message with all her friends? And dare he send an 'x' back? He debated for ages how to respond, but the message had come in over an hour ago and he didn't want to seem as if he wasn't bothering with her, especially as she felt guilty about this whole thing. As much as he analysed her message, she'd undoubtedly do the same with his.

'Hey Tammy missing you too. Thought you'd like this picture x', and attached a snap of Belle lying on his bed, yawning. Since she'd sent him a kiss – how could he not send one back?

He couldn't help but stare at the phone. She'd received it immediately, and was typing back.

'She's absolutely adorable!! I'm in love!! How did you get on today? x'

'Fuck – me – running', he thought. Who's she in love with? Belle – of course.

'2 broken ribs :(will be off school for a few days :) Back next week sometime. x'

'So sorry. Anything I can do? x'

Justin took his time to think about this one, and boy – did his mind wander. But there was only one thing he *could* ask for. 'Send me a picture of you would you please? x'

'Tada!' A reply in about ten seconds. But this time, he noticed there was no kiss. She had attached a picture that she'd only just taken, and she was blowing him a kiss. This was even better. This medicine was better than the knockout drugs the hospital had given him.

'Gorgeous! Got to go for dinner Thanx Tammy x' Not being in-person provided the bravery he needed to compliment her looks – she deserved it.

'Bye x'

Even the shortest of texts sounded great from her. As he scrolled through those messages again in bed, he couldn't help thinking that maybe something was beginning to develop between them. As he fantasised, the drugs kicked in hard and he fell asleep holding the phone. Tomorrow would be a day of working from home, and he had a storm to draw for the exhibition.

When he woke, it was Friday morning. He still felt sore, but not *as* sore. He pulled away the covers, and sat on the edge of the mattress, putting his hands up and to the side, as if he was doing yoga, gauging *how* sore this was today compared to yesterday.

He was on the mend – so the storm was on and it was time to get to work, but only after breakfast. When he'd been moving around, he heard his tummy rumbling and he could never draw on an empty stomach. Breakky first – then drawing.

Chapter 26

After breakfast, Justin got his dad to drive him to an industrial estate in Redleaf to see if he could find a suitable backdrop for his picture and decide what angle to draw it from. He wanted somewhere unique, not a mainstream thing. When he returned home, he got straight to work sketching it from the pictures he'd taken with his camera.

There were a few businesses in the background, and he'd concentrated on making sure that the detail shown in his photograph – now on his laptop, was clear in his sketch. He'd changed the light, from sunny daytime to a troubled sky, with hardly any light getting through, and huge black clouds menacing above. Driving rain was bouncing high off the sidewalk and splashing in the puddles they'd made below, and a fork lightning bolt, zig zagging its own path to the ground, hitting an electricity pylon, causing sparks to fly all around and the cable to snap and dangle free. The lightning created immense light all around, and created unique shadows elsewhere.

It was all coming together. The more he worked on it, the more complete it became. The more complete it became, the more he worked on it, but he had to stop. Coats of paint needed drying, and his fatigued grip-hand and ribs needed a break. It was time to rest up and be proud of what he'd achieved so far. With no school, he worked on this and this alone all day, with no other classes and no interruptions from anyone, except Belle. He could now focus on this project only, dialled-in as he concentrated to get everything perfect. Typically a fast sketcher, he took his time with this, feeling a new sense of pride in Redleaf, and this was the very first picture he'd made of somewhere in his new town that he felt a connection with. He spent Saturday working on it too, scheduling play time with Belle as the paint dried.

"Belle!" She looked up from her basket. "What do you think?" But she just looked at him, waiting for a command.

His mom pushed the door open, knocking gently. "Wow – that's amazing. Is that somewhere *here* – in Redleaf?" She'd always taken a fond, but wary interest in his artwork.

"Yeah, it's in town mom, just off Nelson Street. Like it?"

"Absolutely. Wow!", pausing to admire it. But it wasn't the reason she visited.

"It's nowhere near finished yet. Got to have it ready for Friday."

"Oh… ", she clicked, "… *this* is the picture for the *exhibition*?" Looking closer, "The detail is superb, son. Hey, how are you feeling now?" He did look a bit chirpier.

"Still sore – better though. Belle's looking after me!"

"Let's see." She couldn't help herself. That overly-demanding curiosity needed answers.

He lifted his T-shirt to reveal the bruising, which had faded a bit now, but still looked worryingly sore, especially to a child's mother. She looked at it again, comparing its shape and colour to the last time she saw it, and asked him not to work anymore that day. Dinner would be ready soon and she wanted him to bathe after that and just get ready for bed.

On Sunday afternoon, not too long after lunch, there was a knock at the Howard's front door. Justin was in his room and his parents were in the sitting room watching TV. Mike was closest, so he opened the door. Tammy was standing outside.

"Hi sir. Sorry… I'm looking for Justin. Is this where he lives?"

Mike smiled at her politeness. "Yes. Justin's upstairs. Are you… Tammy?" Justin had mentioned during dinner he was paired up with a girl from school named Tammy, and watched as she nodded shyly. "Well lovely to meet you Tammy. Come on in love.", he said warmly, and stepped back to allow her inside. "Grab a seat and I'll let him know you're here."

"I'm Deborah, Justin's mom.", Deborah said with a smile, showing her where to sit with her hand. "Have a seat Tammy."

She sat across from Debbie, and watched Mike vanish up the stairs, veering off to the right towards Justin's room.

"Justin says you two are paired in art."

"Yes mam. Justin's the lead. I'm just following his instructions", she said with a laugh, downplaying her involvement. "He's *really* good."

"Yes he is. He says you're really good too though." Tammy broke eye contact with Deborah as she relayed the compliment. "And he says you came up with all the ideas for the project too."

"Not really. That was nice of him to say though. We both decided on it actually."

As they were chatting, they could just about hear Mike's muffled voice above, but couldn't quite make out what was being said. Mike had quietly knocked Justin's half-closed door, and it pushed open further when he knocked.

"Hey son. Tammy's here to see you!" He spoke through an enormous grin. He could have shouted from below, but he was desperate to deliver this one in person.

"Tammy's here?"

Mike excitedly nodded to clarify.

"She's here – for me?"

Mike nodded again, grinning ear to ear, soaking up his son's expression. A perfect blend of shock and panic. Mike was trying to decide which shone through more, but he remembered the time when all these feelings happened to him.

"She's downstairs?"

"So quickly get ready and I'll let her know you'll be down in a bit, okay?" Mike parked his grin upstairs and when he returned, his wife and Tammy were already drinking tea and chatting, mainly about school. "He'll be down in a few minutes. He's just getting ready."

He sat down beside Deborah. "Did he forget you were coming round, honey? These pain killers make him a bit confused."

"No. I thought I'd just pop over and see how he was."

"Aw sweetheart. That was really nice of you!", said Debbie.

"How is he?", Tammy asked, looking at both of them as she spoke. Mike replied first.

"He's getting better every day. Still a bit sore though, but he's on the mend."

Justin appeared from the top of the stairs, holding the handrail as he came down. He was only about half-way down when Tammy came into sight. "Hey Tammy. You okay?" He'd been a bit worried for her.

Mike intervened. "Actually, we're just popping out for a bit. We've got to pick something up… from the hardware shop."

Justin looked confused. So did his mom, but she clicked and played along. He couldn't instantly recall them speaking of buying something else, or ordering something they'd have to pick up. They'd moved in not long ago, and needed quite a lot of things, and most stuff just got delivered to the house, but maybe he'd missed this. The medicine messed with his memory.

"And I need to get gas too.", he added. "We'll leave you guys to it. We'll be back in about an hour. Lovely to meet you Tammy – you're welcome here anytime, sweetheart."

"Thank you sir. Lovely to meet you all too."

"Just Mike and Debbie, from now on.", he smiled, closing the door behind them.

"Your mom and dad are really nice.", Tammy said. It was the easiest way to start.

"Yeah they're… always looking after me. Are you okay?", he repeated.

"I'm fine."

"How did you know where I live?"

"I got it from Ray."

Justin sat down on a warm patch where his parents had been sitting across from Tammy, and let out a sigh as he did, which Tammy heard. She left her seat and sat next to him.

"I want to know how *you're* doing", she insisted. "Can I see?", finger-pointing to his side. He gave a cautious nod. She carefully peeled up his top, knowing how bad it had looked before. When the bruising was revealed, her concern lessened a little, as it was visibly getting better. The strapping covered the broken ribs, but not all of the bruising.

"Getting better.", Justin said casually, trying not to steal all the attention. She had her own troubles.

"I'm so sorry Justin. I'd no idea this was going to happen." She didn't. She'd only just turned eighteen and was naive about how the other sex battle over a mate. But she was now realising that Curtis was exercising his so-called, alpha-male status among others at school, and woe betide anyone who ventures close to *his* mate.

"It's okay Tammy. It's not your fault."

Half-relieved and half-convinced that he was on the road to recovery, she felt able to say something else. Ever so gently, she felt the bruising to gauge any pain, then the strapping. As she placed her hand on the side of his chest, she looked him in the eyes. He didn't grimace, but she noticed Justin's breathing get faster. 'Damn, she smells good!', registering her scent. Sitting right next to him with her hand holding up his top revealing most of his chest, looking directly into his eyes… "Justin – do you want to know the *real* reason why I came over?"

Justin nodded ominously, delaying a gulp. He was a virgin, and his parents were out. He felt half naked, and now this beautiful girl was undressing him on the sofa.

"I'm here to see Belle!", and kissed him quickly on his cheek. She knew she'd taken advantage of the moment and flirted with him, but he wasn't complaining, and saw the funny side of it. "Where is she?"

"Come and I'll show you. She's in my room, most likely sleeping… or chewing something!"

He led Tammy upstairs to his room. As she stepped in, Belle trotted up to her, sleepy-eyed, and she squatted down to meet her at floor level.

"Oh my *God* – she's *gorgeous!* Aw Justin, she's *tiny!* Hello Belle!", petting the pup's coat.

There was an instant bond between them, and Justin watched on with a huge smile, as the two of them enjoyed a playful moment on the carpet. Only now, Justin noticed what she was wearing, as she rolled about with the dog. She had on a pair of white jogging pants and a sweater top. He'd tried hard not to look when she was on the sofa a few minutes earlier, but her attention was diverted elsewhere now. Till then, he'd only seen her with her school uniform on.

As she spent a few minutes on the floor with the pup, Justin observed her, and when she moved, he noticed how the light above reflected on her hair. He noticed the scale of the dog compared to her and that her skin tone almost matched part of the dog's coat – but this wasn't for a picture, or a drawing he would make with a colour palette. This was to slot into a private memory file.

"Aw, Justin, look! She's licking my hand!" The dog had picked up the scent of something and was having a taste of it. "Ha-ha. It tickles!" Belle didn't stop.

Justin almost didn't hear what she said. He was engrossed in observing her kneeling on the floor in front of Belle. Here was one of the most beautiful girls he'd ever seen, and she was in his bedroom, five minutes after putting her hand up his shirt. 'There seems to have been a role reversal', he thought. He'd been online and he'd seen some adult material and he'd watched some porn – loads actually – it was everywhere. Although a virgin, he wasn't *quite* as innocent as he let on to Tammy, while he very nearly drew blood from his lip as he chewed the fuck out it.

'Licking your hand? If I had the chance, I'd be licking more than your hand!' He almost spoke it out loud.

He couldn't help but notice her body – his eyes just went there. He knew it was wrong to look, but fuck that. What else were they supposed to do? Wow, how her female shape differed. He loved her soft body curves flowing effortlessly from top to bottom. He'd never had any sexual feelings for anyone in his life, until now – until right now. These feelings were racing in, rushing in, flooding in like a tsunami, and he wanted soaked. If this is what desire is, then he was all-in, staking everything on it.

But she was Curt's girl, for now at least. And surely there were other guys in the queue. Justin had only known her a couple of weeks now, but hadn't noticed a single thing about her that was bad or wrong, or even just 'iffy'. She had no flaws. How could someone so small, so petite, have a dynamite impact? She was just five foot three inches, but she packed a heavyweight's knockout punch with no training.

This was the beginnings of infatuation. Justin knew all too well he wasn't good enough for her, not even in the same league, so why was she here? Just being nice? She belonged with Curtis. She turned around to ask Justin something, and as she did, she may have caught him looking at her bum.

"Is it okay to give her a chewy stick?", she asked, noticing Justin's eyes flicking up to her waiting ones. He couldn't help himself from looking. Her body made him do what his eyes were ordained to do – to feed him information. Then with a different type of smile, one he'd never seen before, she added, "I bought this at a pet shop yesterday."

Justin knew he'd been caught. He tried to play it cool but didn't know how to, and she didn't make a big thing of it. Maybe she wanted him to look? Maybe she was deliberately testing him, teasing him, to see what he'd do, to see if he was interested? Of course, he'd never ask, and she'd never say, so he'd never find out. 'Why are girls so fuckin complicated', he thought?

But what he did know for sure, is that there wasn't a pet shop in Redleaf, so she must have travelled out from town to get this.

"Yeah, no problem – just the one though."

She took out the packet from her pocket. Belle immediately noticed her doing this. As Tammy knelt on the floor and began tearing open the packet, Belle sat attentively on the floor directly in front of Tammy, her eyes glued to the wrapping, and her short tail sweeping the carpet behind her, as the scent of chicken filled the room that only she could really smell. Belle had picked up this routine quickly.

She slowly took the stick from Tammy's hand, being careful not to bite her, and returned to her bed with it. Tammy looked on in admiration, as she nibbled away.

"Can I take her home with me?", she asked cheekily.

"Eh – no!"

Belle had stolen the attention up till then, but she'd retreated to her bed with the chew stick. Tammy began looking around Justin's room. She noticed the storm painting that Justin was working on, and walked up to it.

"Wow, oh wow, Justin!" She turned to look at him. She puffed her cheeks out. No more joking now. No more funnies. Credit where it's due and this was stunning, even though it was only half-finished.

"This work Justin – there's… emotion in it. I can feel it."

Justin had gone through many feelings in the past week, and he'd tried to convey that in this painting. He'd put his best into it, and it was paying off. Desperate to impress her, he loved it that she appreciated his work, but also that she'd sensed its mood.

It showed a different place, away from the typical mainstream, with the weather rapidly changing from a serene calmness to a raging tempest, like an ambush had happened and the creator was God, no less. He wanted it to speak out something like, 'Beware – things can quickly change.' Tammy seemed to understand.

She scanned the picture, letting her eyes wander for themselves as they feasted on the story that was being told.

"I love it, Justin." He'd joined her now and was standing right beside her at the easel. She looked at him intently, pausing to select the right words. "I get it, Justin.", and she touched his arm. "It's powerful." So was her touch. "Do you think you'll have it finished in time?"

"I'll make sure it's finished.", he said, sensing her touch, but not looking down to see it.

"That reminds me!" She looked disappointed in herself for forgetting. "I've got something for you too." She went back into her purse and found what she was looking for. Now, she handed Justin another photograph – this was the real thing – an even older picture than the last, showing her family tribe from generations ago, with horses in the background. It showed their clothing, footwear and how the horses were dressed.

"I'll guard this one with my life!"

Chapter 27

Justin's parents had come home from wherever they'd been. They'd just given the two youngsters a bit of parent-free time, and had brought home some groceries so it didn't look too obvious. Justin and Tammy were already downstairs by the time they'd arrived back, and were just chatting and playing with Belle, waiting for their return.

The moment they got back, Justin said, "Hey. We're taking Belle for a quick walk in the park."

Young Belle had only been allowed in the garden up till now, so this would be a first. His mom didn't want to cause a fuss and argue strict safety rules in front of Tammy, so she just allowed it. "Son", she said, "Remember she's just a puppy. Don't allow her off the lead, just yet. Are you sure you feel up to it?"

"Tammy's going to hold the lead, mom. It'd be good for me to get a bit of fresh air."

His parents looked at each other. Neither of them really had any issues with this and they were glad Justin seemed to have a friend over. They couldn't wait to interrogate him after Tammy had left, grill him about this secret romance. They'd already been discussing Tammy when they were out.

"Okay. Don't be out too long, son. Remember this is her first time out away from the home."

And with that, they left with Belle leading the way, even though she didn't know the route or where they were heading. It was just a quick walk round the park and back, and they'd taken a few treats for Belle and a poop bag. Tammy held onto Belle the whole time, and while they walked, Belle was desperate to bound along faster than they did, never allowing any slack to develop on the leash.

They chatted constantly and had discussed the project they'd been paired up to do and had made a plan. Tammy would bring it over to Justin's home in her car the next day they had art, and he would do some work on it there. It would only be for a couple of days, as he felt he could return to school before the end of next week.

"C'mon Belle!", Tammy said. Close to home, an excited Tammy alerted Justin. "Look Justin, she knows her home already! Good girl!"

Before she left, Tammy thanked everyone for their hospitality and wished them goodbye. As she was putting her seatbelt on, Justin walked up to the car, and she rolled down the window.

"Thanks for coming over. Hey…", it just dawned on him as he was speaking, "You've been my first visitor!"

"I've had a great time. And I *love* Belle!"

"Yeah me too. She's a gem."

"Maybe, one day, we could take her somewhere else? She could go in the back."

Tammy drove an old Honda Civic estate, and Belle could absolutely have her little bed in the back, as they drove somewhere different. This almost sounded like a second date, but he was conscious she was already taken. Was she just being nice? On meds, it was too hard to work out, and he sensed that both his parents would be peering out from the window, trying not to be seen. Were they going to kiss?

"That would be brilliant Tammy. Listen, drive safe."

Tammy gave a final smile, and pressed the 'up' button for the window to close. There was no kiss but she gave a little wave as she slowly drove off, and Justin watched the car all the way until it turned out the street. As he swivelled round, he saw his parents scamper away from the window, and the drapes gently sway back to normal.

Chapter 28

Justin and Tammy had texted each other all week, mostly about Belle, but also about boring school stuff, especially history, which Tammy wasn't enjoying, and of course, their project. She hadn't managed to pop over with the painting they were working on, as she couldn't get permission to remove it from class. It wasn't a problem though – she'd done her best with her part – the horses in the foreground. She'd texted him a picture of it, and he said it looked great.

But it was now Friday, and Justin decided to return to school, strapping and all. He'd been working on his storm picture all week and was super proud of it. He couldn't miss the deadline, and, of course, he wanted to show Tammy and Ray, what he was really capable of.

As he walked into art class, the other students noticed his return. Rumours had spread about his absence. He walked up to his desk and slowly uncovered his masterpiece. Tammy saw it first.

"Wow!" She leaned in, absorbing everything. Trying to comprehend it all and what the picture was representing in Justin's life, she was speechless. Impressed beyond words, it took a few moments for it to sink-in that Justin really was the creator of this, but she knew he was. She'd only known Justin a short while now, but already she liked him, admired him, trusted him. Something she couldn't say about her boyfriend.

It magnetised others in the class, slowly pulling them in to gather round and gaze. Mr Henderson also made his way to their table and gorged his eyes.

"This is an excellent piece, Justin.", he finally said, never taking his eyes off the painting. "The garage and the business's shown are so lifelike." He scanned across. "The effect that the clouds have on shadows that would otherwise have been there, are instantly recognisable." The compliments didn't stop there. "I can almost feel the heat from the lightning! Remarkable!" He turned to Justin. "Well! This will *definitely* sell. That is, of course, only if you *want* to sell it!"

Justin hadn't really thought about selling it or not. It wasn't the money side of things for him. He just wanted to submit something that showed his best work, and this piece did exactly that.

"It *is* finished?"

"It's finished, sir."

"Then I'll put it with the others. You'll just need to select a frame." As he carefully lifted it from the desk, he treated himself to another look. "Well done, son!"

And with that, the painting was securely locked in the cupboard with the others, and the room went noisy with conversations. After around half an hour, the teacher interrupted.

"Right class… ", pausing until the noise dropped. "Good news! As promised, today we're going to finish early. This is to allow a little extra time for those of you who submitted something for tonight's exhibition to go home, have dinner, and get ready for the event. Remember, last year's exhibition was a huge success, with many students going on to bigger and greater things, and I anticipate tonight will be no different. A reminder we'll start at seven pm, in the gym, and your presence is required at least fifteen minutes before we start – if you've submitted a piece. Wear whatever you like, but *please* dress appropriately!"

After a few sniggers died down, he finished with a final moment of reflection for his artists.

"One last thing. Your piece may sell. Think about all the hard work that went into conjuring up what you made, all the stages of creating your masterpiece, how long it took you and all the sacrifices you made to be with your piece – instead of out partying somewhere! Consider the connection you have with it – what this particular piece means to you, and, of course, how much you want for it. *That* part – is completely up to you. Off you go, and good luck for tonight."

The room started emptying. But Tammy stayed, looking intently at Justin as he gathered his things. Her admiring smile he didn't see, perhaps not just for his painting. She knew people would be fighting over it. It's a one-off. He could name his price – within reason. Whoever saw it first, would undoubtedly make him an offer. She thought all this, but said nothing. It didn't need saying. Her look, that he finally noticed, told him.

"Are you coming tonight Tammy?" Justin knew she hadn't submitted anything.

"*Definitely*! Wouldn't miss it.", still beaming.

Justin noticed that Curtis had appeared. He'd been waiting right outside the class for Tammy, and had swam against the tide of exiting students, and was now propping up the doorframe. With his eyes, Justin signalled to Tammy to look behind her. When she saw him, Justin heard her tutting. This hadn't been arranged.

"I'm just coming!", and turned back around to Justin, her pissed eyes darting up, disappearing under her eyelids. He'd come to 'collect' her this time.

She felt smothered, and Justin knew it. Following a restricted smile that Curt didn't get to see, he said, "On you go… ", diffusing this before anything happened. "I'll see you tonight."

She sent Justin a private smile, then turned to face her waiting boyfriend. As she walked toward the door, head down, Curtis sent Justin a condescending sneer. However, Tammy stormed straight out the door and passed Curtis without saying a word. Statement made, as the smile on Curtis's face, lept across the room onto Justin's.

Chapter 29

A rejuvenated Tammy arrived before the seven o'clock opening time, eager to show support for her new art partner.

"Hey, there's Tammy!", Debbie alerted everyone as Tammy appeared. Tammy walked straight up to Justin and instantly gave him a hug. She knew his ribs were still sore, so it was a gentle hug. Justin looked over Tammy's shoulder, x-raying the room for Curtis.

"Good luck tonight", came a warm whisper in his ear as she clutched him. "Hi Mrs Howard – Mr Howard."

"Hi honey! And Mike and Debbie to you sweetheart! Okay?", his dad insisted.

She nodded. "Thank you – Mike. Hey, it's going to be a really busy night – the queue outside is huge!"

All the student's pieces had been hung around the room and the room was brightly lit to show them off. There were quite a few paintings, but some uncoloured drawings were also on display, as was a clay model of a diplodocus dinosaur, and a spinner dolphin which had been made from wax. Centrepiece was a large spherical globe wrapped in film, with the countries of the world all made from broken pieces of recycled glass and the oceans made from blue coloured jelly which reflected light as it gently rotated on its chilled display.

Justin's painting was situated at the far end of the room, opposite the main entrance. All the students had a chance to see each other's work before the crowds embarked, and they looked even better hung on the wall, than on a desk.

The doors suddenly opened, and people started flooding in, greeted by a teacher and an array of colours on display all around the gym hall that replaced the humdrum normality the students were accustomed to. The finished pieces snatching their attention, spoiling them for choice, as they circulated.

Just like all artists, Justin and his parents were hovering around his showpiece, eagerly waiting for people to arrive. Tammy could have left and wandered around the room with the crowds, but she didn't.

They saw the room slowly fill up, and watched as people casually made their way round to them, pit-stopping at each of the student's work, discussing their piece. Some went clockwise, some anticlockwise and Justin's eyes were darting from left to right, trying to discover which side he'd be approached from first.

"Wow! This is superb. Who made this?", said a woman he hadn't noticed, a mother to one of the other student's who'd left her daughter's zone to have a nosey around.

Tammy extended her hand to the left, proudly presenting Justin.

The woman's near-disbelieving eyes crept left, stunned at the age of the painter. "This is excellent. So real. Just like a photo. It really draws you in." She looked at Justin once more. To her, the painter and the painting didn't match. "Stunning!"

Then she left, but as soon as she did, another person arrived, then more. The room was alive, buzzing with chatter and discussions, but it was now Justin's time for focus, and crowds from both sides of the room met up at his thunderstorm painting, and many stayed for a while.

Mike was chatting to another parent when he noticed Deborah staring at something. She was watching a lady who'd just visited them, on the phone to someone else, and telling them to get round to the school as soon as they could.

As it turned out, she was the owner of the garage in Justin's painting, and she'd contacted her husband. After a few minutes, she walked back round to Justin and his parents. "Is this for sale?", she asked. "It would look great on our wall."

"Hi", offered Mike, "I'm Justin's father. He's the talented one!", robotically turning to the creator. "Is it for sale son?" Mike didn't know if Justin wanted to part with it or not. He'd seen how attached he'd become to it. This one seemed to mean more than just another picture. Surely he wouldn't sell it for just a few dollars. But the decision wasn't his to make.

"Do you like it?", asked Justin.

"I love it!", came an unexpected reply from someone else who was there. The woman looked around to see a man who'd butted in. She was disgusted that he'd rudely interrupted their private conversation. "I don't see a price, but I'll give you a hundred dollars for it."

Everyone looked at Justin for his response. Before he could say anything that may form some kind of contract, the woman said, "I'll give you *five* hundred dollars for it."

People in the crowd gasped at this offer – looking at each other. This was an exhibition – not an auction, but students had been told that they would be free to sell their work if they wanted.

"I'll pay you a *thousand* dollars for it", came his counter-offer.

The woman's husband ran into the room, and he pushed his way to the front of the crowd so he could see what his wife had been so charged up about. He instantly connected with it, putting his hands close to the frame. He knew this opportunity wouldn't come round again but his connection was interrupted.

"Son, I'll pay you one thousand dollars for it – right now – cash.", he repeated.

The garage owner realised his wife's urgency. He saw Justin quietly discussing this with his father.

"Are you the artist?", he asked Justin.

"Yes, sir."

He too, was drawn-in by the image and the story it was telling. "It's simply mind blowing."

Justin smiled, a bit nervous about where things seemed to be going.

"Son, the garage you've painted, is my garage. I've ran it over twenty years. It was my father's business – he left it to me in his will. He died inside this very garage, and he died on a night just like what you've drawn. I absolutely love your painting. Would you sell it to me – for ten thousand dollars? And I'll pay you that right now."

Everyone heard what he said, and louder gasps were inhaled.

Justin took a moment's pause, but not to allow a chance for the other man to out-bid him, who hung on that pause.

"Sir... if it means that much to you, then yes, you can have it."

Cheers went up around the room, but Justin wasn't finished.

"… but I can't take your money for it sir – not like this. It would be an honour for me if you took it, and took care of it. That would mean more to me than the money."

Justin's parents looked at each other in puzzlement, but neither stepped in. Instead of being angry at not taking the money, they were both proud of him for his gesture, and so was the garage owner, who couldn't hide his emotions.

After putting his fingers to his eyes, he said, "Then let me service your car for free."

"Deal!", replied Justin instantly, and they shook on it.

"I have a couple of paintings, but *nothing* like this. You're going to be a big star one day, and I'm just glad I have your first painting."

They uncoupled it from the wall and he had a closer look. He shook his head with awe at the piece, but then he thought it might appear he'd just conned a young lad. He took out his wallet, and counted one thousand dollars in hundred dollar bills, and handed that to Justin.

"I can't take it for free son. Use this to help pay for… for paint for your next painting."

They agreed upon a smile, and he offered Justin a hug with outstretched arms. Justin walked up to him and felt his arms pat his back. People started clapping, including Tammy, who was bursting with pride.

"Oh!", taking a step back from Justin, "You've got to sign it. That makes it officially, one of your *original* pieces!"

Mike and Debbie looked at each other with matching concern.

"Of course I will!", and before anyone could say something, he was handed a pen for signing the artwork. He removed it from the frame, and made his mark on the bottom right-hand corner.

"So you're... Justin Howard – I'll remember the name. Thank you son. This means a lot to me."

And after shaking his parent's hands, and reminding them of his promise, he proudly made his way off with it. He was delighted, but oblivious to what was just about to happen.

Chapter 30

Mike drove Tammy home, and all four of them chatted about the exhibition until they arrived at her house. He stopped the car a little in front of her home, to give them privacy to say goodnight without prying eyes. Justin walked her to her front door.

"That was *such* a kind offer you made Justin – *and* to a complete stranger!" Tammy touched Justin's arm again. "That's the nicest thing I've ever seen. I'm *so* proud of you!"

Justin smiled back. He felt her touch and glanced down to make sure it wasn't his imagination. And although it was *just* her hand on his arm, it felt like she was telling him something, but he was confused. Was he looking into her simple gesture too deeply? He wanted more than this, but he knew she was taken. As he was thinking this through, and trying to make sense of it all, she leaned forward and gave him a quick kiss on the cheek.

"I've got to go. Text me later."

"Yeah, of course."

She opened the door and sweetly wriggled her fingers before closing it gently.

Like his papa, Justin had always been a deep thinker, and Tammy was becoming a hard puzzle to work out. With anyone else, he wouldn't even bother trying to decipher mixed messages. But right there on her doorstep, it made sense. He didn't know exactly what Tammy wanted from him, and he daren't ask. He was getting nowhere when he thought about it. But the very fact that he was still frantically trying to work it out, meant something. She was worth the effort, and he now realised that he'd been falling for her.

She must have been safely inside at least a minute, and it wasn't until the porch light automatically went out, that he realised he was still there, and his parents were waiting in the car. He hadn't even heard the engine running, until now.

As he was walking back to the car, Justin noticed something else, and squinted his eyes. Was that Curtis's car he saw parked up in the distance? Although it was now getting dark, it did look like his convertible Audi. There were no lights on, and he just couldn't make out if someone was in the driver's seat? This is all he needs. He didn't let on he saw this, and casually made his way back to his parent's car and got in the back. As they made their way off, they didn't pass the Audi, but Justin peered out the rear window from time to time as they drove.

After he got home and had taken Belle out to the back garden to let her do the toilet, he got out his phone and continued the WhatsApp trail.

'Home now. Been out with Belle. Thanx for coming tonight x'

typing…

'It was a brilliant night J - & so very generous! What a sweet gesture you made to that man. You'll have to go with your parents when they get their car serviced – just to see your painting again! Haha x'

'I've still got it in my mind Won't forget what it looks like x'

'Nor me! How's my gorgeous Belle? x'

He sent a picture of Belle curling up on her bed in his room.

'Missing her :0(x'

'What you doing tomorrow? x'

typing…

Justin anxiously waited on the next message coming through. But it didn't arrive quickly.

typing…

'Not sure. x'

Justin thought that if Tammy took over a minute for that, then she must have typed something else, then deleted what she originally wrote. He'd only left her about half an hour ago, but was already desperate to see her again. He decided to take a risk.

'Taking Belle for a longer walk in the park around noon. Want to come? x' His dog seemed like a cheater's way in.

'Love to. Want me to come round to yours just before? x'

'Brilliant! Want to go for a burger afterwards? x' Justin paused before pressing 'send'. If he was reading her right, then hopefully she'll go.

typing…

'Can't – sorry :0(Busy afterwards :0(x'

'Okay Still on for tomorrow? x'

'Of course see you then. Night. x'

'Night x'

'x'

Justin thought to himself. 'If she was *my* girl, I wouldn't be happy if she was texting other guys and adding kisses at the end of every message.' Surely she was about to dump Curtis. Maybe she was just testing the waters with him before sacking that piece of shit? He lay in bed and thought about it until he fell asleep.

Chapter 31

Tammy arrived just before twelve, and stayed for a cup of tea while Justin was getting ready. She chatted with Mike, while Debbie helped Justin get ready and refresh his strapping.

"That was crazy last night!"

"Thought about it all night, Mike. That man will be so happy with the painting – I bet he's hung it up already!"

"Yeah I bet he has as well."

"Justin's going to be a big star. A famous artist!"

"I hope so – then he can pay off our mortgage!", Debbie added.

"You two taking Belle out today?"

"Yeah. Just to the park again. She's so adorable."

Belle came bounding down the stairs and immediately ran up to Tammy's open arms. The wag of her impatient tail earned her the chewy stick her nose had told her was hiding inside Tammy's pocket.

"Is it okay to give her this?", Tammy asked, presenting it.

"Of course it is honey!"

Belle sat proudly to attention, her eyes fixed on it, and she gently accepted it from Tammy's hand and left.

"Aw. She's so cute!"

"Have you got any pets, Tammy?", Mike asked.

"No. I'd love to though."

Justin appeared. "Hey."

"Hi. How you feeling today?"

"Better. Not as sore."

"Hey you two – watch the weather today, it looks a bit overcast. If you're taking Belle out, maybe best to head off soon."

Outside did look as Deborah had described. Unusually bleak for this time of year, and no weather warnings had been given. Strange.

"Ready?", Tammy asked Justin.

"Let's go."

Tammy fixed the lead onto Belle's collar and off they went, with Belle leading the way. When they got to the park, Justin noticed that Tammy wasn't quite herself. She hadn't been saying too much, and her thoughts seemed elsewhere.

"Hey – you okay?", Justin asked, sensing she wasn't.

"Can we speak later?"

"Of course – but are you okay Tammy?", he repeated.

She turned away from Justin and just nodded her head. Justin noticed her hands rise to her face.

"Jesus, Tammy!", and gave her a cuddle from behind. He took the leash from Tammy's hand to allow her some time to fix herself in private. It was a welcome gesture.

"Sorry."

"Don't be."

On cue, Belle came round to her. It was as if she knew Tammy was upset. Tammy squatted down to ground level and cried a happy tear as she gave Belle's ears a thank-you scratch. It broke the awkwardness. Tammy felt that both of them were looking out for her.

After the visit to the park, Justin walked Tammy home. He knew Tammy was itching to say something, and he'd been wondering what.

"Justin… "

'Shit! Here comes the split', he thought.

"I'm meeting Curtis later on. That's why I can't go out with you afterwards. I'm sorry."

"It's okay."

"No it's not."

"I'm not sure I follow, Tammy. He's your boyfriend. It's none of my business."

"Yeah, but…" She couldn't find the words, but Justin allowed her time to think. "There's something you don't know – about Curtis."

"Tammy, that's none of my business either."

She sighed. This wasn't going to be easy. "Will you listen if I tell you? I *need* to tell you this. I need to tell *someone* this."

He'd never seen her this serious. "Tammy, of course I'll listen – you know that."

It was her time to be on the spot. Justin noticed she was arranging the words she needed to say in the right order, before she blurted them out loud. "Curtis…", she started, "… He's a bully…"

Justin butted in, "Yeah I kinda know that! I've got the scars to prove it."

"I'm trying to tell you!"

"Sorry!"

"He's got… mental health issues. He was bullied at his other school, before he got transferred here. That's *why* he got transferred."

"So he thinks it's okay for him to do that to others!"

"That's not all…" She grabbed Justin's hand and attention simultaneously. "He says he'll kill himself if I leave him."

"For fuck sake, Tammy! So you're staying with him… because of, what? A threat? A threat he's making to *you*? Jesus!"

"It isn't just a threat. He'll do it."

"How do you know?"

"… because I tried to break up with him before and he took some sort of pills. He ended up in hospital."

Justin stopped walking. She did too. "Tammy, can I tell *you* something?"

She now stood with less dignity, nodding with shame at the ground.

"Tammy – what he's…. *threatening* to do … it's all wrong. Listen – every time I see you with him, every time I hear you talking about him, you look upset. He's only bringing you down. You're not *yourself* with him. You're not the person I see when you're here." He took her other hand. "Tammy, if he's got *mental health* issues, then he's got to sort that out for himself. He needs to get help. But what he's doing is blackmailing you – that's not fair on *you*, Tammy."

"He's jealous too."

"Yeah, don't I know it!"

"He's probably been watching us in the park."

"Oh for fuck sake!"

"I've seen him watching me before. Outside my home. I saw him there for hours."

"Seriously?"

"Yeah."

"This guy's a looney, Tammy. Dangerous, maybe!"

She didn't disagree.

"… and you need to take care. You need to look out for yourself."

Justin realised that it may well have been Curtis outside Tammy's home last night, and sensed he may also be watching the pair of them – right now. He realised his advice to Tammy would also apply to himself. He'd already been to hospital. Next time he'd be in a box. He looked around, expecting to see Curt in his car – or right behind him wielding a pickaxe. Now this shit was making Justin paranoid.

They started walking again and continued onwards. Justin thought carefully about what he would say next. Spending time with Tammy was becoming more risky by the day.

"Do you love him?"

Tammy looked at Justin, as if he'd asked a stupid question. But as far as Justin was concerned, it wasn't stupid. He didn't know.

"I thought I did", she sighed. "He was sweet at first."

Justin knew it was downhill from here, so he made certain he wouldn't interrupt her again. He wanted her to say just how shitty this guy really was.

"… then he just began showing off. When there's a crowd, he's worse. Acting like he's invincible or something. I hate that."

Justin just nodded in silence, hoping there was more to come, but she'd stumbled to a corner. Maybe she was recalling good times with him? If that happened, it'd be time to step in.

"Something happened. He done something… to me."

"What happened Tammy?"

"Justin, no. Sorry. Maybe another time."

She put her hands to her face, and wiped away some tears that had fallen suddenly. It smeared a bit of light make-up she had on. Justin gave her a needy hug.

"So what are you telling me Tammy? What do you want to do?"

"I know what I *have* to do. Give me a little time to sort it out, would you?"

They'd reached Tammy's home. She'd been as open with him as she dared, and he thought he knew what she meant. Surely she'd bin this creep, and text Justin later on that she had. Once that WhatsApp message came through, Justin and Belle would do a victory lap of his garden.

Chapter 32

Tammy got picked up by Curtis later that day. He never went inside Tammy's home. Instead, he always just peeped the horn from the road. Her mom hated that about him. He took her for a drive and parked up somewhere too far away for her to walk home. It was further from his normal parking spot he usually took her to.

"What you been up to earlier on?", he asked, tense jaw muscles showing through his cheeks.

"Studying." She didn't look him in the eye. If she had, she'd have seen that he knew otherwise – and his anger, prepped for another fight. She faced him to say something else, but then, out of nowhere, clouds started to blacken.

Daylight from above quickly dimmed until it looked like night-time. The first few spits of rain fell gently on the windshield, and they rapidly became heavier, then heavier still. The speed they fell at seemed faster than gravity, and the unique acoustics of driving rain pounding off the car's fabric roof worried them both. Tammy looked outside, and saw the rain bouncing high off the ground and forming puddles. Big rings formed in those puddles as more rain pelted down. In no time, it resembled a monsoon.

"Drive Curt.", nervously checking the sky, "We can't stay here."

Curtis put his wipers on full speed. Even when parked, he could hardly see outside. It would be worse when driving.

"Take me home, Curt. Right now!"

"Honey, it's just a bit of rain."

A lightning bolt broke through the dark sky and zapped the earth on the horizon.

"It's not just rain! Take me home." A massive crack of thunder followed a few seconds later. It rumbled on, interrupting Curt's train of thought. The storm was close. "For God's sake, *drive*!"

"Okay, okay!" Curtis started the engine and waited a few seconds until the steam on the windshield cleared. Another bolt of lightning spiked to the ground. It looked as if it landed in the direction of Redleaf, just where they'd come from.

The rain was bucketing down now. It had been a decent day earlier on when she'd been out with the dog, but the weather had violently turned, showing them what mother nature was really capable of. Quickly following the strike, came another rumble of thunder sounding off, this time much louder than the first.

Curtis got worried. "Where the fuck is this coming from?" He pulled away, but very slowly and carefully. Tammy noticed his hands starting to shake.

There weren't many cars out, so the roads were near empty. As they drove, they saw two other cars that had stopped at the side of the road and had their hazard warning lights flashing. 'Maybe they'd crashed into each other', Tammy thought, but Curtis wasn't stopping to help.

The car wheels were dredging through deep water flooding the roads, as rain was falling faster than the drains could cope. Those drains were becoming blocked, and the standing water was worsening to dangerous levels.

As they travelled back towards Redleaf, yet another bolt of lightning stormed down. It was around half a mile away, and this one was massive. It was thicker than the rest and forked out in different directions before it hit ground. Tammy let out a scream as it flashed, drowned out by its deafening thunder crack.

"Shit – we're right in the middle of it!", Curt said, feeling surrounded.

"Slow down!", snapped Tammy. He was already going slowly, but they were heading into where the storm was greatest.

"FUCK ME!", as he passed downed electricity lines. Water was gushing along the roads with urgency, as if a dam had burst. Neither of them had seen anything like this before, and Curtis steadily drove through their village, both of them disbelieving their eyes as they slowly trekked to where Tammy lived. When they got there, she said she'd text him later, and told him to go home safely – then lept out and ran inside. What she wanted to say to him – would need to wait.

When she got inside, her mom was looking out through the window. Tammy ran up to her room, picked up her other phone and immediately started writing a text to Justin.

'Are you seeing the rain? x'

'Yeah its wild outside. Are you somewhere safe? x'

'I am now x'

typing…

'Justin – you drew this happening! x'

'Yeah! What a coincidence! x'

'Its happening exactly as you drew it? Its May! x'

'Sorry. I've jinxed the weather! x'

'x'

A single 'x' was their way of ending a text conversation. It was a bit abrupt this time though. Justin joined his parents who were downstairs looking outside as the torrents fell. After a few more minutes, it lessened a bit, then suddenly got lighter as quickly as it had gotten heavier earlier on. Within minutes, the black clouds that had ominously floated above Redleaf, turned light grey, then vanished. What had been in those clouds, was now in Redleaf drains, and the beginnings of sunlight peeped through. Before long, it was bright and sunny again.

"What just happened dad?", still staring outside.

"Shit!" Mike eyed Debbie. "We feared this may happen, son."

"Feared what?"

"We can't explain it, honey", said his mom. "We've spoken – me and your father – we've spoken about this many times. Listen, the best thing to do, is for you to go back and visit your papa. He's the only one who can explain. He'll tell you everything you need to know – and you *do* need to know!"

"We need to leave *right now* son", added Mike. "Get yourself ready."

Chapter 33

Mike drove Justin all the way back to Westfield without stopping, and it was getting late by the time they arrived.

"I wondered when I'd be seeing *you* again!", Justin's papa said when they stepped inside.

"It's happened again.", Mike said, interrupting his dad's and his son's embrace. The clunk the door made when it closed startled Stuart to what he was saying.

The smile remained on Mike's father's face, but it was less enthusiastically held in place now. Although anticipated at some point, he'd never fully prepared himself for this.

"*What's* happened papa? Dad's not said anything."

Mike interjected. "Listen, I'm gonna leave you two to talk in private. I'm going to Mac's Diner. I'll be back in an hour or so, but then we'll have to head back. One hour, dad!"

After he closed the door behind him, Justin sat down on the sofa. Although there were two sofas, his grandfather joined him on the same one.

Justin looked around the room, seeing the space his chessboard used to fill on the table in the corner. "I've decided to put flowers there. Got a vase looked out."

"How are things papa? You know… without gram." The decency to ask about his papa first, impressed his papa. He'd been thinking about her along the journey.

"I'm okay son. But I miss her. Every single day I miss her – I can't escape it. In truth, I don't want to either. I know you're hurting too." He patted Justin on his knee. "*Hey*, but let's focus on my *grandson*! We've only got an hour!", he winked. "Tell me what's happened." He already knew.

Justin blew out a big sigh. "Well… I drew a picture, and… and… *somehow*, it came to life! That's why I'm here."

Stuart steadied himself. "You've drawn pictures before, haven't you?"

He shrugged. "Yeah, tons!"

"So why did *they* not… *come to life*?"

Justin was stumped. "I don't know. That's why we came to see you."

"Think about it. What happened with this picture that was different from the rest?"

He thought, but drew a blank. "Well… I spent a lot of time on it papa. This one was really good."

"I'm sure it was son, but however much time you spent on it… that doesn't matter – irrelevant. What did you do after finishing it?"

"Oh! I gave it away. Well actually, a man paid me for it."

"That doesn't matter either. Now listen to me *very* carefully son. Did you sign it?"

"Oh yes! The man told me to."

"… and you've never signed any of your drawings before, have you?"

Justin tried to recall if he had signed any of his work before. "No, I don't think so papa. Why would I? I was waiting to see if I could open a shop or something before I signed anything!"

His papa knew *that* dream all too well – one that wouldn't come true. "What did you draw?"

"It was a storm… in the town of Redleaf – where we moved to."

"A *thunderstorm*?", he clarified.

Justin replied with a confused nod.

"… and a thunderstorm *did* happen, didn't it?"

"Yeah, it did. But that was just coincidence!"

"No it wasn't! After you signed it, did the thunderstorm happen for real – within a day?"

Justin paused to think. "I signed it last night… about half seven. The storm happened earlier this afternoon."

Stuart proudly smiled and shook his head at the same time. "Then you *do* have the gift, son. It's been passed on."

Justin's mind was muddled. He watched his papa get up and open the fridge, as he opened the safe in his mind where he'd locked up memories that he just couldn't have freely floating around. "What gift, papa?"

Stuart tugged on the ring-pull of a can of beer, and gave one to Justin. "Here, you'd better drink this."

Justin opened the can and took a big gulp, burping a second later.

"You have to listen very, *very* carefully to what I'm about to tell you. We might only have this one opportunity to talk. Right?"

Justin nodded and slurped another drink from the can. His papa paused until he had Justin's full attention. "I *know* the thunderstorm happened.", he said, leaning in. "I felt it too – all the way over here!" Justin shuffled himself on the sofa. "You see son, me and you are alike – I've always known it! We have the same gift. More of a *curse*, really – and it will bite back, believe me. Are you listening?"

Justin nodded nervously.

"I found out by accident. It was *way* back – when I was about your age, my math teacher was an arsehole. *Far* too strict. He shouted, and made a mockery of me just because I couldn't do the sums. Other kids made fun of me too. He gave me the belt in front of everyone. And I got lines too! He was evil, and he was bad tempered. On the way home from school, someone actually said, 'He's got no heart', which stuck in my head. Later that evening, as I was getting my art stuff ready for the next day, I drew him clutching his chest, as if his heart was suddenly missing and he'd only just realised it. I signed it, just to finish it off. You see, *that's* the key. Once you sign it – it can't be stopped. It can't be paused either. Think of it like not being able to put the genie back inside. You still with me?"

Justin nodded again, shrugging heavier shoulders now.

"*Instantly* upon signing, I blacked out – BANG! Unconscious. While I was out, I visualised this thing happening – it played out for me to see. I called them '*pre-visions*'. They showed me everything. I felt the pain. It was as if the Devil himself was now showing me what was going to happen. What I'd sketched, was going to happen for *real*, and it was going to happen soon. Afterwards, when I woke up and came to, I would get the most awful headaches."

Sitting on the edge of the sofa, Justin's ears were recording this, as his mind rewound. He'd never concentrated so hard to a story.

"The whole thing knocked me off my feet. It was just meant to be a laugh – not for real. But then, the next day at math, he was the same rude, evil bastard he always was, making fun of me again – and other kids. I think he enjoyed picking on us – getting us to fear him. Nowadays, you'd be sacked for that shit, but back in the seventies – nobody gave a toss. It was all to keep the kids in check. Then, suddenly, just out of the blue, he stopped talking while at the blackboard. He fell to his knees, clutching his chest, hardly breathing. Nobody knew what was going on – but I knew. A girl screamed – I can still hear that scream now, Justin. Someone called the school's first aider, but they didn't know what to do. An ambulance took him away. And just like that… he was gone. He died later that day in hospital." He took a few casual gulps from the can.

"You didn't make that happen papa!"

"Yes I did! YES I DID! I didn't know that *then*, but I found out for sure afterwards. No one expected it, as he was in decent health. Nothing wrong with him *physically*. He did smoke though, so people just put it down to that. A heart attack, they said. Bullshit! Fifty-seven he was."

As Justin's mind took a wander, Stuart took a long drink from his can.

"And these – *visions* – Justin – they'll keep *you* in check, reminding you that this IS on, and there's no going back. Sometimes they'll happen straight away – sometimes they'll take over your dream when you're sleeping – and they can be brutal. These visions – they'll be imprinted in your mind. It's part of the curse, I think – being forced to remember all the shit we've done – all the suffering we've inflicted… and when you wake – that's when the headaches thump you like a freight train."

He twisted open a bottle of vodka and gulped down a mouthful straight from the bottle.

"I did the same as you, and went looking for answers. My papa explained it to me – my Papa William. He didn't tell me *everything* at once though – he felt he couldn't. He had this thing too, and he suffered for it, big time. At first, he used it to play pranks on kids at school and amaze people at stupid, unnatural events that couldn't happen, like a rainbow appearing when there was no rain, or hailstones in the middle of a heatwave, signing his drawing each time… and it all happened – and kids doubted their eyes – doubted what their teachers had told them – what they'd read in books. Then one day, after a run-in with a kid at school, he drew himself at the riverside, punching that kid into the water, the kid all dazed as the water swallowed him up. That night, he went to bed as normal, all confident and assured of himself. He had a great sleep. The next day, he challenged that kid to a fight, next to the river. The lad accepted, and after school, they went there. Straight away, this kid punches my papa in the stomach. It folded him over. Things were maybe not going as planned. However, the fight was not over yet. He tried to get up, but before he could, the lad kicked him in the face. My papa fell to the ground, blood pouring from his mouth. Then, he got on top of him, and used the strap of his school bag to strangle him. Papa struggled and choked. 'Give in?' the lad yelled. Papa nodded – being strangled, he couldn't speak. His face was all red and puffy. The guy released his grip, and left papa sprawled on the grass – gasping to get his breath back. So my question to you is this… Why didn't his drawing work?"

Justin couldn't think. "I don't know?"

"He made a fatal error. He forgot to sign the drawing he made. Don't make that mistake. He got cocky. But he learned from that… and then, he used it again – and again to get payback on that lad… and others. He used it a lot, so he *paid* for it a lot. He died age fifty-five."

"Fifty-five! Jesus! How so young papa?"

"This is crucial Justin. You've gotta remember this. You have the same ability, son – this power. But it comes at a huge cost. Each time you use it, you'll pay a price for using it."

"A price?"

"Losing time. *Time,* Justin – right here, on earth. He never told me this bit until his death bed. By then, it was too late for me, but I'm telling you everything now. He thought that each time he used his ability, he'd only suffer a vision – a bad dream of it happening and wake up covered in sweat, or just black-out for a while. But that's only half of it, son. Be *extremely* careful, before doing what you do. Think it through first. For everything we do, we lose time here. It's the last thing he told me. He took someone's life, and he lost however much time that person had left – before they would have died. You see, if it's an old man in hospital, and you put him out of his suffering, you'll not lose much time I suppose. BUT, if it's a young, healthy boy – or girl – with their whole life ahead of them – then *you'll* lose what *they* lose – he did. At least that's what I think. Hey – I'm not saying you'll ever want someone *killed*, but you never know what's round the corner."

"Papa – if I've got this thing, whatever it is – I'm never killing anyone."

Stuart sighed a proud smile. Before him, was a good lad, but he knows that sometimes – shit just happens in life. Who knows what tomorrow will bring?

"You *do* have this thing. Check this. When you were in kindergarten, all the kids were asked to draw an animal. All the kids drew dogs, cats, fluffy sheep. One kid drew a mouse – you drew a fuckin snake! All the drawings were to be taken home to show the parents, so you were all asked to put your name on the back, so they didn't get mixed up."

Justin couldn't remember. "What happened?"

"Well you put your name on it – just like all the kids did. Your mom picked you up that day, and showed the picture to your dad. It was on the back of a numbers colour thing your parents always gave them! Your parents took a day off work the next day, and looked after you themselves. Word has it, that a python found its way into the classroom through an open window. Everyone was terrorised – teachers running about, screaming. The place was evacuated! Snake catchers called in. It *wasn't* a coincidence, son. That was your *first* time."

Stuart continued with his warning. "But my Papa Will, he got flashbacks of all the shit he caused. They would happen at any time, even through the day and they didn't stop happening. It fucked him up badly. People thought he was crazy. He died in a mental institution. It stole *years*. He got addicted son, and used it *way* too much. Don't make that mistake."

Stuart handed Justin another can of beer as he'd finished that one already. He knew that Justin had questions for him. What bad things had Stuart done? He wanted to confess, before he was asked to confess.

"But Justin – for me? I used this unwisely. That math teacher is gonna catch up with me I suppose. I also used it to get rid of someone – an old friend of mine, a guy called Damian Keefer and send him to jail. Although extreme, this was my way out. We'd done some things before and stole things – I'm ashamed of all of it now. This man Damian... he's a sick bloke son – unsympathetic, never shows mercy. A right nasty bastard."

The wind picked up a bit outside and some leaves spun round in a circle. Justin imagined an invisible food mixer making this whirlwind show. The stiff breeze forced a window to blow open, and Stuart got up to close it, locking it tightly, pausing before he turned round. They both noticed this happening out of the blue. The wind hadn't been gradually picking up.

"I set the whole thing up. I did it because I knew he'd come after me for... for a terrible thing I did. It's too bad to say, so don't ask. But after we robbed a place, he'd piss on the beds of those we robbed. I mean, come on! Only a sick, twisted, fuck does that!"

Stuart saw Justin's face turn sour as he imagined the act and the smell. He then told Justin the story of the bank job they'd done together, and how he sketched the cops arriving – so he knew they'd get caught. He told Justin everything about the court case too, and the evidence he gave.

"So he got put away – but now he's out."

Justin stood up. He'd put two and two together. "Wait a minute... so it was him that peed over *your* bed?"

"Yes." Stuart stepped right up to his grandson and put a hand on his shoulder to prepare him for this one. "Justin – son – it was him that killed your Grammy Sarah. He tampered with her car."

186

"Jesus papa!" He remembered being told. "Why don't you get your drawing stuff back out and make him pay?" Justin saw his papa's fingers scratching opposite arms at the same time.

"He *has* paid, son. That was his revenge on *me* – for taking away all those years from *him*."

"Bastard!", Justin let out, scanning the room for options. "But... you *have* thought about it?"

And as Stuart emptied the can down his throat and open another, Justin looked closely and noticed his papa's eyes consider it. "I... don't think I still have the ability anyway – it's been so long. It might not even work and I'm not sure if I want to either. This revenge thing, Justin – it's got to stop somewhere. We've both paid heavily."

No words came to Justin in that moment. Processing this was difficult.

"... and ever since he got out of prison... this is gonna sound strange... I've *sensed* him. He's menacing the town. This was a good town – Westfield... it was good. Ever since he returned, shit's happened again – children have been kidnapped and he goes out searching for them. He even wears a cross round his neck now – it's all a smokescreen. He's infected these good people, son – corrupted their minds too. They all drove you out."

He watched in silence as his grandson fetched those memories from his half-locked safe.

"Doing this has consequences – *severe* consequences. I can't take it anymore Justin. Do you think we can just alter God's natural pathway of events – and get away with it? We're altering *time,* son! It has to be re-adjusted!"

Both of them slurped from their cans.

"I think… if we make things happen, *certain* things son… it can take *months* to fix. Of course I don't know for certain, but I think that if we make things happen that wouldn't have happened, then the length of time it takes to re-adjust things back to some kind of normality, is the amount of time we lose on earth. I'm ageing faster than my years, Justin. I feel around 90 inside!"

Justin nervously tipped up his second can, and hid his face behind it as the last drops fell on his tongue.

"My papa died young. I'm feeling weak now too, and I'm only fifty-two. My time is coming to an end, Justin."

Justin dropped his shoulders. "Papa, don't say that!"

"You can't control the visions – but let me help prepare you for what's coming. Each time you use this, you'll get a vision of if happening – *before* it happens. It can happen any time – through the day or during your sleep." Stuart saw Justin getting a bit fidgety. "You've had one of these already, haven't you?"

He watched as Justin nodded, recalling the bad dream he'd had last night.

"It seemed *so* real papa!", he confessed, staring aimlessly through the window, imagining the same thing happening outside right now.

"Oh I know it does, son."

"Papa, I saw the sky flashing… the lightning blinded me for a bit." He shut his eyes tightly. "The thunder crack was so loud! I was wading slowly through a river, up to my waist, trying to get to safety, imagining crocodiles sliding in from the riverbanks as they sensed my movements."

Stuart was captivated by Justin's vision, nervously re-living it with complete empathy.

"I felt the water wave differently as the crocs thrashed their tails. Then... then both of my arms got grabbed. I felt bear traps clamping my arms, piercing my skin, then those crocs twisted in opposite directions." Justin started convulsing standing up.

"Justin!" His papa grabbed his shoulders and shook him back to the riverbank.

"What just happened?"

"You slid away, son. *Too* deep, Jesus! *Never* recall pre-visions so deeply."

Justin was in a trance, visibly shaken by this new experience.

"Sit down son! Breathe – breathe – relax. Jesus fuck!" He poured a shot of vodka. "Swallow this now!" As he watched Justin tip up the glass, he remembered the same thing happening to him many years ago, and *his* papa saving *him*. "You're safe now – but we need to keep going. There may not be another time to do this. No more talking – let me tell *you* a little story about your Great, Great Papa Will... a story he told me."

Stuart told the story about a bully his Papa Will sorted – a bully that was in his class. "This guy was the type of guy that's full of himself all the time. Picking on younger people, and stealing their dinner money. Spitting on people. A real piece of shit. One evening, Will had gone home and had drawn this guy pissing himself in class – his pants all wet and a 'piss puddle' on the floor – all yellow and steaming hot. The next day, Will challenged him to a fight in full view of everyone – and he accepted. He said he kept turning round to stare right at this bully in the classroom. Around twenty minutes later, he peed himself – just like he drew it.

Everyone was pointing at him, laughing. The smell was stinking. Of course, he went straight home – he had to walk, as they wouldn't let him on the bus. So he never turned up for the fight either! He never got over that. He was seen as all talk and no action – seen as a pussy! He feared it may happen again. That story got round the whole school in no time, and he never bullied again – in fact he got bullied by others for that very incident. It fucked him up. You see, you can change the future, Justin. But be wary – yes, he was a bully, but he *could* have changed. He *could* have turned into a decent guy. But what my papa did – it changed that guy's entire life."

Justin thought about the guys in school that had beaten him up recently.

Stuart sighed, "I got the bullies to suffer. Bullies are not tough guys, Justin. They are just hopeless kids who prey on younger, smaller kids, knowing they'll have the upper hand with them. They are pathetic. I punished them Justin. When I did, I saw it as the Devil's work I was doing, because I got rewarded for it. Even the Devil hates bullies."

"Rewarded?", Justin asked.

"For getting payback on them.", Stuart said. "You see, when I drew them – I got their features. I wasn't always this handsome you know!", modestly winking at Justin. "I changed. Let's just leave it at that. Oh, and when I was young, I had a stutter. There was this one guy in particular, who just wouldn't stop making fun of me, and he took the piss all the time."

"You had a stutter, papa? No way!"

"Uhu. And this guy, he took every opportunity to walk up to me and start stuttering – even though he didn't have a stutter himself. So I sketched him, and sketched him struggling to speak – so he could realise just what it's like. And then I signed it – I knew what I was doing. The next day, he came up to me again, and took the piss again. In class, he put his hand up and asked permission from the teacher to go to the bathroom. But he couldn't spit out the words. It was, 'Mi Mi Miss. Co co co could I go t t to the b bath b bath b b bathroom.' Everyone else couldn't believe it, and thought he was just joking – but he wasn't. It was real. Just like that – my stutter had completely vanished. The stutter left me, and jumped into him. The poor fuck still stutters today!"

Stuart handed Justin another can of beer. This particular evening needed it.

"Deaths – however, will haunt you and torment you – even in the future. You'll be the author and witness to the events, and you will feel their pain. The pain is temporary, yes, but the mental torment afterwards… " He turned to look out the window for the rest, "… well that's heavy. It may haunt you for all time. Even now, I keep getting flashbacks of things I've done. And that's *God's* punishment, I think – so I don't forget."

Stuart poured a large vodka and drank it straight. Then he cracked open another can. "Scary stuff isn't it?"

As Justin worryingly nodded, his eyes stared right through Stuart's body as if he wasn't there.

"How are you getting on at the new school?"

Justin quickly re-set from imagining what his papa had done. Then, he told him about his new school, about Ray and that he likes Tammy but she's got a boyfriend, but thinks she'll dump him. But he didn't mention anything about being bullied and his visit to hospital. Papa didn't need to know that. Maybe his papa *already* knew about the bullies?

Maybe he felt Justin's pain as it was happening? Maybe he could feel Justin's longing for Tammy? Maybe it worked that way, and words didn't really need speaking? But he did speak fondly of Tammy and asked his papa for the advice he couldn't ask his father.

"Be yourself with her. If she likes you – she'll let you know. Follow your heart son – she'll follow hers."

They both heard Mike's car pulling up outside.

"Listen. The flashbacks from previous things I've done – you might get them too. It's our cross to bear, son. Learn to deal with them."

The engine stopped. Mike would be inside imminently.

"I never told Sarah.", he blurted out in a hurry. "That's one of my biggest regrets on this earth. I never found the way to tell her. By *not* telling her, I lied to her – and I can't put that right. Don't make that same mistake with Tammy, Justin. Promise me."

Justin nodded. "Papa – what if we've been given this thing... *intentionally*, so we can do something positive with it?"

"I've been trying to find out the answer to this shit my whole life. You'll work it out, son, you're smarter than me. You can change the future – it's a gift, so use it wisely, but use it scarcely. Remember this – it's just a picture, till you sign it."

Mike rushed in, wet from the rain that had started. "You guys finished? Almost ready son?"

"Yeah – Justin was just telling me about his new puppy, Belle." Mike didn't see the wink his father gave Justin as he spoke.

Justin was flabbergasted. 'How the fuck did he know about her?' The time had passed so quickly, he simply hadn't got round to it.

As for Stuart, he'd finally let out this long-held secret, and he instantly felt the better for it.

"Thanks papa!" Justin was enthralled at his papa's psychic ability. It was all starting to make sense now – this was done on purpose. "We… better make tracks."

Stuart nodded, and Justin hugged his grandfather. They both had a firm grip of each other in knowledge that, just perhaps, this may be the last hug they ever had. Mike noticed his father whisper something in Justin's ear.

Mike gave his father a tight hug too. Stuart held that hug a little longer than Mike anticipated.

"Nice car!", he said, as Mike thumbed the fob and its lights flashed. "Drive safely", and waved what might prove to be his final wave to them both.

As they drove off, Justin waved a special goodbye. He'd absorbed all this from the only other person who has this gift. Sure, Stuart had offloaded this thing he'd been burdened with, but he'd lied to Justin too. He hadn't told his grandson about the time when he killed a baby, growing inside its mother's tummy. He couldn't share that with anyone, and he knew he'd be taking that one, and all the guilt, to the grave.

It was only when Mike had reached the main Highway heading home before he asked his son what Stuart had said to him just before they left.

He shook his head. "That one's private, dad."

Chapter 34

Just before dinnertime, Justin sat in his room deep in thought. He'd been there all afternoon since Tammy had left. Just after breakfast, she'd came round again, and helped take Belle out for her walk in the park. While out, she'd confided in Justin that last night, while he'd been away seeing his papa back in Indiana, she'd texted Curtis and told him she needed a break. That put Justin on a state of readiness.

But once again, he felt as if someone had been spying on them while they'd been out. Maybe paranoia was setting in? Maybe he was going crazy? Tammy had left hours ago, and Belle was sound asleep, curled up on Justin's bed. He knelt on the carpet, leaning over the bed beside her, with an arm cuddling her back, watching as her outstretched paws occasionally flinched with a bad dream of her own, and wondered if Belle sensed what he did. He gently held one of her paws, reassuring her that he was there to protect her from the baddies in her dream.

As he knelt there, he looked around his new room, but something caught his eye. One of the white pawns on the chessboard had fallen over and was lying in the centre of the board. 'How long's it been like that?' The game he was devising hadn't even started yet, yet this piece was already down. After the kicking he took from the guys at school, he imagined himself as that pawn – needing to get up and fight. Was this a sign?

Justin had thought long and hard about what his papa had told him the previous evening, and he'd made up his mind on what to do. If he did nothing, things would surely just remain the same old shitty way they were, and he wasn't about to let that happen when he felt himself on the cusp of something. You only get one shot at *this* game. Now, armed with his papa's advice, he was more certain than ever about what he needed to do. Now – he was ready for battle.

Justin lept off his bed, which startled Belle. "Oh – sorry baby! Back to sleep."

After taking the pawn off the board, he fetched out his sketch pad and carefully placed it on his desk. He pondered about what to draw – several times coming close to making a start. Then a cheeky grin gradually formed. 'Maybe? Just maybe?'

Sam was one of Curt's friends, and the one who'd field kicked him all the way into a hospital ward. Unlike Justin, Sam didn't have any acne – but all that was about to change. Justin drew Sam sitting on a bench in the boy's changing room with a towel round his waist, wet from a shower. He drew spots all over Sam's face and neck – just like his. Then he drew himself sitting next to Sam, but with no acne at all.

"Fuck you! Pizza face!", and sniggered, as he signed the sketch. And that was it – done. Only not quite. Papa Stuart had told him within twenty four hours. But Justin was in a hurry now and had instantly become child-like impatient. He eagerly looked in his bedroom mirror, but nothing had changed. The usual spots were still there, all in the same positions and all the same colours.

Only now, did he take an interest in them, their shapes, their heights, their individual sizes and shades. Only now, did he notice a grouping – around a dozen or so little spots in a little pattern on his left cheek. Now – they had character. To him, they looked like little meerkats, hanging around on a desert plain, all standing to attention, wary of a threat. There was a join-the-dots to be done, like he did as a child. Only now, did he notice that this little collection of spots on his left cheek would have vaguely resembled a map of Africa, if only he'd got his pens out and connected them. Was today going to be the last time he'd see those African meerkats? How he'd miss them! "Good luck, guys!", he said in the mirror, suspecting he'd see them elsewhere.

That night, he dreamed about Tammy. She was in his room, and it was her that noticed his skin was all cleared up. She put both hands on his spot-free face and kissed him for the first time, while his hands were pulling her in towards his body, one hand on the back of her neck, the other on the small of her back, feeling her breasts press against his bare chest, her hair flowing in the breeze from an open window. She put her moist tongue in his mouth which went searching for his.

"For fuck sake Belle!", he said, pushing her off him, his face all wet with her slavers. Still half-asleep, he stumbled his way to the bathroom and ran the water. He collected some water with cupped hands, and raised them to wash his face. But after washing the dog's licks away, he looked closer at his reflection. All spots had gone. Zero acne, just like it was before that evil, puberty monster visited him a few years ago, then fucked off, mocking him.

It was Monday. "Morning son – breakfast is on the table. You're a little bit late. I'll run you in.", said his father walking past. He hadn't noticed Justin's face yet. And although it was *only* the vanishing of a few spots, it was a magic trick to Justin – a big deal. His smile shone through, and made his model cheeks puff up at each side.

Today, he hadn't washed with his usual dermo-lotion that he'd faithfully applied every single fuckin day and every single fuckin night for years on end – and gotten nowhere at all. Today, was the beginning of a new wash-time era – plain water.

Marching into school, he strode confident strides. He could have been on the catwalk with a jacket draped over his shoulder. Before, he wanted to merge-in with the shadows, but now, he was hiding from no one. This demanded the spotlight.

"Hey homey, how you doing?", Ray said at the corridor lockers, referring to Justin's broken ribs. It was too early in the morning to notice Justin's complexion.

"Actually, much better today, cap'n! Hardly even notice them now. In fact, I could probably take off the strapping any day."

"That Sam's evil scum, you know. It's only a matter of time before he picks on the wrong dude, and he gets the kicking of a lifetime... and I want front row tickets to see it happen. I'll even bring popcorn!"

Justin sniggered inside and outwardly too. In fact, so much, that he had to wipe some spit away. Maybe that day has already arrived?

"Shit!", Ray said with less volume, and even less enthusiasm. "There's the prick there, and he's coming this way."

That caught Justin's attention, and he felt his heart sink a little bit to his belly. Butterflies? Yes. Nervous? Not quite, but intensely dialled-in.

Sam walked up to the lockers where the boys were. Ray noticed that he seemed to be hiding his face from them. Justin noticed too.

"Hey Sam", Justin said, hoping he'd turn round so they could catch a glimpse of his face. "You okay?" Ray couldn't believe Justin was even talking to him.

There was a hesitation. "… Fine. You?" The locker door hid his face.

"Yeah, I'm great!" He held up a finger to Ray, indicating to him to stay where he was and not to say anything. He wandered round the other side of Sam's locker. Sam slammed the door home, and turned the lock. Immediately after that, he just turned and looked directly at Justin. All the students were going to see him at some point anyway – so what's the point hiding?

But when he did, he noticed that Justin's normal, spotty face was perfectly clear now. Justin immediately saw that Sam's normal spot-free skin, was now acne-ridden, and just the way, and in just the same patterns as he'd drawn it only last night.

"Hello meerkats!"

As they stared at each other, Justin noticed Sam's confusion. It seemed he was trying to work out how, in the space of a single day, one of them had gone from perfect skin, to a 'hard-not-to-take-the-piss' skin, and the other had the same transformation, only in reverse.

"I've got some acne cream left over, if you want it. I won't be needing it anymore." A clear fuck-you to his enemy – a bishop, that he'd remove from the board later. It was only Ray that saw the funny side of things. Sam didn't say a word and just left.

"Homey – fuckin *meerkats!*"

"Private joke – tell you later."

"Dude – what the fuck just happened? Cos it looks like he stole your spots, and glued them to his dish."

"He was the one that called me pizza face."

Ray was confused, but happy for his friend, who was now daydreaming. Justin had realised something, and it was stark. He didn't just get clearer skin. As his spots left him, they appeared on Sam. That's what his papa had been trying to tell him, and it may work differently for him than it did for his papa, and his papa.

He now realised, that he'd have to be careful what he planned, as there'd be risks for sure – just like chess, so calculate them beforehand. If he'll swap traits, then he'd have to be sure with his victims. He could have fun with this, and the only limits he'd have, is his own imagination, and he'd never lacked there. One down, two to go. It was now time to plan his next move.

Chapter 35

It was Monday evening and Justin hadn't met Tammy that day, as she had called in sick. '*Female troubles'*, read the cryptic, but tell-all insertion in the School's 'Student Attendance' record. Justin genuinely missed her. School was dull without her, and he'd been desperate to show her his clear face. Out of everyone, Tammy was the only person he wanted to impress.

Justin's mind slipped away to gain a few private moments of reflection. His very own eyes had borne witness to this double transformation and he was feeling emotions he'd never experienced before. He'd lost something – but it wasn't time to grieve. Meerkats are welcome to leave… bye! This was hard-hitting for Sam no doubt, but he deserved it – and more. But that was nothing. The next one would be *much* harder hitting, and Justin was now starving for payback. This thing actually works, and if the next one works too – then it'll fuck-up this guy's entire life.

Given what Tammy had said about Curtis, Justin decided to leave him, at least for the time being. His next target was now Zac, and he recalled what Zac had said about him. Zac called him a wimp. That's okay when you're over six feet, and built like an Adonis, with good looks and perfect hair. Justin's hair was tight and wiry. No matter what he did with it, the best it ever looked was a bit less wavy. Although it pained Justin to admit it, Zac was a good looking bloke.

'Fuck'im', he said to himself. 'He's next.'

That evening, Justin's mind wandered away from the dinner table, as he subconsciously sliced his carrots into tinier and tinier slivers, while gnawing endlessly on a slice of beef, that an attentive Belle hoped might get dropped her way. What would be the best way to approach this, and could he really fuck-up Zac? Yes – was the short answer, but this one required a considered approach before putting pencil to paper. There was a real need to keep this thing moving, and not give the trio a moment to catch on to his attack.

"Son! You okay?", his worried father asked, watching his son chew away a journey, and snap back from it.

"What? Eh, sorry. Can I leave the table, please?" He'd hardly touched his roast beef slices, and his peppercorn sauce had gathered a skin. He hadn't heard a word they'd said the last few minutes.

"On you go.", his father nodded, eyeing Debbie. His dad knew.

That night, after having a one-way debate with Belle in the garden, Justin sat down again at his desk and wondered. Belle innocently looked up from below, still panting from her evening tour of the decking and flowers. He'd decided, and began carefully and accurately drawing Zac. It was indeed Zac – no doubt about that. But noticeably skinnier, 'air-brushed' all the way to a land called anorexia – and but for a few tufts of hair over each ear, he'd gone bald.

Justin included himself in the picture, but with a more developed physique, and his hair was now longer and straighter. This would be two trait swaps this time, and was that even possible? Was it asking too much from whatever greater power there was? He needed to know its limits. He'd never really bothered too much about his looks before, or how he appeared to others. He just wasn't that vain. But he'd change this game's rules now, and more than anything, he wished that Tammy was his girlfriend. And if something's there for the taking, then take it.

He gave a final look to Belle, stood up and then signed it. Almost immediately, he felt dizzy and sat back down. A 'pre-vision' of this was bulleting to his mind as fast as the lightning, and it would hit him any second. He'd expected its arrival, but not instantly.

The light dimmed in his room. Justin found his foot nervously tapping on the floor in anticipation of what was about to happen. Belle stopped panting, and looked behind her. Right then, it arrived. It smashed right through him, and just like a heavyweight boxer's knockout punch, he went stiff. Belle disappeared, as did his room. In fact, all eyesight had left him, and he went blind. But in this lonely darkness, he saw a figure walking towards him, and as it neared, he realised it was the person he'd just drawn.

As Zac slowly came into focus, he looked like he did in Justin's sketch. Zac looked severely pissed off with Justin, as if he knew that it was Justin who had made this happen. As he got closer, he yelled out 'Bastard!' and lunged towards him, grasping Justin's throat with both hands and they fell to the ground. Justin panicked, and grabbed his hands to try and release them from his neck, but he didn't have the strength. The more he tried to release Zac's grip, the tighter his grip became, and Justin was choking. No air was getting in. No air was getting out.

Although noticeably slimmer than he was before, he was still stronger than Justin was, and he was livid. Justin looked up at his opponent and saw Zac's fury as he bit down hard on his teeth. They both noticed a few hairs slowly falling down onto Justin's eyes, but the thing that mattered most, was that Zac's thumbs felt like they were now piercing his throat, right through his skin and crushing his windpipe.

Desperate for oxygen, his legs were now shuddering, and Zac finally had a wicked smile of glory on his face, sensing his victory and Justin's demise. This was the end of everything, and there was nothing he could do about it – apart from stare into his opponent's eyes as he finished him off. That would be the last thing he ever saw. Now, he wasn't even trying to breathe – there was no point trying. This was his termination, and he just accepted it.

But out of nowhere, the grip released, and Justin looked up. It was as if he'd been swimming way too deep, and was on his way back up to the surface, but rapidly running out of time and he could hear Zac's voice of reality saying, 'you're not going to make it!' But he did make it – only just, and took the biggest breath he'd ever taken when he hit the surface.

"Calm down son!" Justin blinked hard and saw his father kneeling above him on the floor. He'd swapped faces with Zac. "Justin – are you okay?"

That moment of panic had passed, but he was still spooked at what had just happened.

"You were choking yourself, son. I tried to pull your hands away, but I couldn't – not at first. Son, you had such a firm grip of yourself. I didn't even know you were that strong."

Justin looked distant. Had he been in a gateway to somewhere else? If his father hadn't rescued him, would he have perished? At that precise moment, he didn't even want to know, and just spidered backwards until he felt wall on his back, still seeing half of Zac in his dad's face.

"You shouted out, son.", said his dad, still kneeling on the floor.

Justin felt round to make sure nothing was round his neck. "What did I say?" His voice was coarse.

"You shouted, BASTARD – *really* loudly!"

His father could see the dread in his son's face as he was thinking it through, and that worried him. Thankfully, he didn't see Justin's drawing that had fallen down, and had floated its way under Justin's bed. But his father had suspicions. He couldn't forget that he'd driven his son to visit Stuart to untangle the mystery of this curse they'd hidden from him.

"I'm okay, dad."

"Christ son! You don't look okay." Mike was right – he didn't. And it wasn't just the marks on his neck or his tormented eyes. Marks would fade in an hour or so, but this curse that had been passed onto his son – well that wasn't visiting and passing through – that was here to stay, just like it did with his own father. You can't shake it off, or wish it away.

Justin's eyes darted from side to side as he tried to work it out. Although he'd survived – this time – it could have been a shit load worse. But for his dad arriving, he most probably would have died. Papa told him about the risks, but this was unexpected. It did work differently for him.

Chapter 36

The next day, Justin walked to school by himself. As he was approaching the school grounds, his eyes robotically scanned everything that moved, desperately seeking out the second bullshit-bishop. He saw the entire school – all the students, all the teachers, all of the parents who drove their kids to school – even a squirrel zipping up a tree, but no Zac. Maybe he was already inside? The curiosity was killing him, and it needed satisfying.

But it wasn't until lunch, while innocently chatting with Ray, that Justin finally caught a glimpse of Zac. At the far end of the dinner hall, he was there with Curtis and Sam, his back to Justin. The trio were discussing things among themselves when Curtis suddenly raised his voice in anger. "Fuck sake! Get a grip!" It was heard by everyone in the hall, prompting curious heads to turn in their direction. Zac looked ill – but he wasn't ill. His clothes were just a tad loose on him now. He put his hand through his hair and brushed it away from his eye. A girl behind him was still looking and she let out a gasp. As Zac went to pick up his sandwich from the table, he noticed some black hairs in his hand. Some hairs had been combed-out by his fingers, and when he looked closer, more hairs had fallen to the table.

It prompted Zac to stand up and stare at all the hairs sticking to his hand, which almost resembled the hand of a werewolf. As he stood, Justin's focus zoomed in. It would appear that his muscley physique has already started to deflate too. Maybe he'd already noticed.

"Have you done something to me?", Zac shouted, pointing at Justin with a hairy hand.

Justin spread out his arms, looked directly at him, but said nothing.

Zac stormed out the room, and went home. That was him for the day.

"Homey – what the fuck's that twat talking about?", asked Ray.

"I think he's feeling poorly!", said Justin, seeing that people at other tables were undoubtedly asking the same thing.

"What's happened to his hair? Did someone… spike his drink or something?"

"Who knows. Hey, maybe he's worried too much about end of year exams!"

They both sniggered, but as they were on that subject, Justin noticed Ray glancing towards his head. "Hey, man. Have you done something with *your* hair? It looks a bit different."

"Just styled it different." Justin leaned forward so others wouldn't hear his whisper. "Don't tell anyone. Used my mom's hair straighteners!"

"Well it looks cool, bud."

Right there, it hit him. Justin realised that people would notice him changing. That included Tammy, and he couldn't tell her about this – about obtaining other people's better characteristics as they lost it, stealing it from them and watching their misery. She'd want nothing more to do with him if she ever found that out. No wonder his Papa Stuart never told his wife about this thing. This was getting complicated.

"Hey man – what you doing after school?" Justin had to change the subject.

Ray shrugged.

"I'm going to the gym. Want to come?"

Ray blurted out a laugh. "The fuckin *gym*! Nah – you're all right. Too much like hard work!"

"I *need* to go Ray. Been a wimp too long."

Justin needed a cover-up. He'd already noticed his body changing, and if he was going to get any bigger, then everyone would notice, and they'd want to know how he got that way. Before sketching this thing, he'd already considered that it might just be the case that however much muscle Zac would lose, he might gain that exact amount, and that simply wouldn't happen on its own. Justin *had* to go to the gym, and people had to see him there. The more people that saw him squat and fly, the better the chances of the word spreading around that he was pumping up.

After school, the gymnasium was open to all students. Fortunately, the gym was quite busy and he immediately got to work on the bench press machine, that being the staple diet of any budding bodybuilder. He'd done a bit of research too, watching a few videos online of how to use free weights, and learning gym-lingo – 'sets' and 'reps', so he knew the basics, but no more. If things went to plan, he'd not really need to know much anyway.

Justin also worked on his arms and his back, doing a few sets for each body part, then went home. He'd put in a decent amount of effort, and had surprised himself about how much weight he'd been able to move around for a newcomer.

When the alarm woke Justin the following morning, he leaped out of bed and took off the T-shirt he'd been sleeping in. "Fuck me!", he said to his reflection in the mirror. His doppelganger with a different physique was revealing himself to its new owner, and he liked it. His arms were noticeably a little bigger, his chest and shoulders more prominent and the new muscle seemed to have eaten its way through his belly-fat as he slept, sculpting an athlete's build.

He'd never seen Zac without his top on, but he knew he went to the gym. As he twisted to see himself from different angles in the mirror, he thought to himself. This clearly wasn't Zac's entire physique he'd obtained overnight, but he'd definitely grown, and if this was from just one day, he couldn't wait to see tomorrow's results.

When getting ready and going to the shower, he made sure he kept covered up with towels, so his parents didn't see him this time. But he only just made it into his shirt, and he knew he'd have to buy bigger clothes at lunchtime that day. This transformation wouldn't be waiting for him to get ready – this was happening right now, day by day, hour by hour – whether he liked it or not. 'Once it's started, there's no stopping it.', he recalled.

After school, he went to the gym again – this time working different body parts with weights, and finishing on the exercise bike, before he walked home alone. School had been such a drag without Tammy. After dinner, he continued their text chat.

'Missing you at school :(x'

'Me too. Just a couple more days off I think. x'

'How are you feeling. x'

'I'm fine. Just sore tummy stuff   :(Hows school? x'

'School sucks! Been going to the gym after tho x' Justin knew that when Tammy saw him next, she'd notice everything – she always did. He knew he had to prepare her.

'Gym? Pumping up? x'

'Yeah! Needed to! Going well so far. You can come too when you're better. x'

'Don't be silly. U R fine the way U R x'

typing…

'Just want to feel better about myself. Dont just now :(x'

Tammy was lying on her bed, thinking about how best to respond. There were things about her that she wished she could change. She'd always hated her skinny legs.

typing…

'Its OKAY to feel that way Justin. Hey, I'm here for you when you need me. Say goodnight to Belle x' She mostly said the right thing. She mostly texted the right thing too.

'Thanks partner! Belle misses you. See you in a few days. Take care x'

'x'

That night, Justin could hardly get to sleep. His thoughts had been mixed up before – but now, he was *aching* to see Tammy again – that's how he knew. He'd always loved spending time with her, but this time, he had a new, muscly body to pull clothes over and he was loving the way it was developing. He couldn't wait to see her reaction when she next saw him. And as he finally drifted off, he wished he'd still had cracked ribs, so she'd take his top off again.

Chapter 37

Over the last few days, things had taken a turn for the worse for Zac. He'd taken a shower at home, and watched-on helplessly as the majority of his hair washed out and spun in circles around the bath's plug hole. He hadn't returned to school after walking out on the Monday, so Justin was absolutely desperate to see what he looked like now.

Justin had grown impatient, but it wasn't until Friday, that both Zac, but also Tammy returned to school, and Justin noticed them both as they marched from different angles. This was awesome. But however much he realised he was becoming infatuated with Tammy, for now Zac was his focus. Zac had been dropped off by his mother, who's look of dread could be mistaken for one dropping him off at hospital. She waited in the car until he'd slowly walked inside.

Zac had lost almost all of his hair now and only a few threads remained. He'd clearly lost a lot of weight too, so much, that he looked old. He was now just a shadow of the guy he used to be, and as Justin absorbed it all in, he actually felt sorry for him. That is, until he remembered about his role in destroying Tammy's irreplaceable family picture and of course, sending him to hospital.

Justin walked up towards Tammy as she approached the school. "Hey, you!"

"Hey, Justin. Wow… ", looking him up and down, "… you *have* been working out!"

"Every day – after school", trying to assert it's been down to hard work.

"You're not taking *steroids*, are you!"

"Of course not! Just hard graft."

"I like your hair too. What have you done with it?"

"Just a bit of gel."

Now he seemed to be making excuses. He had been night and day different from Zac, so maybe he shouldn't have targeted him? And maybe he shouldn't have done the double? This was proving to be such a change, that it was going to be hard to justify.

"Anyway, how's you? Better?"

"Yeah. Glad to be back I suppose. Hey thanks for sending me pictures of Belle. That cheered me up."

As they walked together into school, agreeing to meet up for lunch, lurking from behind a tree was Curtis, and his jealous stare. A few weeks ago, he pitied Justin. Now, he envied the way his girlfriend looked at him. She hadn't returned all of Curtis's texts over the last few days, and just told him she was in bed sick. Curtis hadn't gone to her house either. He'd never even met her mom, so he felt too awkward to go to the door and ask to see her. Tammy was slipping through his furious hands, and into the arms of his foe. An archenemy he'd underestimated. Something would have to be done.

At lunchtime, Tammy sat with Justin and Ray. All three of them freely chatting and laughing belly laughs, Ray spilling the beans, teasing Justin about his shiny hair and about how he styles it after stealing his mom's straighteners. It was good banter. Teasing with fun, and being taken that way.

Curtis was at another table with Sam when Zac walked over to them. The noise level dropped a bit and people looked up to see what had caused the hush. Zac looked like an old man, like he'd came from the future. He gingerly sat down, and the chatter slowly returned.

Justin so badly wanted to tease him, dying to ask Zac in front of everyone if he had AIDS or something. But it wasn't in his nature to do that, and he'd lose brownie points with Tammy if he did. A glory gaze directly into Zac's eyes, was prize enough.

Tammy gasped into her hands. "Oh my God! Is that Zac?"

"Yeah – he's ill I think?", said Justin, still gazing over, inwardly triumphant – but poker-faced.

"What's happened to him?"

"I think he's shaved his head, or something. No one knows!", said Ray. "Who cares? Fuckin prick anyway.", biting into a sandwich.

"I suppose he had it coming.", added Justin.

Tammy wore the beginnings of a confused look, mixed with worry. Maybe he *had* deserved something, but he'd gone downhill so rapidly, his prognosis surely wouldn't make happy reading. Tammy sighed it off, then got up. She had history next, then art.

"See you in art?", asked Justin.

"Yeah… see you then.", sending another concerned smile – but it wasn't because of Zac.

Justin seen she'd been troubled for Zac, so how would she react when he played out the revenge he had in store for Curt? That was ready to go, but now, on retrospect, maybe what he'd planned for him was *too* severe. A slightly milder,

'Plan B' was needed for Curt, so he'd need to re-think. Maybe after removing the second black bishop from the board, it would come to him.

Chapter 38

Mr Wallace, Tammy's history teacher was a young lad, fresh out of University, and at only twenty-three years old, this job at Auburn Junior High School was his first post as a fully qualified teacher. Tammy had always felt a bit uncomfortable around him, as she'd noticed him staring at her on more than a few occasions. She'd always made a point of deliberately flocking within the moving herd into and out of the classroom, so she was never in the class with him alone. She'd taken this class, due to an interest she had in American History, and she needed to pass to have her grades adequate enough for college.

That week, the subject matter had changed. They'd now moved onto the topic of indigenous people of the USA – Native Americans and the settlers to America who'd travelled there from elsewhere was now being taught. Mr Wallace had told of the battles that had commenced over areas of land, and described how the Natives, sometimes referred to as 'Red Indians' had fought poorly, were easily overcome, and that the Tribal leader, Chief Honnillow was a coward and had easily surrendered without putting up much of a fight.

Tammy, being the only student who was a descendent of any Native American tribe, took offence and he knew she would. She couldn't just sit quietly like the ignorant others.

"That's not true.", she said out loud, drawing the attention of the entire class.

"Eh… sorry.", pretending to be surprised. "What's not true, Tammy?"

"Your *version* of what happened. That's not what happened."

"Tammy, what happened is in numerous history books from decades ago. They all say the same thing."

"It's offensive, and… discriminatory. These people are my ancestors. What you're saying may have happened, but it's the *way* you're saying it happened – it didn't happen that way."

"All right Miss Yazzie – tell us how it happened?", said Mr Wallace, folding his arms now.

"They were not *cowards* – don't call them cowards.", she scorned. The stage was hers. She looked around the class, and saw everyone looking directly at their new teacher. The room was silent, poised for her expert contribution.

"The original Natives – all the tribes, they lived peacefully – lived off the land. The clothes they wore – they came from the land too. They weren't cowards – they took down *mammoths – and* other giants, and there were no such things as guns then. America was *their* land, until people from elsewhere flooded in when it got safe, and tried to steal what they'd fought for, for what belonged to them. They all came with guns and rifles – *they* were the cowards – hiding a safe distance behind a rifle! The tribes didn't have guns – yet they *still* fought back. They just had knives, arrows, horses… each other. They were out-armoured and out-numbered. They fought bravely but they didn't stand a chance… so many died."

"So how *did* they fight, Tammy?", asked one of the students, called Steve.

"They *scalped* their enemies!", smirked Mr Wallace, attracting a few sniggers.

"If you'd been there – they would have scalped *YOU*!" In fact, *I* would have done it!" Tammy boasted, looking intently at the teacher. Students gasped out loud – followed by a moment of silence as they awaited a response – eyes darting left and right, like watching tennis. It seemed like a veiled threat, and the smirk instantly vanished from Mr Wallace's young face.

Tammy sat back down. As the teacher was digesting what she'd just said, the bell rang. It woke Mr Wallace from distant thoughts, as he saw his tribe of students doing their own retreat from the room.

"Tammy, one moment. Wait behind a minute, please."

Once everyone had left, Mr Wallace closed over the door. "We need to stick with the coursework text Tammy."

"What – even if it's wrong?", she snapped.

"I'm sorry." He saw Tammy looking down at the floor.

"Sorry, sir. I can't go along with it – if I know it's not what happened."

"Even at the expense of failing history?"

She looked confused. "How could I fail history? This is just one element."

"You may fail other parts too. Your attendance isn't great, and your attitude – well that little outburst just there – that felt like a threat to me."

Tammy didn't say anything in reply.

"What would your father say?", knowing he'd passed, and looking on as she shook her head. "I could make it all go away."

She looked up from the floor. "What do you mean?"

"Tammy, I've got a… kind of offer for you. I do private tuition sessions – after-hours schooling. I think you could benefit from some." He began slowly walking around the room. "Why don't you come round to my house around seven o'clock tonight, and we'll talk it through. I'm the last house on Bankhill Street, the one with the black door. Assuming all goes well, then… we'll just take it from there."

Tammy seen through this. The 'private tuition' was all bullshit. He could have done that in the school grounds. If anyone found out about this, it would be her, voluntarily going round to her teacher's home, as if she had a crush on him. He didn't even mention a fee.

"It's just one hour, Tammy", he added, "… and if all is okay, then I could make things go well for you – write up a great report." He knew she needed to pass history. She'd already dropped out of one of her other subjects, so she needed to pass the remaining ones to have college worthy grades.

Piece of shit. "Let me think about it."

Chapter 39

"Not getting a run with Curtis?", Justin asked, as Tammy jogged up behind him.

"No", came the abrupt reply. "So this is the new Justin?", referring to his new, and quite obviously, improved physique.

"Late puberty, I suppose.", smiling his reply. "Hey, are you all right Tammy." He'd noticed her blank response.

On the walk home, Tammy felt she could open up to Justin and tell him everything about her teacher and what had happened in class earlier. She included that there were no witnesses, and that she knew the teacher would fail her if she refused his advances. She couldn't see a way out. Justin was disgusted with what she was saying, but quickly had an idea.

"Do you want me to see if I can do something?"

"Do what?" Did he mean a set-up? Was he going to put secret cameras in her bag to record what Mr Wallace said and done if she went to his house later tonight? Surely not.

"You're not going tonight?"

"Of course not!", she said sternly.

"Do you trust me?", he asked, hoping she'd reply instantly. She did, but not verbally. She just nodded nervously.

"Then let me see what I can do. Leave it to me, Tammy, alright?"

They'd reached the junction where they'd go their separate ways, and on her way home alone, Tammy couldn't help wondering what he thought he could do to stop this guy, especially with no proof of his proposal.

After dinner, Justin got to work once more. This teacher needed sorting out and he knew exactly what to do with him. 'From crook – to rook', he imagined. He brought out some magazines he'd been reading recently. These he could use. To ridicule Tammy in front of others, was a mistake. To blackmail her and get her to go to his home, looking like a desperate teenager, with her undersexed hormones swarming over him with a sexual fantasy, when it was his perverse idea all along, was a bigger one, and this teacher needed to be taught a lesson.

Although revolted with Mr Wallace, he grinned. This guy has to be stopped and Justin had to make sure he wouldn't do anything like this ever again. This creature that he'd only ever seen in passing, carting books under his arm to the circular history room, was going to regret the day he ever met Tammy. No one fucks with her.

"Just me and you, Belle!", twisting a pencil in a sharpener, "Someone's about to make history!", winking at her as he closed his bedroom door, and he got to work outlining his next sketch to be signed – but not tonight. By God – the next day this beast taught his history class, was going to be a whole lot of fun – for everyone else that is. Well worth recording, but what a shame this battle had to wait until Monday.

Chapter 40

Tammy popped round again on Sunday, and she helped Justin walk Belle. She loved Justin's company and the conversations they had seemed effortless. He didn't just let her speak, he listened to her, and understood her – something Curtis never even attempted. And once back in his room, she felt safe enough to take a risk – get something off her chest that had been building up for months. She needed the ears of another boy.

"Can I tell you something?"

"Sounds... ominous!", Justin replied, but quickly gave her his full attention – after making sure his door was closed over completely, trapping Belle.

"It's been driving me mad. I've got to tell someone."

"Tammy. Are you okay?" He immediately noticed that tears were forming in her eyes, and fetched some tissues from his top drawer. This would be the first time ever, his tissues would be getting used for tears. He sat next to her at the end of his bed.

"It's Curtis.", she said, hitting the bed. "Hands! Hands! Fucking hands! All over me, all the time! All he ever wants is... " She struggled to complete it – then, she bravely spat it out. "All he wants is sex. I'm sick of it."

"I thought you guys were having a break?"

"I met him yesterday." It was almost apologetic.

Replying to this would be tough. Justin could empathise with Curtis here. Although he hated this guy, and he had the girl of his dreams as his girlfriend, at the very least, he could understand Curt's craving. But knowing Curtis the way he did, a fear popped into his head.

"He's not *forcing* you to do anything, is he?"

Tammy looked away. With the amount of time she took before replying, it was obvious that he had. What a bastard. Justin noticed her eyes moving about, searching for those times.

Tammy sighed. "A few times he has, yes." Somehow, it sounded like *she* was apologising. This was getting serious, but now she'd let him in, he had to hear what she was really trying to tell him. Maybe, it was too hard to say, but Justin felt close enough to ask.

"Tammy – tell me he's not… raped you."

Again she paused. During the silence, as she thought how to say it, Justin felt his tummy spin.

"He tried to… once."

"Jesus Christ!"

"… in his room. We were just making out, but then I felt him unzip my dress, and he tried to take it off. I *told* him to stop, and I wasn't ready for that yet, but it was as if he didn't hear me. Then he just kept trying to slide it up over my shoulders. So I slapped him. He didn't like that."

"What happened next Tammy?"

"Then he grabbed my wrists – *really* hard. Threw me on his bed and climbed on top. I heard him unzipping his pants – then I knew it was for real. I kneed him in his nuts and managed to escape from under him. When I tried to open the door, he was right behind me. He shook me. Called me a… " She shook her head, not wanting to speak it, "… he called me a cock-teaser. Told me I'd been leading him on, and it was my fault. I *wasn't* teasing him, Justin. We were just kissing!"

"I believe you Tammy." It was difficult to hear stories of anyone making out with Tammy, especially this bastard.

"I was scared. His parents were out, and I thought he was going to force me – force himself on me. He looked as if he was going to. But then…"

Now, he had bat's ears. Justin leaned closer, anticipating what was coming next, desperate to hear how this ended.

"… then he released his grip. Told me to fuck off. That's what I did. Just zipped myself back up and left. The next day, he apologised. Said it was his temper going off."

"This guy, Tammy. He's been – *violent* to you then?" Justin needed her to realise what he'd just heard from her. He wanted Tammy to bin this shit-head. The more he could do to summarise what a creep Curtis was, the better it would be all round. "Has he done that kind of thing again – since then?"

She shook her head. "Just that time."

"So you've never… " This sounded like fishing – it was.

"Heck no!" She sounded disgusted he'd even suggested it.

Banked! Justin knew this was a chance – probably his one and only chance to give her advice while they were on the subject. Undoubtedly, they'd never discuss this again. But he quickly decided that it wasn't his place to tell her what to do. She already knew what to do.

"But you're *still* with him.", he said. Of all the conversations they'd had, this was the only subject which caused Justin to worry for her. It was her decision to make, and he respected that.

"Not for much longer. It's just hard to... "

"Tammy, he's the one thing in your life that's shit. Because of him, you're not the girl I know you could be. Seriously, once you break up with him – *if* you break up with him, you're gonna feel much better about yourself. Guaranteed you will."

The look she gave him, revealed complexities around this break-up thing. Telling Curtis it's over would, most probably, be a tipping point for him. How would he react to that? That news had to come, sooner or later. But for now, the subject needed changing.

"Hey, how's your ribs now?"

"Only a wee bit sore. Fed up just lying on my back every night! In fact, I woke up a few nights ago sore. I'd turned over in my sleep, and it was as if I was lying on a hard stone!"

He closed his eyes the moment he'd said it, but he hadn't meant it the way it came out. Tammy saw the funny side, but it wasn't a time for laughing. Before she got up, she cuddled Justin a friend's cuddle to say thanks for listening. She looked round to see his easel had a cover over what he'd been working on. She got curious – but this one wasn't for her eyes.

"Can I take a peek?", already making towards it.

"Sorry, Tammy. That one's private."

She didn't push it. It'd been their first difficult conversation, and she was just glad it was over. Instead, she lay on the carpet beside Belle's bed and scratched her chin, and she stretched her head up when Tammy began rubbing. "This little baby looked as if she needed a scratch!"

They both looked adoringly at Belle. "Do you want to stay over with Auntie Tammy?" But she just collapsed in her bed.

Justin walked Tammy home, and their chat continued to her porch. She thanked him for being there for her the last few days, and apologised for dumping way too much baggage on him. He imagined the pressure she was feeling, and bottling these things up had troubled her, but sharing them had been only half a twist of the cap.

On the way home, Justin made a detour. He put the hood of his jumper over his head and wandered past the home of Mr Wallace, before calmly putting a letter in his mailbox. He'd made a note to this teacher which shouted a clear message. Justin saw this as 'check'. Was he willing to play on?

And once back in his room, his drawing was oven-ready. All it needed was his mark. Signing his artwork was becoming like loading ammunition in a revolver. Once he'd slid those bullets in the chamber, his work was dangerous. But no one knew exactly *when* the trigger would be pulled, not even the artist himself. Serving up revenge for those who just asked for it, made him smile. He also knew he'd pay for it, and no one knew exactly when he'd pay, and butterflies wiped that smile away. These were bittersweet moments, but it was worth it, because this time, he was doing it for Tammy.

Chapter 41

Hyper-charged, he had trouble sleeping. A ticking time bomb it was, but with no visible timer, and no clues to how much explosives this one came with either. It was right to be wary. Anything less would be disrespectful of this thing's power.

But his thoughts soon switched to Tammy and she was controlling the rhythm of his heart, sounding off like a tom-tom as she palmed it. She'd needed someone to listen to her. That much was obvious. And although he felt privileged that she'd decided she could trust him with her highly private truths, he just couldn't help wondering if there was something he was missing. Of all the people she could have gone to, she'd chosen him to confide in. From the very girl he ached for, he had to endure stories of her and Curtis making out, of him trying to strip her, trying to force his way to her body, and God only knows what else happened, and that stung.

But then he had another thought. He seen it from the point of view that only the next in line to the throne would see it. What if Tammy was telling him blunders that Curt made, so he wouldn't make those same mistakes? Was it a head-start? Maybe she knew he liked her and this was her way of saying, 'Don't go too fast', 'Don't try to take advantage of me just because I'm small.'

She'd be the boss in their relationship, no doubt about that. Justin had always wanted a 50-50 relationship, but she'd be *more* than that. Yes she was tiny. Five foot, three and not even a hundred pounds with her rucksack on, yet she'd be in charge. Boy – he dug this girl, and her roots. He imagined her wearing full tribal dress, with stripes painted on her cheeks and dancing a dance round a blazing fire with rocks all round. He heard the crackle of that fire, and felt its heat, as others joined the chanting to the drum, while the flames performed their own dance.

His eyes shot open and he sat up. Then he saw the drapes move. Shit… someone's in the room. The tom-tom's had stopped, as a dark figure, wearing all black and a balaclava appeared from behind them. The figure walked confidently towards him, silently treading barefoot past Belle's sleepy bed, and stopping at his, then slowly removed the balaclava, tossing it aside, revealing the intruder's face. Tammy hadn't gone to bed. She'd driven back over and had sneaked in, through his unlocked window.

She shook her hair free, eyes focussed only on him, intent on intimacy, and she wasn't leaving empty handed. She leaned over him, one knee on his bed, her lips gradually getting closer to his. The gap narrowed and she slowly licked her lips to wet them as she opened her mouth, now looking at *his* willing lips, as she gently bit his lower one.

He couldn't help himself look down at her boobs. Then she pushed his chest and he toppled onto his pillow again. She climbed aboard, now straddling him with a knee either side, as she put her hands on his bare chest, feeling his heart thumping as she blew him a kiss with her pouted red lips. She slowly dragged her nails gently downwards towards his naval, never breaking eye contact. Like a magnet, his hands shot to her thighs, and he found himself stroking her ninja-black leggings, up to her bum as she smiled permission.

She leaned backwards, and slowly unzipped her top as she winked at him. There was nothing underneath. She put both hands behind her back, as if she was being constrained. Maybe she was hinting her desire to be tied-up? Justin had seen this online – plenty. Still straddling him, she leaned over to kiss him again, girl on top and her bare skin pressing against his. Her lips tasted awesome, and he felt her tongue searching for his as she firmly gripped his hair.

In her hand, above his head, she'd concealed a knife. She put a finger to his lips to signal to him to be quiet. Justin heard a sound he was familiar with, but it didn't come from Tammy – high pitched whistle-yelling in the distance, but getting louder. This spelled danger in her Native language, and his throbbing dick receded – just a tad. Still grabbing his hair, she took her knife to his head. Only now, did he notice the look of terror in his eyes from the blade's shiny reflection. Without hesitation, she began sawing at his scalp. Blood instantly squirted out and ran down, through his hair. He felt paralysed and couldn't stop her.

"This isn't *your* hair!", she scorned. All he could move now, were his eyes and he looked around for whoever was making this noise. Justin screamed, but only inwardly, as she continued with the task.

Justin panicked, but Tammy the assassin was confidently smiling. He felt blood on his cheeks now, and his body was convulsing, desperately trying to escape the paralysis. Getting nowhere, he shut his eyes tightly, held his breath and screamed again. When he opened his eyes, Tammy had escaped. She'd been replaced by Belle, who was straddling him. She'd learned the ropes from his dad, and she had slobbered him with drool again. The sound had been her yelping, noticing Justin needed help.

"Jesus *fucking* Christ Belle! I'm gonna lock you in a fuckin cage at night."

Justin looked around, and it took a few moments to realise what had just happened. He went to the bathroom, just to satisfy himself that his new hair was still firmly attached. It was. His strapping was still there too – as was a semi. His watch told him it was just after 2am. Time to get back to bed and although he needed a shower – a cold one, that could wait till morning. This had been terrifying and if this was a taster for what was about to come tomorrow – or rather, later today – then he was already taking pity on Mr Wallace.

Chapter 42

Tammy walked into history among the crowd as usual. She had refused her teacher's offer, and she knew he'd have it in for her. Whatever was coming now, had been started and she'd just have to wait and see what happens. When she sat down at her desk, she casually got out the history book they'd been reading and a pen from her bag. Eventually, she had to look at him, and when she did, she noticed the blank look he was sending her way. Smiling at everyone else was the giveaway. What a loser.

"Steven", Mr Wallace said, "You start us off today, would you? Turn to page 82 of your textbook, and start reading from the second line, where it begins, '*When Christopher Columbus and the early settlers sailed to America in 1492…*' – start from there please."

As everyone busied themselves flicking to page 82, Tammy noticed the teacher looking directly at her as he was finishing off what he was saying. It gave her the shivers. This was a bully, starting his shit with her already, and it chilled her.

Young Steven started reading as instructed, and Mr Wallace sat down, scanning his students, but spending considerably more time looking at Tammy. All the student's eyes were down, following the text as Steven spoke it aloud. She just stared back at him, as if to say, 'Well fuck you – sir'. Both of them were oblivious of what was about to happen, but Justin was all too aware. Just like last night, his heart-rate started racing, nervously awaiting screams from the history class that Tammy was in just a few rooms down from where he was. But this time, it wouldn't be Tammy who did his scalping – she'd just be a spectator.

As Steven reached the third page of his reading, Tammy noticed something happening with her teacher. So did some other students. Mr Wallace quietly got up from his chair, and walked a couple of steps to his desk, where he slid open a drawer. Steven noticed this and it made him lose concentration for a moment, but he continued to read. Mr Wallace returned to his chair and sat back down on it. Something wasn't quite right with him and Tammy noticed his eyes were funny. It was as if he was under a spell.

She noticed he now had a pair of scissors in his hand and was fiddling with them the wrong way. Then, it snapped as he pried the two bits apart. The sound was loud enough to stop Steven in his tracks, and as he stopped reading, Mr Wallace didn't even notice. One by one, the students began looking up, wondering what was going on, looking at each other to see if they knew. This class was never silent, but it was now.

People were now getting concerned. As they wondered what was going on, Mr Wallace dropped one part of the scissors on the floor. It seemed to bounce around, taking ages to settle. That shattered the silence and gained their full attention for what was just about to happen. Everyone watched him as he calmly raised the scissor's blade to his head, still completely expressionless and worry-free, unlike most of the students. Now staring at Tammy, he sliced his forehead open – yelling out as he cut into himself. Blood instantly began pouring down into his eyes as he pulled the blade across his head time and time again, to make a deeper cut. Some students were screaming, and others covered their eyes, not wanting to witness this. As he wasn't stopping, a girl ran out the classroom screaming. The room began to empty, as others fled the scene too, not wanting to be scarred from this memory.

But Tammy stayed behind, and she watched everything. She watched on as he grabbed his loose flap of skin and tore it backwards, then cut it off completely, revealing a bloodied skull bone. Wells of blood were on the floor below him and his shirt was soaked with it too.

Two other teachers ran in, to see him holding his scalped hair aloft, smiling as he'd completed the job – as if he'd been ordered to do it and succeeded. One of them pressed the school's fire alarm button, and the noise from the sirens seemed to wake Mr Wallace out the spell he was under.

He looked confused. With his hand up, he looked as if he wanted to ask questions, until he saw what he was holding in the air with his left hand. Then, reality hit home, and pain kicked in. He was sitting in his own blood, and no one wanted to touch him.

"Mr Wallace – put the scissors down.", came the instruction. One of the school's Police Officers had been alerted by one of the fleeing students and had raced to the scene. With a trembling hand adjacent to his side-arm, he gave the instruction again, and the bloodied blade dropped to the floor and bounced toward its other half, which remained clean and shiny.

The other Officer put handcuffs on Mr Wallace, in case he had any other weapons on him. It was now Game Over.

The Principal ran in, only to be horrified by the aftermath. "Tammy, leave now." She'd been the only student that had remained till the end.

All day, the school was hyped. Buzzing with differing stories of Mr Wallace and how he'd turned looney in front of everyone, and how he got carted away in an ambulance.

That's a career ender, for sure, but the Principal had ordered an emergency assembly meeting for the entire school just before lunch and made it mandatory for all students to attend. His aim was to provide re-assurance that Mr Wallace was okay and had been taken care of, but also to strictly forbid anyone from posting any videos that may have been taken. But it was too late. Someone had already done that, and it was circulating around, gathering momentum and comments.

The person had been identified as one of the history students who captured the whole thing on her phone, despite school rules demanding they be switched off in class. The girl got suspended right there and then, and ordered to take the video down, but only after the Principal had seen it himself.

Later that day as Tammy and Justin walked home together, curiosity got the better of her and took over. She just had to ask.

"Did you hear what happened to my history teacher?"

Justin didn't want to lie. The last thing he needed to do was to bullshit her. "Did you see it Tammy?", not committing himself, answering her question with his.

She told him everything. Justin hadn't seen the video, but had heard rumours before the assembly at school. He'd endured the very same thing just a matter of hours ago and he was now face to face with *his* scalper.

"He'll be fine.", he re-assured her. "Hey, you saw it all. Are *you* okay?"

"Just a bit shocked he'd do that to himself."

"Maybe he just went crazy or something?"

She slowed the pace down a bit to get serious about something.

"Listen… I don't know if you've… You said you were going to do something."

Justin knew his reply would make or break his chances with Tammy, so he had to be careful what he told her. Could he half-let her in?

"Tammy… he done that shit to himself. You saw it all!", watching her re-envisage it. They reached their parting point and had stopped walking. "But I *did* reach out to him. Believe me, you won't get any more grief from him again. I can assure you of that."

She needed more than this vagueness. "What happened, Justin? What did you do?"

But he couldn't tell her. She'd think he was as wicked as her teacher. But in some cases, you have to fight fire with fire.

"Trust me Tammy – you don't want to know."

Chapter 43

On Wednesday, Mr Wallace, returned home from the hospital around mid-day. He'd been kept in for two nights and had his carpet of skin and hair stitched back on. Although young, he'd been starting to show signs of male pattern baldness and didn't have much hair on top, but it just about covered the stitches, which were scheduled to be removed in another week.

He'd also been assessed by a psychiatric nurse, and apart from what he'd just done to himself, she'd found no other reason not to allow him to go home. 'Temporary insanity' – it had seemed like, after he'd assured her he wasn't suicidal and felt perfectly normal now.

When he arrived back home, he immediately went to a drawer that he'd stored a letter in on Sunday evening and took it out to read once more. He read it word by word for a second time now. It wasn't a threat, but a premonition.

TOMORROW – YOU'LL HURT YOURSELF IN PUBLIC. APOLOGISE TO TAMMY. SHE PASSES HISTORY. OTHERWISE THINGS WILL GET WORSE AND YOU WILL SELF-HARM EVERY SINGLE DAY UNTIL YOU GET LOCKED UP IN A MENTAL HOSPITAL

It was all spelled out in individual cut-outs from newspapers and magazines and glued to paper, so no handwriting could be identified. Because of this, Mr Wallace suspected this would be from someone he would recognise the handwriting of – a student. It could only have been Tammy, he thought. Then he thought deeper. Was she an Indian Shaman? Did she have powers handed down from ancestors? Surely not – he didn't believe in all that stuff. But then again, he stared at what he was holding in his hands. He couldn't think straight, as his thoughts were impeded by pain-killers the hospital had given him.

The single letter he'd returned to, told him he'd been placed on sick leave. Ordered by the Principal to stay off for the next month until they met for a review. One month and counting – for him to complete *his* homework, and work out who'd sent it.

His weary mind needed a break. Time for something strong he thought, and he reached out to his cabinet and pulled a bottle of Absinthe he'd been keeping for a rainy day, and today, in his mind it was pouring. He cracked it open and poured some into a crystal glass, and just stood there, staring straight down at his jaded reflection slowly becoming motionless. This particular moment needed a straight one, and clear thoughts would investigate later. He swallowed down the first, large shot in one go, the aftershock vibrating his head.

Surely this was the work of Tammy? Maybe her boyfriend, Curt? Who else could it be? Then he remembered that Tammy got comfy when everyone else left. She'd stayed for the credits.

"Tammy if this was you – then you're FUCKING DEAD, bitch!", and threw the empty glass to the floor, shattering it into tiny diamonds.

Chapter 44

Mr Wallace woke up the following afternoon, and found himself lying on the sofa, dried blood on his cheek and hands. The bottle of Absinthe was half-empty, and he'd managed his way through a bottle of red wine too. Shards of glass everywhere. Not a great look if someone from the school would pay a courtesy visit, so the next few hours demanded a clean-up and sober-up.

After a painful shower, a few strong coffees, and deciding to get a Chinese takeaway for his dinner, his blurred reflection told him he still wasn't sober enough to drive, but it wasn't far, and the fresh air would do him good anyway. On his way back from the Chinese, he walked through the park. His half-blurry eyes noticed a couple heading towards him. A few more steps towards each other revealed that it was Justin and Tammy, and they were too close now for him to turn round or detour. They were heading back to Justin's home with Belle.

His wrath from last night had simmered down. He'd been desperate to confront Tammy, but what he'd sworn he'd say to her, had now been forgotten in the drunken haze of last night's half-marathon booze session, and he just wanted home now.

"Hey sir. Are you okay?", asked Tammy with sincerity, as she got closer and realised who it was they'd be passing. The woolly hat he wore covered everything.

"Yes, I'm fine… Tammy…. Thanks… for asking." Upon saying it, it began to sink in, that it was him, and only him, who'd been responsible for what he did to himself that day. She'd been there, but he did the cutting. Now he actually felt guilty for giving her something to have nightmares about, but also for blaming her in his mind for this – accusing her of being the conductor. "Taking a few weeks off."

He wasn't stopping for a chat, and swiftly walked past the pair of them. Belle had to be tugged back as she followed Mr Wallace, the first time she wasn't leading the way home.

"Hope you're feeling better, sir.", Tammy said after he'd passed them.

Of course he heard her, but embarrassment kept him walking. But she'd seen him much worse than this… Justin imagined a castling move – no surrender yet.

"Tammy!", cried Mr Wallace suddenly, realising the opportunity may not repeat itself anytime soon, turned – and walked back towards the pair. When he caught back up with them, he didn't quite know what to say. Justin's curious ears honed in.

"Sir?"

He hesitated. It was awkward enough – but even worse with Justin there. "Tammy, I, er… what I said in class… I want to apologise… to you. *And…* also for what I did in front of you.", as his shame-ridden, bloodshot eyes rose from her shoes. "It won't happen again – I promise."

Tammy nodded. "Come on honey.", as she tugged Belle's leash. It was indeed awkward, and knowing the type of person he was, she hadn't expected an apology. Justin had though. Now he could tear up that ready-made drawing that had been stuck on pause-mode, just awaiting his mark to kick off round two. This rook was a rookie – black castle destroyed.

Then, with his bagged dinner, he swiftly walked away and out of sight. In the still of the night, the smell had remained in their nostrils but he'd gone.

When he was out of ear-shot, Justin jested, "Chicken chow Mein?"

"Nah – beef stir fry!"

That moment needed something, and as they continued onwards towards home to drop off Belle, discussing the day's events so far, Justin stopped abruptly. Tammy was so deep in conversation that she hadn't noticed. He was looking around, but specifically at the bushes and trees, drawn to them and squinting his eyes to try to spot something he knew was there.

"Justin? What's up?", she said, and began looking where he was looking. Belle started barking. Although she didn't know what was there, her protective instincts knew no limits.

After a few moments, he gave up. "I thought I saw something.", he said, "It must be nothing."

He knew fine what it was. Curtis was in those trees. He was on Justin's radar, and he was next in line to get fucked-up. But despite not seeing him, he could sense his presence, like Belle sensed a chewy. Although he hadn't sketched Curtis yet, he had plans to do so imminently, and the connection was already there.

"Let's get this wee pup home."

Afterwards, while Justin was walking Tammy home, she reached under his hand and locked fingers with his. She noticed Justin's smile as she did. He was well aware that Curtis may also be watching them at this moment, and inside he smiled bigger.

Neither of them unlocked the grip until they reached her home, and at her doorstep, she thanked him for walking her home safely again.

"It's been a bit of a weird day!", said Tammy. "But I've had a great time."

"So have I."

He took a step closer to her and slowly leaned in towards her, hoping for a kiss. When he got close, she snatched the last gap. She made sure it was a brief kiss – just for now. There would still be things to do before this could go any further.

"Come over here tomorrow after school?"

"Really?" Justin said, surprised at the unexpected progress.

"Yeah.", she confirmed, nodding. "See you at school.", and gave him another quick kiss on his cheek before nipping inside.

Justin's walk home was full of thoughts about what had happened that day. If only his mom was a history teacher. But now that he knew Tammy liked him, this was the green light to make Curtis pay, and he had a backup plan for him.

Chapter 45

The following evening, Justin walked over to Tammy's home. He didn't mind that it had been pouring, but he was soaked though when he got there.

"Hey, you didn't make *this* happen did you!", Tammy said when she opened the door, referring to the rain, and pretending – just for a second, to be serious. He liked her new sense of humour. The real Tammy was beginning to show herself.

Tammy handed him a towel she had fetched. "Mom, this is Justin."

Justin walked up to her, making sure his hand was completely dry before shaking hers.

"Nice to meet you, mam.", he said.

"It's lovely to meet you too Justin. Nice to put a face to your name at last."

Justin turned to Tammy.

"Tammy's told me lots about you. Sit down son. Tea?"

"Only if you're having one. Don't go to any trouble, mam. Do you want a hand?"

"No trouble at all. Tammy will help."

When they reached the kitchen, Tammy noticed her mom smiling at the kettle as it boiled – carrying that same smile to her daughter in the privacy the kitchen allowed. It communicated how nice Justin seemed and how polite he'd been. She was happy for Tammy and immediately took to him, and Tammy sensed her approval – and that was a must.

They soon returned with tea and a tray of biscuits and chatted about nothing in particular for around an hour. The recent downpour, school in general and the art project they were completing together, his new puppy that Tammy adored and of course Justin's talent for art.

"What do you do, Mrs Yazzie?"

"I don't work son. Not since Tammy's father died, seven years ago."

"Oh, mam, I'm sorry. I didn't know." In the time they'd spent together, Tammy had never spoken a word about her father dying. It was only now that he realised he'd never asked, and that made him feel awful.

"It's okay son, but thanks for saying. Hey, how's your tea?" She'd noticed he'd hardly touched it.

"It's…", he didn't want to lie to her either, "… *different* to what I've had before."

"Takes a bit of getting used to!", she replied. "Home-made, it is."

"You *made* this yourself?"

"Generations old recipe", she said proudly.

Justin took another sip. "Wait a minute, is that lemongrass you've put in it?"

"Well done Justin – and more."

"Ah. I knew I could taste something familiar.", taking another sip.

"So, when did the two of you start dating?"

The two of them looked at each other. Justin didn't know what to say, but Tammy stepped in.

"We've only just started dating, mom."

Justin sent Tammy a strange smile.

"Well I think you make a *lovely* pair.", rubber-stamping her approval, as she put down her empty cup. "I'll get the dishes."

"Come on, I'll show you my room."

"Thank you Mrs Yazzie – for making that tea."

When walking into her room for the first time, Justin's eyes were treated to an advanced history lesson. He instantly saw all the decorations and was fascinated. It was a private lesson – just for him and he listened intently as she told him stories she'd been told, as they lay on her bed. Her ancestors were tribal Natives – indigenousness people – the real thing, and possibly related to Clovis people. He saw her passion as she talked of how they made their homes, how they hunted and ate from the land and made their clothes from what they killed.

"I only know what I've read.", Justin admitted.

"Many books – they get it wrong. Bloody history!", she smirked as their eyes met. "There were numerous dances for different events and they wore different dresses. The sounds were not from hands over the mouth garbage! It came from whistling and from the back of the throat. I can't do it.", sighing a little laugh, as Justin mirrored her. "The spirits they believed in, are much more complex than a few lines of text. The rituals had *deeply* sacred meanings Justin – totems do too. They put their trust in things they *couldn't* see

– things no one can see." She turned to see him nodding, listening empathically, visualising it – he was almost there.

"Sometimes, they communicated with the spirits." She showed him some memorabilia she had in her wardrobe – a totem and some clothes, which have been in her family for generations.

"This is broken… God's sake! But it *was* a totem.", as she held up the skull of a Golden Eagle.

"Wow! How's it broken?", not seeing anything wrong with it.

"It's cracked, see?", turning it around. "Curtis dropped it. He said it was an accident! My father gave it to me. I should never even have taken it out the house."

"Don't blame yourself."

Tammy looked at Justin. She was deciding if she should tell him something very personal. Then it happened.

"I tried to connect with my father." The shaking of her head revealed it hadn't worked. "I think it was a fake anyway!"

Justin knew this moment called for a respectful reply. "Tammy… I'm sure he knows you tried."

"My Great, Great, Great, Great Grandfather was a Shaman. A spiritual leader of his tribe. He could do it – communicate with those who have passed from living to dead."

"Really?" Justin was hooked.

"Really. And when I was younger, my father told me that I've been passed down the gift too. It's never worked though. I even tried a voodoo doll on Mr Wallace!"

Justin could hardly believe it. He'd been passed down a gift too – but he hadn't found the way to tell Tammy yet. Maybe it was time now?

"Curtis hates all this stuff. *Dark* stuff, he calls it. Spirits, totems, dead skulls!" She let out a little snigger.

"Yeah, dead skulls are a bit spooky I suppose!" They had a connection in humour too.

"*There's no higher power*, he told me once. But I think there is."

"I believe there is too."

"He never takes me anywhere because of it. I think he thinks I'll tell his friends about cooking frogs in my cauldron or bring tarot cards or something! He hates it all and wants me to get rid of everything."

"What? Jeeso! I'd never ask anyone to… not be themselves or change. Tammy, this stuff… it states who you are!"

"I know I'm different." She seemed sad about admitting it.

"Tammy, you *are* different. But you're different in a brilliant way. It's *good* to be different… I *love* who you are!" He was also different, and hopefully she'd accept him when he told her – *if* he told her.

She slid out a box from under her bed. "Hey, this has been handed down to me for safe keeping. I'm taking care of it for now.", and removed its lid.

"Oh wow!", referring to a neatly folded dress. "Tammy, you've *got* to put that on! I'd *love* to see you in it!"

"Really?"

"*Absolutely* really!"

"Curtis made fun of me when I showed him a picture. He never wanted anything to do with it."

"And look what he missed out on Tammy. That stuff is awesome. Put it on would you… please?"

She paused a bit to think. Hers was just a small bedroom, and she didn't have a separate bathroom to get changed in privately. "Well no looking!"

Justin lay belly down on her bed as instructed. He couldn't help but smell her sheets, and boy did she smell good. He heard clothes being dropped on the floor, and his mind galloped ahead of him. 'Fuck sake don't turn round' – he kept repeating to himself as he lay there. 'There's your new girlfriend beside you… stark naked… but you can't look!'

For fun, she quickly swiped on two black lines across her cheeks, then wiped her fingers clean. "Ready?", she asked, and Justin rolled over.

"Holy shit!", he gasped, promptly sitting up. She was wearing a brown dress, that had tassels at the chest and the waist, hand-stitched triangles around the bottom. She had matching boots too, that showed off her olive-toned, super smooth legs. Feathers had been sewn into a white band of stretchy fabric she had around her forehead. This time, thank God he had permission to look at her, something he'd been itching to do. Finally, he saw her naked shoulders and he noticed how dainty and delicate they looked.

"Wow – oh wow, Tammy! You look *stunning*!" His words were authentic, and she knew he meant it. "Is that suede?"

"Yeah. We'd dance in this dress."

Justin saw the opportunity. "Show me how you'd dance."

She smiled, her eyes blinking left, considering his proposal – but she was already half-way there. Then she walked over to her stereo and pressed play on a cassette she'd inserted in the slot. As the music sounded off, Justin heard chanting and some tom-tom drums being hit. It was a real recording of a real event. Other people would have burst out laughing, ridiculing this whole thing, but not Justin. He was hooked instantly, and loved learning about other people and their ways. Who better to demonstrate, than his *almost*-girlfriend, super-sexy in her genuine outfit.

She moved with the music's beat, swaying her hips, moving her hands as she did, all the time looking directly into Justin's eyes, never breaking contact. The music was slower than he imagined it would be. Her moves were just as slow, and totally deliberate. It was erotic, and it was just for him. It was sensational – *she* was sensational, she was magical he thought, as his eyes soaked up everything. She *must* know magic – she was removing the bend from his manhood, and she hadn't even touched him. He clutched one of her cushions to hide it from her – fuck, that smelled great too. She turned around from him, still moving slowly and gyrating her hips as she dance-walked toward the wall, moving her hands in pre-rehearsed directions. Then she turned round to face him once more, and watched his eyes dart upwards again, meeting hers, as she slowly made her way back, directly to him. Nothing else in the room mattered. It was all for him. This was, by a country mile, the sexiest encounter he'd ever had.

As she got close to him, the music stopped abruptly. So did she, and this tribal dance demo was over, and she held her final pose for a few seconds.

"That was brilliant Tammy. Oh my God, that was brilliant!" She was like catnip, and he was a tomcat with three balls, on the prowl for a mate. It wasn't *quite* a lap-dance, but tell that to his weeping boner.

"That's just part of it. I'm not that good", as she watched Justin's head shake in disagreement. Tammy felt great that she'd finally done this. Self-mocking, "It's not all *bows and arrows* you know! And we *didn't* yell, Woo-Woo-Woo either!", as she pulsed her hand against her mouth.

Her mom shouted from downstairs to see if everything was okay, and they both burst out laughing.

"Yes mom... we're fine!"

Justin looked at his watch. "Oh shit! Tammy, I've got to get home. I've got to see to Belle."

She noticed the time too. It'd sped by so quickly. "I'll drive you home", she said.

When they reached Justin's home, she stopped the engine.

"Tammy, it's just been the best night. Thanks for – making it really special. I'm never going to forget that dance, you know!"

"That was a mating dance.", she added. "Young women would perform that dance to try and attract the man she wants."

She leant over and kissed Justin on the lips. Her passion matching the dance she'd done for him earlier. Justin was aware that they may be getting watched and pulled back. "Tammy, I don't want to rush things with you."

"Wow. No one's done that before – they all want to rush!" She felt she'd spoiled the night. "I'm sorry."

"But I do want you as my girlfriend.", he added, and watched her beam a smile. "What will your boyfriend say?"

"Curtis? He's not my boyfriend anymore. I'm done with him. I'm telling him tonight."

"Things will be different then.", he said, and gave her a quick goodbye kiss. How he'd yearned for her to decide that, and he was the first to know.

When Tammy got back home, she kept true to her word, and texted Curtis.

'Its over. I'm breaking up with you. We're finished.' The inevitable incoming reply text was on its way.

'WTF are you talking about? I love you.'

'I don't love you Curtis. I'm sorry.'

'doing this by text?'

'I've tried – but you didn't hear me'

'Are you seeing that Justin wank?'

Tammy read her ex-boyfriend's text, over and over. How can she reply? It felt like just a few seconds had gone by, then…

'Are you???'

'That's none of your business now.' Tammy knew this would go on all night, so switched off that phone. It had been a waste of nine months or so, but this had been a learning curve. There was no way she'd ever let another nine months of her young life get washed away with a guy she didn't want to be with, just because it was good for him. She had to think what was best for her, and now, she was sure she'd found it.

Chapter 46

Tammy took the following two days off school, just needing some 'Tammy-Time'. She appeared at school on Wednesday, all the better for her absence – but feeling sick about the prospect of being confronted by Curtis. She hadn't switched that phone back on, fearing escalation of his rage for dumping him, and had, in fact, thrown it in the bin – along with any feelings she still had for him. He'd bought it for her so he could keep in touch, but recently – he'd just been pestering her. Good riddance to it all.

Seeing Justin first, was a welcome relief and he asked if she wanted to go to the local diner that night, just to catch up on things. At school, wherever they went, was within earshot of scores of kids, but once at the diner, they felt more able to talk. Tammy asked why they'd moved State to Redleaf, and Justin just spilled it all out. Although he had a secret he hadn't yet told her, this expanding web of deceit he'd been caught in – simply had to stop. So he told of the trouble they had in Westfield, the kidnappings, the break-in and how his only grandmother had died. But he omitted certain facts. They could come later – if only he could find the way to tell her.

He also told Tammy that he received some money from the death of his grandmother, and he was, for now at least, keeping what's left in the bank. The money was nice to have, but it didn't make up for losing her, and Tammy saw that.

"How are you?"

Justin looked surprised. "No one... ever asks me that!", he said as the waitress rested burgers on the table. "It's hard to concentrate in school sometimes. I tell you what Tammy, the last thing I needed was Curt and his mob."

"I don't want to talk about him, okay?" She clearly didn't. Justin offered his hands across the table and she gripped them firmly. The strength of her grip showing Justin just how serious she was – maybe just how much that guy had hurt her. It seemed she'd seen the last of him, but Justin would definitely be seeing him again.

After their cheeseburgers, and sipping their milkshakes, Tammy opened up and told him about her father and how he died mysteriously while trying to call spirits one night when she was young. That's why she's been trying to connect with him, but she knows it's a dangerous thing to do.

"I never got to say goodbye." Tammy wiped a tear from each side. "I still feel him close to me, Justin. That's daft isn't it?"

"Not to me, it's not. Maybe he feels you too?"

Sucking on the straws sounded off that the milkshakes were finished.

"We've both had losses, Tammy. We're all gonna die sometime. That's why I want to live a good life. No regrets. Hey, do you want another one?", referring to her drink. She didn't, and it was time to go, but not before arranging their next date. Justin suggested an Indian restaurant in the city he'd heard was great, for Friday after school, but they'd have to get the bus.

After Justin paid the cheque, Tammy insisted she'd drive them there. It'd be the first time she'd driven that far a journey, but was willing to throw caution right out her driver's-side window. This was the new Tammy, and she liked herself for who she was becoming. After school, Justin arrived at Tammy's home by taxi on Friday for their date.

"Hey Justin – come in son. She's almost ready. I'll let her know you're here."

"Mrs Yazzie, these are for you, mam.", handing her a bunch of flowers with a big blue bow on the front.

"For me?" The gesture took her breath away. "Oh they're beautiful! Oh, son, thank you so much."

"You welcomed me into your home, and… it just made me feel good. Thank you."

Mrs Yazzie put her hand on her chest. "That's such a lovely thing to say, son!"

Tammy glided down the stairs, dressed in black jeans and a black halter-neck top and her hair tied up, with a few strands dangling down each side. Justin's shoulders dropped as his lungs deflated. This was the first time he'd seen her with make-up, and she looked sensationally pretty. She oozed confidence as she descended the steps, seeing Justin's jaw open.

"Are those flowers for me?", she enquired.

Mrs Yazzie stepped in. "Actually, this young man brought them for me!", still clutching them. "And how did you know lilies are my favourite flowers?"

"Just a good guess I suppose mam – a picture helped. Hey Tammy. You look… lovely." It was an understatement.

"Doesn't she just! Here, I'll put these in water.", and took them to the kitchen, searching for a vase.

Tammy walked up to Justin beaming a huge smile, showing she's impressed by his gesture, and gave him a cuddle. "I thought they were for me!", she whispered in his ear as they hugged, trying not to sound too disappointed.

"Sorry, Tammy. Not today… but I do have something for you too!" He fetched a bag that he'd brought into the home along with the flowers, and had slyly placed to the side of the sofa.

"I had to do a bit of research into this. I went to see someone who knows about these things. He passed me onto another bloke, who got me in touch with the guy that had one of these. Apparently, they're quite rare."

He handed her the box. "Be careful – it's delicate… and it's old." Tammy's intrigued hands carefully removed the lid, stunning her at what lay inside.

"I bought it for you to try to… hopefully, achieve what was impossible before – perhaps to somehow communicate with your father?"

Inside the box was a real Golden Eagle's skull. Tammy immediately knew its authenticity, like an art dealer would recognise a genuine Da Vinci.

"It didn't work before because it was a replica totem. This is the real thing. It's a used one, and there's no guarantees it'll work – but it's got to be worth a go, right?"

Overwhelmed tears spilled down Tammy's perfectly blushed cheeks. The very first gift from her new boyfriend was the most thoughtful and considerate gift she'd ever had. Over-awed and speechless in the moment, and so taken by the gesture, she didn't even feel those tears forming. She threw her arms around Justin's neck, soaking his shirt with them.

"No one's ever done anything like this before!"

"I'm sorry Tammy. Didn't mean to upset you."

"I'm not upset. I… just…" She couldn't finish – emotion stole those words.

"Hey, it's okay."

"You don't even know what this means."

"No… I don't Tammy – but I want to. Tell me. Teach me."

Tammy gazed over his shoulder and into a half-lost culture, seeing a strong tribal family care for the land and each other, with ancient, sacred spiritual beliefs and rituals – their ways so honest, so pure, so tough – so different to today's easy TV, fast food and cell phones. "Maybe one day."

She felt so safe in his arms, which felt as if they were all the way round her, twice. From the kitchen, Mrs Yazzie saw them cuddling, and chose to stay there. Her daughter's happy. For the first time ever, she's crying happy tears.

"You look sensational!" He'd kept this for her alone. "Tears will ruin your make up!"

She laughed. "Okay. Give me two minutes.", and ran back to her room to fix herself.

At the restaurant in the city, Justin sensed prying eyes checking out his date. She deserved it. Every direction he glanced, he saw a head quickly returning to face their own date. She was emerging from a girl into a woman, and although all dressed in black, she was no plain moth. Now immersed in each other and the conversations about the totem and what doors it may open – a potential gateway for impossible communications, they hardly noticed anyone else. Now she was that girl in the green scarf.

Safely home and back on her porch doorstep, Justin felt confident enough to ask her to go out again tomorrow, this time for a picnic, and Belle was invited too.

"It's just been the best night, Justin." Tammy leaned toward him, her passion showing through her eyes, displaying her eagerness for his kiss. Doorstep snog greatly accepted. And just like he felt her arms around his neck, he felt another presence nearby, but an uninvited one and it was getting stronger. It might just be an eventful walk home.

Chapter 47

"Hey gorgeous!", Tammy said to Belle as she knelt down and gave her a chicken flavour chewy stick she knew Belle loved most. She tutted an adoring tut. "She took it so gently!"

Tammy had arrived bang on noon, and Justin had already taken Belle for a walk, so she'd be okay for the lengthy journey. Both Justin's parents took to Tammy, and loved that she was just genuine. No frills, no bragging, no bullshit… she was just as you saw her. Her family was poor, but it simply didn't matter.

"Be careful driving! Have you got everything?"

"Yes mom! See you tonight.", yelled Justin with a reassuring smile from the passenger seat, just before the window slid closed and put an end to verbals.

They were only going for a day trip, but deep inside, Debbie already had feelings that this girl may well be the one to take her son away from her for good.

"Stop in here, Tammy.", Justin directed, pointing her into the gas station a few miles into their journey. "Fill it up."

Belle refuelled happily in her bed most of the way to the park. It was around thirty miles away, and was chosen so hopefully they'd not meet anyone either of them knew. Justin had packed a little bit of everything. There was cheese, biscuits, jam, pancakes, bananas, bottles of fizzy juice, and of course Belle's food with a few chewy sticks and a water bowl.

"Can you afford all this? That totem alone must have cost a fortune.", Tammy asked, lying on her side on the blanket he'd lay down.

"Money's for spending Tammy. I want to tell you something.", as he settled beside her. "My parents gave me $15,000 when my gram died. I can't think of a better way to spend some of it than on this."

Tammy was silent a few seconds, as her thoughts drifted to a place that stole her smile. "I'm not even going to say his name. He never spent a dime on me. Everything went on his precious car… clothes and his stupid, poxy tattoos!" It wasn't a sulk – but more of a reflection, and a hidden compliment for her new boyfriend. "It's real… the totem, I mean – it's real." She stopped petting Belle and faced Justin. That threw him.

"How can you tell?"

"I *know* it's real. Late last night, in bed – I *felt* it. It was as if… as if it was telling me something. Sending me… almost sending me a message to use it. That sounds stupid."

"Tammy, believe me – it's not stupid to *me*." Justin was desperate to do what his papa had told him to do and tell someone. Who better to tell than Tammy? He knew he had to wait until the time was right. Was it now?

"Tammy, I'm sure you have the talent. I'm sure you have whatever power or… ability it needs – I feel it in you too." He had to be careful not to scare her – this was just date No 2. "I suppose you just didn't have the tools before with that broken totem – but you do now. If you can feel it – I believe you." He got closer to her and gripped both her hands. "Use it, and you'll do wonderful things. It *will* work, Tammy. *You'll* make it work."

"You're serious. You're not making fun of me?"

Justin turned *very* serious. "Tammy, I don't do that. I believe you – 100%. I **know** there's a higher power. I've seen it with my own eyes."

Maybe this was the time, but Tammy seemed to miss that last part. She hadn't had anyone believe in her. Not Curtis, not anyone at school, not any of the teachers. The only person who'd believed her was her father.

"Do you know why I wanted to come here?" He'd allowed her to choose.

A simple 'No' was a cop-out. So he thought and guessed. "You've came here before… Your dad used to take you here?"

"Holy shit! *You're* the psychic one! He was a gentle giant, you know."

"Tell me about him Tammy." Justin was as eager to hear, as she was to tell. He sat enthralled by passionately recounted family tales of her father, things he'd taught her and amazing acts he'd achieved with his totem. Justin listened, showing respect for her father, and honing-in on how fondly she spoke of this great man. No wonder he had attracted such a beautiful wife. A quarter of an hour had whizzed by, and Justin could almost picture him in his mind.

As she poured some fresh water for Belle, Justin wanted to know something. "Here, what made you buy a station wagon anyway? Instead of a sedan, I mean?"

She laughed. "It was my father's car. He bought it as it had more storage. He'd always bring back something from when he went out. My mom doesn't drive, and couldn't bear to part with it, so we just kept it. Mom let me have it when I turned 18. Just as well, I couldn't afford to buy my own car anyway!"

"I don't care about that, Tammy." As he'd declared that instantly, it was fact. "I just love being here with you… and Belle!"

"I'm not used to going out anywhere Justin."

He knew she'd been referring to Curtis, but didn't want to say his name. This was *their* date, and this was *their* time together. Talking about ex-boyfriends, no matter how 'ex' they recently had become, would spoil the day. But she had to get him out her system, Justin thought. If they were going to move onwards, he'd have to allow her space to do that. And even if it was when they were together, it would be best to listen and be there for her. It might not be easy for her, and he thought she might need a prompt – one of consent.

"I don't understand that Tammy. He had *you* – and he never took you anywhere?"

"He made fun of me for having my totem… *and* when I mentioned about my dress. Come to think of it, when I spoke of my interest in other stuff – witchcraft… you know – spells, potions, tarot cards… he always just rolled his eyes and changed the subject. He thought I'd embarrass him in front of his friends, and he couldn't stand the thought of it. He was always putting me down."

"Wait a minute Tammy. He thought YOU'D embarrass HIM? He got that *so* back to front!"

The merited compliments she'd missed out on before, were now stacking up. Embarrassment began building in her eyes and she turned to focus on a sandwich.

"I'm *proud* to be seen with you Tammy – I *love* being here with you. I want to take you to the cinema or a drive through movie, to restaurants, to MacDonalds, to a mall and go shopping."

"Well *he* didn't. Most of it went on his car."

Justin remembered his Audi. It was a beautiful looking car – but Tammy was miles prettier. "I want to buy a car when I'm old enough – just to get about."

"Well – you can afford it! Sure he can, honey?"

Just then, it started raining. Time to pack up everything and shelter in the car.

"Come on Belle!", Tammy said, hoping she'd manage the jump in the back by herself, but she had to be lifted up, wet bum and all. They made it inside, just before the worst of it came down.

"Wait a minute!", he said, noticing a shift in the centre of gravity, and got out the car to have a look around. "Damn!" He brushed the rain from his jacket once back inside. "You've got a flat. Do you have a spare?"

"I don't know. Sugar!"

After laughing it off, they decided it would be best to wait until the rain stopped, but it just kept coming down, and the dark clouds made it look later than it actually was. After about an hour of solid rain bucketing down with no signs of stopping, Tammy had a suggestion.

"Justin, it's not going to stop. Why don't we just bunker down… in the back. We've brought cushions and a blanket – Belle's got her bed. We'll keep the doors locked."

"… and change the wheel in the morning?"

Tammy nodded. "Text your mom. I'll do the same. Don't want them worrying about us. You know what my mom's like!"

And that was them for the night. With the back seats folded down, they lay in the back and were a bit squashed, but it was comfy enough, and no one complained. Cuddled up together, with her head on his chest, they chatted all night to the sound of the raindrops hitting the car. Eventually, she'd fallen asleep, safe in her new boyfriend's arms and with Belle keeping her feet warm.

The following morning broke with silence, and Tammy was still in the same position as she'd slept in all night. Belle seemed to have waited until one of them woke up, before trampling over Justin on her way to lick Tammy's face. It was time for her morning walk, and they quickly made a deal. Justin made a start on changing the wheel – only after a call to his dad, while Tammy took Belle out on her leash, poop bag in hand.

Chapter 48

Tammy and Justin chatted all the way home, and they'd both texted their parents again to let them know that they were safe and on the way back. She'd had a great time, even though it hadn't cost much. But Tammy had spent more than she'd let on, and when they'd stopped at Justin's home, and Belle had raced inside to tell Justin's parents about the trip, Tammy fished out something from the car that she'd hidden from sight.

"Hey – before I go – I've got a little something for you."

"You've got something for *me*?" Justin knew Tammy and her mom were only just getting by, struggling with everyday bills and living hand to mouth.

Tammy opened up the door and, from under the driver's seat, she slid out a package. "This is for you." She was eager to see how he'd react.

He opened up the package, and found a box inside. A box he was immediately familiar with, and his eyes seemed to unwrap the rest while he knew what was inside. But it was still obligatory to open it up, and as he did, he sighed out loud. "Tammy, you didn't have to do that!" He gave her a massive hug of appreciation. "These are superb. Thank you so much." Then he comprehended just how much they would cost her. "Tammy, you can't afford these."

"I have some savings too, you know."

Inside the box, was a set of fine art brushes and inks. Justin was speechless as he held them in his hands. "I don't even know what to say."

"You don't have to say anything."

"Why?"

"To say thanks… for everything." She spoke sincerely. The price she'd paid for this was a lot for her, and she'd felt quite a bit behind, compared to what Justin had done for her.

Belle bounced straight towards Tammy. She was showing off a different chew stick that Justin's parents had awarded her. "Oh I'm gonna miss you, sweetie! Auntie Tammy see you the next time?" Tammy squatted down to pet Belle with both hands. She'd been a pleasure to be with, great company, a through-the-night guard dog, and a foot warmer. She was multi-talented and Tammy loved her innocent cuteness.

"Tammy… thank you. Seriously." He'd had a great time, and this was a special gift from his perfect girlfriend. "Hey – do you mind if I call you T?"

"Haha. Not at all… I think I like that!" Curtis hadn't done that, so she liked it all the more.

"You better get going. Tell your mom I'm asking for her, would you?", he said.

Curtis hadn't ever said that either! This guy seemed perfect for her. Some pennies just fit the slot. Some were designed not to. Her ex was the latter. Just out of a relationship, she wanted to take things slowly this time, and didn't want to rush and spoil it all. But then again, she couldn't treat Justin with cautious hands, just because things with her last boyfriend hadn't worked out. "Of course I will.", stealing another hug, thinking about how her mom would receive the unfamiliar gesture. The kiss on his porch was just a quick one, but a special one.

"Drive home safe.", he said, as she got in her old car and strapped her seatbelt round. With a toot of the horn, she was heading off to Mrs Yazzie, leaving behind her besotted boyfriend.

Later on, as Justin was walking Belle in the park, he received a text message from Tammy.

'Thank you for everything J Loved our stay over at the Hilton Honda! See you at school tomorrow. x'

'Loved it too. Thanks again for my brush set. WAY too much. WAY too kind. Will definitely use them! x'

Each were so eager to receive the next text message from each other, no matter what it said. Just staying in touch, and knowing that when they were typing a message, they were only thinking of each other as they tapped their screens.

But Justin had noticed that Belle hadn't done her business in the park, so when they arrived back at his home, he let her out in the garden while he tapped a couple more messages.

After a few more minutes he called her in. "Belle – come on sweetie. Time for bed."

But Justin saw Belle chewing something, and wandered over to her to see what it was. It was a different kind of chew stick that he normally bought for her, a much tougher kind, meant for large dogs, and she was just a little thing.

He prized it from her, and threw it over the fence. "Come-on baby – inside now", and closed the door behind them both. Belle followed him upstairs to his room and into her bed. It was now 'lights-out'. Bedtime was normally around half past ten for Justin, and Belle was becoming accustomed to the routine.

A few hours later, as Justin's eyes darted around in REM mode, he was awoken by whining sounds. Belle was in some discomfort, and letting her master know. He was shattered, and hoped she would settle down and go back to sleep. But she didn't. Her whining only got louder, and as that happened, Justin only got more concerned – and more awake.

"Belle… honey… are you okay?" Despite asking, he seemed to know the answer. She wasn't okay – anything but.

Justin became more worried and more concerned. What was up with her? Had she picked up a little bug somewhere? She'd had all her injections, as he'd read up on that and had made sure she had been fully immunised for a dog her age, and he was very careful about what he fed her.

"Hey baby, it's okay", he said in hope, trying to convince himself this was the case. He got down by her bed and lay on his side beside her, stroking her coat gently. As the minutes slowly and agonisingly ticked by, Belle gradually got less vocal and more motionless. Justin picked Belle up from her bed and sat her on top of his, where he tried to see what was up with her. He put his arms around her, desperately trying to protect her from any outside threats, but it was too late – they'd already beaten him to the post.

"Mom, dad", he yelled. "**MOM – DAD**", he shouted a few seconds later, as they hadn't appeared instantly.

"Justin… do you know what time it is?", his mom said in frustration, the first to arrive in his room. Mike had also been woken and alerted to the drama, but was hoping they'd sort things without him and he'd get back to sleep in a few minutes. Belle coughed up some sick on Justin's bed. She'd been sick before, but this seemed sore for her. And it smelled horrible.

"Justin, what's up with her?", his mom asked. She was now concerned, looking around for Mike to appear over her shoulder, but he was under the covers.

"Mom, I *DON'T know*…", panicking. "BELLE!", he shouted, as her eyes rolled backwards, upwards towards the ceiling." She seemed to be slipping in and out of consciousness. "BELLE", Justin shouted again, watching her eyes – her loyal eyes, roll to meet his, then collapse to the side. Her front paw twitched, as if she was trying to reach out to him, then it froze still.

"Oh Belle, no! Mom, call the vet."

Debbie glanced at her watch. "Justin, the vet's not open, son. It's almost three in the morning."

"Then call him anyway. They'll do… an emergency call-out, won't they? I'll pay for it."

"I'll try son. Get her to drink some water", and ran out the room to make the call.

Justin picked her up from the bed and carried her downstairs. With each step he took, his eyes were fixed on hers, as she flopped about in his arms lifelessly.

"No, Belle! Stay awake. Help's coming baby – help's coming." When he got to the sofa, he lay her on it and he heard his mom speaking on the phone, but he didn't hear her words. He ran to get her bowl and quickly ran the cold tap for a second and put some water in it. He'd only been gone a few moments, but by the time he got back, it was too late – she was gone. Kneeling beside her, he dipped his fingers in her bowl and opened up her mouth. He smeared some water on her lifeless tongue. "Belle – drink baby."

"The vet's on his way." But Debbie watched on hopelessly, one hand on her chest, the other covering her mouth, sensing finality.

"BELLE! Mom, what's happened to her?"

She didn't answer. She was fighting back tears and couldn't speak. Mike had heard all the commotion and had now joined them. Justin hadn't even noticed him come down the creaky staircase. Mike saw the empty look on his wife's face and the silent shake of her head. As he took everything in, he wished he'd got out of bed straight away. He knelt down beside his son, realising it was the end, and put his hand on his shoulder. The pain didn't belong to Justin alone. Mike tried to hold it in, but he burst out crying.

"She's gone son." Justin kept staring at Belle. "She's gone."

Chapter 49

Justin had stayed kneeling beside Belle until the vet arrived. The vet confirmed she had died, and there was nothing he could do for her. Out of respect, he'd only stayed a short while. He bagged a sample of her vomit and told Mrs Howard that he suspected she'd been poisoned, then he left, leaving nothing but a large bag and his condolences.

This hadn't sunk-in yet, but Justin knew that when it did, he'd be completely devastated. She was only in his life a short while, but she'd been gold. He'd realise just how much he loved her when it struck home later, but for now, not being able to blink, and with the vet mentioning poison, his mind played in reverse to last night. Poison? Was it that chew stick he took from her? Was this done on purpose? He snapped out of it and lept up. "I threw it away! It'll still be there!", and sprinted outside. He scrambled over the newly painted fence to the grasslands behind his home – but he couldn't find it. Maybe a bird had taken it? Maybe a fox or a deer? Regardless of what happened – it was gone now.

Tammy pulled up outside. She'd been notified by Justin's mom after dawn, and she'd driven over, crying all the way. She ran into the home and saw Justin on the sofa, with Belle resting on his lap. He'd cradled her for hours. He was still stroking her, talking to her as he gently rocked back and forth.

"Oh Justin… I came as soon as I heard." He was delicately holding one of her front paws, the last one he saw move, before she became limp. He was distraught and his T-shirt soaked with tears. She burst out crying, seeing the pup motionless for the first time. Still crying, she knelt down in front of him, and put her head on his knees. She was heartbroken too. He hadn't even noticed Tammy's presence until she asked, "What happened Justin? She was fine yesterday."

"She's gone Tammy …………… poisoned."

Tammy was stunned. As her muddled mind tried to think who would do such a heinous thing to a little puppy, she felt a shiver zap her body. She got up and sat beside Justin, leaned over and kissed Belle on her forehead.

He looked directly into Tammy's eyes, "Whoever did this – did it on purpose.", showing he already had suspect No 1 in mind.

She wrapped her arms around him tightly. "I don't know what to say Justin. I just don't."

"Thanks for coming." He tried to force a smile, but it didn't work. Then he realised the day and time. "You should be in school."

"I know. Took the day off.", wiping snot from her nose that just kept running. "Couldn't go."

She put both hands on Justin's face and turned his head towards her. "Who would do this?"

"I already *know* who done it. I *feel* it… ", he said. "… and I feel him trembling. He *should* tremble – I'll be coming for him."

"Justin, you're scaring me. Who done this?"

"Tammy – I've gave that cunt a pass up till now. Only because he's your ex."

"You think *Curtis* done this?"

Justin was desperate to tell her everything, but right now, just wasn't the time. He gently gave Belle a long kiss on her little button nose. It was cold. He knew he couldn't just leave her on the sofa, and had to bury her, and the longer he postponed that, the stronger that awful smell would get and he didn't want those kind of memories, so he made the decision right there and then to make a start. His father helped him get Belle into the bag and seal it up before he carried her to the garden and rested her so very gently on the grass.

Mike fetched a spade from the shed and asked Justin where he'd prefer her to be buried, then started digging the hole.

"She's going to need these." While Mike had been digging, Justin had fetched her bed from his room and her favourite toy she always seemed to drag about the house.

Mike sighed with pride. "That's a nice touch, son.", as he saw Tammy break down completely, and Debbie cuddling her. "Is this deep enough?"

Justin leaned over the hole and nodded a resigned nod. He got in and placed Belle's bed in first, adjusting it to make sure it rested evenly on the bottom.

"Are you ready for her?", Mike asked.

Justin couldn't speak, so he nodded again. With each thing that happened, he knew it would be the last time it happened. His beautiful, loyal pup… gone. Cruelly taken from him – for what? A guy with a grudge? His father lowered Belle down to him and he held her in his arms for a while, not wanting to let go. He didn't have a free hand to wipe away new tears which, by now were running down his neck. Mike watched on as his son tenderly held his dead dog close to his heart. Seeing his son grieving and hurting so much was torment, and he longed for this moment to end, but he knew Justin needed it, so gave him a little more time.

"Justin." It was a soft call. No more words required. Justin heard his father, but didn't look up. This would be his last ever moment with Belle.

"Just a few moments longer.", his son begged. They would be precious moments, as he recalled the good times – the slobbers, her devotion, loyalty, watching him paint, protecting him – even in his sleep. Then, ever so gently, he lowered her down to her bed for the last time. Caught half-way between feeling immense grief – and the full-on rage which would come later, his tongue didn't work. He couldn't find the right words to speak, but maybe Belle sensed what he wanted to say?

He took the toy from his back pocket and placed it between her and the side of the bed. As much as he didn't want to leave her, he had to. It was now time.

Mike handed Justin the spade and, after a reluctant pause and some deep breaths, the first load of soil went in. Soon, the hole was no more and memories were all that remained.

"She's… at peace now.", Mike managed. "Want to say a few words?"

Justin felt Tammy's arm cuddle his. She was there for him and he needed her to be. She gave him all the time he needed for this moment, and after a minute or two, he spoke.

"Belle, we were just together for a short while – but you were my best friend. I can't believe you're gone. Losing you was my fault – I was responsible for looking after you, and I failed. I'm so sorry. I hope you can forgive me. I love you, so – *so* much, and I'll never forget you. See you in my dreams."

His parents left so he could have the last, precious moments alone with his dog, but Tammy stayed.

"She was part of the family", she sobbed.

"She was brilliant… always excited when I came back from school. She never let me down."

Tammy tightened her grip on his arm. "She was the best."

"I never told her I loved her. Not to her face I didn't."

"She *knew* you did, Justin."

Raindrops started coming down. It seemed like a sign to Justin.

"You'll get soaked. You've just done your hair as well. Get inside – I just need a few more minutes alone with her."

Tammy nodded, and gave him a kiss on his cheek before running inside. The three of them watched on from the kitchen window as Justin remained at the bottom of the garden with the rain getting heavier.

"Whoever done this – made one huge mistake Belle. He'll pay for this – I *promise* you that. Sleep tight baby – I'll visit every day." He could arrange for him to be in a car crash, get beaten up with a baseball bat or fall down his own stairs. But broken bones heal in a few short weeks, and Belle had taken her last breath. The gloves were truly off, fists were clenched tight and revenge was called for. But despite having all this power, nothing he could do would ever bring her back. It didn't work that way. "I love you Belle."

It was a painful walk back to the house, and Justin immediately pulled off his wet T-shirt and dropped it on the kitchen floor. "I'm staying off school." Nobody argued. "I'll be back in a second.", and went to grab a dry shirt.

"I'll let your papa know, son.", Mike said.

"He *already* knows", Justin said – under his breath.

That night, after Tammy left, Justin stared at his chessboard. He lay in bed thinking how to make Curtis – the dog killer – pay, and he'd made up his mind. He didn't know for *certain* Curt done this, but he felt it deep inside that he had. This piece of shit needed put in his place anyway, so 'Fuck'im', he thought. They'd both dug holes in the last 48 hours, but Justin had dug his for someone else.

Chapter 50

Broken bones only grow back stronger, so Plan B was out and Justin had to decide on something a shed-load more severe. He now wanted Curtis punished severely and had racked his brains about what mattered to him. Nothing much, it seemed. But then it hit him and he'd now decided, and this would be long lasting. There was now an evolving, shady side to this innocent young man, and it was going to reveal itself soon. Curt had brought out the worst in him too.

With the day off school, it was time to get to work, and he'd spent most of the day, busy in his room, undisturbed by his parents. Perhaps they were aware of what he was doing up there. They knew he needed time alone so hadn't disturbed him, apart for dinner when they'd forced themselves to break the agonising silence, but it was *still* silence – Justin couldn't hear them. Chat was meaningless anyway – it would be for a while. Staring at nothing, he'd hardly heard them speak at all – white noise in the background, as he toyed with his food with a fork, glancing down to see Belle wasn't sitting beneath him – ready to hoover up.

His room was quieter than before, and a lot duller. The unique smiles he couldn't help but make adoringly to his new best friend – he didn't make anymore. He couldn't even force one. She'd filled his room with pleasure, happy just to be at her owner's side, obedient to whatever he said, ever-alert to his next command. She'd be sorely missed, and this was the start of lonely days again. Another dog wasn't even on the cards. Belle was irreplaceable – a one-off painting.

That was another tough day. A few days ago, he had Belle and Tammy in his life, looking forward to going places, doing something – anything. What was there to look forward to now? Both his parents were hurting. Tammy was devastated – she absolutely adored Belle and was great with her. Justin also felt his Papa Stuart's grief. He'd never met Belle, but he could feel Justin's hurt – and that *did* work both ways.

With one single hit, Curtis had taken them all out – like a bowler had spun a ball down the alley and made a strike. His time was coming – and watch the fuck out. He wanted to kill Curt – eye for an eye – but that would cut his own life short too. After a lot of thought, Justin had painted his work now. He hadn't benefitted from the calming inspiration from his ever-faithful companion, so had drawn angry. Justin had let him be for now, but it was Curt that had thrown down the gauntlet. Accepted. Gratefully. This guy was in for it big time, and he'd no idea what was coming.

His parents heard him crying through the wall as they lay in bed. He stared at the empty space he'd made for her, now just a hollow void again and it matched his feelings. He turned and looked at the painting as it dried, partly rewinding to fond times with his dog, partly playing out a merciless Round 3 and the turmoil it'd bring, as he bit down. He knew he'd pay a price again – but so be it. He owed Belle that much.

Chapter 51

His thoughts were elsewhere as he approached the school grounds – shorter, vacant steps being the give-away. Then he heard what he'd predicted.

"What's up… Just-in?" Turning around, he saw Curt snigger. The innocent shrug of his shoulders and silly look on his face identified him as the guilty one of the three sitting on a wall who'd spoken it.

'Fuck – me – running…' – Justin thought, '… he doesn't even need provoking!' This was a bonanza moment, one he couldn't pass up – but he didn't need to. Curt had already bumped himself off the wall and was menacingly heading over, full of swagger. 'He just doesn't know when to stop!', shaking his head with disbelief – good disbelief though. He was wandering right into Justin's trap, and he hadn't even laid it yet.

As he approached his locker, Curtis and his worse-for-wear duo neared him, just a bit too close for comfort. 'Fuck it – send it on!' His mind was ticking the first few boxes, and racing a few steps ahead to what was next. 'This twat *is* as daft as he looks.'

Curt wore a cocky smile, over folded arms. A smile identifying he was the poisoner, and he was self-indulgently wallowing in the level of pain it was causing, the best bit being – there was no proof and he'd never get caught.

"Everything good?", he gloated. But Justin restrained himself and just went about sorting things in his locker. "Aw, what's up?"

"Fuck you! You know damn-well what's up."

"Well, you've got me there!", Curt said, turning to his friends, smiling. "I've *no idea* what on earth you're talking about!"

It was now time. "My dog's dead."

"Oh, I'm REALLY sorry to hear that... ", came the patronising reply. "... and I suppose you think I did it?"

"I fucking *know* you did it... *and* you're going to pay for it too."

Curt started laughing, but nothing was funny. "You're accusing *me!* You little nerd."

"Laugh now... while you can... because later, you certainly won't be laughing. That's a fuckin promise!"

Curtis couldn't take a step backwards – not in front of his, so-called friends. "Tell you what, let's settle this the old fashioned way. After school – me and you. Over there, on that grass."

Hook – line – fuckin – sinker. An own-goal! "Abso-fuckin-lutely. In the park – after school today. I'll tell you what I'm going to do to you as well. I'm going to knock your perfect, shiny, white teeth – right down your fuckin throat!"

Curtis laughed, but it was noticeably tainted with concern. Being new to the school, Justin was an unknown quantity. Why was he so quick to accept his duel? Was he a martial artist or something? Justin was raging with fury and that made him dangerous. The scales of confidence were beginning to tilt in the underdog's favour – but he had to say something. "Oh, do you think so?"

"Enough talk. Talking won't smash in your teeth… but my fuckin fist will… ", gritting his teeth as he swore, and clenching his fist which was held up for the small crowd that had started to gather. Enough people to spread the word to a few others, who'd do the same.

It hadn't slipped Curt's attention that Justin had got the better of *both* his side-kicks, and left them wondering what the fuck had happened. So although putting on a brave and confident face to the kids and the lofted phones that had hurriedly surrounded them, inside he was wondering if he'd also bitten off too much.

But there was no going back now. It was set. But just to make sure… "… and no dodging the beating – if you run home to your mommy, you'll be forever known as the gay pussy that you are!" Justin made a point of addressing the crowd as he spoke.

By now, with just a few drawings already successfully in the bag, he was oozing confidence that this thing will work like the rest. So much so, he was prepared to make sacrifices. His own looks – his own safety, certain his plan – this untested *new* plan, will work, and he showed this confidence as he cooly swaggered away, knowing his nemesis would be watching his exit.

At lunchtime, Tammy found Justin in the dining hall with Ray and rushed over. "Justin what's going on? Arranging a fight with Curt after school from what I hear!" News travels fast.

Justin looked around before he spoke. He noticed that loads of pairs of excited eyes were on him, the volume of the hall a bit higher than usual, alive with gossip of this fight.

"Tammy… what was it that you… "

"That you've challenged him to a fight straight after school! Everyone knows!"

He hadn't planned for this conversation. Why wasn't she off school today with period cramps or something? This was going to be awkward.

"Tammy, listen to me…", leaning towards her, his hands reaching for hers. "Whatever you've heard, whatever people have said… I'm not fighting!"

"Justin – don't *lie* to me! *Everyone* heard you!" She leaned back and yanked her hands away.

"Tammy – I'm not lying to you. Please believe me. I *promise* you – I won't fight."

Tammy was confused. Her unconvinced eyes telepathically sending that message. Justin reached out to grip her hands back. "Tammy… don't worry about me. And after school, *you* promise *me* that you'll go home. I've *got* to meet him – but I'm not fighting. And I don't want you to see."

"You know he's mad, don't you?" He saw Tammy was shaking her head, stuck somewhere between what she'd heard Curt would do and what Justin was re-assuring her of, unsure what to believe. She knew what he was like. "Justin…", she began.

"Tammy – don't do this." He grabbed her hands securely, but gently. "Trust me. After school – go straight home – don't go anywhere else. I'll text you later, and I'll see you here tomorrow."

She was clearly distressed. She'd just lost Belle – they all had. If he was wild enough to do that to a little puppy, then what was he going to do with a guy that had stolen his girlfriend, made his friends look stupid and just insulted him in front of other kids – and the cameras?

"I've *got* to do this..." He twitched his hands so she'd look him in the eyes again.

The sound of the school bell ringing notified all that afternoon classes were now summoning their students, and classes would start in five minutes. As Tammy left, she left nothing behind but a faint scent of perfume, but in Justin's mind, her worry lingered stronger. What she didn't know – what he hadn't told her yet, was hurting her and Justin realised it. No wonder it caused so much grief for his papa. What he'd advised about offloading to someone, had been sound advice.

That afternoon troubled Curtis. Normally a decent student with decent grades, nothing sank-in during his afternoon classes. He was there – but not *really* there, as he played, and replayed the events of earlier. Someone was going to get the better of the other. That was certain, but before now, he'd been 100% certain he'd be the victor. Now doubts crept in. He thought of Sam and Zac and wondered what on earth had happened to those poor fucks. He noticed a girl next to him looking at his knee as it bounced up and down with the constant tapping of his foot. He hadn't been aware of it till then.

His positivity had diminished in just a couple of hours. He'd watched his teacher's lips move, but unlike the rest of the class, he hadn't heard a word, as if he had headphones on. Others had taken notes, but just as the final bell tolled, he looked down at his notepad to see what his nervous hand had doodled. He hadn't even meant to do it, but somehow, sub-consciously, he saw that he'd drawn what looked like a fence. He noticed others packing up their bags for the day and leaving to walk home, glancing a grin his way as they passed. Then it hit him. He'd be walking to the ring, to face a younger, weaker opponent and he'd simply have to win.

He bore the weight of scores of eyes on him, everyone eagerly smirking but him. Only now, with this fight imminent, did he feel butterflies. But he couldn't walk away. He couldn't back down. He couldn't apologise. This fight was on, and his enemy was probably already there waiting, and the crowd would be gathering in numbers, jeering, placing bets.

He just couldn't be the last to leave the classroom. That would look as if he was stalling – having second thoughts, looking for a secret turning bookcase to hide. It would look as if his belly wasn't really up to it, and he'd offer a gentleman's handshake instead.

He stormed out the room, jumped down the stairs and walked angrily along the corridors to the exits. As he approached the venue, he saw masses of kids. Fuck walking home – they were staying put for the main event of the evening. Excitement had been building, and then he heard someone shouting, "He's turned up!", realising they'd been referring to him.

The ring of people parted like the Red Sea, commanding his presence, and as he waded in, the tide of kids rapidly gushed closed behind him. Justin looked casual. It was Curtis that was the nervier of the pair, looking drowned as he noticed people around swapping dollars.

"I'm surprised you've appeared! I thought you'd shit-it!"

"Fuck you", came Curt's reply.

"Tammy left you because you're a fuckin loser. But she's happy now."

"Belle's not happy I hear."

"You should know – you killed her. Now I'm going to fuck you up. I'm going to punch your teeth out."

"Not a chance!" Curtis dropped his bag beside him on the grass. "Come on then!", nervously chewing freshly unwrapped gum, and waved Justin towards him.

Justin smiled, and walked up to his rival who'd made a plan of his own. He appeared ready to pounce, like the panther had been in his mind. But Justin lowered his hands as he neared, and unclenched his fists. His casual manner didn't fool Curtis though – not for an instant. Curtis clenched his fist and took a looping swing at Justin. It hit Justin on the jaw. There hadn't been a guard to get through. This was easier than he'd been expecting. Justin's head swivelled to the side, as everyone looked on, but returned to centre.

"Fuckin hell! Is that all you've got?" People started laughing. "No wonder Tammy left you! You ARE a pussy!"

Curtis hit him again, and the same thing happened.

"Fuck me – did you just *slap* me?"

"Fuck him up – Fuck him up", chanted the crowd, taunting the attacker. Curtis looked down at his fist. Then he stepped in and head-butted Justin. That dropped him, and Curtis quickly lept on top.

"Call me a pussy?", punching him on the face again, this time with his other fist, then again and again to the jeering crowd.

"Is that all you've got?", Justin said, blood now trickling from his mouth.

As Curtis's hands were becoming sore, he remembered what he'd brought with him, and reached around to his bag. He brought out an unopened can of Pepsi and held it up. With his other hand choking Justin he said, "… and you said you're going to smash *my* teeth in!"

"Do it – do it – do it!", the crowd chanted, wanting it, needing it. Nothing less would go viral.

"Fuckin do it – pussy!", echoed the taunt from below, through the choking hand. Curt didn't have to be told again, and he held the full can above Justin's face.

"DO IT!", ordered Justin.

Curt nervously looked around. There was nothing to stop him. No adults – no teachers, just kids jeering. He gripped the can tightly, then rammed it down, battering Justin's mouth with the edge of it. Justin's lip burst open with the first strike and squirted blood over his face.

"Call *me* a pussy?", he shouted in rage, and he hit Justin in the mouth with the full can again, and again, each time with force his teeth couldn't stand.

"Ha Ha Ha", came the noise from under the blood. "HA – HA – HA!"

Curtis was now doubting this guy's sanity. Regardless, he raised the can higher and struck again with brutal force. Then again. Then again. Then again, panting as he did so. Justin finally put his hand up to indicate 'stop', but he took a few more hits before it ended, more out of Curt needing a breather than anything else.

Justin turned his head to the side, and spat out some red teeth on the grass. Justin noticed that the eagerness on some of the crowd's faces had turned to dismay. Others were confused, frantically urging him to fight back. Then he looked up again. "You hit like a little girl!", he shouted again, blood all over his face and in his eyes which were wide open. Through the blood, he smiled at Curt showing gaps. Curtis screamed out as he hit him again with the can, and again, and again – all full force.

Justin hadn't fought back, nor resisted. People in the crowd had turned away. Some covered their eyes. One girl had been sick. "Right – that's enough Curt", someone said.

Curtis stopped as he caught his breath, and looked around. "No fuck it", and rammed the edge of the can into Justin's mouth. With his free hand, he hammered it further in. He'd felt the resistance drop as another tooth gave way. Despite punching it in, the can couldn't go any further, and his disbelieving eyes watched on as Justin breathed through his bloodied nose.

He took it out and watched as Justin coughed up a cocktail of blood and teeth. With two fingers of each hand he scooped some blood from Justin's cheeks and smeared it over his own – mocking his ex, as he noticed Justin's tongue swipe from side to side, searching for remaining teeth.

"Jesus, man, he's had enough!", shouted Sam. "You'll fuckin kill him!" Sam thought he'd have to pull Curt off him, but he stood up himself. Some skin from both fists were hanging off, cut by Justin's teeth.

"Well, I just knocked *your* teeth out, you little fuck!", and he got up, raising his hands aloft. But no one cheered. The savage brutality of it all was sickening. He leaned over Justin so he'd hear his final words. He rubbed the can on his jeans to wipe clean the blood and grass. "I saw your Pepsi drawing on the art wall… ", as he opened it up and took a drink after the fizz had stopped trickling over Justin below. "Nice."

Sam took Curt's arm and led him away. "Let's get the fuck out of here – the pigs will be here any minute."

"Is that it? Finish the job, pussy."

Those from the crowd who'd stayed behind were amazed. Departing others turned round. Curtis looked back to see Justin provoking a toothless grin at him. He yanked his arm free from Sam's and stomped back to Justin. "You just don't know when to stop – do you?" And with that, he raised his foot over Justin's face, and stamped down hard.

Someone had called the cops and sirens were now wailing. Sam grabbed him again. "The fuckin pigs are coming! Move!", and the pair of them managed to escape around the corner just before the cops arrived, leaving Justin sprawled on the grass, with his face a bloody mess. His face, his hair and shirt were now all soaked in his own blood and some of his teeth were on the grass too, but he softly laughed away to himself.

"Okay son, step back.", one of the Police Officers ordered Ray, who'd only saw the last few moments and had ran to his friend's aid once Curtis left.

"It's okay Officer – he's my friend.", Justin just about managed to say, still brushing the grass with his hand, trying to retrieve as many teeth as he could.

"Holy moly", the cop said when he saw Justin's face. "I'm calling an ambulance."

"Don't – it's not as bad as it looks."

"Who done this, son?", but Justin didn't answer. Neither did Ray, who was still busy nursing his friend. Silence blanketed the lingering crowd – most of them feeling shame. "I take it some of this lot will have recorded it?", pointing to the remainers and walking up to them.

"A bigger lad done it.", came a voice from one. "Never seen him before."

"Well he'll be online in a few minutes! Always the way nowadays!"

"I'm not pressing charges, sir." Justin was a bit wobbly as he got back to his feet, but Ray held onto him. "I'm fine. Honestly. Thanks for coming.", and started walking home.

The cop admitted defeat, and once he'd driven off, Ray said, "Justin, you're anything *but* fine. You're fucked up man!"

"Yeah, it's fucking sore!", Justin tittered through a red mess. But he was the only one laughing. As they walked, Ray couldn't help but notice the slight tapping sound that Justin's teeth in his pocket made, bizarrely akin to some change jingling around. Ray walked with him all the way to his home, not bothering a sod about getting blood onto his own clothes.

"Thanks buddy. You're a good friend."

"J – get yourself inside and call a doctor… *and* a fucking dentist. Want me to come in?"

"I'll be fine, mate. Get your clothes in the wash smartly – that might stain. See you tomorrow at school.", and winked at Ray just before he turned to go inside. Ray listened out for it, and sure as shit, he heard the screams from Justin's mom only a few seconds after he got in.

Before that door re-opened, it was time for his swift disappearance, and on the way home, he couldn't help but remember what his friend had said… '*See you tomorrow?*' See you in a *month*, more like!

Justin had told his mother he'd fallen down the stairs at school, and it was his own fault. The last thing he needed was her making phone calls to the school again – and investigating things. Fuck that. It was an early bed, and despite just taking the beating of a lifetime, he was in good spirits. Tammy had kept her word and hadn't gone to the fight, but she might have been sent a video or seen it online somewhere? He'd need an alibi for that.

The face he'd tried to shield from his mother's following eyes was throbbing sore, no doubt about it, but he had some wicked painkillers left. Underneath the blood, he was eager to see what the damage was. He ran the water and patted a wet towel to his face. Eventually, all the blood had been washed down the sink and he leaned forward to get close to the mirror, and opened up his mouth. "Fuck me!" Almost all his teeth were gone, apart from a few at the back. He knew that anyway, as he'd been talking like an old man without his dentures.

He placed the rinsed teeth in a circle on his bed like souvenirs – mementos of the occasion, but it was still a shock to look at your teeth from a different viewpoint. He'd only ever seen their reflection in the mirror before. He chuckled away to himself as he almost put them under his pillow, reminiscing about waking to find 10 cents. This haul would net a few dollars.

An hour after he swallowed the second lot of painkillers that robbed the edge off the excruciating pain of his almost certainly broken jaw, he slowly opened up again in the mirror. 'Holy fuck! It's working!', as he saw an array of little toothlings, just beginning to sprout. Phase 1 complete.

And as he lay in bed, he texted Tammy not to worry, and he'd see her at school tomorrow.

Chapter 52

Justin arrived by car on Wednesday. His overly protective mother had insisted. Even she couldn't believe how well he looked compared to yesterday. He saw Ray speaking with Tammy on a bench, both hands on his head, and sneaked up behind them. "Surprise!"

Tammy immediately got up and gave him the monster of all cuddles. "Jesus – are you okay? I saw a video on YouTube and it looked as…"

"… Tammy – I'm fine!" She hadn't let go of him yet. "Christ! Ribs are a tiny bit sore though."

"Sorry", as she let go, inspecting the damage.

"What… How did… Eh… Did you go to a dentist?"

He'd thought about making up some bullshit like, '*it's not as bad as it looked*' kind of thing, but it *was* as bad as it looked. That lie wouldn't work, and as much as he hated lying to her, here we go again…

"Yeah, actually. My dad knows a dentist and he gave me a set of implants, right there and then!" Justin opened his mouth so they could both see.

"Seriously?", said Ray.

"Are they okay?" His eyes went searching for Tammy's approval.

"They're… perfect. Wow!" Inside, she knew this couldn't happen overnight.

"I had the money saved, so…"

Tammy hugged him again. "But *you're* okay?" Explanations could come later.

"I'm fine. Nowhere near as bad as the video looked. I saw it too."

"But there was blood everywhere!"

"Yeah, I just bit a piece of my tongue!"

"But I saw him hitting you with a"

He had to cut her off. "Tammy!" With his eyes half-closed, "I – AM – FINE! Never better, actually! Told you I wasn't fighting."

The bell rang and Tammy was told to go, but only after one, last, gentle hug. "I'll see you at lunch.", and ran off.

"What the FUCK Justin?", Ray said, after she was out of sight. "You're a lying bastard. FINE – my arse. I picked up some of your teeth, for fuck sake!"

"They're probably Curt's! I got a few shots off myself."

"He jumped on your face!"

Justin pulled him aside. "Keep your voice down!", holding onto Ray's arms as he thought. "CHRIST!", he whispered aloud. "Listen… I'll tell you later on – but if I do, it's between me and you, right?"

Ray nodded worryingly. For Justin, at least 'later' would buy him some time to make up another bullshit, cover-up story. Maybe he'll just boycott 'later'.

"Fuck!", he sighed after Ray left. Quite simply, he'd *have* to tell him – there was no other way. Actually, letting someone in, might, perhaps, be a good thing.

When Curtis swaggered into the dinner hall, he immediately scanned the place, searching for Justin. He shouldn't be there. When he spotted him, sitting happily, eating with Tammy and Ray, cracking jokes together, he looked on in utter disbelief, as if he'd somehow managed to escape from hospital. This defied logic. Zac and Sam were equally stunned. They'd been there and seen the absolute thumping this lad had taken. It was as if yesterday hadn't happened – or Justin had a twin.

Curt's bemused face was working out why there wasn't a mark on Justin. Of course, there wasn't a mark on him either. Curtis cautiously walked up to where they were sitting. His perplexed eyes almost convinced him that Justin's doppelganger sat before him.

Justin gave Curtis a massive smile, showing off his perfectly straight and shiny teeth, identical to his, licking the top ones. He pointed to them and bragged, "Told you – you hit like a pussy!", and casually bit into his baguette. "Now fuck off!", and continued speaking to Ray.

Curtis almost said something, and he opened his mouth to do so, but he'd been stunned into silence. He was doubting what his eyes were telling him. He was doubting his *own* sanity now. Wariness was growing again. 'Who the fuck is this guy?' Zac and Sam waltzed over to gloat, but they were dumbfounded.

Noticing Curt still hanging around, Justin pointed with his thumb to tell the unwanted trio to leave. And that's what they did. He'd fucked with their minds, and won. He'd got the better of all three of them, one after the other, and he wasn't finished yet. And although he'd shown them the door, Justin didn't want them to leave completely. The real show was about to begin.

The trio sat down just a few tables away, and Justin noticed all three of them glancing over from time to time, still disbelieving their eyes. He couldn't quite make out what they were saying, but it didn't matter. He knew.

He could now tell the future and knew what was about to happen. The dinner hall was full and this would be the perfect time. Tammy was chatting away, but she didn't get his full attention – not at this particular moment – Justin's ears were elsewhere. His eyes flickering over to them from time to time. He was itching for it to happen now – right now, in front of everyone, and oh what joy that would bring.

He heard Curtis arguing with Zac over something, then he banged the table with his fist. That got most people's attention. "Who the fuck are you looking at?", he snapped, looking around to see an army of eyes on him. He bit into an apple, and Justin put his hand up. This was to shut up Tammy, and get her attention for the show. Curtis froze still. With the apple still in his mouth, his eyes squinted down as he tried to focus on what he'd bitten into. Very carefully – very slowly, he removed the apple from his mouth – but both his front teeth remained in it.

He was now looking at his teeth which were sticking out the apple. His tongue went searching for them, touching the large gap they'd occupied, and noticed another one was wobbly. "Fuck me!", he said, but it didn't come out right without them. What did come out, was another tooth. Understandably, a girl gasped. Then a few people laughed. The legs of chairs were heard scraping the floor as more and more people stood up to get a closer look. Phones got unlocked.

"SHIT", he said, becoming frantic now. Panic was the new look and he quickly grabbed the apple and collected the other tooth, in hope they'd get re-inserted. He ran out the room, with his hand over his mouth. He probably hadn't heard, but almost the entirety of the room was in fits. He'd got what was coming. If anyone deserved it, he did.

"So – *did* you get a few hits at him?", Ray asked, puzzled by the whole thing.

He shook his head, noticing Tammy watching his response. "Didn't touch him! You saw the video."

Once back in his room, Justin removed the black queen from the board and held it up, "And I'm nowhere *near* finished with you."

Chapter 53

The next day at school, Curtis kept himself to himself. A dim shadow of his former self, he wasn't cocky anymore, not showing off now, keener to lurk about out of sight – out the limelight that Tammy by his side had attracted. Yesterday, he'd left school immediately and had managed to get an emergency appointment with a dentist. Replacing his once-perfect teeth – one of the things Tammy had liked most about him – were emergency dentures, only for now, and until he'd decided on a more permanent solution.

In a few short weeks, he'd lost it all, and lying in bed last night, he'd reflected on where it all went wrong – and who's to blame. He'd never blame himself. He was now, hell bent on getting payback. Justin Howard was his sworn enemy, and he'd stolen everything that mattered. When he thought about Tammy cuddling or kissing Justin, it enraged him. He recalled the scorned looks she'd frequently sent him, compared to the admiring looks she always seemed to have for the new boy. Did she have feelings for Justin? She might just be a week or two away from telling him three words, words she'd never uttered to him.

He was still in love with her, but did she still have any feelings for him, even though it'd been her choice to end it? He thought if he could only get Justin out the way, maybe he could get her back. That would be a hammer blow to Justin, a stake through his heart. He saw the two of them again at lunch in the school grounds, holding hands as they strolled. She was *his* girl, and this intruder had stolen her. With his mind made up, he waited outside the school grounds when finishing time arrived, and made sure he was in a place where Justin would walk past.

"Hey shithead!", he shouted as Justin came close. "Rematch."

"What the fuck are you talking about?"

"I'm going to kick you into next week, you little fuck!"

"What right here, in front of the teachers!" Curtis turned to see one of the teachers who'd heard his words and had stopped to observe. Curtis walked right up to Justin so she wouldn't hear. "Okay. Tomorrow then. Straight after school, in Gordon Park, away from the school. No rules! This time, I'm really gonna fuck you up."

"Yeah, you said that the last time, bitch – and look at me! Then look at you."

Curtis paused for a few moments. Justin was toying with him. Why was he so confident? Why wasn't he scared, when everyone else he'd ever beaten up had been?

As he was de-coding, Justin said, "But you're on. Got to go – walking my girlfriend home.", and winked at him.

"What's going on?", Tammy asked as she arrived.

No more lies. Too many cover-up stories needed already. "Your ex just challenged me to another fight – and I accepted."

"Aw for *God's sake*, Justin. You *know* I hate fighting. I had too much macho bullshit when I was with *him* – I don't want that anymore! You said NO, didn't you?"

He stopped walking. "Tammy – I am going, but I *won't* fight him. I PROMISE." He already had a masterplan – something he'd buried, but now it was time to unearth it.

Rich boy Curt could get new teeth, implants or whatever, but there was no cure for this.

He was hoping she wouldn't quiz him much more, and their walk home wouldn't be conversing about her ex-boyfriend, or fighting with him. But a thought quickly came to him. Just as well, because he noticed she was about to say something.

"Tell you what... last time, I told you I didn't want you going. But this is different. This time, I *want* you to be there, and see what happens. It's tomorrow, straight after school, in Gordon Park – away from the teachers."

"Justin, I can't watch you get beaten up. If anything happens to you... "

"That's not gonna happen.", he interrupted. He didn't want her thoughts going there. His smile boasted how confident he was.

"Ray", Justin shouted when he spotted him. "Come round to mine tonight."

Chapter 54

"Please don't touch that.", as Ray approached the chessboard, undoubtedly to re-set the pieces.

"You… in the middle of a game?"

"Yeah." For now, it was the only answer he'd be getting. But none of this was a game to Justin. The board – and the pieces on it, was like an aide-mémoire – a simple display of a complex situation. Ray must have noticed that no white pieces had been moved. Justin couldn't bring himself to remove a piece for Belle. If he had – it would have been his queen.

"So what the hell's going on, J?"

"Sit down.", and waited until he did. Even then, it was hard to find the words to start. And after a massive breath and sigh, he was ready.

"Well you know what happened to Zac?"

"Christ on a bike! Yeah – he's fucked *right* up!"

"… and you know what happened to Sam?"

"U…Hu?", slowly recalling it. "Absolutely *riddled* with spots!"

"… *and* Curt?"

"Wait – with his teeth falling out?"

Justin nodded.

"… so what you saying partner?" He was suspecting foul play. "YOU? You did something to them?"

"… *and* Mr Wallace"

"Fuck me, yeah, he just went mental or something."

Justin shook his head as Ray was speaking. "He didn't go mental."

For the first time, Justin was now feeling a mixture of shame and embarrassment. How could he possibly tell Tammy the same thing. How would she take it?

"WOAH! Fuck-me, man. SHIT!… how did… what happened?"

What was the best way to break this news, and would his new bestie believe him? It simply had to be the truth. That's what his papa told him. A sigh started it off.

"You're not gonna believe this."

"Maybe fuckin *not*, dude! What?"

"I did all that." Ray looked on, quizzed. "I can make *anything* happen."

"You had something to do with all that?"

"No – I had *everything* to do with it! I *made* it happen, Ray – and the storm too." He watched as Ray's eyes recalled the storm's untimely visit and its rapid departure, and hunted for nature's explanation.

"Justin – what you saying man? This is fucked-up."

"Everything that happened – I done it all. I don't expect you to believe me yet, but you will. You absolutely will. Know how I'm fighting Curt tomorrow?"

"I heard!"

"Well there's worse yet, still to come. Listen, I'm not even gonna touch him, but he's gonna shit himself – right in front of everyone. Wait to you see it happen. I'm *making* that happen and Ray – it *will* happen. That's why you'll believe me, because you'll be there and you'll witness it happening – just like I'm telling you now."

"This is scary shit man."

"Don't tell a soul, Ray." It wasn't a request. He watched for Ray's response and his confused nod gave his word for him.

"Come here tomorrow – *after* the fight. I'll have something to show you. It'll be ready by then."

Chapter 55

The next day, Ray strode to school a little taller. He'd now been let-in to the inner-circle, but only half-in. All night long he'd thought about what Justin said, and none of it made sense, but all these things happening didn't make any sense either. Did his friend know magic? Or had he found a ouija board and had conjured up all this to wreak havoc on those who'd crossed him?

These things that had happened in Redleaf recently, were nothing less than chaos, and his friend was confessing to all of it! He wanted so much to believe, but he just couldn't.

However, the big test was going to be later today, after school. This was going to be mega. His friend had already specified *exactly* what to expect, and if things unravelled as forecast, then he'd have no choice but to believe. Curt shitting himself? Fuck off! No way! He was a tough-guy and he never even got scared, or showed a shaky hand or anything. If he shits himself, then the only diagnosis would be someone laxed his lunch.

Ray met up with Justin and Tammy for lunch and the three of them chatted about the showdown in the park later that day. Tammy tried in vain to talk him out of it, but Justin's smile of confidence revealed he was not concerned for his own safety. Ultra-casual he was, and Tammy just couldn't understand why – but Ray could. If his friend was, as he suspected, some kind of sorcerer, or wizard, then that may explain things, but come-on – *Justin?*

"Remember – after school – Gordon Park", as he walked past Curtis and the usual morons.

The school bell rang early that day, signalling the last Friday of the month had arrived. Instead of finishing at the usual 3pm, it was just 2.15pm.

Justin looked at Ray. "Showtime!" He was super-confident of the outcome in advance of it. It was as if Curtis had rolled both dice, and only Justin had seen the numbers. The outcome had been pre-determined quite some time ago, and Curtis hadn't even been party to the planning.

Masses of crowds had caught wind of the news and were making their way to Gordon Park, instead of plodding their usual route. Friday's main event – 'Justin v Curt 2' – wasn't to be missed.

Justin casually made his way there, heart rate normal, not sweating, not bothering about potential consequences. He'd been chatting to Ray about school-work and his project with Tammy along the way. By the time they'd arrived, Curtis was already there, waiting for his nemesis. He was punching his own hand, torso-twisting, warming up his shoulders for the match like a boxer who'd entered the ring first.

Curtis was madder than before. He threw down his denim jacket with rage, showing just how angry he was and how he'd mistreat his opponent. Justin noticed Tammy with a friend of hers, and noticed how nervous she looked. With a super-confident, and care-free smile, he walked inside the ring of school-kids and rolled his eyes. He looked up at the sky and smiled again. People in the crowd couldn't believe his confidence and the contempt he was showing for his seemingly unworthy challenger.

Justin spoke first. "Are you sure you want to go through with this? This is your last chance to simply walk away unhurt."

"FUCK YOU! You're gonna *die* today, dick-head!"

Justin burst out laughing. "Not from *your* hands, I'm not. Tell you what, why don't I keep both *my* hands behind my back at all times? Maybe give you a bit of a chance?"

Awkward chuckles sounded from all directions. Right then, Curtis put his hand behind his *own* back. He reached into his jeans shorts, and pulled out a raggedy-edged dagger.

"J – he's got a knife!", Ray screamed after spotting its dazzle in the sunlight.

"Of course he has Ray", came Justin's casual reply, turning his head towards Ray, but keeping his eyes on his enemy, as he began his advance directly to the action. Curtis tossed the dagger from right hand to left, with his own smile forming now through gritted dentures, almost foaming with fury, his confidence brimming over the edge.

"I hope you know how to use that knife. Cos I'm gonna take it off you and STICK IT ALL THE WAY UP YOUR ARSE!"

Curtis's smile sagged a bit. He wasn't *quite* withering yet, but Ray noticed he wasn't quite as confident either. Ray wondered – "Did he mind-fuck them all?"

"I'm going to carve you right up!"

Justin waved him forwards – then put his hands behind him again. "Well fuckin do it!"

But Curtis didn't move forward, so Justin started making towards him instead. Surprised at this, Curtis looked around at the onlookers. With the knife held high, Curtis began breathing more heavily, as weary adrenalin sped through him. Justin closed the gap, bit by bit, with his hands now clasped behind his neck.

Justin thought he wasn't going to get stabbed – he hadn't drawn this. But because he hadn't drawn it, doesn't mean it isn't going to happen. From previous episodes, things had happened that he hadn't drawn. That concept hit him right at that very moment, but there was no escaping now. The ring of excited punters had firmly shut now, enveloping them both. However, nothing good happens from never taking any risk, and he was ready to tackle this risk head-on.

Ray saw Curt's enthusiasm diminishing. But he couldn't back down – neither of them were going to, not in front of everyone. Curtis looked again at his friends who'd turned up to see the fight, maybe looking for corner pointers, but both of them had blank looks. This wasn't supposed to happen. Justin confidently edged himself closer, until he'd reached arms-length.

"I'm gonna fuckin kill you!"

"Yeah, you *said* that. And everyone heard you – and they hear you now.", egging him on, as he inched his way forwards, allowing ample time for the fatal strike to happen. The jostling crowd made their views heard, mostly on Justin's side, desperate for this bully to get some more of his own. With each movement Justin made towards Curtis, the blade got lowered a degree, like the second hand of a ticking watch. As he passed more of the crowd's gauntlet, those behind him seen that his hands were clasped tightly behind his neck, and he didn't have any weapons.

The knife was now at three o'clock, lowered to stomach level, the tip of it now aimed directly at Justin, but Justin continued his slow, inward steps.

They were only a single step away from each other, and as face to face as they'd ever been. Justin looked him directly in the eyes, and made to take the final step. As he did so, the knife pushed his belly inwards, but it didn't go through his skin. Curtis was the nervy one, and Justin didn't even look down.

"STICK HIM!", shouted Sam desperately, "Do it now!" Zac motioned a stabbing, egging him on.

"Yeah, stick me! *If* you've got the tummy for it, that is." Curtis gulped, sensing a trap but couldn't see it. Some traps are hidden. "Do it – FUCKIN PUSSY!", screamed Justin, both hands still behind him, as he'd vowed.

That was it. Do or die. He'd never live this down if he didn't do it now. He took a fresh grasp of the knife in his right hand, psyching himself up for the kill. The crowd were alive, everyone with different views, shouting different things. He saw people jumping up and down, desperate to see if Curtis would cease the moment presented to him.

This was his to take. Stab time, and it wasn't just a threat. His brain instructed his hand to take the knife underhand and stab all the way in, then twist upwards to his heart. But it didn't move. His arm froze, as if he was paralysed.

With his hand not doing as commanded, he made to take a lunge forward towards Justin and through him, but as he took that step, the knife didn't move and he stopped dead in his tracks, one foot forward – one stuck where it'd been. The focus from his eyes, which had been on Justin, un-zoomed backwards to himself and his pupils widened with urgency. He knew what had just happened, but the crowd didn't – not just yet. He gulped again, this time for a whole different reason.

"No fuckin way!", one of the kids shouted. People were looking at each other, struggling to discover what was going on. "Fuck me! He shit himself! Curt shit himself – and *he's* the one with the knife!"

"Holy fuck", another said to the sound of shutters, many filming it for the inevitable upload to the ever-hungry world.

Loose brown splatters of shit started trickling down his left leg to his socks. People were laughing, some were feeling sick by the sight of it, and by its awful smell that the wind had carried. The fight that was promised, was off, perhaps cancelled. Curtis acknowledged he was being filmed. This was utter humiliation. Times like these call for a rapid departure, but there was no revolving bookcase or trap door here. He turned and started trudging away, his shorts now visibly soaked with his own runny, loose brown shit.

As he approached the circle, people gratefully gave way, desperate not to get any of his stinking crap on them. It was disgusting, and he was mortified. "Grose!", said a nearby girl, clamping her nose.

"Nobody better post any fuckin video of this – I swear to Christ, you better not."

As this disgraced gladiator made the solo march of defeated shame out the amphitheatre, Justin made after him, but no one else did. They were all too busy laughing and posting.

He jogged up and in front of him and they both stopped. Now they were alone. "I want you to know something. *I* did this to you. I *made* this happen. Remember what happened to both your sidekicks? I did that too – *and* fucked up your teeth."

For the first time in his life, Curtis was now scared. He'd been bullied before, but this was different. He was truly beginning to believe Justin *was* behind all this. There just wasn't any other explanation.

"Oh! I almost forgot. Mr Wallace threatened Tammy, and… well let's say this – things didn't go well for him… "

"What have you done?", Curt asked.

This piece of dirt didn't deserve an answer – certainly not the truth. "It's *magic*!", came an overly-facetious reply. "Don't think losing Tammy is the worst thing that can happen to you."

Justin turned to walk away, but instantly turned back. "And if you EVER try ANYTHING – and I do mean ANY FUCKIN THING, to Tammy, Ray – family or any of my friends, I'll see to it that you shit yourself every single fucking day for the rest of your miserable life. It will *define* you. Understand? I will fuck you up *so bad*, you'll regret the day you met me. Want to wake up with a one inch dick to play with the rest of your life? Oh and by the way, tomorrow, you're going to shit yourself again – at *exactly* – three o'clock – just so you know I'm for real."

He saw terror accumulate in Curt's eyes, just as expected. "You've not seen my full power yet. You've NO FUCKIN IDEA what I'm capable of – you couldn't even comprehend it. You killed my dog – I felt it. And for that, I'm sending you to hell for a day – very soon. You'll not even know when it's coming… but *by Christ* – you'll know when you're there."

Justin observed him – like analysing another artist's sculpture, to register glimpses from other angles – register all the flaws in this case. "Oh, and don't like it *too* much – they might never let you go."

Curtis was speechless – sweating. He was glued to the spot – not from the shit that had made its way to his shoes, but from inflicted terror. This guy had fucked-up *him*, and his friends – and stolen his girlfriend too. Despite the knife that was still in his hand, he felt defenceless. Justin was inches from him, yet he didn't fear being stabbed.

Terror barged its way in. "What the fuck are you?"

Justin got right in his face. "A fuckin anomaly!" He grinned, even though he was admitting he was less than human. "I'm your worst nightmare. I'm the ruthless, evil guy in your scary dream that's still there when you wake up. Oh, and don't think you can hide among those bushes! There's no hiding from me, I can get to you *anywhere* – even in your sleep."

Justin turned and walked back to the buzzing crowd, holding three fingers aloft so Curtis could see his reminder. Their ovation showed that this guy had it coming, and it was appreciated that someone had eventually stood up to him.

Sam and Zac had departed, taking their dizzied minds with them, and realising their little pack needed a re-shuffle to find a new leader. Justin spread his arms wide as if to say, 'Well that was easy!'

Chapter 56

Once the stink had left, and after Justin had told Tammy he'd come round to hers later that evening, he left the park with Ray. Ray was now bouncing.

"I thought he was gonna stab you J – I really did, man!"

"He was never going to do that."

"Here, you should have seen Sam and Zac's faces after he shat himself! Oh homey!" Ray was still pumped, hyper with adrenalin shuddering its way through every fibre. "It happened exactly as you said it would, man! How are you so calm, J?"

"Wait until we get inside. There's something I've got to show you."

When they arrived at Justin's home, they were alone. His parents had gone out for a while. They went to Justin's bedroom and he told Ray to calm down.

"Ready?", as he approached the easel.

Ray nodded, not really being ready at all, but willing to accept whatever was coming his way. Justin grabbed the cover and flipped it backwards.

"Jumpin fuck!" Ray lept off the bed and walked up to the drawing. "No – fuckin – way! Jesus – the knife as well! Wait a minute – you predicted that?"

"Not *quite*.", he said. "I *made* it happen. Ray – I can make *anything* happen."

"Fuck right off!", watching Justin's calm expression. "J – I'm spooked. You've got to let me in!"

The two lads stayed in Justin's bedroom for over an hour, as Justin decanted everything. Telling Ray of all the history about this, the drawings, the pre-visions he had to suffer and of course, the dire consequences of his life expectancy cut short, actually felt good. However, this debrief was also a pilot run, an experiment of sorts, for when he'd have to do it all over again, and finally come clean with his girlfriend.

"Come on", grabbing his jacket, "I'm heading to Tammy's. Remember pal – not a single sole."

Chapter 57

Stuart had bought a bottle of Jack on his walk home. With his chequered jacket on, he ferried the bottle to his thinking chair and pulled it from the brown bag. No glass required – it's already got one, as he took the first few big gulps. He immediately felt his stomach getting blow torched as he rocked gently. This self-harm was nothing – compared to what's coming.

The liquor was helping him relax and his thoughts align, but in a while they'd be blurred as the bottle got lighter in his hand. Better get those thoughts in quick…

It was him who now felt ousted by the town folks. His wife was gone, and his son and his family had all fled this merciless, judgemental town, while Damian had returned there. Damian Keefer was their new self-imposed hero, seen to be helping to find those missing kids, and rescue them from whatever perils awaited. Stuart was absent, and he'd never joined-in on any of the searches, and that got people talking. Why not? Why wasn't he searching?

The pendulum had swung. Damian had been winning over the townies, vindicated by the court's recent ruling, and he felt welcome. If anything, the townies were now suspecting Stuart of something sinister, maybe even directly involved in the kid's disappearances, and they'd made their opinions clear when they'd spotted Stuart braving out – in a shop getting groceries or gassing his tank.

But this pestering, this finger-pointing from the angry mob – it had to stop. He'd recently lost his wife and although the shattering, suicide-invoking pain had simmered down with the passing of the weeks, a dull emptiness now battled against his every thought.

Since his wife departed, he felt as if the earth had stopped rotating, and while it did, and before it spun again, there was a stillness in the air, an ambience of tranquillity, and the currents in the rivers had stopped – not knowing which way to start flowing again. Everything simply carried on, but nothing really did. And before he allowed his globe to spin again, he had actions to take, and he felt a calling. Inside, his burning stomach was spinning too and he knew his actions would signal the end. It was time to fetch out his dusty easel and uncover it for the last time.

Taking another swig, and seeing more bubbles bounce off each other, snaking their way through his gold-brown poison of choice, he distinctly remembered snooping on Damian an hour ago, and had seen him parking up outside the bowling alley, and taking a little bag inside to practice without a care in the world. Since his wife died, he hadn't even known what fuckin day of the week it was – it just didn't matter. But this confirmed it was a Wednesday, and he needed to make a start. This wasn't going to end well.

This town could soon be plagued again, blighted with a generation's old, tit-for-tat feud, but the end of all that was in sight now – he owed it to Sarah. When he'd walked home earlier, Damian was oblivious to the forthcoming danger, rolling ball after ball down a lane, and high-fiving a new friend when they all scattered. His wife had been oblivious to the danger when Damian had cut *her* brake-line, and by fuck, that was tempting – but no. And as Stuart marched his way homewards via the liquor store, he heard a ball angrily smash the pins and empty the lane, then the typical roar of applause. He wouldn't be cheering for long.

Another gulp or two with the bottle upside down, momentarily mesmerised by more bubbles, watching them squiggle their way to the top – joining the others already there, their one and only purpose in life – everything's got a goal. He thought about his family's goals. They could all have a good future – but only once things were sorted, and he found his thoughts jumping to their worry-free months and years ahead...

He saw his son and his wife, cut loose of the chase, burden-free and happy at last. They were now getting on with the normal life they'd been robbed of, mingling with neighbours at barbeques, clinking beer bottles as they laughed to jokes and told stories their poison had dared them to share.

He envisaged Debbie finally finding herself again, her mind slowly returning to what it once was, before all this happened, now able to converse with people, confidently looking them in the eye. She's oozing the vigour she'd lost, after shaking off the listlessness that had clung to her for so long, imprisoning her in a near-constant state of lethargy. In so many ways, she'd benefited from those therapy sessions, and her inner beauty and humour returning bit by bit, day by day, to what Mike had fallen in love with. He'd been loyal to her and his wedding vows, despite all that deserting her. He just loved her too much.

He saw Justin and Tammy, walking through a park, free from danger, free from this world's wickedness, free from hunter's eyes, unchained at last and starting a future that only they knew. Papa Stuart wasn't going to interfere with any of that. Let those chips fall as they may.

These were welcome thoughts. It rubber-stamped his already made-up mind, and he watched more bubbles fight each other in their little race to the top – or were they all helping each other get there? How simple a life a bubble has.

One to be envied, compared to the shit that reality throws at you outside the bottle of dreams.

Then he imagined his wife again, the way she'd always been, the way she'd always looked, before her face got bashed in by the absence of an air-bag. Home isn't home without her, and he'd decided he couldn't stay anymore.

But as he closed over those sleepy eyes, he saw a figure emerge from the distance – one he couldn't place. An out of towner, calling on Redleaf with a tinged past and a score to settle.

It wasn't until the following afternoon, that Stuart woke up. The sun had made its way to the side of his home and the light had uninvitingly forced its way through some half-drawn drapes, drunkenly flung together the previous night – or morning at whatever time. Time simply didn't matter anymore, now his wife was gone. But today was different. For the last time ever, he needed it to be Thursday, and once he'd switched on the TV news channel and realised it was Thursday, he knew today was the day he'd finish his last ever piece.

It was time to soak up last night's liquor with the greasiest breakfast grill he could make, and an egg as well. And as he started eating, sausage among grilled mushrooms, beans keeping toast warm and pancake under poached egg, it felt like a blood transfusion. One poison would leave his body as another entered his thoughts. Time to get to work and make amends.

"Now I'm ready, honey. I'll find you.", and helped the last mouthful down with coffee.

Chapter 58

Damian had invited Mr and Mrs Preston round to his home to pray for their daughter's safe return. The church could only do so much. They'd turned up, and drank tea while discussing the areas the groups had searched. Ultimately, there had to be a point where spades were required and this needed breaking to the Prestons. A difficult conversation it would be, as it may signal the end of hope. He wanted to gauge their reaction.

"Let's keep going. Keep the searches up.", as he gulped down the last of his tea.

"Mr Keefer, I want to say thank you… for all your help." It was a tearful response.

"No bother at all, Mrs Preston. Listen – we'll find all three. I feel it in my heart. We've got Jesus on our side, mam."

"She's alive and well. I just know she is.", Mr Preston said, grasping his wife's hand.

"I *know* she is too, sir. Jesus tells me she's alive and well. Let's pray for them all.", suggested Damian, and reached over the table, inviting them to link hands.

"Dear Jesus", he began, eyes closed tightly, looking down inside them, "This little town of Westfield needs your love and your guidance. You'll already know that three of our little angels are missing – stolen from us. Their parents love them so very much, the way we love you…"

Mrs Preston tightened her grip as she began to weep.

"Families need them back – you'll understand. The town needs them back. Please provide us with the strength we need on this agonising journey, and guide us to success. Shine your light on us and show us the path to where these children are, and we'd be forever in your debt. Amen."

"Amen."

Damian kept hold of their hands just a few moments longer, as Mrs Preston smiled and said, "That was beautiful. Thank you."

"Can I use your bathroom?" asked Mr Preston.

"Of course. Down the hallway, and last on your left sir." Damian watched on as he walked away. It was a dangerous game, and while he was away, Damian considered whether or not it was time to propose that the teams start digging.

Chapter 59

Around half an hour before the end of class, the teacher butted-in, "Okay everyone… ", said Mr Henderson, alerting everyone with a single clap, visibly more excited than most of his art students that had bothered to turn up for the school's final day. It was the end of the week too and most of the students had party plans – some most likely already there.

"As you know, today is the day that I announce the winners of my *mystery* prize. There were some *excellent* submissions, and thank you for everyone that did. As you know, there is only one winner – no prizes for second place here!"

Although the contest was a fun thing, this final moment was worth waiting for. There were quite a few excellent artists among them.

Despite already knowing the winner, excitement filled his face. "Well, gather round then!", and waited until they approached and stood in front of the desks. "OKAY – drum roll please!… ", as he went to unveil the triumphant piece that was already hanging up as promised. Everyone tapped the desks, as he made his way to the wall. Tammy and Justin looked at each other, both smiling in anticipation.

"The winners are…….. Janet and Ray for their painting of a World War Two Navy battleship firing its cannons, with sailors busy about the deck!" He clapped in their direction. "Well done the pair of you!"

A clapping Justin Howard immediately went over to Ray and shook his hand. It was a genuine and heartfelt applause to a worthy winner. Everyone else showed their appreciation too, as they all took a closer look at the painting and the amount of detail that had been included.

"Well done homey! That's mega!", as Justin examined the piece in awe.

"Deserved winners Janet!", Tammy added, cuddling them both.

The room was busy with comment and conversation, but Mr Henderson interrupted it. "Right folks! This one will remain on my wall, and in exchange for that, and as I promised, there is a prize for the winners. For everyone else, you can take them home with you today. But for the *winners*, Janet and Ray, they will both receive personal recommendations from me, to be allowed into college – that is – should they *wish* to study at the School of the Art Institute of Chicago!"

A few of the students were heard gasping. They didn't think it was going to be a prize with such magnitude, and the applause started again.

"Well done the both of you!", the teacher added. "Right. Come on – it's the last day of school, so let's leave a bit early! Off you go, enjoy the holidays and best of luck with whatever you're doing next."

People started tearing out the room and away home. Justin stayed behind just a moment longer to congratulate Ray in private and to thank the teacher for helping him settle in the last couple of months. Justin told Tammy to take the picture home with her, and as they walked out of the school together, there was a sense of closure on that term, and it wouldn't seem long before another one started. As he walked home with Tammy, discussing the next nine school-free weeks and what they'd be doing, Justin stopped suddenly.

"No! Fuck no!", he cried. It stung him, pierced right through him as if someone else was holding Curtis's knife but actually having the balls to use it.

"Jesus, *PLEASE*!", he shrieked, falling to his knees. Tammy screamed. They'd just been chatting away when he collapsed, all excited about the end of term. She realised he couldn't hear her screams. All he could hear was this deafeningly sharp, ear-piercing, high-pitch squelch, but everyone else was on the other side of that sound-proof booth. It was like a dog's whistle in a million watt amplifier, and the mother of all migraines was charging to him right now. Tammy felt helpless, and her bag fell on the grass as she panicked about what to do.

A few kids gathered around. Some just walked by, clearly wanting nothing to do with whatever this is. They saw what he did at the fight, and this guy wasn't wired right. Maybe best to just stay clear and not get involved.

Justin immediately knew he was being sent a sign. A pre-vision of sorts, but it wasn't his. The noise started fading, and by Christ it had gotten his attention. Replacing the shriek, was an image, equally as appalling in nature, and as it hijacked his thoughts, his pupils slowly dilated all the way. His eyes were now like a shark's, all black and lifeless, and Tammy lept back with the shock it gave her, realising he was being possessed. He blacked-out completely, and his lifeless body lay on the grass. She called his name and shook him, but no response. She slapped him gently in his face, shouting his name over and over, but it was no good. He simply had to endure this show, and it wasn't for spectators.

Tammy stayed with him, shouting his name, and talking to him, letting him know she hadn't abandoned him. He could feel the gentle stroke of her hand on his, and heard her faint calling way off in the distance, but could do nothing about it. He was completely paralysed, numb from head to toe, and couldn't even speak now, being compelled to watch the show from beginning to end, in the privacy he owed for possessing this curse.

Tammy was trembling, as she put Justin's head on her lap, stroking his hair, feeling useless. Looking down his body, she noticed his chest cavity turn motionless now, and the back of her hand went looking for any signs of shallow breaths. But it never came. She screamed at the top of her voice for someone around to call a medic, instead of filming. As she did, Justin's eyes turned red – just momentarily – and she didn't see this – then return back to black.

A full minute had now passed since Justin took his last breath. He lay sprawled on the grass and hadn't moved. She carefully took his head from her lap and lowered it on the grass so she could start CPR. More kids started to gather, watching on inquisitively as Tammy, muttered, "One – two – three – four – five – six – seven – eight – nine – ten – eleven – twelve – thirteen – fourteen – fifteen, and she pushed down on his sternum with clenched hands, exactly as the school had taught them, then pinched open his mouth to breathe for him. Everyone watched as Justin's chest raised and fell, raised and fell again as she breathed, then re-started the count.

"One – two – three – four – what's happening with that ambulance? – seven – eight…" Justin wasn't responding. "Stay with me Justin." She took off her jacket and flung it aside. "… ten – eleven – twelve – thirteen – fourteen – fifteen. Justin – don't you leave me. You hear?"

Two more breaths, and fifteen more compression later, he still hadn't responded. She continued the routine once more, forehead sweating, and swapping which hand clenched the other. A schoolteacher arrived on the scene, and saw what was going on, noticing some kids looking downwards. As Tammy carried on, she heard the teacher ask something and someone replied, "About five minutes, mam."

The teacher watched on as Tammy gave it her best for yet another round. She would have intervened, but Tammy wasn't doing anything wrong.

Tammy paused to get her breath back after another fifteen heart pumps, and wiped her forehead, before blowing into him again.

"JUSTIN", she shouted frantically, and she started pushing again.

"TAMMY!", said the teacher finally. Tammy knew the teacher, and knew she wanted to help, but she wasn't giving up on her boyfriend. She'd already lost his puppy.

Another round of breaths and compressions, and breaths again. Everyone looked for Justin coughing, or breathing on his own but the only movement was his chest falling flat after Tammy's breaths, then nothing.

"Tammy – sweetheart! Tammy – he's gone." She looked up to see the Teacher, a blur through her teary eyes.

She wiped them clean. "NO!", she said. "He's not dying today." She put her hands where she'd been trained all those months ago, and started the routine again.

The teacher looked around at the other kids. None were laughing. None were filming now. All were respectful, and some could bare to look no more. She knelt down opposite from Tammy. "Then let me compress for you.", and took her hands away. "You do the breaths."

Another round started, this time with them sharing the workload. As the teacher compressed, Tammy spoke into Justin's ear. "Justin, don't you dare leave me – do you hear? I love you. Don't leave me." She was now pleading with whatever higher power there may be, and willing to swap her troubled soul for his. As the teacher compressed again, Tammy spoke to him – but not through words. She felt it in her heart that he'd receive her unspoken words – telepathy – or whatever, but he'd hear her voice. She told him something very private, wiping away more tears as she did.

After breathing for him once more, a voice was heard. "Coming through. Let us through" Someone had alerted the school and they'd ran over with a defibrillator. "Keep going", he said as he took the lid off the box and cut Justin's shirt open. He attached the sticky pads to Justin's chest. "Right – everyone clear", he said with authority, and his shaky hand pressed the button on the device. The machine repeated his command.

Justin's body jumped with the zap. It reminded Tammy of the time when Sam kicked him hard in the ribs. Nothing. The machine whined as it recharged, "Again", he shouted, finger in the air, "CLEAR!" Tammy looked on as the current forced his body to convulse again.

"Tammy", said the teacher. "He's gone sweetheart."

Reality was beginning to set into Tammy's mind too. "… No – *again*!", she insisted. "He's still with me. I *know* he is."

She watched on as the button got pressed again, this time with hopeless looks all round. He'd been dead twelve minutes now, as the shock arched his back once more. Nothing.

"Take that thing off him.", and she blew her breaths into his mouth again. Then again. Then another breath.

"One – two – three – four – five – six….. FIGHT, JUSTIN FIGHT", she shouted. She blew some exhausted breaths into him again. No movement. Nothing, as everyone looked at each other.

Someone had to call it a day, and they were hunting for the person with that authority, or the courage to say it.

As they were searching, someone shouted, "Wait! Look!" Tammy twisted around to see a finger point at Justin. She looked back at him, and saw his chest slowly moving upwards, starting to take his first shallow breath. Then exhale for himself.

"That's it Justin, breath for me!", she said, remaining kneeling by his side. "It's Tammy. Breathe!" Her orders were clear, as she placed her hand on his forehead, letting him know she was there.

His shallow inhalations continued for a few seconds more, hardly enough to carry oxygen anywhere but breaths, nonetheless. Then, as if he'd been held underwater, he took a huge gasp, then sat up. Tammy's T-shirt was a soaking mix of tears and sweat, but she didn't care a bit.

"What happened?", he said, noticing yet another ring of kids around him. For one moment, he thought Curtis had knocked him out at the fight and this was him fighting his way out a coma. A cheer went up and people started hugging each other, even people they didn't know. Someone shouted, "What happened? You fuckin died dude! … oh sorry miss."

Tammy flung her arms around him, instantly bursting out crying again, but these were happy tears. "I'll tell you all about it when I get you home.", whispering in his ear.

"Actually, Tammy, when you get me home, there's something *I've* got to tell *you*."

Chapter 60

"Hi son. Hi Tammy – are you staying for dinner, honey?", asked Debbie, as the pair hurried themselves through the door.

He answered for her. "We're not staying for dinner, mom – we'll be in my room for a bit." Justin took Tammy by the hand and led her upstairs. The instant she stepped inside, he closed the door and locked it shut.

"Tammy, you don't need to tell me anything. I *know* what happened – I know everything."

"Justin, you almost died! No – you *did* die!", sitting on his bed. "What the hell's going on?"

He sat beside her, and took both her hands in his. "Tammy, I didn't die – but this whole thing has been killing me. I needed time before I could tell you this. I needed to be sure."

"Tell me what?"

This was a difficult thing to express. It's not every day you tell your girlfriend you possess a curse. "This... thing... these things – these odd things, that have been happening..." He took a huge breath. "... that was me."

"You're not making any sense, Justin. *What* was you?"

"Everything!" This may not have been the ideal time and place to confess, but it had to happen here and now.

"Do you guys want some drinks?", shouted Debbie from downstairs.

"We're fine mom. Thanks.", he shouted back. "Tammy, time is running out. You've got to believe me. What I'm gonna tell you – you've got to believe me."

"Then tell me.", clinching his hands even tighter.

"Tammy, what if there's more than just good and bad? What if there's more than God and the Devil? What if there's something else – something in between?"

"Justin, I don't even have a clue what you're on about."

"Tammy… I'm plagued – with a curse. The fight with Curt, what happened to Sam and Zac, what happened to Mr Wallace… it was me. I set it all up. I made it happen." He went to his drawing easel and flipped over the cover. "Here, look." He turned the page, showing Curtis in hell, but unsigned, the next page back, was one of him shitting himself at 3pm, the next page was another one of him shitting himself at the fight, then he turned another page, this one showing Mr Wallace scalping himself in class, and continued turning to show Tammy all his drawings. He showed her his sketch pad too. "Tammy, these were all drawn – *before* they happened. Whatever I draw, happens."

"Aw Justin… come on!"

"Tammy, I *am* cursed. I didn't ask for this – I just have it. Think about it… Zac going skinny as I get a better physique… Sam going through puberty – *twice*! He goes spotty again, while my spots *completely* disappear – overnight!"

"Oh my God, Justin."

"I got revenge on them – for what they did to me. I got payback on Mr Wallace for what he did to *you*. And Curt? Well, fuck sake, you know what happened to him. That was for Belle."

"Belle?"

He had to tell her. "Tammy, Curt poisoned Belle."

"Jesus, Justin. This is WAY too much.", and made her way to the door.

"Tammy wait! You told me you love me." That stopped her in her tracks. "When I was on the grass, you told me that. I wasn't dead. I was just... away. I heard everything you said."

She turned round, confused but ready to listen. "But you weren't even breathing! You died!"

He grabbed her hands back. "Tammy, listen. I love you too – you must surely feel it? I'm crazy about you. I fell for you the minute I saw you in class. What I'm saying is true – all of it. When I visited my papa, he told me about this... *gift* I have. He has it too. Listen to me very carefully... tonight, there's gonna be a huge crash – a helicopter crash... into a bowling alley. Not here, but in Westfield, in Indiana – where I used to live."

She withdrew her hands from his. "Justin, what are you talking about? How do you know this?"

"I've seen it."

"That's daft Justin, you can't see things that haven't happened yet!"

"I can. I've had a vision. I'm not *making* this crash happen – but I can do that too. I know, it sounds terrible. Listen, I've found out I've being doing... Jesus... maybe doing the Devil's work for him... punishing bad people?"

"Justin, you're not making sense! If there even *is* a Devil, then why would he want bad people punished – if they are so bad? Surely, that's how he'd want them to be?"

"What do I know Tammy? Maybe they weren't bad *enough*? Maybe they were just *slightly* bad? Evil people kill – not one of *them* killed – none of them were *truly* evil, they were just… pricks." I'm just his slave on earth, I suppose – a 'punisher'. My *papa's* making this crash happen tonight. I saw everything when I blacked out. That's how I know it's gonna happen."

She wasn't any less confused, but willing to listen. "Why, Justin?"

"He's doing this to kill the man who killed his wife. It's a Police helicopter, and it's looking for Sarah-Jane, a little school-girl that's been missing there for months. They're swooping on this guy Damian Keefer, due to new leads. T, I know this is heavy. You see… oh God… when a death is made, we pay a heavy price. Tammy, my papa will die because of this. Whatever power he had left in him, he's used it up, knowing it would be the last time. He must have drawn this yesterday. This is happening in just a few hours – when it's dark. Time's running short. I've got to warn people."

"Christ, I've got a cousin there! Carol… and her fiancé, Stephan."

"In Westfield? Does she go to the Bowling Alley?"

"I don't know. Sometimes I think, yeah. There's not much else there. *And* it's Friday, so maybe?"

"Get her on the phone – you've got to warn her."

She opened her phone and started thumbing the screen. "What the hell am I meant to say?"

"Just tell her not to go. Or go somewhere else."

"No answer. Straight to answerphone."

"Shit! Fuck it! We've got to go."

"Where? Indiana? Tonight?"

"Now – *right* now – this is imminent. I'll gas your tank, but we've got to head off now if we're gonna make it. Listen, I'll tell you everything on the way, and I won't lie to you. I promise you that."

And armed with just a few sandwiches and Justin's favourite Pepsi Max, they started out on the four-hour journey east. Along the way, Justin kept his promise and told Tammy everything there was to know. There was no stopping this thing once it's in motion, and seeing is believing, and she'd soon see this for herself. Then, there would be no doubt. Although a sick thought, Justin needed her to see this happening so he knew she'd believe him 100%.

Tammy managed to contact her cousin and simply said she had a bad feeling about the bowling alley and not to go. Instead, they'd drive to her home, have the two lads meet up, and treat them to something special at MAC's Diner in Westfield around 8pm. MAC's was less than a mile from the Bowling Alley.

Chapter 61

Later that evening, after his hour long search with 'Alpha' group, Damian went to the bowling alley. He'd taken the sport up after his release and had bought his own ball and glove. This was a twice-a-week thing and Friday night was indeed the other bowling night, and a night he'd usually meet up with an old friend he'd shared a cell with inside prison. This guy, Bobby Meston, had got out a few months before he had, and on Friday's, they played for rounds of Scotch.

"Hey brother!", he said to Damian as he swaggered cooly into the alley, sporting his fancy new shirt. "Thought you'd called it off!"

"Nah. Just had, eh... some things to attend to." It was mysterious, but Bobby knew better than to pry. Damian was a bit late – but let's just leave it at that. During hard time inside, Damian had told him stories about the scores he'd taken down and the beatings he'd given out, some so severe that the average person wouldn't go into graphic details of the gruesome and agonising injuries – but he relished that part.

He'd told of the time he broke into a home with the owners still asleep, creaked up the stairs and entered their room, raking drawers, looking for sparkly stuff as they slept just feet away. When the man woke up, he cracked him in the jaw with the butt of a revolver he had, and told him to face the wall. As the old man obeyed, he reached round his neck and cut his throat with a knife he'd brought to open locked drawers. It was the sound of snapping that lock that had woken the man. His wife started screaming – but not for long. She suffered the same fate.

Damian boasted of the time when he met a random bloke who was just wandering through his neighbourhood, and had asked Damian for directions. After stealing his wallet, he started choking him, and continued until the burbles stopped. He'd already got the guy's credit cards and his paper, but wanted to teach him a lesson, never to wander through his patch again. It worked.

Damian had also bragged of the botched bank job, and the lies the cops had agreed upon that had, ultimately sealed his doom. He'd told Bobby of the time he'd hit a female bank teller in the face with his shotgun, but her nose hadn't shattered the way he'd thought it would, so he hit her again, even though she was on the floor, obeying orders. The next time he hit her, it was much harder, and that last blow shattered her nose, and her blood instantly started gushing. He told Bobby of the relief he'd felt when that worked.

"I see you've started getting in some sneaky practice already – before I turned up!", Damian added, seeing the pins get arranged in their uniform 'V' shape by the machine, forgetting he was twenty minutes late.

"I got you a couple of beers. Drink up, they're getting warm."

"Hey Damian, mind if we join you for a game?", asked one of the young Westfielders, with his girlfriend under his arm. "This is the guy I told you about", he said proudly, "… the one that's leading the searches."

And as the four of them rolled bowls down a lane, Damian was finally mingling with the families he once robbed. Stuart watched on – telepathically, from his home.

"You need a strike, pal!", Bobby said, and watched as Damian steadied himself. He danced up to the lane's edge, letting go of the ball with his gloved hand in the air, the rose inside it spinning like a top. The other three looked on anxiously as it headed towards the pins and crashed into the side of the head one. Pins went flying everywhere, except one.

"Damn!", he said, never liking to lose.

"Wahay! You're round!"

And as he got to the bar and ordered two rounds of whatever they were having for all four of them, he reached round for his wallet, but it wasn't there.

"Sorry pal – back in a minute. Must have left my wallet in the car." As he got inside his car and started looking in the glove compartment and on the floor for his wallet, he heard a noise from above. When he looked up, he noticed it was a Police helicopter above the building he'd just left, clearly in distress – spinning around in circles like his rose had been, and losing altitude.

"Fuck me!", he said – getting out the car. A second later, it plummeted straight down, and through the roof of the alley. Its rotors scattered debris everywhere, and a piece landed nearby. It whistled as it fell, and as it landed inside, it caused a huge fireball to explode. He heard screams from inside, but he wasn't going in.

Seconds later, another explosion happened, and the whole building was now an inferno, flames shooting through the windows that had been smashed with the force. Some people managed to escape, but not many, their faces blackened and cut. Screams from inside lessened, then fell silent.

Damian only had to think for a moment. Police helicopter above a bowling alley? From memories not too distant, he suspected what was going on, and shouted, "STUART, you missed me. You're fucked now!"

Tammy had picked up Carol and Stephan from her home. Although blood related, the cousins weren't related in heritage and Carol was white. While Tammy drove to MAC's, the four of them couldn't help but see the commotion in the streets outside. Police cars, fire engines and ambulances were racing to where smoke was bellowing from, their sirens screamed that a major incident was nearby. Tammy looked at Justin, and ominously told her to follow them so they could all see what it was – but the front two already knew.

By the time they got there, Damian had vanished. This wasn't a warning – it was a miss. This was a real attempt on his life, and he knew who, and he knew why. Damian didn't give a fuck about those inside – those who perished, not even his semi-trusty old cell mate. For only a brief moment, he'd considered going back inside, but only for his ball.

Justin gave instructions. "Don't stop, Tammy – just drive by. They've got all the help they need."

"Holy shit! We were going to go there tonight!", Carol gasped to her cousin. "You said you had a bad feeling about that place, Tammy!"

"Are you psychic, or something Tammy?", asked Stephan, his twisted neck staring at the wreckage and the fire hoses spraying water everywhere. Tammy didn't answer – she couldn't. All Tammy could do was look to Justin. This served up the proof he had to provide. Whatever doubts she may have had before, she can get rid of them now. Now, she knew he was for real.

A dose of nausea set in for Justin. Still, "Come on, let's get to MAC's", he said.

Stuart had blacked-out, but when he came to, he discovered he was responsible for the deaths of eight innocent people at the alley. All out for a good night, but it'd turned to tragedy. The Paramedic's efforts and defib had saved none of them. Many more had been injured too, but Damian escaped. It had been on the 10 o'clock news.

Stuart wept for those whose lives he'd changed. It would have been bad enough if he'd got Damian along with those other poor souls – collateral damage. But his one and only target walked free, yet again. He couldn't take it back and he couldn't sort things. It doesn't work like that. What's done stays done, and this was a mess.

Chapter 62

On Sunday, Stuart was surprised he'd woken up at all. Saturday hadn't even arrived, and Friday's carnage had ended a blur. Empty bottles lay strewn on the floor beside the sofa he'd crashed on. Now, there was only one place he could go.

Church may provide answers. It may provide solace. This may be a long journey to forgiveness, a place he'd never found before. It would take years and years, and years he didn't have. Still, if he was doomed to hell, then so be it, but he had to visit God's home first, while he had the chance to pray his *own* prayer to Him – nothing out their book. Tell Him his side of the story. He hadn't asked for this curse, any more than Justin had.

He felt a hundred years old now, and on his inside, things were much weaker. It was raining, matching his mood. He hobbled his way to the Church, a place he simply had to be. He had to pray for those who perished, and those who suffered, but he could never admit to arranging it. That was a step too far.

The organ was playing a hymn when he went inside, and people were embracing each other as they sang. As he found a quiet seat, he noticed Damian there, among the grieving families.

"He's the evil one! He's Satan!", he screamed, pointing a wrinkled finger straight at Damian.

"Shut up man. You're making a fool of yourself.", Damian replied.

"He *is* evil. You all know what he did – right?"

Damian stood up. "You've got it back to front. *You're* the evil one.", now stomping towards his former friend. "YOU caused the helicopter to crash – *YOU* did… and people died, Stuart."

Gasps were heard as people inhaled sharply.

"Don't listen to him", Stuart ordered the crowd. "*He's* the criminal. *Everything* he says is lies."

As Damian approached Stuart, he grabbed him by his coat, and they stumbled down the steps. "Right that's enough. Out you go."

But Stuart grabbed him too, and he wouldn't let go. "You're a fuckin piece of shit. Jail is where you belong, scumbag."

Damian instinctively headbutted Stuart. It stunned him backwards and he fell on the wet grass. "Just like old times then!", as he wiped blood from under his nose.

"You tried to kill me on Friday. But look at all the misery *you* caused. In there!", pointing back at the Church. "People are devastated!"

"It was meant for *you!*" This was the confession he hadn't intended to make. But it was only for Damian's ears.

This was all he needed and he raged up to Stuart and got on top. Stuart hardly resisted as punch after punch rained down. Damian noticed a few people now watching, as the Church door was still open but they hadn't ventured outside in the rain – hadn't ventured out to get a closer look of the 'changed' man. He grabbed Stuart by the collar, dragging him along the wet grass and around the corner to the rear of the building where no one ever went, completely out of sight.

Stuart turned over to spit blood out his mouth, and as he did, Damian reached around and put his forearm under his throat in a choke hold, and pushed on the back of Stuart's head, crushing his windpipe. Stuart didn't have the strength to do anything about it. He couldn't breathe and he couldn't speak.

"Gotcha!", snarled Damian.

Out of instinct, Stuart tapped Damian on the leg – a submission move from a hundred years ago. A submission move they both knew, but it was ignored. He tapped again, this time quicker and more panicky than the first, but it wasn't heeded either. There was no escape. The hands that tried to free himself, tried in vain. And as the seconds passed, he just gurgled. But the gurgling soon stopped, and his struggle fell away after a final jerk of his leg. Even so, Damian kept the choke on a little bit longer, just to be sure. Then, with his floppy, lifeless ex-friend in his clutches, Damian cautiously released the squeeze. There was no sign of movement at all, but the realisation of taking another man's life quickly set in, as did the prospect of going back to that prison cell for the rest of his life.

After making sure none of the Churchie's had followed them, he grabbed Stuart by the ankles and dragged him deep into the nearby bushes. He tossed him over and mounted him one last time, for a last, victorious look – a look for his old pal 'Howie' to fade away to. Perhaps a few more moments of life still remained in him? Maybe enough to take his final words with him, to wherever the fuck this cursed being would go.

"You took from me – I took from you." Drops of rain falling on his face via Damian's messed-up hair but perfect grin, would be the last vision he'd take with him. Although a few drops fell directly into Stuart's eyeballs, he didn't blink.

But Damian's head turned round like an owl's, his paranoid eyes now scanning around to see what his ears told him to see – to see what caused that twig to snap. But it was dark in those bushes, and the tree branches were swaying a dance in the rain and wind they'd caught. Damian's half century eyes had already witnessed a lifetime of pain and misery, hurt and counter-hurt, beatings and backstabbing. And as Stuart's paralysed eyes stared aimlessly into the abyss of Damian's betrayed ones above, gone was his usual expressionless glare. A sly, triumphant demeanour now counter-grinned downwards, hardly bothered about the trees – or what's in them.

Before he left him, Damian took off Stuart's watch, to make it look like a robbery gone wrong. He leaned closer. "And we aint even yet", he scorned into his face, then spat in it. Maybe they'll meet in an afterlife where a deciding round could play out. It was all a game to him. He turned him over again and left him lying face-down, to stare at the ground he'd soon be returning to. It was still pouring down, and he pulled some bushes over him, before making his invisible escape by going in further, past those bushes and through the forest trees behind them.

Immediately after Stuart had died, Justin began sensing what his papa had just gone through only moments earlier. This wasn't a 'pre-vision'. There was no chance of warning him in advance – not this time. This had already occurred. He'd been waiting at home for Tammy arriving, and as she approached the home, it happened.

Justin fell to the floor face down, and blacked out. He witnessed everything his papa had just went through, like it had been recorded especially for him. He saw and felt the strangulation first-hand that his papa had suffered only moments ago – but with a difference. No one is behind him, choking the life out of him.

Tammy rang the doorbell but there was no answer. As she looked through the window, she saw Justin on the floor, writhing about. At first, she thought he was kidding, but soon realised he wasn't as he got dragged backwards along the floor by an invisible man. Hysteria rushed in, and she yelled out as she watched Justin attempting to release whatever was around his neck – rope, a chain or hands that simply weren't there. Through his papa's eyes, Justin looked to the side, and saw Damian's grinning face – his forehead veins prominently throbbing with the physical effort, as if he'd been strangled himself, or had a tourniquet round *his* neck. This enforced re-run, let him discover that it had been Damian who had strangled his Papa Stuart – and now him.

Tammy tried the door handle again but the door was locked. She took a chair from the veranda, threw it through the side window, and managed to clamber through it. She ran to him – then he stopped moving completely. As he stopped moving, she did too, creating silence. Her ears were like radars, as they scanned the waves, searching for the slightest clue he may be sending her.

Squatting beside him, she said calmly, "Justin, it's Tammy. I'm here. Tell me what to do." She noticed he was breathing, but only shallowly. Being choked, he gave no reply. She felt for something around his bare neck and sensed a thick rope, even although she couldn't see it. It was tight but she pushed it over the back of his head, then rolled him over so he lay on his back with his head on her lap. She felt around for the rope, but nothing was there.

He was now unresponsive – but breathing, and she stayed with him until he sparked back into life with a massive breath. She noticed his eyes flip open, and they're looking for answers.

"Jesus Christ, Justin! Are you okay?"

Justin looked around as he came-to, looking for Damian. "He's gone, Tammy."

"What do you mean?"

"Stuart. My papa – he's gone. Damian just killed him!"

He tried to get up, but Tammy wouldn't allow it just yet, embracing him with a hug as strong as the rope. "You're safe Justin", she whispered, "You're safe now. Tell me what happened.", and the pair lay there while he tried to explain, finding it a bit easier to open up while not speaking this crazy stuff directly to her face.

One of the Church elders had realised that neither Damian or Stuart had come back to the Church, and after the service had finished and everyone had gone home, he went back to the Church grounds once more, with grave suspicions. He searched around, but didn't find anything. Damian had been too well versed to leave a body easily spottable. Stuart's motionless body lay on the ground, dragged well out of sight with some branches over him.

Eager to do the right thing, he called the Police and waited back at the Church until they arrived. The cops were interested in the man's story, especially as Keefer was involved.

"So sir, two men had a scuffle?"

"It was more than a scuffle. This was serious, I tell you."

"Did anyone else see this?", one of the Officers asked, hoping it was a no.

He realised that although he'd called the Police, there was no real crime committed. It was just a fight. But he had a thought. "Wait a minute! Our CCTV would have captured it." Leading the two Officers to the Church office, he rewound the tape and played it back.

"Look, right there!", pointing to the corner of the screen, before they went out of reach of the camera. It looked blurry and they'd used the same cassette over and over again, and so wavy lines spoiled the playback view further.

"Sir, this VHS *tape* recording…", he turned his head to his partner, rolling his eyes out of sight of the Elder, "… it's just too grainy! You don't have *digital* CCTV do you?"

"No. This is all we've ever had. It was donated to the Church a few years ago."

The other Officer intervened. "And you don't have any footage from another camera?"

The Elder shook his head.

"Sir, we'll take the tape with us. But if we can't make anything out, it's not really much use to us. Thanks for reporting this though. If anyone gets reported missing, we'll come back."

As the Officers drove away, they both chuckled. An old-timer using ancient equipment. "Fuckin hell man!", tossing the cassette in the back, "… they couldn't even use that shit for a break-in to claim insurance!"

"We'd get crucified again if we press charges against Keefer with that crap! Chief would go bananas."

"Yeah. Bin the paperwork."

Chapter 63

Exactly nine days later, Justin turned sixteen. Nobody felt like celebrating, partying, dancing. This wasn't the time.

"Hey Tammy.", as Justin let her inside. Tammy gave his parents a brief cuddle too, witnessing a more gaunt Deborah than before, noticeably so in her now prominent cheek bones, but saying nothing about it. This day should have been a good day. Rather, there was a cold serenity in the air, and it took over.

"How are you, honey?", asked Mike.

"Has there been any word on when the funeral is?", she asked him. "Whenever it is, I'll go with you."

"Take a look at this.", said Justin, and handed Tammy a card. "I only received it a few days ago."

"Justin, open up to Tammy! No secrets – no regrets. And I forgot to say, choose carefully – sometimes the visions can sting. I love you, Papa xx"

"Oh my God. He must have sent it before… " She couldn't say the words.

"Friday – for the funeral, love. Listen… we know he's gone. Justin's certain. I called and called." He was shaking his head in disbelief at the words he was speaking. "No answer. I drove over and used my spare key to get in. He wasn't home, but the TV was still on. Nobody cares over there… and you're *more* than welcome to come sweetheart.", attempting a smile.

"It's the last time I'm going back.", said Deborah to the floor. She didn't need to say why. There were just too many bad memories. They were jinxed in that town. To her, it felt like the very streets themselves had debated and arranged their demise and lit the touch-paper, secretly watching how it all sparked off from the cover of darkness. Whatever it was, the Howards just weren't a good fit for Westfield, and they were better off away from it. Going back, sent shivers through her existence and Justin saw it all. He'd seen her fears growing over the last week, and noticed she'd steadily gotten worse. She'd hardly eaten a thing in the realisation that she'd have to go back.

Tammy carefully handed the card back. "I'll definitely go.", forcing a return smile for Mike. "Here, I got you this for your birthday.", and gave Justin a box covered in wrapping paper, with a tag that simply read, 'Love from Tammy X'. Justin opened it immediately. Inside was a book, and he read to his parents… "*How to take your painting to the next level*. Thank you Tammy." She didn't have much money, and this was a faultless gift.

"Oh, and I got you these too." From her pocket, she took out a small packet of fine soft drawing pastels. "The man said these will enable you to see things from a whole different perspective."

"Oh, Jesus Tammy! Mom, they're *Rembrandt* pastels!", tilting the box her way. "Tammy, you can't afford these! *I* can't afford these!" He hugged her tightly, unashamed that his parents were there.

Justin took Tammy up to his room, realising both couples were needing some privacy. Tammy had made provisional arrangements for her and Justin to stay over with her cousin in Westfield after the funeral, and complete the journey back home the following day, and told Justin she'd take her car again. Once confirmed, she just needed to text Carol the day they'd arrive, and she did that immediately.

For the next three days, Justin didn't see Tammy again, but had texted her in the evenings. Her arrival on Friday morning astonished him. The usual, casually-dressed Tammy, had transformed effortlessly into a stunning beauty. His eyes scanned her from top to bottom without her permission, but it was okay. She wore a long black dress, and her straight, glossy hair hung down around its tight neck and over her narrow shoulders that Justin adored. She had small silver earrings on, the first time Justin had seen her wear any. The dress's arms were cut off at three quarters, showing half her forearms, and a dainty little watch of her mom's. She wore plain black shoes, with a small heel. From their conversations, she knew Justin hated pumps, and she knew he hated lots of make-up, so she'd kept that to a minimum.

"Tammy. Wow! You look *stunning*." And he meant it. This was his girlfriend standing before him, looking as if she'd just stepped out of a stretch limo and onto the red carpet, on her way to the Oscars with paparazzi jostling for prime position, flashes pulsing from all directions, as they called her name. If he hadn't fully realised it before, he did now, and it was actually a worry. She was an 'A' lister, and he was nothing. All she needed was a diamond necklace and a film star on her arm. She was *way* too pretty for a guy like him – a nobody with troubles and a dodgy past creeping up on him. This could just be a short-lived romance, until she inevitably coupled up with someone actually worthy of her – it certainly wasn't him. This fantasy may soon be over, and that was tough to take. He dug this girl so much, that he didn't even want to think about a time when all he had left, were memories.

She looked at him as he eyed her. She'd never seen him in anything apart from school uniform, jeans or casual stuff, so seeing this young man in a dark suit was a bit strange, but her growing smile revealed he was winning her approval.

Justin had told his parents their plans to travel in Tammy's car, and that they'd be staying over with her cousin for a night. Among all this misery, this would be good for him and they knew how much Tammy meant to him. His bag was already packed, and he placed it right beside hers in the trunk.

The two cars set off on the four hour journey, for what they hoped would be the very last time in their old hometown. As Tammy followed Mike's car along the way, she and Justin spoke fondly of his papa and he recalled the best times he had with him, from bouncy castle and trampolines, train sets, weekend get-aways to the fishing trips – he didn't have a bad word to say. The journey seemed quicker than it was, but it was still late-afternoon when they arrived at the crematorium.

As Justin got out of the car, he immediately felt a strange feeling. He heard a buzzing noise and felt a presence like never before. This surrounded him. It was all over him, all around him, even inside him. He felt wobbly on his feet. A newborn mountain billy-goat had got out the car, but with vertigo, and Tammy had to steady him.

"Are you feeling OKAY?"

He lied. "Yeah, I'm fine. Sitting down too long!" He looked around him, but there was no one there. Were his eyes deceiving him?

"Justin!", Tammy said, prompting him.

"Yeah, I'm – I'm coming." His hard blink didn't make any difference, but as he made his way inside, the buzzing receded. Tammy sat beside him, holding his arm.

When the service started, no townies had turned up for the event. It would seem that the folk of Westfield hadn't been informed, or got the days mixed up. Maybe they were in fear? There was a mixture of disgust for these people for their no-show, and anger for wrongly accusing this family for the sickening events that happened there, but it rang a truth bell. Although appalling, Deborah realised a benefit, because if people had turned up, then she'd be compelled to converse with them again, thank them for coming and all that stuff and she just wanted to get this done and leave town, and she wouldn't feel safe until they were in the car heading west.

Tammy grabbed Justin's hand as the celebrant began speaking the committal readings, as pre-arranged by Mike and Deborah.

Justin knew his parents back to front, and knew neither of them would be able to speak, and he'd prepared a eulogy in tribute to his papa – missing, but known to be dead. This thing had bonded them closer, and he'd only recently discovered it.

"Papa", he started, "You were the best papa ever to me. You were a man of principles and you always told the truth, and taught me to do the same, even if it got me in bother. When I needed you, you were always there for me, and I know you'll still be there. Only recently, I discovered that we're connected in ways others can't even begin to comprehend. I want you to know I got your card. Those were wise words indeed, and I know exactly what you meant. You have my word, and trust me that I will keep my promises. Rest now, and guide me from above."

He stepped back and held Tammy's hand, detecting it was wet with tears she'd wiped away. In less than an hour, it was all over, and a milestone had been reached. Something significant had ended, but stepping into the fresh air outside, Justin knew his time was only beginning. He now felt as if the baton had been passed to him. There just aren't words for this precise moment, and the worry his parents borne for him went unsaid. But as they held that embrace with each other outside the crematorium, he heard their thoughts.

And after telling Tammy to drive safe, they set about their onward journeys. Another foursome with Carol and Stephan had already been arranged and they went to a newly opened Chinese restaurant that had been given great reviews. A taxi would enable them all to have a couple of drinks first, and maybe one at the Chinese, unless the waiter asked for identification.

Before they met up with Tammy's cousin, they'd made a pledge. A compact detailing that chat about spirits or magic was off the table and out of bounds. It would only lead to darker paths. He'd let his girlfriend into his family secret, and in contrast to the rice and crackers, this wasn't for sharing. After all, who wants to hear about how Justin single-handedly fucked-up three, older school bullies, sending all three of them home crying to their mamas? Who wants to hear Justin retelling freshly made tales of unfathomable witchcraft and spells that he'd cast, wreaking revenge on three of the worst bullies the school had ever seen, inflicting all of them – and a pervert teacher – with life-changing illnesses? Far from keeping the chit chat going, that's a conversation stopper. No one wants to know they're sitting next to someone who could do the same to them, should they dare to cross him?

Plan 'A' was to have a better night. A night where secrets remained that way. A tipsy night where everyone is relaxed, chilled and giggling, talking about nothing in particular, and that wouldn't happen if the truth got out. The stopper was firmly on the facts bottle and it couldn't get spilled, at any cost. Freshly washed and changed after his papa's funeral, it was time to relax and unwind, yet he couldn't. Justin had to have his guard up at all times.

And as he sat and nibbled away at the chicken curry and duck spring rolls he'd ordered, he listened-in, but kept mostly out of the conversations, occasionally adding the odd token remark, in agreement with the others. As the food piles dropped and belts tightened, reality set in. This would be an act he'd have to keep up his entire life, the way his own papa had.

But right now, he was more than happy just to listen and learn about how his girlfriend and Carol had grown up, meeting occasionally, mainly at family get-togethers and weddings and how the naughty pair escaped the adults and played together.

At that table, he discovered a younger Tammy. A pure and innocent girl, who'd never even noticed the discriminatory remarks some adults had made – and other kids. The taunts from kids, remarks and jokes not punished by their parents – not punished by teachers. The remarks from other parents, the gestures – not allowing their child to mix, not challenged by their spouse. The near empty birthday party Tammy had, and the lack of invites to others? Oblivious to it all? Or rode the storm with class, with dignity – the young lady she'd grown into? Tammy was proud of her roots, but as a youngster growing up in the nineties and noughties, things were said, cruel things. People had judged her and her family, discriminated against them and shunned them, making fun of them all whenever the opportunity arose and her father had absorbed everything, protecting them like the great man she said he was. With him gone, Tammy had grown strong. She'd stood up to Mr Wallace in front of the entire class – done it with her head held high despite a few background sniggers. With a childhood of taunting, it sounded as if she should have been living in shame instead of pride – the pride for being who you are, pride for not fighting back, pride for remaining, the pride for not changing just to 'belong'. Right there, he felt an immense pride for belonging to her – being her boyfriend. Now, he was the one carrying shame, embarrassed for his ancestors who'd tormented minorities for as long as history tells us – regardless of who they are – regardless of what they are, just because they're not one of the bigger group. The greatest shame of all, lives on the other side. Bigger group shame he didn't ask for, but combined with this curse he didn't ask for, and all the secret baggage *that* came with that he'd never be able to put down, it was nothing compared to what Tammy and her family had endured. If only we could swap – and see it – live it – endure it from their side, then maybe one day things might change?

Listening to the girls reminiscing fondly about yesteryear, recalling stories of pranks they'd done together, something sinister arrived on his plate and it wasn't the fortune cookie he hadn't opened. This stared him right in the face. It shouted to him that this town wasn't jinxed. They were all having a nice time. His new town of Redleaf, where all the recent shit had just gone down, well it wasn't jinxed either. Both towns were just the same – it's the people in them that make it what it is. They make the town a place you want to be or a place you want to be leaving. The towns weren't bad. His family possessed a curse and it had been the Howards that had damned it for everyone. Now Justin bore that sole responsibility. All by himself, he'd taken the bait and had spread evil in Redleaf, leaving the locals stuck in a conundrum.

And no matter where he went, he'd bring that same doom with him, fucking each virgin town, contaminating them all like a plague. Tammy was smart – smarter than he was and smart enough to eventually cotton-on to this. He dreaded the day when she finally twigged, and knew she'd be off. No wonder his papa kept this to himself. Maybe his earlier confession to Tammy had been hasty?

Chapter 64

Tammy and Justin got the spare room to themselves. Her older cousin's apartment only had two bedrooms, and they'd moved there when things had got serious between her and Stephan just under a year earlier. Upon their arrival back at the apartment after the Chinese, they'd all enjoyed another drink and a few laughs – the boys got on well. With everything that had gone on that day, it never really grabbed Justin's thoughts until now, but the single bed, with two pillows seemed to be standing out, demanding answers to the question they both were now considering.

Apart from the fact that it wasn't really big enough for the both of them, they'd only been dating a few weeks and weren't at that stage yet. It hadn't even been discussed, and as Tammy began undressing, ready for her pyjamas, Justin fought against himself not to look. As he turned away, holding onto a chair, she noticed his eyes peeking at her in Carol's make-up mirror that was on the bedside table.

"Justin! Are you watching me?" Her smooth velvet tone gave up the fact that she knew fine he was. Caught, red handed and guilty as charged. He froze, awaiting his sentence, ensuring he didn't look at the mirror again. "It's okay to turn round babe." Seriously? Bingo! The green light he craved had finally illuminated. And as he slowly turned and saw her eyes, her sexy dark eyes, they spoke out to him, giving him permission and telling him to feast. He didn't need to look down as he could already see that all she had on was her pyjama top and it wasn't buttoned. But he simply had to look. His mind was demanding clarity. Not this, out-of-focus peripheral blur.

He looked downwards. Every inch of her was stunning. His girlfriend was standing in front of him, stark naked, apart from a little top she'd deliberately left open to tease him more. As he fed his eyes and mind with all of her, she stepped in and closed the gap. "Someone's happy", she said, feeling his hard-on pressing against her tummy. She kissed him while rubbing him through his jeans. She stepped one foot up onto the chair, and pulled his hand into her groin, guiding his fingers to where she wanted them. She kissed him firmer, the passion she'd built up over the weeks had tortured her. It needed a release and it was time. This was all new for Justin, and he was now acting out what he'd watched on his phone in his bedroom with his free hand.

Tammy's hips were gyrating, and as she squirmed with his fingers inside her, she freed herself from his kiss to moan, biting gently into his neck instead. He withdrew his hand from inside her and pulled open her top, revealing her dark nipples, just as erect as his shaft was. He pulled the top halfway down her back, so her hands were gently bound behind her, but she didn't try to free herself. He rubbed her juices over one of her nipples, then started licking it, tasting just how good she was.

She wanted to taste him too, and she slipped free from her restraint, then knelt down in front of him, and started tugging at his belt. As she was unbuttoning his jeans, she looked up at his eyes, which were fixated on her lips, and he wanted that plum-red lipstick all over his manhood so badly. She pulled his jeans down, and then his underpants. He was leaning back on the dressing table behind him with, both forearms resting on it, as he watched on intensely, letting her do whatever she wanted.

She slowly licked his length, from bottom to top, looking at his eyes all the time and never breaking contact, desperate to see his reactions as she stuck her tongue out all the way. She knew he was loving this, but knew he wanted her to suck him in her mouth. She pulled down his cock so it was angled straight at her mouth, and, very slowly, with her mouth relaxed open and tongue hanging down, she leaned in, closing her lips and sucking him as it went inside her mouth. She felt his jerky throbs, as his manhood pulsed involuntarily in her warm mouth as she went back and forth, her hand around its base at his abdomen.

This was Justin's first blowjob, and he didn't want it to end. He put his hand on the back of her head, making sure not to force her in, but letting her know he was loving this. Tammy was loving it too, knowing her partner was in extasy. Her hair was so silky-smooth and tangle-free and some of it tickled his balls as she sucked him gently. As she stood back up, she pulled him close and kissed him again, her tongue licking his, and he tasted himself off her.

"Do you want to fuck me, Justin?", she asked. There was only one answer to this, and as she lay back on the bed, one hand in her hair, the other rubbing herself, he quickly joined her there – but there was an issue. This had initially looked like a one way street, but as sexy as she was, and as tempting as all this was, Justin had second thoughts.

"Tammy...", he started. "I don't want to... ", he was choosing his next words carefully when he saw her eyebrows rise. "... to take advantage of you. Not after drinking."

She smiled at him. "It's okay Justin. I want to."

He lay beside her on the bed. "Tammy, this would be our first time. This is *my* first time. I don't want alcohol to play any part in it... not for our *first* time."

She wasn't drunk, but certainly tipsy and she knew it. "You *do* like me, don't you?", she asked shyly, pulling a pillow over her, hiding her body now.

"Tammy, oh my God – I'm fuckin *nuts* about you. I love *everything* about you. And… you're *so* damn sexy it's unbelievable. But I just want us both to be… to be thinking a hundred percent clear when this happens. So there's no regrets."

He cuddled into Tammy, her warm, naked body quickly re-aroused his erection that had retreated, thinking a false-alarm had been called. Every cell in his body was arguing with him, ordering him to charge ahead. If the veins on his boner could speak, they'd be screaming. He was letting his entire team down, and they'd remember this moment. These opportunities don't come round too often and this felt like Haley's comet was now finally here, but he wouldn't pull out his telescope.

But this wasn't about having sex with her, just so he could reach a certain base. Although to him, she was sensationally pretty, and ultra-sexy, his ultimate temptress-deluxe, drawing him in like a vacuum, earlier that day had been his grandfather's funeral, and that was a tough one to take. He just needed to delay things until he felt the moment was right for both of them. When he explained this to her, she felt bad for not appreciating his feelings more.

Nonetheless, the two of them spooned up in the single bed and he noticed that Tammy took no time at all to fall asleep. She was more petite than the normal girl, and the drink most probably had, in fact, had a boosted effect on her libido. As she slept, he cuddled in some more, preciously stroking her silky smooth skin, holding his beauty in his arms, keeping her feeling warm and safe inside whatever dream she dared to dream, and sheltering her from the evils that he knew lurked around in the shadows outside.

Once she was sound, he silently slipped out the bed so she could have it to herself and get a proper sleep, without his ever-eager hard-on, jabbing her in the back all night. The cold floor would sort that out. He put on some clothes and stole one of the pillows, and as he lay on top of some towels, with some more covering him, his thoughts switching from Tammy, Belle, his papa and his parents, the night out they'd just had and all the crap back home in Redleaf – but mainly Tammy, he smiled. He knew, as difficult as it had been to call a stop, he'd done the right thing. If Tammy was as keen on him as he was about her, there would be more times ahead, and he'd be a team player then, but if he rejected her again, that could be a showstopper to their relationship. In the meantime, he took the opportunity to smell his fingers. 'Jesus – fuckin – Christ!', he thought. Out of all the smells, all the tastes there is, this was eureka, the missing jigsaw piece he'd been hunting for his whole life. He hadn't edged to this online.

The following day, Carol had made sure they'd all had a small breakfast in them, prior to their departure, and the two boys were chatting in the kitchen as Tammy and Carol sat gossiping in the living room. Both pairs had spoken about the bowling hall and were wondering how bad the damage would be when the smoke cleared and revealed whatever would remain.

But while Carol had Tammy in private, sitting next to her on the sofa, she had a bit more to say. "Well, did you guys sleep okay last night?"

"Shut up!", came a half-giggled reply.

Carol hid through the steam of her tea. "… Well – did you?"

The lads heard the laughs of the girls in the next room. When Tammy quietly explained that they've not been going out that long, and 'nothing' happened, she actually felt good about saying that.

Carol nudged her cousin. "*Nothing* happened?"

Tammy knew it would be okay to let a little out. "Well – a few things happened!" The boys heard them laughing harder now. "But I'm not saying what!"

"Has he got a big dick?", whispered Carol, eyes wide open, ready to receive the answer. Tammy coughed on the tea she'd half-inhaled, her hand catching most of the spray from spoiling her new flowery dress, both girls in hysterics.

The girls laughed even louder as the boys joined them in the living room. Both boys saw a funny side, and Stephan kind of sussed what topic they'd discussed. Justin knew. He already had a kitchen towel in his hand and passed it to his giggling girlfriend, now polar oppositely shy from last night. "We better head soon", he smiled a private smile. "I've checked the forecast. Heavy rain's coming." He was wearing shorts he'd packed for the return journey, but as they'd be in the car, the rain wouldn't matter, or dampen his spirits. And after a last-minute catch up chat with her cousin, it was late morning before they finally left for Divernon.

Around two hours after setting off, they were still in the State of Indiana, so they'd agreed to stop to get a burger and chips for the rest of the journey. In order to save time, they'd not stop in the restaurant, but just get a drive through and take it with them.

A mile or so down the road, Tammy spotted a place where they could stop the car and eat, so she pulled in and switched off the engine. The burgers went quickly and they washed it down with cola and orangeade.

"T, thanks for doing this – for coming all the way, I mean. And being here for me."

Tammy drew a smiley face on her window that had fogged up with the food. "*T* says you're welcome!", she said, thumbing towards her picture.

"Oh! T's got a happy face?"

She palmed clear the first picture and drew another, this one with a straight lined mouth."

"Aww. So T's *not* happy! What would make T happy?"

"Really?", she asked.

"Yeah, really."

She pressed the central locking button to lock all the doors, then raised her perfectly white sneakers on the dashboard, and removed her knickers, throwing them in the back, all the time eyeing him. He looked around to see if there were any other vehicles, but could hardly see out the steamed-up windows. She climbed over to his seat, straddling him, her hair falling around his neck as she kissed him, her hands on his seat rest.

Feeling his hard-on inflating, she then clambered over to the back seats, and signalled with a curled finger for him to join her there.

He saw the scrunched-up burger wrappers on the floor below her, but she was offering him the feast of his life. A banquet lay before him, a la carte, and he could choose whatever he wanted. Suddenly, he was hungry again. Fuck thinking about it, and climbed over his seat to the back where she was lying. As he positioned himself awkwardly on top of her, they kissed again and she grabbed his bum with both hands, pulling him tighter.

"Take these off.", referring to his shorts. He did as commanded, this time just going with it. She nodded permission, and as his stiff length entered her, her eyes closed a little and she twitched.

"Are you okay?"

"Yeah. Just a little sore."

"Then we stop. I don't want to hurt you." And pulled out of her.

"No. It's – it's my first time." As she looked at him from underneath, with her arms round his neck, she pulled him closer with her heels. "Don't stop." With him calling it off the previous night, and showing her he didn't want to cause her any pain, she knew that although he'd done bad things with his ability, he wasn't bad. Inside, was a good lad, a very good and talented lad, with a heart of gold. She'd never experienced reluctance with any of her previous boyfriends.

As he entered her again, she moaned. She was feeling every inch of his above average penis dilating her, and she wasn't holding back showing him it. "Oh yes Justin, that's it – that feels so good!" After a few minutes, she told him she wanted to change positions. She wanted to be on top, like she'd seen online. As she straddled him again, she took hold of one of the car's grab handles, and kissed him again, releasing the passion that had built up. He reached up under her dress and grabbed hold of both breasts, gently feeling their shape and rubbing her nipples. It wasn't too much longer before the inevitable happened.

"Oh Tammy… you're gonna make me cum.", he said. But she was on top, and she wasn't for stopping. She wanted to please him. She wanted him to reach orgasm so badly, that she kept bouncing on him, eyeing him intently for signs of it happening. As he was climaxing, she stopped bouncing and circled her hips slowly, grinding on him instead, coaxing out every bit of sperm he had.

"Oh Jesus Tammy." He couldn't decide whether to thank her for this, or to apologise for climaxing so quickly. It had only been a few minutes, but it had been a brilliant few minutes. "Sorry Tammy – I couldn't help it."

She panted a giggle. "Don't apologise. I wanted you to cum."

Justin laughed. "I tried as hard as I could *not* to!" And as she sat glued to him, he knew this was his best feeling so far. His sexy girlfriend, sitting on top of him, just after climaxing. But then, very abruptly, he realised something. It was quite obvious that she hadn't reached orgasm. There was simply no point asking if she had – she hadn't. Full stop. And if there was to be a repeat of this, he'd better read up on how to make that happen, because as much as she wanted him to cum, he wanted the same for her.

As the two of them got dressed again, and were fixing themselves, there came a few taps on the other side of the steamed-up window. Tammy pressed the button for the electric window to slide down, and the two of them got a bit of a shock when they saw who was on the outside.

"Hey mam – are you all right?", asked a Police Officer noticing Justin beside her in the back. He'd stopped out of curiosity when he'd seen the stationary vehicle.

"Yes sir. I'm fine thanks. *We're* fine!" Her reply wasn't convincing. She was still a bit out of breath and he couldn't miss the sweat on her forehead. She felt a bit shocked about a cop right outside her car, and her embarrassed tone seemed to be trying to mask the fact that two youngsters were in the back, and had just finished romping.

He torched the car's floor, looking for contraband. "All right, kids – break out some ID."

"Shit Tammy... ", Justin whispered out the side of his mouth. "I've just turned sixteen."

"Don't worry about it. Hand over your ID card.", Tammy said, handing over her driving license.

The Officer looked at their ID's, then checked the faces of the two in the back, and as he did so, he saw that Tammy's dress was not sitting right, and she was fixing it. "Mam... is, erm... is this... *your* car?"

"Yes sir... we're just heading home soon.", confident they'd done nothing wrong.

The Officer worked the dates in his head. "Then mam, drive home safely to Illinois.", handing back their ID's. "Have a nice day.", he smiled awkwardly, and left them to it.

As she closed the window again, the two of them burst out laughing, half out of the cop's embarrassment and half out of sheer relief. But although it'd been fun, Justin was now lost. "Tammy, how did that happen? The age of consent is seventeen!"

"Yeah – but we're still in Indiana. It's *sixteen* here."

Justin thought for a few moments, then he clicked. They were only a few miles from crossing the state line. "Wait a minute... did you plan this all along?"

She giggled a naughty giggle. "I might have!"

Chapter 65

Tammy wanted to give Justin space – just a few days to himself, to allow him time to grieve for his grandfather in peace. Despite not meeting up, the pair had texted each other to keep in touch. But the peacefulness Tammy longed for Justin wouldn't last long, because while mourning his papa, something hit him.

In those thinking hours, Justin had also made a plan, knowing it would cost him but he couldn't see another way and those grains of sand seemed to be falling faster now. His papa had come close to wiping Damian out with the helicopter crash, but it had backfired somehow and, as well as eight pawns, it was his papa that died – 'White knight leaves table' – and during a blurry haze, he'd now removed all the white pieces from the board that hadn't made it so far. His pieces were now extra vulnerable. However, in reality, 'revenge follows revenge' – there's no other way – and that very concept would sharpen Damian's focus into thinking Stuart's successor would now be seeking him out – like a metal detector hunted a bad penny – and Justin would be mad at the killing of his grandfather.

But Justin knew Damian wouldn't just let that day arrive – not with his ability. Damian knew Justin was only a young lad, but Damian wasn't stupid, and he couldn't take chances – not for a second time. He'd underestimated Stuart and he wasn't about to make the same mistake with Justin. The next move would depend on who cottoned-on to the other's strategy. Justin had to act first, before his new opponent did.

Despite having Jesus round his neck, he knew Damian was pure evil. But in the same way that Damian killed Sarah to teach Stuart a lesson and get even, something finally struck him, and it was terrifying. They'd both be thinking endgame, and it was now a race against each other – a race against time, and he twisted the hourglass over. Just like the lightning bolt he'd ordered to strike Redleaf town, he now felt an electrifying shock as if he'd been plugged into the passing chair. Tammy's life was at risk, and Justin thought to himself – 'There's no fuckin way that's going to happen.' He'd already made the drawing, but now a sick, blurry concept had barged into the foreground. To eliminate Damian while he was at his most vulnerable, he'd drawn Damian's house ablaze. An unsurvivable inferno, with fire gusting out every window. He'd planned it for Saturday.

After clearing it with his parents, he'd called Tammy and had asked her to stay a few days. That would be enough time to finish this for good. He'd explain everything later. Tammy arrived with her holdall with a change of clothes, and needing explanations.

"Thank god you're okay.", he said. Concern was etched on his face, as he ushered her inside, safe from whatever was lurking in the trees, perhaps a rifle pointing straight at her.

"Justin, what's going on?"

"Tammy, listen – no more secrets, right?" He had to let her in completely. With his bedroom door closed over, he showed Tammy the drawing he'd made.

"Jesus! Come on Justin – this is wrong!" Approval denied. "What? You're asking me to sanction murder?"

"Tammy, he's evil and you know it."

"Yeah, he's a bad apple, but… "

"Tammy, my Grandma Sarah – Damian killed her."

She gave him a questionable look. How could he possibly know?

"… *and* my Papa Stuart. He killed him *too*. I FELT IT! Remember in Indianna, I felt something? I *know* he done it."

She acknowledged everything he'd been through – she'd been with him for most of it. "Justin, you're not thinking straight."

"Tammy, if he killed Sarah, he could do the same to you! Just to punish me – to warn me off."

Tammy walked in to take a closer look at the picture.

"Tammy – I'm *forced* to do this!"

"What if he hurts you?"

"He won't."

"God sake, Justin. How can you be so… blasé? You're taking a big chance here!"

"I've *got* to do this."

"No you don't! Not this time! You're *literally* playing with fire, Justin!" He saw her glance at the picture once more. "When's this planned for anyway?"

"Tomorrow. He goes out drinking on Fridays."

She shook her head, showing disgust. "So this is signed tonight? He'll die tomorrow? Sorry, I can't be any part of this!", and lifted the bag she'd just brought up to his room. As she left down the stairs, Justin thought about trying to call her back, but he didn't have a counter argument that topped hers. From his bedroom window, he watched her get into her car and speed off.

"Shit", he said sighing, opening up the same type of beer that he'd had with his grandfather. But the plan was still on. It simply had to be – it was kill or be killed.

Justin awoke the following day just after noon. The cans of beer that he'd planned to share with Tammy as she stayed over, were crushed empty. As he tried to blink away a self-induced headache, reality delivered panic. This was happening now – it may already have started. After quickly getting showered, he ran over to Tammy's home, top speed. Her car was in the driveway when he got there.

"Hey Mrs Yazzie. Is Tammy home?", he puffed.

"Hi son. Yes she's up in her room – just go up."

He carefully scaled the steps, being respectful not to cause too much noise, as if she was sleeping.

"I thought you'd come round.", she said, much more calm than he was.

"Tammy, put the TV on would you?", he said from the door, "Channel 13." It was the Indiana state news channel, but she already had it on. As he sat beside her on her bed, he immediately saw what he knew would be coming. From a bird's eye view, came the news helicopter's video lead. The chopper was circling around the home of Damian Keefer, 'a known convict' they were reporting, among other things that had happened in that town.

The story was getting meaty, and as they avoided the smoke from the blaze, they were zooming in on the fire at his home, now fully destroyed and being extinguished by the fire teams that had been there for an hour or so. What was also being reported was that there had been a barbeque being held there by the owner, for his niece, Amanda-Jo for her 13th birthday party, and there'd been a few of her school friends round for a barbeque lunch. The news crew had people on the ground and they were all providing updates on the extent of the burn injuries to kids who had been there when the fire broke out.

Justin put his hand to his mouth. "My GOD!" This hadn't been accounted for. "Aw Tammy. I had no idea kids would be there!" He could hardly breathe. "How did I miss this?"

She didn't answer him – but her disgusted eyes did. The two of them stared at the TV and watched in dismay as one of the house's walls collapsed.

"Oh Jesus! Tell me there's no kids inside Tammy." But she just looked at the TV, watching on, spellbound, as the updates kept scrolling along the bottom of the screen. He put his head in his hands and started crying. "Tammy, I didn't mean for this. I swear."

"I know, Justin. I know." She was much calmer than he was, and she needed to be. As they continued to watch the channel, something major happened. From the bellows of smoke, a firefighter appeared, carrying a girl over her shoulder.

"Oh fuck no! Tell me she's not dead?" With tunnel vision, they watched as the firefighter carried the girl to a waiting ambulance, and within a few seconds, it drove off with its sirens blaring. This would bring a new type of hangover, one that wouldn't wash away with coffee, or fade in the sun. One that would haunt him for the rest of his life. Tammy herself would hammer in the last nail in his coffin.

In disbelief, Justin's horror-filled eyes watched on, staring through the telly, his mind elsewhere and his whole body out of tandem with reality.

"Did you hear that?" He hardly felt her nudge. Tammy nudged him again, "Justin – did you hear what was said? Damian has not been found."

Wishing he could turn back the clock, regret was visiting his thoughts. This was murder, or double murder now, plain and straight. There was no denying it, and there was no going back. Tammy had seen compelling evidence last night and she'd know for certain he was guilty, and that was worse than any Court jury. She'd been reading the updates as the words rolled along.

"Justin, for God's sake – snap out!" She'd seen him like this before and knew it needed a bit more than gentle coaxing. She nudged him so hard, he almost fell off the bed. His senses snapped back into action as he reached the tipping point.

"What?" Everything came back into focus. He'd fled the scene, but was back in the room now.

"Look!", ordered Tammy, pointing to the repeating words.

'BREAKING: Girl pulled from burning home rushed to hospital.'

"Jesus Christ! I'm going to prison."

"Keep watching!" Her tone commanded full compliance.

Then, the on-screen text read something unexpected. 'BREAKING: Sarah-Jane Preston, Westfield girl missing since January found in basement of burning home.'

The two of them looked at each other. A bomb had dropped and hadn't exploded, demanding their silence – their full attention. The text continued, 'BREAKING: 15 year old girl pulled alive from home of ex-convict, Damian Keefer.' She'd turned fifteen in captivity.

This was a game changer. "The fuckin dirty *bastard!*" Justin stood up. "That prick pretended to – to *look* for her… to *search* for her… when he had her locked up in his basement all the time? The dirty *bastard*!"

Tammy palmed her forehead, as she watched Justin spin around on the spot, like a dog looking for its tail.

"Well where the fuck is he then?", he demanded – seemingly from the reporter. Tammy didn't think he was asking her, until he continued. "Tammy! Where's Damian?"

She'd been watching the channel earlier and noticed his Ford Mustang wasn't anywhere to be seen. "He's fled Justin. *Look!*" Her inpatient finger jabbing at the words on the telly that wouldn't be there long…

'Have you seen this man?' There was now a picture of Damian on screen, and a whole lot of details about him. The TV reporter said, "If you see this man, do not approach him. He may be armed and should be considered highly dangerous. Instead, call 911 immediately."

"Fuck me! He's on the run!"

Tammy could hardly believe what she was witnessing, but it was all live pictures. She knew most of the townies in Westfield would also be watching this, and that the Howards would finally be vindicated.

But in that moment, when Justin's hangover was muddying his already dazed rationale, putting the brakes on his thought process and winning that battle, she knew that one of them had to be thinking straight. It simply had to be her. A wanted man and a dangerous fugitive was now on the run, and when he put two and two together, he'd surely be heading to Redleaf.

Chapter 66

Later that day, the local Police Chief gave an update on live TV. As he approached the microphone, the sea of waiting reporters and camera crews abandoned their own little nests at the back and jostled for forward positions again. They were shouting over each other, desperate to be the one who got their questions out first.

"I want to make a brief statement, and after that I will answer questions, so please leave them until I've finished."

The reporters were just feet away, like coiled springs, waiting to jump into action, with pen in hand or a voice recorder in the air. Tammy and Justin sat to attention as the Chief took a deep breath, half blinded by camera flashes.

"Earlier today, around 1215hrs, fire department crews were called to a blaze at a home in Ashton, Westfield. The fire seems to have started in the kitchen. When the fire crews arrived, they tackled the blaze. As this was happening, a search of the home commenced and seven children were found in and around the property. I am glad to report that *none* of the children rescued have suffered severe burn injuries. All children are safe and well and are being monitored at Hospital – as a precaution, and all their parents have been informed of the situation. When it was deemed safe to do so, the fire crews made a subsequent search of the home itself to see if there were any other children trapped there. It was during this *further* search, a female firefighter found a local girl, named as Sarah-Jane Preston, who had been reported missing as from 18th January this year. She was found in the basement, and was found gagged, and handcuffed to a radiator. Although she *has* been injured – she is still alive and is receiving the very best medical treatment in Laport Hospital, and is under armed guard there. Although some of the children have suffered smoke inhalation, there have been no fatalities. The owner of the home, a Mr Damian Keefer, is said to have fled the scene and is now of interest to the Police. I must stress this… **do not** approach this man if you see him. Instead call 911 immediately. I will now take questions."

The reporters sprang alive again. "How did the fire start, sir?", one shouted.

"We're unsure. However, there was a grill being used in the kitchen. Burned food was found under it. Next question."

"Is the fugitive Damian Keefer, an ex-convict for armed robbery?"

"Yes. He's spent time inside prison for armed robbery and should be considered extremely dangerous."

"Sir, how many people were on the premises in total?"

"Seven girls were initially rescued, and Sarah-Jane Preston, so eight girls in total – plus Mr Keefer."

"Sir, were any girls injured *by* Mr Keefer?"

"At this time, we don't know. All girls are being questioned and looked after."

"What condition is Sarah-Jane Preston in?"

"It would be fair to say she was in a bad state when she was rescued. She was found drugged and handcuffed. But she's being looked after by our very best medical practitioners and she's likely to make a full recovery. Her parents have been notified."

"Has she been raped, sir?"

"Come on!", warning the reporter. "You know I can't go into that. Okay, last few questions."

"Where is Mr Keefer, sir, and how dangerous is he?

"Damian Keefer should be considered *extremely* dangerous. At this moment, we have local Police teams out searching for him. I repeat… **do not** approach him if you see him. He may well be armed."

"Is this connected to the two boys who also went missing in Westfield?"

"Mam, at this point, there's nothing to suggest they're connected, but we're keeping an open mind. And I'm sorry to say that the missing boys have not been found yet. They're certainly not in the property. Thank you."

As he turned his back on the press to leave, they reverted back to their usual disorganised bedlam, selfishly swarming around each other to swap notes, and juice-up their stories to as close to defamation as law permits. In a small town, this was big news and would dominate the headlines till its conclusion.

Since December, the Howards had been suspects. Although it was just the girl that had been found, there was huge relief for Justin. However, the biggest relief was that none of the girls at the party had been injured or badly burned, but that was just potluck.

"I have to tell my parents.", he told Tammy as he tied his shoelaces.

"Wait a minute. He might be on his way here – could be driving right now. We need to do something."

Justin nodded a confused nod – still thinking it through. This time, there could be no mistakes. This was too important to screw up, but there would be severe consequences for him should he go through with this, but he couldn't see another way out. Dozens of images flicked though his mind, ones he'd pre-arranged for a moment like this. But he knew he needed to be at home for this next step, hopefully a final step.

Forcing a smile for her, he leaned over and kissed her. "I'll think of something. Text you later."

Chapter 67

Justin ran home and told his parents that the missing girl had been found in Damian's basement, and that it was on the news. As they turned on the TV, scanning for the channel reporting it, Justin went upstairs to his room.

When he got there, he lifted the easel's cover, ready to make a start. Tammy was right. Damian may be heading here, and could be in the State right now. If he's already here, any drawing he made wouldn't work – it may not have time to. And although Damian would be stupid to travel anywhere – hunted by the cops, Justin had heard how much of a loose cannon he was. Maybe, it should be them that hid?

Regardless, he felt he had to act. As he flipped to the last drawing he made, the one of the fire at Damian's home – he froze. This picture was different to every other. Somehow, he'd forgotten to sign it. 'How can that be?', he thought. The very thing he'd spent ages devising in his mind, then creating in detail on this very paper in front of him, *had* happened – *just* like he sketched it.

He checked the drawing again, looking closer to see if his signature had been rubbed out, or he'd signed at a different corner – but there were no signs of either. He turned it over to see if he'd signed the back instead, while half-drunk last night, but no. "What the fuck is going on?"

This was heavy. *Way* too much to be a coincidence, and he couldn't make sense of it. With his phone, he took a picture of the drawing, and thought about sending it to Tammy – then binned that idea. He knew that doing so would leave a trail, so he'd have to go back over in person. Tammy saw the confusion in him before he caught his breath and spoke, but it didn't matter. She knew what he was going to say anyway.

"I didn't sign it!", he said, once in her room, showing her the picture. This was the most sincere she'd ever seen him. She absorbed his facial expression, his body language, stance, tone of voice, everything – for the next time. Next time he was like this, she'd know he was telling the truth. "... and yet it happened *exactly* as I drew it!"

"No it bloody well didn't!", pointing to his phone, then folding her arms tightly. She was infuriated, and it was because of him. "Where were the kids? They were right *there* Justin! You didn't do your homework!"

"Well how was I supposed to know they'd be there?"

"For God's sake! Just be thankful none of those kids were hurt. They could all have been killed." She seemed to have her thoughts elsewhere now as she folded her clothes up. "No one died. Thank God for that!"

"Tammy... listen, I'm sorry. I'm fucked-up right now. I can't think straight!" He sat on her bed, and she saw him grabbing his hair with both hands. "Tammy, we've got another problem – a big one. Damian is nowhere to be found. I think he's on his way here. If he gets here and I've not... prepared anything, then he'll fuckin kill us – of that I'm sure!

He turned and spoke directly to her. "He won't stop – he never has before. He'll never stop until one of us is dead. Tammy, I need your help. Tell me what to do!"

"Go home." She couldn't have been more serious if she tried. "If he's on his way here, and he most probably is, he could be here in the next hour, I suppose. Go home, and tell your parents to leave town. Don't tell *anyone* where you're going."

"Then come with us Tammy."

She shook her head. "I've got plans of my own. I've got my mom to look after, like you have. Don't worry about us – we'll be okay." She gave his cheek an anxious good-luck peck. "Get up – I'll drive you home.", pulling him off her bed. His parents were unaware of the danger, and it was all his doing.

It was now beginning to get dark, and if Damian was nearing Redleaf, there were countless places for him to hide. Damian was a master of ambushes, but this time the tables were turned. This time, Justin knew he was coming. He could feel Damian's unwanted presence deep inside him, and it was growing stronger by the minute like a cancer. He could sense that Damian was travelling fast, speeding away from the scene of the crime, and heading towards their peaceful little town, ready to shatter it.

When Justin told his parents about this, they took the threat seriously and all three of them left town in Mike's car, after grabbing a few things. They couldn't waste time packing and Damian may already be close to Redleaf. They were now being stalked again, Debbie feeling the strain of this cat-and-mouse thing more than Mike, who she noticed repeatedly glancing in the mirrors as they drove Westward. Fleeing town was Déjà vu, but hopefully for the last time.

Justin had brought a sketchpad with him, and was already busy doodling away in the back of the car, as his dad took to some back roads, making this a stealth mission. As he pencilled away, he promised himself that he'd end this, no matter what – his mom couldn't take much more. From time to time, he looked out the windows, looking for Damian's Mustang as they sped along.

Justin texted Tammy, to let her know they were okay and had left home, and telling her to keep safe. As he pressed the 'send' button, he glanced out the window again. When he did, he thought he saw Damian's car pulling out from a side street, and starting to follow them. Debbie noticed too. "He's coming after us!", cupping her hands round her face.

"He's coming after *me*, mom." Justin noticed his dad's eyes in the rear view mirror switch to Debbie's as he said it.

But when he looked out of the rear window, seeing it behind, it turned, following it's blinkers and disappeared down a different street. Panic over. There must be hundreds of Ford Mustangs out there, and continually looking out the windows would scare his parents – especially his mom. 'Calm down' – was the advice he remembered his papa had given.

As they journeyed along, Mike suspected they must be well in front of Damian, and that's if he was dumb enough to hunt them down. Even so, as he took a hand off the steering wheel to comfort Debbie with it, they both saw it tremble. He wasn't up for this.

The sun was half-way out of sight as they neared another town, and they'd decided to stay in a hotel that Deborah had found on her phone, just for the night. As they neared the hotel, they got stopped at a cross junction by the traffic lights. As they sat motionless, their idling car obeying the red glow, they agonisingly watched on as other cars coming from left and right crossed the junction in front of them.

"Wait!", said Mike, as the lateral traffic stopped. "Straight ahead – facing us. Is that a black Mustang?" His wife and son both looked ahead. Just the other side of the junction, also waiting for the lights to turn green was what did indeed look like a black Mustang. It was too dark and too far away to see, or make out who was driving, but Mike wasn't taking any chances. "Turn the light off.", he ordered – Debbie had been using it to plug in her phone. Just in case he needed to take action, Mike put both hands firmly on the steering wheel and got ready to turn. "Everyone got seatbelts on?"

Watching intently, nobody broke the silence. Deborah's heart was pounding. The sideways traffic had come to a stop. Red lights had halted their lanes, and people standing on the sidewalk started walking across the roads. Justin leaned forward and took a picture. Soon their lights would glow green again. The seconds agonisingly ticked by as the last of them made their way safely across to the other sidewalk. It was like the last grains of sand falling.

"It's not Damian. It's not a Mustang.", he said. "It's a Dodge", he confirmed as he zoomed his snap, extending his arm for those in front to see.

Suddenly, the Dodge shot forward, tyres screeching. The driver had jumped the lights, and had now adjusted the steering so was on a collision course with them. There wasn't time to do anything, and Mike couldn't reverse as he'd noticed cars had gathered behind. All three watched on as the Dodge was going to ram them, head on.

"HOLD ON!", Mike shouted over his wife's screaming. Just before impact, he closed his eyes, and she did the same. But from the back seat, Justin didn't. He watched everything. As the Dodge launched, catapulting its way to them, his eyes needed to see Damian Keefer in person – not hide from him. Justin's eyes were as much laser-focussed on him, as the driver's enraged eyes were on their car, that neither of them saw the speeding truck arrive from the left, straight through red lights with two Police cars chasing it. It had been stolen, and was involved in a heist around twenty minutes earlier, and had been hurtling through all junctions, red lights or green, and nothing could stop it – until now.

It T-boned the stolen hot-rod, shunting it into the air, and it tumbled over and over until coming to a rest, thirty feet or so away, upside down, smoke hissing out it. Cops decanted from the two pursuing vehicles and immediately spread out, covering the truck driver and the car it had smashed into. One radioed for help and emergency vehicles arrived at the scene in minutes.

As the Dodge rested on its roof, its wheels still spinning freely in the air, the driver didn't even try to get out. It had been a massive shunt and car's airbags had went off, and there was glass everywhere. As other Police arrived on the scene, they soon noticed that the license plates on the Dodge Charger matched that on their wanted system, unholstered their sidearms, then barked their commands at the barely-alive driver as they cautiously approached the wreckage.

"He's got a gun!", one of the cops shouted. Gunfire sounded immediately, overwhelming what may have come from the car, and more glass shattered as the driver went limp, dangling from his seatbelt. As one of the cops got cleared to open the door, the driver's arm flopped out. It was the tattooed arm of Damian Keefer.

Chapter 68

Damian suffered horrific injuries in the car crash, and had been operated on in hospital. He'd been placed in a coma, but was alive. He had suffered severe facial injuries, a combination of smashed glass from the side-on impact and the vehicle tumbling over, the report detailed. In addition, the surgeons decided that the best thing to do would be to amputate his leg, as it was beyond saving. Damian only realised his left leg was gone when he woke from his coma.

"Arrghh! Justin, you *BASTARD*!" He'd tried to reach down to feel the leg that wasn't there, but both his wrists had been handcuffed to the bedframe. Police were sent to the hospital to be on continual guard, and one cop remained outside his room at all times.

A few days later, after Tammy and Justin had thought it through, they decided to visit him in hospital before he got transferred to prison. They knew that once deemed medically fit enough, he'd be occupying a remand bunk, and they wanted to confront him while they could. After the Police Officer had searched the gloomy pair, they walked into his room, but neither said a word.

Damian looked Justin up and down as he went inside. "So you're the new guy? Stuart 2.0?"

"Something like that, yeah. Only Stuart was your friend at one point – that's why he took it easy on you. I'm not your friend."

"I suppose you've got no friends?" He noticed Justin looking at the floor. "Thought as much."

Damian saw Tammy looking around at all the machinery he was connected to, all of them monitoring something. "Suppose you've come here to gloat?"

Justin looked at his restraints, and the flat spot on the sheets where his left leg would have been. "Not to gloat. Just to have a look at you before you go to prison."

"Don't make me laugh boy! It's sore enough with a hole through my cheek. See the girl they found at my house – she *asked* to stay with me. Her stepdad was abusing her, you know. I let her in so she'd be safe. Rent free… and my word against hers. You see son, I'll be walking the streets again in no time… and then I'll be coming after you – and her."

"No you won't. You won't be walking anywhere – not with one leg. You'll only be hopping around your prison cell."

"I'm not going to jail son!", he scorned. "The cops are shit-scared of me. They won't even charge me – they've fucked that up before! Oh, but of course, you didn't know that! In fact, my lawyer says I should be suing them – right now… *and* I've already arranged for a prosthetic leg. I've got the money."

"Bullshit! Everyone knows what you done now. And you can't hide with *that* face. Poetic justice, I'd call it, actually."

"Just like what happened to your papa? Oh, which, of course – no one saw? Must have been weird going to a cremation – when there's no one inside the box!" His smug comments were sent out to level any hints of a smirk.

Tammy noticed that Justin wasn't winning this verbal battle. "I think I'm a witness at your trial.", she added. "I saw the whole thing as it happened. Can't wait to tell the jury how you dragged an old, defenceless man round the side of the church, strangled him, ditched his body in the bushes and stole the watch he got for his fiftieth birthday, that's hidden under the floorboards in *your* basement." Her steady, confident words came coupled with a magnanimous tone and the sound of a cell door slamming home sounded in Damian's mind. "I told the cops to look under the floorboards in the corner of the burned basement to find his Tag Heuer."

Both Damian and also Justin were simultaneously thinking the same thing at the same time. "How the *fuck* – could she know all this?" But Justin's fake smile concealed from Damian that he didn't know, while Damian's stumbling thoughts revealed his cluelessness. He'd been certain there were no witnesses. He'd made sure he dragged Stuart away and out of sight from the camera he spotted at an earlier visit to the Church.

"The cops are on their way – right now, to find Mr Howard's body. I told them – *exactly* – where to find him.", she added. "Your DNA will be all over him. Murder one, that'll be. This time it's life Mr Keefer – life without parole."

She didn't even say goodbye as she left the room – he didn't deserve it. They'd been searched before they entered the private ward, and they were searched again on the way out, but the only thing the cop found was a happier couple. Justin was desperate for answers, but he'd wait until the privacy her car provided. Once outside, and on the way back to her car, Tammy bent over. "Sorry Justin.", she said, holding onto him, before being sick.

Justin gave her a paper towel he had in his pocket. "Hey – you okay?" She couldn't reply as she wrenched again. "Sorry, Tammy. I should never have dragged you here. It's closure for me. I should have come alone."

She took a breath between throwing up. "It's okay. I needed to come."

As Justin got inside her car, he noticed a newspaper on the floor in the back. He recognised that it was the 'Westfield Times'. Just as things seemed to be sorting themselves out, this was now something else that he simply didn't need to be working out. "Tammy, what's that?"

She didn't want to lie to him either. But sometimes, the truth – the full truth, everything – is better left untold. She sighed. "I've been getting it delivered. You know, to see what's going on with the missing kids." It sounded plausible, even if a bit strange. But it'd be hypocritical of him to accuse anyone of acting strangely.

"It's finally over… ", she said, interrupting on purpose where his thoughts were heading. "You're safe now."

"We all are." It was a speedy reply, but his thoughts were stumbling. She started the engine, then turned it off. "Justin." She didn't have to wait long for his full attention. "It was me."

"*What* was you?" Surely she didn't have anything to do with the missing twins. "… and how did you know all that stuff?"

"I can't have you killing people. I couldn't be with you, knowing that."

"Tammy, I didn't kill *anyone* – I *swear*."

"No, you didn't – I *know* you didn't, but you *would* have done! That's the thing. You tried to kill Damian. With those kids there, that was reckless!"

As usual, she was spot on. He hadn't heeded his papa's advice. He hadn't thought it through.

"This gift you have… it's become a first choice for you, every time."

That silenced him. Hearing shitty news about yourself from the girlfriend you're trying to impress, is always hard to take.

"I got Damian."

"Honey, no. His car just got hit by…"

"Justin…", she interrupted, "… listen to me. There wasn't time for you to make a drawing. By the time we found out what was going on, it was too late for that. I used the totem you got me. It works – it's genuine."

"It works?"

"It may not have worked for someone else, but it works with me. I made that happen – *and* the fire at Damian's home. I made that happen too – but I made sure those kids were safe. You just lit a match! Thank *God* you hadn't signed it."

"Wait a minute… that skull thing – *actually* works?"

"You didn't think you're the only one in the world with a gift, did you?" She waited on his response, but he didn't have one. "There's loads of people that can do *something*, Justin – most don't even know it. They live out their entire lives oblivious to it all. My dad told me that."

The unsolvable parts to the puzzle had just been solved. It was all starting to slot into place, and as he joined the dots, he realised something else. The one person that he thought could do no wrong – had done wrong. She'd dug him out of a hole. She used her own talent to stop a wicked man, but for the right reasons.

"I never saw that coming Tammy."

"It was wrong. I feel awful for doing it."

"Don't. There's... no bad in you, Tammy."

"There's a little bit of bad in all of us Justin – you've just got to learn to control it. *You've* got to learn to control the power you have – instead of *it* controlling *you*. This guy *had* to be stopped. I was *forced* to do it."

Then he remembered he'd drawn a picture of a savage hell. And in a tall stone chair, eagerly awaiting the arrival of this pitiful Curt specimen, Satan sits grinning with his own agenda. But he never signed it. He'd let Curt off the hook. As pathetic as he was, he'd been punished enough. He'd got the message, so no need to go overboard. He'd resisted the urge to sign that one. He *could* control this thing after all.

Although Tammy had used an old, ritualised power, he wasn't scared. There's bad in her, and there is good in him. She already knew it – but he hadn't. And in that moment, she knew what he was about to say next. Why had it taken her so long to use it, if his family was in danger?

"You've been one step ahead all along. Why didn't I think of that before?"

"For *God's* sake Justin! You're talking about *using* me! I *hated* using it for that! You know, that was the *very first* time I tried it – just like my father had shown me before he died. His tribe – they didn't do this kind of thing – *ever*! What's the first thing I do? Set fire to a stranger's home then disable him. My father will be looking at me from above with shame. I feel ill!"

Justin had no response. Nothing that made any sense anyway. Nothing that could repair this damage – the damage he was responsible for. It was permanent, and there was no going back. Before, he could say anything, she started the engine again, and pulled away. On the journey home, neither of them said a word, but Justin was privately rehearsing conversations in his mind, desperately searching to find a scenario that would lessen her hurt. And on the cusp of finding something, she pulled into his street.

"Tammy, I'm sorry."

"Me too. I need time to think."

His heart imploded. "Are we... still going out?"

She'd kept the engine running up till now, but turned it off for her reply. He saw her draw a huge breath as she shook her head. "Justin. For God's sake! I feel *used*. I used this to help *you*. You've used your gift for *you* all along – not for me – not for anyone else. You always think of yourself. I've had too much of that already. I can't be with someone like that."

Justin knew there was no point arguing. She was right. It had been all about him – what he wanted – what he needed to happen. From getting a partner at art, getting all the tyrants at school sorted out and stopping Damian. He couldn't stand the thought of using her in a relationship, or even her thinking that way. And although Tammy admitted she had bad inside her, he'd seen most of it while partnered with him. He now realised that, just as Curt had been a bad influence on her, he'd been a bad influence too, and she'd be better off without him. More time she'd wasted. Opportunity had knocked, and he'd blown it. As much as that thought crushed him, it was best for her.

"I need time to think this through – so do you. I'll get back to you when I'm ready. And Justin – don't even *think* about texting me. Don't do it!" As he sat ashamed in silence, thinking where it had gone wrong, she ordered him out the car without ordering him. "I need to go."

And after getting out, searching for a reply, one that may salvage something, she drove off. He hadn't even closed the door over, but as she sped away, it closed over itself.

Chapter 69

It was almost five weeks later when Tammy came round to see Justin. As warned, he hadn't texted her, but he had started typing many a time, only to watch his gutted finger delete those characters. He'd been desperate to text, telling her to use the totem to try and make contact with her father, but that got deleted too. Robbed of enthusiasm, he'd only done the bare minimum of cleaning in his room. Even the chessboard had been left the same – game finished with the black king lying on side.

With each numb day that had come and gone, another percentage point was added to the odds against them getting back together, and he was now resigned to the fact it was over. Accepting this, even just in his mind, had been the hardest thing he'd ever done.

His summer break had been awful without her being part of it, and it broke his parents, seeing their boy mope around the house miserable, as relief finally shone on them. He'd thought about drawing something that could, perhaps, get her back – but that would've been the wrong thing to do. She'd probably know he'd done it anyway. There was no other option but simply to wait it out, and waiting in the dark was torture.

With hair wrapped in a towel, and a bigger one round her body, it had been Debbie that answered the door early one Saturday morning, and welcomed Tammy inside. It wasn't her place to ask, but she was hoping Tammy would bring good news. "Hey, Tammy. Come on in honey."

As Tammy stepped over the threshold, dozens of memories rushed back to her and she turned around to hide her emotions.

"Are you okay Tammy?" She dare not cuddle her. It would be wrong on several levels.

"I'm fine Debbie.", she insisted, her moist cheek that reflected the ceiling light suggested otherwise.

"It's good to see you again. Sorry, I'm just out the shower. He went in after me. I think he's in the bath."

And after making Tammy a tea, she went upstairs to tell him that she'd come round. Tammy was a bit nervous, her tea steaming away as she paced the room. Belle had always demanded her attention the very instant she arrived, but the place was empty without her – their home just glowed less. But now she noticed something odd. She'd never noticed before, but without Belle to tend to, her return brought a new pair of eyes. There were no family pictures on the wall, or any shelf. She peered around the corner to look at the dining room walls, but they were bare too. What she did see there, was an open drawer and a photo album sticking out of it.

Curiosity got the better of her and she had to peek inside. No harm in that. Inside were family pictures, ones that included Justin's Grammy Sarah. This was the first time she was seeing her as Justin never had any family pictures hung up on his bedroom walls either. She turned the page and saw a photo of the Howard family, taken a few years ago, everyone happy.

The next one showed the entire family, a snap taken at Christmas around four years ago, when everyone had gathered to celebrate. Turning over again, was a photo of Justin and his grandfather. At first, Tammy gave a warm smile. That is, until something stole her attention. As she looked closer, both of them had red eyes in the picture. Nothing strange in that, but as she flipped back over at the family picture, it was *only* Justin and Stuart who's eyes were red – no one else. She checked this with a few other pictures, but it was the same with all of them.

Something made her check through some old selfies of Justin and her she'd taken on her phone, and it was exactly the same thing. She'd never even noticed before, but as she zoomed in, it boldly stood out now.

"That's why we don't hang them up.", said Deborah, closing the book over.

"Jees! You gave me a fright."

"He's my son. I've loved him from the moment he was born, and I'll love him forever, regardless of what he does. Regardless of what he is."

Tammy had spent the last five weeks trying to understand things, but the time apart hadn't really helped. Here was his mother right in front of her, and if anyone would know, it'd be her. "Debbie, I don't understand. What is he?"

"No one knows Tammy. Not even him."

"Not even who?"

Tammy saw that Justin was half-way down the stairs with a large towel wrapped around his waist. "We need to talk, Justin."

"Yeah – of course. Come on up." He got to his room before she started climbing the stairs and had put on shorts before she stepped inside. She noticed that he'd kept Belle's other bed in his room, as if she was out on a walk and would be back anytime.

She twisted round after closing the door shut. "I'm pregnant.", she blurted out.

Yet another young birth in the Howard family – it was almost inevitable. She expected some kind of a response, either a cuddle or a verbal reply, but he was neck deep in thoughts.

"Justin – I need to know something… "

"Your answer's NO."

Before he could say or do anything, she shook her head and ran out, down the stairs.

"Shit!" Tammy was leaving, most likely forever, and he couldn't just let her go. "Tammy!", he shouted, but she was now at her car.

He flung a T-shirt over his damp body and it wasn't sitting right. His hair was still soaking wet and he'd not even put on socks, but he tore after her. He simply couldn't let her drive out of his life. Too many things had happened recently that didn't need to have happened, and they'd all been permanent. This could be another.

The engine was running, but she hadn't driven off, eyes seemingly staring through the steering wheel she was gripping, the selector held in 'P'. Upset and confused, she needed more time to process it all, but still – he was half-invited to stay.

After quietly getting in, he sat down. "T – listen to me. I love you. I've missed you *so* much. I've never met anyone like you in my life. You've got to believe me, I'm not the devil – or a servant for him – I know that now. I can't feel that."

He gently removed her hand from the gear selector and gently kissed its back. "When my papa died – he wanted me to have all the inheritance money – all of it. He's left me his house too. It's mine now and I'd be safe in Westfield – or sell it and move somewhere else – somewhere even safer. But it would mean nothing without you. That was his way of making up for passing this thing onto me. It was a *good* gesture he done, T. He helped me, and I want to help other people too – I feel I can do it."

He dotted away a pristine tear that seemed stuck in limbo, half-way from tipping over, with a decision to make. He saw his reflection in that tear, empathising with its liquidity. "I knew you were pregnant Tammy. I've felt a part of me growing inside you since we parted. It's a girl, you know."

Tammy burst out the cry she'd been holding in for weeks.

"… and if she's anything like her mom, I'll be nuts about her too."

Tammy turned across, seeing him staring, gazing happily into the near future, imagining her.

"Tammy, I couldn't before, but I can see her now. Wow – she's gorgeous. She looks like you, all innocent and playing in our garden with friends – making butterflies, a light blue hair clasp in her short black hair you clipped in. There's a tipi in the garden and her friends are inside."

He paused, going there, as Tammy eye's revealed the pride her heart was feeling. "Tammy, I can almost touch her – she's reaching out to me. I need to hold that soft little hand." He looked at her tummy as he placed his hand there. "I'd do anything for her. I'd give my life for hers – or yours. Know it's true."

She did. "Justin – you've been given the *rarest* of gifts. You don't even know the things you're capable of achieving yet – *great* things, Justin. But you've only done selfish things with it…" she said, dabbing her eyes with a hanky. "…

things for *you*. You've *chosen* to do these things for your own benefit. But I know you're a good guy, Justin. You could have *really* hurt Curt *and* his friends – but you went easy on them. You bought me that totem – to help me try to contact my father – but you never even asked me what happened when I did. If you *ever* use this thing again, you need to start doing good things with it. You've done it before… to find Sarah-Jane? I can't do that."

For the briefest of moments, he thought that if, from now on, he did just that, then maybe he'd gain back some of the time he'd lost. Then he disregarded that thought, and kissed her hand again.

Tammy steadied herself. "Maybe you didn't even realise you were doing good things Justin – but it *was* good. Otherwise, who knows what would have happened to her?"

The gentle squeeze his hand gave hers, tried to assure her of changed priorities, as did his apologising eyes. She decided through a massive sigh. "I'll help you. All magic doesn't have to be used for revenge, you know. Now – there's two little boys that need our help to find them. So let's find them."

REVENGE, ILLUSTRATED

Part 2: the missing twins

Released 2024 –

ABOUT THE AUTHOR

Born on the West coast of Scotland, Barry Cochrane now lives with his wife, son and daughter in Aberdeenshire. A very keen fitness and snooker enthusiast, Barry only took up writing in his fifties.

He started his career in the prison service, and after 'serving' 6 years in a maximum-security prison, he moved into Health and Safety where he worked for some of the most successful companies in the UK. He also went to Robert Gordon University where he started training as a Nurse – but left to pursue other dreams. He's keen on renewables and is passionate about the environment, having devised a solution for the home heating industry that emits no carbon in use.

His key passion now is writing and he has several ideas for his future books and also for TV comedy, however, 'Revenge, Illustrated: Part 1: unearth the underdog' is his first book to be published.

The sequel, 'Revenge, Illustrated: Part 2: the missing twins', is due to be released late 2024, and his final goal for these books is to see, 'Revenge Illustrated' on a steaming service such as Netflix.

Printed in Great Britain
by Amazon